USA TODAY BESTSELLING AUTHOR

DALE MAYER

A Psychic Visions Novel

ITSY BITSY SPIDER

ITSY-BITSY SPIDER
Beverly Dale Mayer
Valley Publishing Ltd.

ISBN-13: 978-1-773360-67-6
Print Edition

Books in This Series:

Tuesday's Child

Hide 'n Go Seek

Maddy's Floor

Garden of Sorrow

Knock Knock…

Rare Find

Eyes to the Soul

Now You See Her

Shattered

Into the Abyss

Seeds of Malice

Eye of the Falcon

Itsy-Bitsy Spider

Unmasked

Deep Beneath

From the Ashes

Stroke of Death

Ice Maiden

Snap, Crackle…

What If…

Talking Bones

String of Tears

Inked Forever

Insanity

Soul Legacy

Coveted

Boxed Sets and Bundles

https://geni.us/Bundlepage

About This Book

Queenie Landry's job as a fortune teller at an amusement park pays the bills but it's a far cry from the respectable psychic advisor role she once filled at the police station where the love of her life, Kirk Wallace, was a detective. A case went bad when she steered the team in the wrong direction and a woman died. Queenie experienced a horrific crisis of faith in her own abilities and pushed everyone away.

Nine months later, alone and denying her psychic gift, she gives birth to a son and feels redeemed. But a happily-ever-after isn't to be. Following a severe illness, Queenie wakes up eighteen months later only to be told her son died. Unable to handle her grief, she opens herself once more to her abilities, desperate to connect with her child. Resigned to telling fortunes at the park, she's stunned when a man walks into her tent and she sees a vision of a woman he's murdered. She realizes she has to contact Kirk again.

Kirk left under duress. Though he regrets his decision, he's never forgotten Queenie or found anyone to replace her. Having to be the one to tell her about her son's death all but destroyed him because he knew it would unhinge her and he isn't sure how she'll ever find stability again.

Unknown to either of them, someone has been watching her for a long time, someone who likes to play games with other people's lives—as he has Queenie's. But even he's confused by the creepy spiders amassing all around her. What message are they trying to convey to her that she's stubbornly refused to hear…and what price will she have to pay if she fails?

Sign up to be notified of all Dale's releases here!

https://geni.us/DaleNews

CHAPTER 1

Saturday Night ...

"HEY, QUEENIE, YOU'VE got a hell of a line outside your tent tonight," Booker called from the Ferris wheel station. "How come you didn't see that coming?" And out came his usual full belly laugh at his own joke.

Queenie waved and smiled as inside she groaned. Somehow this teasing never seemed to get old with this group. And the jokes didn't get any better. At least with the people she worked with here. Then again she was a fortune-teller at an amusement park. She had to expect a certain amount of ribbing.

Still, she did what she could, and, for that, she was grateful to have a job. She finished her ice cream, tossing the last portion of the cone into the garbage. All around her, the noise of the park and the smell of supersticky cotton candy filled the air.

She had to stay focused. This wasn't for her—this was for someone else. She stepped through the back entrance of her tent. After shrugging off her sweater, she picked up the huge headdress that went with the seer's role and placed it on her head. Her crystal ball prop was under the table. She put it on the table in front of her. Then she pulled back her chair and sat down. This booth made money. Because of that, the owner paid to keep her around. Not much money, however, but it was easy work, and she got cheap food as a side benefit.

She'd been here, near Seattle in the state of Washington, for several years now. She was footloose, yet a long way from being fancy-free. Life sucked. But it didn't matter because it was all for the right reason. She leaned across the table and opened the curtains that separated her from her customers. Close to six feet from the tent door, the line had formed, curling to the left. She smiled at the teenage girl standing in front and motioned for her to come forward.

The teen handed over her five-dollar bill. Queenie accepted it with a smile and asked, "What question can I answer for you today?"

"Will I get asked to the prom this year?" She squealed out the question in a breathless voice.

Queenie chuckled inside. "Is there someone in your life already?"

The young woman shook her head. "Not yet. But I'm really hoping you say there will be soon."

"Let's find out." Queenie held out her left hand and said, "Place your hand in mine."

And then she waved her right hand around the crystal ball. As soon as the young woman's hand connected with Queenie's, she smiled. Was there anything fresher than young love? She studied the ball, using it to formulate a story to tell the young woman. The ball was a prop for the people. Queenie could see everything through her eyes right now. She said, "Somebody named Jake, by any chance?"

The young woman cried out again as she gripped Queenie's hand like a lifeline and did a half jump in joy. "Yes, that's him."

"Well then, you needn't worry," Queenie said gently,

happy she could hand out the good news. "Because he's going to ask you to the prom."

The young woman dropped her hand and squealed again, jumped up and down, and then dashed out of the tent.

Queenie smiled and dropped the money into the jar beside her. "Next," she called out.

A man in a business suit walked in, carrying a briefcase.

She studied him and found nothing unnerving about him, but something was off. He appeared to be calm, maybe too calm. He sat down in front of her and said in a quiet voice, "I'm about to lose everything. Is there anything I can do to help myself?"

Now that was interesting. Rarely did people come with a question of what they could do to turn something around.

He handed over his money and said, "I know this is all fake, but you have a certain reputation. I need some advice. A direction to look in? Something? Preferably good news," he said heavily. "I could really use a shot of good news right now."

Interested in spite of herself, Queenie held out her hand and said, "Place your hand in mine."

As soon as he did, tingles went up and down her back. Now she was very interested. Normally she was good at judging the core character of a person. And nothing about him had set off her inner alarms. She waved her hand over the ball as she tried to sort out the images coming to her. But all she could see were metal bars. And then she realized why he had lost his job. She glanced up at him and said, "Are you trying to find work?"

He shook his head sadly. "No. I thought everything was going great … but then …" His voice trailed away.

"But then?"

"Somebody blamed me for something." Pain and discouragement were heavy in his voice.

She studied the bars in the ball and realized they were a jail cell. He was in grave danger of going to jail for the rest of his life. She frowned and looked at him. "Do you know somebody named Mike? Mike Marrow or Munro?" She frowned, trying to get the name clearer in her head.

He leaned forward. "Mike Munro, yes, he's my best friend."

She looked at him sadly. "He's not your best friend. He's the one who framed you. He's the one who's guilty."

The man stared at her in horror. He got to his feet and bolted from the tent.

She dropped his money into the jar. Next thing she knew, three little kids stood before her. They were giggling. One held up a five-dollar bill and placed it on the table. She could see the mom to one—or all—standing in the back. Queenie smiled down at the kids and said, "What would you like to know?"

"What am I going to be when I grow up?"

She held her hand out to the first boy who wore a plaid shirt and cowboy boots.

He placed his hand in hers.

Instantly the answer flooded her mind. She chuckled. "You'll be a fireman."

He gasped and raced toward his mother. "Mommy, Mommy. She said I'm going to be a fireman."

Queenie smiled at the kid's excitement as a little girl stuck out her hand. "What about me?"

"You will work with animals, little one," Queenie said softly, seeing images of this girl as an adult, caring for dogs and cats. "I don't know if it'll be as a veterinarian or as something else. But your path lies with animals."

The little girl dropped her hand, stepped away and waited for the third child, a little boy, to step forward. He held out his hand and said, "What about me?"

But his voice was defiant, almost angry, as if he'd wanted to be the fireman, and he didn't like that his friend had that role. As soon as his hand touched Queenie's, a shock coursed through her system. And then a cone appeared over his head. She swallowed hard at that sign and said, "Wow, you're really hard to read. I'm not sure I see anything."

"You don't have to. I'm going to be a policeman," he yelled. "I'm going to hunt down robbers." He broke contact and raced away, past the adults at the entrance to the tent and roared like a banshee.

She carefully eased her chair backward, and, using some of the antibacterial soap, washed the hand he'd held. It wouldn't change the fact that the little boy would die—and sometime in the next three days.

She shuddered, hating that part of her talent. The last thing she wanted to know was who would die prematurely. Especially when a child.

So far the cone hadn't been wrong. She'd seen enough of them to know. She sat back, sipping water from her bottle, trying to calm her nerves.

Out of the corner of her eye, she saw a spider walk across her table. She looked at it with guarded curiosity. The amusement park was definitely not the cleanest place, and certainly loads of food were here for rodents. But she hadn't seen much in the way of spiders. She wasn't afraid of them, but neither did she like them. As far as she was concerned, if they left her alone, then she'd leave them alone.

This one didn't get the message.

It walked across her table, heading for the fortune-telling ball. She watched, wondering at the odd light around the bug. She saw auras all the time. Rarely around animals though. Never around bugs. But the spider definitely glowed. She smiled at the oddity. "Where are you from?"

Something inside Queenie told her to pick it up. But she hesitated. Just because she wasn't killing the thing at first sight didn't mean she wanted it crawling all over her. The spider went up on its back legs, reaching out one of its front legs to touch the crystal ball. A mist swirled deep inside the ball.

And those eyes … How many eyes did spiders have?

The spider speared her with a look she found fascinating. She leaned forward, studying the bulbous critter carefully. Then, unable to help herself, and yet cringing as she did so, she touched the spider. It scrabbled onto the back of her hand.

Instantly images assailed her.

Blood. A woman giving birth. A toddler—a boy. And a name flashing in neon inside her brain—a name she'd never forget: *Reese.*

Shuddering, she stared at the spider in horror. It stared at her. As if it knew her. As if it knew something about her.

She brushed it off her hand and onto the table and backed away, knocking her chair over in the process, staring at it in horror. "What do you know about Reese?"

Of course the spider didn't answer. How could it? But it gazed at her with that same knowing look. She shuddered again.

Just then a large man stepped through the tent opening, dragging a young boy with him. The man took one look at her and laughed. "Well, look at this. The fortune-teller is scared of spiders." He walked over, flicked the spider to the ground and lifted his leg to step on it.

Before he could, she shooed it off to the side away from him. "I'm not afraid of it," she said quietly. "And I don't kill anything unnecessarily."

He snorted. "You're a charlatan, just like all the rest of the idiots here."

"No, I'm not," she said wearily, having heard it all before. "What can I do for you?"

"Well, seeing as how I'm here, you might as well tell me something. I'm trying to acquire a piece of property. A pretty cabin on a lake. Will I get it or not?"

With a sneer he tossed a five-dollar bill on the table. Too many people like this were in her life with the same attitude. Most of the time she could ignore them. This man, however, … had made himself part of her job.

She hated to reach for his hand, but it was necessary in this case, and his closed around hers, holding her tight. And once again images slammed into her. A mountain lake. A cabin with paths up and down to the lake.

And, in the lake, a woman's face floated just beneath the surface.

Queenie broke contact and sat back down again, holding her hand against her chest, her nerve endings fried, her body already shaking. She didn't know what the hell was happening. But something was wrong. She gazed at the man and said, "The property owner is dead."

His gazed narrowed.

Her gut clenched. She should keep her mouth shut. She didn't need to start anything, … but she couldn't stop her visions or stop speaking of them. Someone had to. For some reason she saw a whole lot more here than she'd like.

Girding herself for his reaction, in a cold voice she added, "But then you already know that, … don't you?"

His visage transformed, a black thundercloud forming. "Bitch," he roared, storming out of the tent and dragging the little boy with him.

Not that it mattered. His face was destined to remain emblazoned in her mind for a long time to come.

But the face from the lake would be there a lot longer. That poor woman had been murdered. And even now floated undetected in the chilly water.

Queenie spun around, grabbed her Closed sign and hung it on the curtain that separated her from the front of her tent, then yanked the curtain closed.

She couldn't do any more of this tonight. She wasn't sure what had changed, but, for some reason, her abilities were heightened to a new level right now. And it scraped along her nerve endings to the point where she couldn't deal with anything. She returned to the table, dropped her headpiece there and picked up her purse.

The spider raced up her arm and onto her shoulder. She involuntarily shuddered and flicked it off. Only it returned to run up her pant leg instead. She danced around, trying to shake it off.

But it was too late.

She'd seen its visions.

Something it knew. Or rather *someone* it knew.

Then, like a weird echo inside her brain, a tiny voice called out to her. *Mommy? Is that you? Where are you?*

She froze …

But that couldn't be. Her son, Reese, had been dead for years now.

Shaking at the unbelievable horror she didn't—couldn't—contemplate, yet one that offered hope on a monumental scale … Unable to stop herself, she pulled out her cell phone and the card she'd kept tucked in the back of the phone case for many years. Unable to trust herself to send a text, she dialed the number on the card.

"Hello."

Her heart slammed into her chest. She hadn't heard that voice in so very long. She'd loved it once, just as she'd loved the man. Then hated both as her life had been ripped to pieces, and he'd been unable to fix what had happened to her son—their son. Whether he knew it or not.

Finally she found her voice. "Kirk?"

A moment's pause followed. Then he said with a heavy sigh, "Hi, Queenie."

Just the sound of his voice had her throat clogging with emotions, her eyes floating in unshed tears.

As her silence lengthened, he asked sharply, "Did something happen?"

She gave a strangled laugh and said, "Yes, but you won't believe me if I explain." And she hung up, sagging into her chair, tears burning the back of her eyes.

KIRK SANDERS SLOWLY placed his phone on the desk. *Queenie? After all this time?* He tried to think back to the last time he'd spoken to her. It must have been at least three years—or just over? How did one reconcile the passage of time when the first time you heard a person's voice again was as if time had never passed?

He sat at his desk, letting the comforting sounds move around him, of everyone else's voices and keyboards clattering in the large room.

Inside he was frozen.

Why had she called? She'd always been tenacious. Almost a bulldog latching onto something and never letting it go. He'd admired that. In fact, he'd loved it. She'd been so driven, and then all hell had broken loose. Her son would be … what? … Five maybe? He'd died at eighteen months. And that had been close to three and a half years ago. Kirk hadn't even known she'd had a son.

He'd loved her from the bottom of his heart. He'd thought he'd found forever, was willing to do anything to bottle it so he could keep it that long. But, like a puff of smoke, it had all blown up.

Like her crazy abilities—which he'd admired—and how he had defended her and them to his colleagues. She'd been fanatical about acting on her information, but sometimes she expected Kirk to jump when he couldn't. There was such a thing as needing evidence before picking up criminals. He was a cop and couldn't go off the reservation or work outside the law. And, when he had been unable to help her with several visions, things between them became strained.

But the Handkerchief Killer case took *strained* to a whole new level.

That case had blown apart their lives, and they'd separated. Over two years later—a rough two years—he had walked into the station one day to hear she'd been hospitalized. Then he'd heard about her son. She'd never mentioned him, and he'd never asked. And now it was too late for all of them. His heart tugged at the thought of the little boy who'd been so sick. She had done everything she could to help him, but, when they had both collapsed, both were rushed to the hospital, her son dying before she'd ever awoken.

Due to some mix-up with the paperwork, her son's body had been cremated and buried. And when Queenie had regained consciousness, they'd almost lost her again when they told her the news.

She couldn't identify the signature on the cremation order—although it was her name. She didn't remember signing the order, but the hospital staff said she had.

He'd seen the signature. Hell, he even had a copy of the cremation order on his desktop. Something he couldn't quite let go of. Somewhere along the line something had happened, as if she'd been unable to deal with the grief, so she'd fed on all kinds of conspiracy theories. She even wanted Kirk to open a missing person's file. He'd tried to explain to her there was no way he could. Her son's death, although painful, was aboveboard. It had been verified by several attending nurses and the physician. His supervisor, when he'd broached the subject of what to do, had said Queenie needed mental assistance and to recommend she get treatment—at least counseling.

That he had privately agreed at the time wasn't something he told her. She'd fought him on it for days as he distanced himself further and further. What did one do in the face of such pain? In the face of such disbelief and the high level of fantasy? She wasn't willing to see his side. How could he possibly see hers? And yet the mystery remained. ... Who had signed the cremation order? Queenie refused to believe she'd done it. Even more so, who had buried the remains?

The mystery was just a little too unsettling for him, and he could see how it fed her own psychosis. But, at the same time, he didn't dare let himself get sucked into it. Unfortunately he'd seen shit like this happen before, way too often.

Maybe somebody had signed it as a good deed, realizing Queenie herself would not likely make it through her own illness. Again, any number of scenarios were possible, but, as far as Queenie was concerned, her son had disappeared from the hospital's care, and they were ultimately responsible.

And it broke his heart all over again. Because that same devotion, that same focus she'd had on various cases, was now something she was locked on to herself. To stay sane, to have any kind of life, she had to let it go.

"Kirk, what the hell's the matter with you?"

Startled, he glanced around and looked at Peter, one of his team of detectives. "Hey, sorry. Just got a weird phone call. Tossed me back for a loop."

"What phone call?" Peter looked at him with a frown. "It takes a lot to shake you. But you sure do look rattled."

With a quirk of his lips, Kirk said, "Queenie."

Peter's eyebrows shot up toward his hairline. "That's not just strange. That's heading into psychotic territory. You stay away from her."

Kirk chuckled. "I haven't had anything to do with her for years, and, out of the blue, she calls me."

"What did she want?"

Kirk said, staring at his monitor moodily, "Nothing. At least she never said."

Peter asked, with a shake of his head, "She's still *out there*, isn't she?"

"I know. I thought, after all this time, she'd have been better."

"I think, when mothers head down that path, absolutely nobody can do anything to help them. They see dead children because they want to see dead children." He smirked. "And, for Queenie, that goes double, as she always sees dead kids."

"You mean, she sees their spirits," Kirk corrected. "Because she wasn't there, she didn't see him die, see his body afterward, so she has no closure on her son's death."

"Hell, when Melissa had a miscarriage," Peter said with a heavy sigh, "I thought she'd gone off permanently. I can't imagine what would have happened if she woke up in the hospital to find out her child was gone, and she not only didn't get a chance to say goodbye but she didn't even see the body or go to a funeral, … nothing."

"Exactly. And, because of that, Queenie couldn't let go of the thought that maybe her son was stolen, maybe somebody did something, and maybe the child was still alive somewhere. But she didn't say anything about Reese this time. It was a weird call actually."

"Can't she contact him with her abilities?"

Kirk nodded. "I imagine she tried. But you know what she was like. She would get all these weird hunches and psychic visions, and sometimes there'd be voices. Sometimes there'd be pictures."

"Nothing was normal about her visions or her abilities," Peter said. "I'm not even sure I believe any of that shit."

"But she did help us close dozens of cases," Kirk said. It had been phenomenal at the time. When she had information, it was usually good information.

"Not at the end," Peter reminded Kirk. "It was stuff somebody else could have gotten from a newspaper or something. Hell, maybe Queenie was listening in at the closest coffee shop where the cops hung out and getting tidbits from there."

Kirk didn't bother answering. They'd had this conversation before, although not for years. He stared at the number on his phone, jotted it down on a sticky note and stuck it to the base of his monitor. He couldn't quite let go of the feeling that something strange was going on—and not just with her phone call.

Her voice had been strained, as if some major trauma had occurred. She'd already been through more than most people had. Yet, he also knew that to go down that path, to even pick up the phone and call her again, was to open up a hornet's nest in his own life, and he didn't want that either.

"You better stay away from her," Peter warned. "She's bad news for you."

Not much Kirk could say to rebut that. She'd been his everything until she broke down and sent him away. But he hated to look at that time too closely. Nor could he forget about her all these years. He'd kept tabs on her after she had lost her son but always from a distance. Then he'd lost track of her. Every six months his calendar reminded him to do another search for Queenie, to find out where she was, if possible. This exercise kept him somewhat connected to Queenie and also reassured him that she was somehow still okay.

"You know what happened when your last girlfriend found out about Queenie."

That had Kirk wincing. His ex-girlfriend Lorraine and he had been going out together for over eight months, with her angling for a ring and permanency, when she found out about Queenie after she'd called him. Lorraine had been horrified about her occupation and him by association. They'd broken up soon afterward.

His email dinged with a new message coming in. He clicked on it.

It was from Queenie. He read the garbled note and realized it was about a vision of some kind. But, once again, no names, no dates, no locations. But she also added the description of a woman who owned property on a mountain who was lying cold under the surface of her nearby lake. The property bordered that lake, and some man was trying to take the property and had murdered the woman to get the property.

Kirk sat back and picked up his cup of coffee, his heart sinking.

The trouble was, he had become a cop because he wanted to help. He then became a detective because he wanted to do *more*. Queenie had abilities that had allowed him to do *even more*. He had turned down a promotion because he wanted to remain in the field. He didn't want to manage people. He didn't want to manage coworkers. He just wanted to do his job.

The others had thought he was crazy. He would get a bigger paycheck, but the job would have been a much bigger headache too. He didn't deal well with the brass above, and he would have become the middleman between them and the detectives, *so* not a position he wanted. But he'd been given raise after raise. Not to mention respect and multiple commendations for a job well done.

Yet, no doubt his record of solving cases had eased back because he no longer had Queenie's assistance.

How sad was that? Most of the guys had no faith in psychics. Except the department knew and worked with a couple who were too good to not believe. Stefan Kronos was one of them. Queenie was another.

He'd asked Queenie about Stefan a time or two, and she'd just given him a blank stare, as if she didn't know anything about him. Kirk would have thought they had an inside line to each other.

Not knowing how to reply to her current email, he shut it down. His reply would expose a door he didn't dare open.

CHAPTER 2

Sunday, Early Morning...

T HE NEXT MORNING, Queenie walked back into her tent at the amusement park. Her gaze searched the floor, the curtains, the tabletop. Where was the spider? Feeling like a fool, she called out quietly, "Are you here?"

No response came. Just the wind, which blew through the thin fabric sides of the tent, making the interior gloomy and lonely. She groaned, pulling out her chair, searching underneath the cot and covered table.

Yesterday had been beyond unnerving between the people who had come for messages and the big man who she suspected had murdered that poor woman in the lake. And then, of course, there was what she thought was the child's voice and the very real phone call to Kirk.

She had barely slept all night.

Any contact with Kirk was guaranteed to jar her nerves for days. He'd been her lifeline, her grounding rod, in a chaotic world of murders and lost children and desperate family members searching for the truth to terrible crimes. Kirk had been instrumental in closing more than a dozen cases for people who had come to her for help. But she'd cared too much... She hadn't any defenses against the wounds of what humanity would inflict upon itself. When the last case blew up, it had broken her. Sure they'd gone on to find the serial killer but not before he'd taken his final victim—a woman she'd been desperate to save … and failed.

She went into hiding, like any animal, refusing to talk to anyone—including Kirk. She'd chased him away—and had further splintered her fragile emotional state into pieces.

She had turned her back on him and the other cops, desperately needing to find some peace inside. She'd ended up at a seaside community, renting a small place. Every day she had just walked the beach, trying so very hard to let go of all the pain and the trauma that had taken up residence in her mind, her brain. The memories were like a disease, festering away at her—she wasn't eating, barely drinking. Her body was a bone rack. But somehow, walking the beach, watching the waves roll over her feet, listening to the seagulls cry above, she could feel some of her own sense of calm returning. But it hadn't been long afterward that another truth had finally sunk in.

At the time, the trauma circling through her brain was so all encompassing that she hadn't seen the signs, hadn't even listened. But a miracle had happened among all that chaos. She was pregnant.

It was obviously Kirk's child, and, yet separated from the man, she clung to that little bit of Kirk, that part of her just so desperate to find some good in all that had gone so wrong. Overjoyed, she'd started to eat better, to sleep more. She knew she looked instantly better just because she was always smiling now. She walked for miles, hours on end, working through the emotional baggage she'd picked up from all her work, read fanatically on how to let go, how to release all the bits of energy clinging to her so she'd be as healthy as possible for this next part of her life. Her pregnancy was important to her, and she planned to do everything right.

She also worked at a retail store part-time, and tried to rest and relax and look after herself the remainder of the time. She had vowed to walk away from the work she'd been doing to keep her stress levels down and to hopefully create a better future for her and her child.

To that end she had sought out free group therapy—from PTSD counseling to handling grief and stress—all to rid herself of the nightmares, and the daytime ones too. She had attended various such meetings around town, run by local doctors who donated their time. She had to laugh how Kirk had earlier urged her to do this, and she had adamantly refused at the time. If only he knew …

Even odder was that more than a couple of those doctors had asked her out. Dr. Jamison was particularly good-hearted, and then there was Dr. Steel. He was all ego. But it didn't matter. She wasn't ready to replace Kirk. She wasn't sure she would ever be ready for that.

Regardless, the group meetings were a necessary diversion and had Queenie among living, breathing people. After all, there was no group therapy for broken psychics. Yet, her biggest improvements came from her discussions with two people not here with her.

It had taken her months of healing—months of talking to the child growing in her womb, months of talking to Kirk in her mind, always apologizing for not letting him know about his child, not letting him know this special person was coming into being. Her connection to her child grew in multiple ways daily.

The pregnancy had been rough. She'd been sick for months, had cramped constantly but had no medical insurance, so her checkups had been nonexistent. Reese's birth, more than three weeks early, had been the most painful and the most magnificent event of her life. Because of the birth's accelerated timing, she had decided to go to the hospital, in case of any complications, then gave birth and awaited the initial medical checkup of Reese, saying all was good with him. She and her son were gone within hours.

She and Reese had slipped out without notice, leaving what little money she had to cover a paltry part of her bill. Upon admittance, she'd given a fake address and phone number, being so broke that she'd been living in a slum hotel. That didn't stop her from dreading any mail that arrived, fearing it would be the rest of her hospital bill. But, when it never materialized over the next year, she finally relaxed.

Her son's arrival was so personal, and their connection was incredible and so damn deep. When Reese had stared out of those huge magnificent dark eyes, her heart had completely melted, and she'd vowed to do everything she could to keep him safe and to show him a whole lot better world than the one she lived in.

But it wasn't to be.

She'd worked steadily, trying several menial jobs, attempting to find a balance between enough money to live on and to raise her son on and yet, not so much work that she was away from him too long. She preferred to take jobs where she could keep him with her. She had cleaning jobs and phone-answering jobs, gardening jobs, always with the condition that her son could come with her. But then she'd gotten sick, and so had he.

Without enough money for early medical treatment, she kept working, doing everything she could to get him the best that he could have, until one night when her landlord had come looking for the overdue rent. Queenie had managed to open the door, and then she'd collapsed.

When she awoke, it was too late. Her son was gone.

She would have done anything to have left this Earth with him because the pain of being left behind was so torturous. She went into a spiraling decline that nobody could talk her out of. Added to that was the hope that her son was alive. She swore she could hear him crying out for her, as if their intimate connection was unbroken—only there was no response on his side. She was knocking, but no one answered. Kind of like her relationship with Kirk.

When her fever broke and she'd finally come to in the hospital days later, her body exhausted but over the worst of it, Kirk stood there to break the news to her. She could see his own pain as he was the one delegated to tell her the harsh truth. While his sympathy was vividly real, and he was helpless but to watch her endure this horrible loss, she also glimpsed his questioning glances, looks. He was doing the mental calculations, wondering …

Not only had her son died but his body had already been cremated. She couldn't comprehend the enormity of the shock, the loss. In her mind all she heard was his cries of pain when she had collapsed at the front door of her apartment. Added to that was the fear her son was alive, taken from her by unknown someones.

Reese's death and funeral already completed, Kirk paid for it as a favor to her. His own son … and he didn't know.

Her recuperation had been slow and lonely. As soon as she returned to her home, she'd set about reawakening her abilities for the sole purpose of contacting Reese. "Didn't I?" she murmured softly.

Yep, and it worked, didn't it? Her son's light laughter around her made her smile, as always, but now she wanted to cry at the same time.

It had taken her a long time to contact Reese, her own abilities rusty and the tunnel between the two that she'd forged was subsequently broken through illness and death. But she'd survived and that connection—different now than it had been—was more precious than anything anyone else could imagine. To know he was there, not always and not for long, but those few moments gave her a sweetness she'd thought she'd lost forever. This kept a smile on her face when nothing else could.

Terrified that if she didn't continue to use her abilities, she'd lose her connection to her son, she worked at the amusement park as the Queen Seer to provide answers for five dollars a question. A misfit of all misfits, she'd felt right at home. And she'd been here ever since.

Only she was stronger now. Her abilities clearer.

Even three and a half years later, whenever she heard about missing children cases, they broke her heart. Or, if little children came into her tent, her heart stuttered in pain—her loss of Reese still so damn hard to fathom. One didn't get over such a tremendous loss easily.

Initially after Reese's death, she had seen grief therapists, three to be exact. Spending her grocery budget on this new expense seemed to be the wiser choice. Yet everyone grieves in their own way. None of the counselors were quite right for her. Two were men, so Queenie had sought out a third, a woman. But still, she wasn't a mother. Funny but the very institution that had never really accepted Queenie had provided her with free counseling after her son's death. And the police department shrink had been by far the best fit. Still, it didn't last for long. Meeting at the police department and reminded of all her losses—Reese, Kirk, her work with the police, her confidence in her gift—wasn't conducive for a proper psychological and emotional healing.

So Queenie sought out some spiritual help. She spoke with two rabbis, a female Methodist preacher, a Catholic priest, a Baptist minister and some nondenominational church leaders. Each were of some solace when she was in their presence, but nothing stuck. Nothing helped afterward.

There was no training for this. No way to rid herself of the guilt that ate incessantly at her soul. She'd promised to look after Reese, but she'd failed. She'd have done anything for her son to get that second chance to keep him safe. To give him a future … In the back of her mind, she wondered, *Had she spoken to Kirk back then, would he have been interested in being a father? Would he have helped?* Only she'd been a mess when they had split. An unstable mess.

That was the last memory he had of her. And she'd been too terrified that he'd take away her son. Afraid she was unfit to be the mother of his child. … Maybe he'd have been right. But she'd tried. Dear Lord, she'd tried. And Kirk didn't know how much she'd changed. He didn't know how much joy having her child in her arms had brought her. How it had turned her life around so much so that she'd finally started looking after herself.

She shook off her memories, focusing on the present. Her gloomy tent. The absence of the curious messenger spider. She looked around for him quickly one more time. No luck. Then she stepped out of the doorway to her tent and took several deep breaths.

Behind her a voice called out. "Hey, are you opening up early today?"

She glanced over at Brutus the Strong Man and tossed him a bright smile. "Nope, certainly not. I came in early to see if I needed to clean up."

The lie came smoothly to her lips. One of the things she didn't like about her current lifestyle was the secret she kept and her need for subterfuge. If she were to tell any of them that she hoped her deceased son was alive, they would look at her as if she were ready to be locked up. How could she explain? But the mother genes inside her wouldn't be silenced. Reese was a reality she wouldn't give up.

Brutus walked in her tent, looked around and said, "What possible cleaning could there be?" He glanced at her sideways. "You look like shit."

She glared at him. "Your manners haven't improved."

"Why the hell should they?" He gave his big shoulders a shrug. "Nobody gives a damn what we do here. You know that."

At those words, she had to nod. "Isn't that the truth?"

"Did you eat?"

The question came out abruptly. Brutus, for all his size and the rough look to him, was really a caregiver. His methodology might leave a little to be desired, but he cared. "I had a banana."

He fisted his hands on his hips. His muscles bulged, and the cords in his neck stood out. "Get your ass over to Betty and make sure you get some food."

"I doubt I could keep anything down," she admitted. "I had a really rough night again."

"Are you pregnant?"

She gave a bitter laugh. "You're kidding, right?"

"Any number of guys here would love to be with you," he said. "You don't have to be alone if you don't want to be."

She wondered at the truth of that. She gave a quick nod.

"Maybe I'm just not ready." She brushed past him, trying to avoid contact.

But he reached out and grabbed her hand. "You can't always be so isolated," he growled.

Visions of his world came, images of Betty and him together. At least they were happy images, joyful images. He released her hand, and she gave him a gentle smile.

"You don't know the truth," she said quietly. "Some things can never be shared." And she walked farther into the sunshine. But she wondered at her own statement. She'd have sworn she could have shared anything with Kirk. But she'd chased him away—something she'd regretted ever since.

Inside, she admitted she'd hoped he would return, but it wasn't to be. And, as she thought about the condition she'd been in, it made sense that he hadn't. She'd been a wreck and likely to take down everyone close to her.

Comparing the inside of her dark tent to the outside was almost symbolic of her world. So much of her life was caught up with everybody else's pain, everybody else's problems. She had to escape that darkness when she was left alone with everybody else's worries and fears.

She walked briskly toward Brutus's trailer that he shared with Betty. They'd been together as a couple for a good dozen years. It wasn't the first time Queenie had had to knock on Betty's door for food. Queenie should have some money coming in, but she would use it now to hire another detective to do another search. She didn't know how the heck to get the type of research she needed. Who the hell knew anything about psychic message-delivering spiders? And where had that little bugger gone anyway?

"There you are, child." Betty was massive. But her smile

was just as big, and her heart outsized both of them.

Queenie sighed. "Brutus sent me over. He says I'm not eating enough."

Betty was wise beyond her years. Although only in her mid-thirties, she had the air of an eighty-year-old about her. "You probably told him you had eaten something to hide the fact that you had nothing, right?"

"How is it you always know?" Queenie grumbled. "I thought I was supposed to be the psychic."

"Oh, you're psychic all right. You just don't want anybody to know you're the real deal," Betty said with a big laugh. And, when she laughed, all her chins waggled and her arms moved as if they were alive.

It was fascinating. And so very different than Queenie's skinny frame.

Betty laughed again and said, "I wish I could give you twenty pounds."

Queenie admitted in a soft voice, "I wish you could too."

Betty pushed the trailer door open wider. "Come on in. We've got leftover pancakes from breakfast."

"Pancakes. I haven't had those since I was here last week," Queenie said, attempting a joke.

"Maybe I made a few extra in case you wanted to stop by. I heard you had a bit of a rough day yesterday."

Her mouth full of flapjacks, Queenie shot her a sideways look but stayed quiet.

"You know you can't hide anything around here." Betty settled her bulk comfortably on the big bench across from Queenie. Betty picked up a coffee carafe and filled a cup. She pushed it toward Queenie.

Queenie stared at it, wanting it almost as much as she

did the flapjacks. She took a breather from inhaling the food and lifted the hot brew, inhaling the aroma. "You make the best coffee."

"And you might even get a second cup if you tell me what the hell went wrong yesterday."

"Who said anything went wrong?"

"Well, Carlos went looking for you when the line at your tent was at least ten deep, and he couldn't find you. At one point he was ranting and raving because you weren't doing your job."

Queenie winced, a motion she tried to hide but knew Betty would have caught it anyway. "Yeah, well, I had a couple rough moments there."

"Care to share?"

Deliberately Queenie cut a big stack of pancakes and shoved it in her mouth. If nothing else it gave her a chance to think. Nobody pulled the wool over Betty's eyes. She was good. But she came from the heart, and that made it even harder to bluff. "Which part? The spider that created visions in my fake crystal ball or the young boy who will die in three days or that last guy I spoke to who had murdered a woman," she finally said, her voice low.

Betty gasped and leaned forward. "Really? Did you get any murder details?"

Queenie shook her head. "Not really. Just a woman floating at one end of a lake caught in the weeds under the surface. But her property is there. It borders the lake itself. This guy was trying to buy it. He asked me if he would get it, and that's when I saw her, and I told him that he already knew the answer to that question. He got really, really angry and pulled the poor little boy he was with out of the tent. But he left an air of evil, and I just couldn't stay afterward."

Betty stared at her, wordless.

Queenie took the moment to eat another large bite.

"And what's this about a spider?"

That was much harder to explain. But typical of Betty to move right along to the next topic. Queenie finished the flapjacks, picked up the coffee, took a big sip and sat back with a happy sigh. "I'm not sure what's with the spider. But there was a spider, and it reached up and touched my crystal ball. And you and I both know that nothing makes the inside of that ball change. But this time the inside of my crystal ball swirled with a white cloud. That last man, the murderer, was going to kill the spider, but I saved it. Then, after the man left, I was trying to flick the spider off. The whole time it's as if he was looking at me – communicating with me, and I thought I heard a little boy in my head calling out, *Mommy, Mommy.*"

A call that had nearly crippled her. But that part wasn't something she could share.

"Honey, you've got to stop following those missing kid cases," Betty said. "They're killing you."

Of course Betty didn't know about Reese. Queenie took a deep breath. "I know. I know that, but it's hard. So many people are in need out there."

An odd silence followed as Betty continued to study Queenie. She had hoped Betty would be satisfied with what she had heard so far. The trouble was, Betty had the natural curiosity of anyone and some of the sight herself. "Did you recognize the child's voice?"

Queenie gave her a bitter smile. "No. It's never that easy, you know? No names ever come, no dates, no locations. Wouldn't it be nice if I could go to the cops and say, *Hey, there's a murdered woman in the lake up at so and so. Here's the longitude and latitude coordinates. You want to run up and grab her? And, by the way, the guy who murdered her is standing beside me with a little kid."*

Her tone was bitter. She'd been through this time and time again with Betty. But she at least understood and had seen the struggle Queenie had gone through.

"Well, you can't just run away again," she said comfortably.

That stopped Queenie in her tracks. "Run away?"

"Honey, you work at an amusement park. Off the grid from the real world. You're either looking for something or running away from something."

"Maybe it's both," Queenie said. She reached across and refilled her coffee cup. She stared down at it. "It still doesn't change the fact I feel like I have to leave soon."

Betty sighed. "I wish you wouldn't."

Queenie's mind immediately said, *I wish I didn't have to.* "I'll try to stay and make it work," Queenie promised. "But you know it yourself. When you get that feeling that you've got to go, then you've got to listen."

"You've got friends here," Betty said. "You can get cheap food, a place to stay if you need to. This is home."

"What kind of a home is it though, for me?" Queenie asked, her voice gentle. "You have Brutus. I don't have anyone. As a future, this isn't a whole lot to look forward to."

"That's just part of what you're running away from. You came to the amusement park world to get away, not to arrive here. Brutus and me, we're here because we want to be. You're here because you don't want to be somewhere else," Betty said quietly. "Maybe you need a change of attitude?"

"Or maybe just a whole new life would be nice too." She

smiled, giving herself a good mental head shake to smarten up. "As usual your cooking is divine."

Betty gave a big belly laugh again. "You can hardly say that. You come here so starving that I don't think it would matter what I fed you. You just want the food to fill that small stomach of yours."

"At least it's awesome food, so I get the pleasure out of that at the same time." Queenie gave her a big grin. She leaned closer and said, "Did Carlos say anything more?"

Betty shook her head. "No. Haven't even seen him this morning."

"Good. I'll head back to my tent and open up and will be there extra long today. If I'm making lots of money, he might forget about yesterday."

"Tell him that you were sick. But don't ever tell him about that murdered woman."

"Right. I know. He'd start selling my services to the police and take a cut for himself," Queenie said. "And I did that for free for long enough."

"Would you do it for money?" Betty asked curiously.

Queenie stopped in the act of getting up from the bench seat. "I don't know. It's easy to say no in theory, but, when you're starving, money can make all the difference." She straightened, walked over to the kitchen counter and placed her plate and cup in the sink.

"Don't bother washing them," Betty said. "I've got to wash up the others anyway."

Queenie turned to look back at her friend and smiled. "You're a good person."

A peculiar look came over Betty's face, no longer with any hint of laughter. "I'm not, you know?" she said. "I was at one time, but I took a wrong path too. I did some things I'm not proud of. And now? Well, now I try to live my life the best way I can, but I know that those mistakes will always be there."

Queenie stared at Betty for a long moment. Queenie didn't know if she should ask more questions or not. It was the first time Betty had ever really opened up about the other areas of her life. So many of the people here had secrets. Then people everywhere had secrets. Including Queenie.

She walked over, squeezed Betty's shoulder and said, "I think the best any of us can do is be the person we want to be, should always have been, from this moment on. I don't know if there's forgiveness in this world. I've seen so much of the ugliness that I hope a great big pit of black lava awaits for those who have been complete assholes. But, since so many of them got a free pass instead, I'm afraid they'll get another pass if there's a life after this. So I can only focus on this moment and hope all the rest takes care of itself."

"You say the right words, girl," Betty said. "But I don't think you're following your own advice. You're so caught up in the past that you can't see the future right in front of you."

Queenie walked to the trailer door, cast a glance back and said, "No, maybe not. But I *am* trying." And she went out and closed the door.

Moving slowly, Queenie walked back to her tent. Her bad night preyed on her, but, now that she'd had some food, the world didn't look quite so rough. And it was foolish. She was certainly capable of feeding herself, but some days she just didn't care. She hated to think other people pitied her. But she'd lost her trust in people a long time ago.

KIRK'S PHONE RANG just then. It was the intake desk out front. "A young woman here says her mother is missing," Sandy said.

"And?" he asked gently. "Is that a current case or an open case?"

"Neither," she replied. "But I think she feels like nobody will believe her. Which makes you the perfect guy for her to talk to."

At the hard *click* on the other end of the phone, he sighed and replaced the receiver. "So Sandy's trying to give me a woman who can't find her mother."

"Ha, ha," Peter said. "Glad Sandy likes you and not me."

"I don't know about that," Kirk said. Standing, he reached for a notepad. "She seems to pigeonhole these people and send them in my direction. I don't get it."

"And yet you always do really well with her assignments." Peter smirked. "Maybe *she's* psychic."

Kirk snorted. After spending enough time with a real psychic, it was pretty hard to miss it in other people, but he didn't think he'd ever seen it with Sandy. Then again, maybe some psychics knew how to hide their abilities. Where Queenie seemed to run on the edge, her abilities completely overwhelming her, Sandy would be the kind of person who would run her day and allow the abilities in only if and when she felt she was ready. He walked out to the intake area and talked to Sandy, getting the daughter's name. Lee-Anne Jenkins. He called out for her.

A young woman stood, clutching her hands together, and walked toward him. He judged her age to be somewhere around her late twenties. He held the door open for her. "Let's go where we can talk." He led her into one of the small interrogation rooms and motioned at the chair for her to sit down. "Now what can I do for you?"

"My mom," she said quietly. "She's missing. Has been missing for weeks."

He thrummed his fingers on the notepad. "When did you last hear from her?"

The young woman winced. "About three weeks ago."

"How often do you speak?"

"We used to talk once every few days to a week. Then we had an argument, and I told her that I wouldn't call her until she decided to be a little more amiable." Tears came to the young woman's eyes. "But I didn't mean it. I was just so angry."

"And then what happened?"

She shrugged. "A couple weeks passed. I'd been sick," she said by way of explanation. "Later I called her but got no answer. And I called again and again and again. Her phone just keeps ringing."

"Did you go see her?"

"No. I don't have a car. She lives on Mable Lake. Her property borders the lake. It's acreage that she's had several offers on because it's so picturesque," the woman said. "But she's never wanted to sell. She plans on staying there until she is old and gray."

"Anybody in particular trying to buy the place?"

The young woman shrugged. "I don't really know names. She got a big offer in the million-dollar range which I wanted her to take. That was the reason behind our fight. My mother is broke. It's all she can do to pay the taxes every year. She needs better food. She can't look after the property the way it needs to be looked after."

"Does she work? Has she missed any work?"

"She used to work but doesn't now. She's an artist and was doing really well for herself, and then her fingers crippled up, and she found it much harder to create the same quality of paintings she used to. But, being an artist, she didn't have a backup plan for getting old. I always assumed selling the property was her backup plan, but she has refused to do so."

"I imagine it can be hard when you've already lost your creativity and your way of making a living," Kirk said gently. "Then to give up the one last thing you'd always counted on that brings you comfort, which is your home."

Lee-Anne looked at him with understanding dawning in the back of her eyes; then she burst into tears.

Kirk sighed and settled back. He reached for something on the counter behind him and pushed a pack of Kleenex toward her. "Here. Use this."

Sobbing quietly, she pulled out several tissues and basically covered her face with them.

"Do you have a picture of your mother?"

Sniffling and wiping her eyes, she nodded. Then she pulled her purse into her lap and dug through it. Various items ended up atop the table.

He was amazed to see hairbrushes and wallets and makeup packs. He wasn't even sure what one thing was and wasn't going to ask. But why did women have to carry so much stuff with them? He never understood. Queenie was the opposite. She was a minimalist by nature. She carried cash or a debit card and her keys, and that was it. But, in this instance, this woman appeared to have everything but the kitchen sink.

Finally Lee-Anne pulled out a small envelope and removed several photos from it. She laid them on the table and turned them around so he could see. "This is my mother, taken years ago."

The woman was in her late twenties with blond hair about shoulder length. She had a big smile on her face, as if everything in her world was right at that moment. He understood that a snapshot was just that. It was a second of a person's life, hopefully at a good time in their life.

He studied several of them and asked, "What about friends? Other family? Have you contacted anyone?"

"There was just her and me." Tears clogged her throat. "That's why I feel so bad. If something happened to her while I was so busy being in a snit, I don't know what I'll do," she wailed.

"Well, I wouldn't start thinking along that line. If you haven't checked at her home, I can call the police or the local sheriff in the area and get them to take a drive up."

She nodded. "Please. I don't understand why she wouldn't have answered her phone."

"Did you ever think maybe she can't afford her phone anymore?" he asked.

Shock and shame filled her gaze. She stared down at the photos. "I hope it is that." Her voice was a little stronger, a little more robust. "Because then I'll start sending her money every month."

"Can you afford to?"

Lee-Anne shrugged. "I'm a graphic designer, so maybe not." She focused on the pictures once more. "Please find her."

He nodded. "Do you have an address? Where is this property located?"

She scribbled down what she knew and the directions to get there. "She has a post office box in the nearby small town. I've contacted them, and they said she hasn't come in to pick up her mail."

"Well, that's something," he said.

She shook her head. "Not really. My mother rarely gets her mail, so she wasn't in the habit of checking in very often."

He nodded. "How long a drive is it?"

"Over an hour," she confessed. "But, as I said, I don't have a car."

"So how do you get back and forth to see her?"

"Normally my mother would come see me. Just not very often."

"But ..."

"She doesn't have any money to make the trip. She hasn't been down in over a year. That's how long since I've seen her."

Kirk sat back and stared at the young woman. They both sounded like they wanted to be together but couldn't find a way to make that happen. "Look. We'll see if somebody can drive out there and take a look. Are you sure you don't know who wanted to buy the property from her?"

She shook her head. "I don't know who. She just said she didn't like him. He was arrogant and mean, and she didn't want him to have anything to do with her beautiful place."

"Is it beautiful?" he asked, wondering about the daughter's own mind-set of the home.

Lee-Anne nodded and smiled. "It really is. It's got a beautiful view of the lake, and I can see that the sprawl of Seattle will catch up there eventually. But, right now, it's more of a holiday home for others than for her."

"What vehicle does she drive?"

"A small Nissan pickup," she said. "About twelve years old."

"We can run the plates and see if she's got it insured. With any luck we can also see if it's at the property. For all you know, she may have gone on a holiday somewhere."

She shook her head. "No, you don't understand. She didn't have money for anything." She stood, grabbing her items, putting them back in her purse. "Can you make copies of those pictures? I don't want to let the originals go."

He nodded. "I can do that."

HE DIDN'T LIKE it here. Except for the spiders. They were his friends. His mommy screamed when she saw them, so he had to keep them out of sight. His daddy squished them.

That wasn't nice.

But Daddy was mean. He hit Mommy and him too. He'd asked the spiders over and over again to stop Daddy, but they couldn't.

The shouting increased overhead. He slapped his hands to his ears to block out the sound, but he still heard Mommy crying.

"That damn kid. I told you not to bring him home. What kind of a loser woman are you that you have to look after someone else's kid instead of having your own?"

The little boy listened to the words, but they weren't making sense.

Mommy never answered. Her weeping didn't stop.

Slap. Smack. Thud.

He scrunched up his face and cried. He knew what that meant. He lay down and pulled the covers over his head, his body freezing in fear.

If Daddy came downstairs, then it was bad, … real bad.

But, if Mommy wasn't his mommy, who was? And could his mommy come and take him away? … He didn't want to live here anymore.

Then he heard it. … Footsteps.

His breath hitched in the back of his throat, and, terrorized, he waited alone in the dark.

CHAPTER 3

Sunday, Midmorning...

I N HER TENT once again, Queenie searched for the spider. Found no sign of him. She placed her Open for Business sign outside, sat down at her table and waited for the customers to flow in. Business was slow today. Probably her punishment for having walked away when there was a line yesterday. She had needed the money too. These last few months had been slow and had barely paid enough to keep her going.

When Carlos walked in a half hour later, his face set as if determined to have something out with her, she smiled at him and said, "Thanks so much for letting me go home sick yesterday."

He froze, and the smile fell off his face. "You were sick?" he asked cautiously.

She nodded. "All of a sudden, I felt like I would throw up. I didn't think having those kinds of germs around this place would be very good for business. Not to mention the fact that vomiting isn't an activity the public wants to see." She spoke with an airy laugh. "But I'm feeling much better now."

He took a cautious step back as if she had germs that would reach out and smack him one. "Are you sure you're feeling okay? We don't want anybody here at the amusement park getting sick."

"I wouldn't have had breakfast with Betty just now if I thought that was the case," she said gently.

"Okay. But you should have given me some warning. There was a line," he whined. "And when we have a line like that, you know how much money we're gonna make."

She did know. She was the one who put the five-dollar bills into the jar. Sometimes she could easily do twenty customers in an hour. Maybe it wasn't big money for a lot of people, but it was for her. Not that she got a whole lot of it. But all business was erratic. There was no rhyme or reason when there would be a good day or a bad day. If her crystal ball could tell her things like that, then she could manage her days off so they were most effective. But her abilities didn't work that way.

As far as Carlos was concerned, she didn't have any abilities. He was all about making it look like she did. The fact that she knew that just made it easier on her. He was also a germophobe, and that gave her irrefutable reasons for leaving the tent unexpectedly.

"I will next time, if I can." She nodded. "Honestly, yesterday was so bad that I wasn't sure I should stick around at all."

Just then they could hear voices approaching from outside. His face lit up. "Hopefully it'll be a good day today. You know? As we lead up toward graduation, we get a lot more people in here."

"You mean, as the summer holidays come through," she said with a laugh. "I'm not sure graduation has anything to do with it."

"We're running a bunch of ads geared toward the grads," he said with a big smirk. "Offering them your abilities to determine what they should be doing in life."

She stared at him. "You did what?"

He waved his hand airily at her. "That's perfect for you. You do such a great job with that already."

She shook her head. "I do for the people who seek me out naturally. I am not at all sure how that'll work when they come in droves."

"What's the difference?" he asked.

He seriously did not understand how that strained her energy levels or how seeing difficult information hurt her on so many levels. But there was really no working with him. He had a mind of his own, and the bottom line for him was money.

He quickly backed away as the first person walked through the tent.

A young girl stood there and smiled. "Is it my turn?" she asked.

Carlos motioned toward Queenie. "She's all yours. Make sure you ask one good question," he cautioned, "because she really does have the answers." And then he disappeared.

The girl looked even more excited than ever, if that was possible. She raced up to Queenie and jabbered about all the colleges she'd applied to, wanting Queenie to tell her which one she would get accepted to because she wanted to make plans. She was really hoping to move to that location soon, so she could spend the summer getting to know everyone. All her friends had heard already, so she figured the mail was just late, but her tone of voice rose up—almost in a panic.

Queenie stared at her, resignation deep in her heart. She was afraid to touch this girl's hand because she could already feel the energy coming toward her. And how did she let the girl down easy? How did she let her know all the applications she'd sent so far were rejected?

"Have you applied to every one you wanted?" Queenie hedged.

"Well, there's still the local one," she said, "but I didn't want to stay in town for the summer."

"Why is that?" Queenie asked, looking for anything to give her a positive outcome. The local college would be a positive outcome. But the girl had to come to that on her own; otherwise it'd be a crushing disappointment.

"My boyfriend broke up with me," she said, her voice just above a whisper. She shoved her fist into her pockets. "But can't you see that?"

"I can see a lot," Queenie said cautiously. "Place your hand in mine, please." She held her hand out, palm upward. The young girl laid her palm down on top of Queenie's. An instant affirmation slammed into her. "I see you staying locally," she said quietly. "And, no, I don't see the same boyfriend back in your life."

The young girl jumped back, pulling her hand away. She glared at Queenie. "That's not what I want to hear," she cried.

"I know that," Queenie said. "Yet it doesn't change the fact that's what I see."

The young woman gave her a hurt look and raced out of the tent.

At least she wasn't sobbing. Queenie would take solace where she could.

Almost immediately a young man walked in, about the same age as the woman who just left. He smiled and said, "I don't think you told her what she wanted to hear."

She looked at him. "I can't deliver good news when it's not."

His smile fell away. "People say you're the real thing," he said abruptly.

She shrugged. "I'd like to think so. I don't deliberately mislead people. That was the problem with the girl who just left. She didn't like the answers."

He cast a backward glance, as if seeing the girl. "She's a year behind me. I graduated a year ago and remember how she was pretty hung up on her boyfriend back then."

Queenie could see the energy flowing from him toward the young woman who had run out before him. "Maybe you should talk to her," she said with a gentle smile. "I can tell you right now that's probably a very good match."

Startled, he glanced at Queenie. "That's not what I came here for."

She shrugged. "Sometimes you get a little more than you asked for."

He hesitated, almost shifting his weight from foot to foot, as if uncertain what to say.

She looked at him. "Place your hand in mine."

He laid a hand atop hers. She could feel the pain and the frustration. Another face showed up in her crystal ball. Truly it was in her mind's eye, but, for the sake of what she was doing, she always said it was the crystal ball.

"You're worried about your brother." She felt his start. But she clasped her hands around his, holding them in place. "He's a drug addict. He's taken too many chances."

The young man froze in front of her, hope and fear worrying on his face.

She sighed and gently released his hand. "He has a tough road ahead of him," she said quietly. "He does have the stuff inside him to make that journey. But he'll need your support."

She wasn't sure anything she'd said was helpful, but the young man's face lit up.

"Does that mean he's done overdosing?"

"You need to get him into rehab," she said. Instantly a name came to her. She pulled out a pad of paper and wrote it down. "Riverdale. Get him into Riverdale. If you can get him there, he'll do much better." She ripped off the piece of paper and handed it to him.

He looked down at it and said, "How am I supposed to pay for it?"

"Talk to them about their charity programs." She smiled as the answers flowed. "They do help a certain number of cases for free. Most of these places do, but they don't tell you about it."

He stared at her in surprise. "They do?"

She nodded. "But, like I said, they don't want anybody to know. *Riverdale.* You contact Riverdale on his behalf and get your brother down there for an assessment."

He took a step back. "I didn't tell you about anything like this."

"I know." She stared at him, her gaze steady and strong.

He took another hesitant step back, his mind obviously overwhelmed with the *what ifs*. And then he turned and bolted out the door.

She smiled until she realized she'd forgotten to ask him for the five dollars. She groaned. "Well, that's your free one for the day," she muttered. She didn't blame the kid. He'd been a little too affected by what was going on to remember.

At the same time, she couldn't keep doing that. She had to put food on her table somehow.

The morning continued on with more odd requests, odd people. Some days it was just girl after girl, looking for boyfriend information; other times mothers looking for information about their children and whether they could have another baby. Today it was everything.

There was a young man afraid to buy a house because the market was so unstable. Privately she thought the market had never been more stable, but she wasn't a financial analyst, so what did she know? It was more a case of he was afraid his girlfriend wouldn't move in with him because she wouldn't like the house.

A woman wanted Queenie's advice on a weight-loss-and-training program. That one really surprised Queenie. She tried to explain to the woman that the program wasn't necessarily the best option, given the money involved. But she hadn't been interested in Queenie's answer. She was looking for validation of her own choice. There was only so much Queenie could say.

By the time she was ready to take a break, she quickly flipped the Open sign to Closed and headed to the coffee stand. There was one thing she did like, and that was her caffeine. She'd been told by enough people that she should stop drinking it, but it was one of the few comforts in her world. And she wasn't up to letting that go too.

Time to get food, right, Reese?

He didn't answer, but a light laugh filled her mind.

She chuckled.

She grabbed a coffee and a hot dog, and headed back to her tent. She stepped inside to see a man with his back toward her. Her voice sharp, she said, "The sign says I'm closed."

The man turned and looked at her. "Hello, Queenie."

KIRK STARED AT Queenie, hating the fear on her face as soon as she saw him.

She stared at him, walked around to the table and sagged into the chair. "What are you doing here?" she asked, her voice trembling.

He stroked a hand through his hair. How did he explain when he wasn't even sure himself? They had so much history. So many highs, so many lows, such a mess of a relationship, so much pain and ugliness … He'd done his damnedest to weather it all, but, in the end, it had broken them. He wasn't even sure what words to give her to make her feel more at ease. "Your email."

He could almost see the wave of fear falling from her shoulders like a shawl she took off and laid on the chair behind her. Why? What was she afraid of?

"What about it?" she asked. "I told you all I knew."

"Did you?"

She glared at him, getting her spunk back.

He loved that. She was never the kind to stay down for long. Even when she was at her absolutely most broken, she'd come out in the ring fighting. Unfortunately it seemed like she'd been fighting everyone, even him. All he'd tried to do was help her, but she couldn't tell who was helping and who wasn't. She'd sent him away, and, to his everlasting regret, he'd gone.

She nodded. "He was only here for a couple minutes. He laughed at me because I was bothered by a spider, but he left, outraged at my words."

His heart slammed against his chest. "You told him something that upset him?" He watched the regret whisper across her face.

"I didn't think before it came out," she said. "I was so

upset at what I saw that I said something to him about him already knowing the owner was dead."

Kirk leaned over, placed his hands firmly on the table in front of her and glared at her. "Did you in any way indicate you knew he'd murdered this woman?"

Her face went blank. And then she shrugged. "I don't think so, but I don't know. You know what it's like when I get the visions. They come and they go. I grasp bits and pieces, but I don't record everything."

He looked around at the table she worked behind and the absolutely ridiculous headdress sitting on the side of it. "What the hell are you even doing here? You have talent, real talent, and you're sitting here, acting like some charlatan."

"I'm doing what I do because it's what I do," she said, her tone hard. "I don't exactly have much in the way of career options. Nor can I keep working for the police when they've decided I was half-cocked and unstable. Plus they never paid for my assistance either—they didn't want anyone to know they were listening to a psychic. So … that doesn't work. … At least not anymore."

He hated the note of accusation in her voice. He understood it, but he hated it. "I didn't have anything to do with that," he said.

Her smile, if anything, went more blank. She stared at him, her eyes, as always, huge wells of deep midnight blue. For the longest time he would succumb to the lure and completely bury himself in those eyes, in her life, their love all-encompassing, their passion all-overwhelming. When they made love, it was completely transported to something else. They forgot their surroundings; they forgot everything but what they were feeling. He wondered if her psychic ability had wrapped him into her same weird slice of life because it never felt the same before or after. He'd had relationships since, more to help him forget what he'd lost, and had never found anything even close.

"Why do you keep putting yourself in danger?" he cried out in frustration.

She looked at him. "Are you serious? Look where I am. What danger am I in?"

"You called out a murderer."

"I don't know that for sure," she said instantly. "Besides, I was … off. … That damn spider had me off my game, so the murderer surprised me."

"Explain." His voice was direct and hard, uncompromising.

She shrugged. "It wasn't much. Just something unusual." At his look, she groaned and explained about the spider's and this man's arrival at the time. "I don't know. I'm still not myself," she muttered.

"But you were sure enough that you contacted me."

Her back stiffened, and she just glared at him.

He was sorry for making it sound so heartless. He knew she came from a place of deep pain, and he wished he could do something to help her. But there wasn't anything. He'd already tried many times. "Back to this man. Can you describe him?"

He watched as she closed her eyes and gave him a recital. "Six foot two, at least 280, most of it chest and belly. Blustery, arrogant, the world is his, and the rules don't apply to him."

"Anything else?"

"Going slightly bald on the top. His hair is dark, almost black, but gray's etching in. His face has a florid complexion, definitely a double chin, dressed well. The child was more easily identifiable."

"What child?"

"He came in with a small boy, holding his hand."

"What can you tell me about the boy?"

"Five-years-old, wearing jeans with the cuffs rolled up, sneakers that had little lights when he walked." Her voice softened as she described the child. "Plaid shirt. He wasn't happy. He didn't like being in the tent, and he didn't like it when the man got angry. He flinched at the tone of voice the man used, and, when they turned, he was dragged out of the tent by the big man."

"What did he tell you exactly?"

"He asked if he would get the property he was after."

Kirk listened while she continued with the message she gave him.

"Tell me what you saw in your vision."

"A woman, early fifties, maybe blond hair, longish, floating around her head. She was just beneath the surface of the lake, maybe an hour's drive from here. Her property borders a lake. There's an old home. She's slim, maybe too slim. But she's at peace."

"What do you mean, *she's at peace?*"

"Her face is peaceful." Queenie stopped, confused. "At least it feels that way."

"She's dead," he said. "Right?"

Queenie nodded. "She's dead. And it was not a natural death."

"How do you know that?"

"Her throat has been sliced," she said quietly. "But it's still not enough for you to go on. It never is."

He stood back, his fingers jiggling the coins in his pocket as he studied her. "Something's different this time though."

She stared at him. "What?"

He lifted his gaze to a point in the tent behind her. "I had a young woman come in, reporting her mother as missing. Her property borders a lake. And it's about an hour out of town."

Queenie stared at him. Then she held out her hand. He hated this part. It didn't always happen when they touched—and it never happened, at least he didn't think it ever happened, when they had sex—but, when she wanted to know something, it was her way of accessing it. He stared down at her hand.

"Scared?" she challenged.

He extended his hand and placed it on hers, hating she could still get that response from him. It wasn't that he was scared; it was—

"It's her," Queenie said softly. "It's her mother."

"Every time you do that is so damn freaky." Cautiously he added, "So you're saying, if we go to that property ... How will we find the mother's body?"

Queenie gave a sad smile. "She's under the lake's surface. You won't see her unless you are almost on top of her. But she's not close to her property. She's on the far side of the lake."

"How did she get there?"

"He used the woman's boat, rowed it across and dumped her out. Other houses are around. He believes nobody saw him."

"*Believes?*" he pounced. He watched her eyes unfocus, going wide and black. Another process of hers that always unnerved him. "Who?" he asked urgently. "You know we need witnesses."

But no answer was immediately forthcoming.

He slowly went to pull away his hand, but she grasped it firmly. He waited, not sure what she was up to. With Queenie, one never knew.

Her voice changed, became someone else's voice. A *man's* voice. "Somebody else saw him," she said, almost trancelike.

He stared at her, instinctively pulling back, but she wouldn't let Kirk go.

"Somebody not of this world. Somebody with abilities like mine. Somebody who's watching him."

"Watching who?"

"Watching the killer."

"Why would he do that?" They'd handled a couple twisted cases earlier on. Cases he still had trouble sleeping with. The last thing he wanted was to have another one.

"It's a game to him." She opened her eyes, dropped his hand and stared at him, her eyes coming around, focusing on Kirk. "I didn't just say that, did I?"

He nodded. "Oh, hell yeah, you did." He shook his head. "But I sure wish you hadn't. You need to tell me who *he* is."

"I don't know," she said in a flat tone. "I don't know who he is."

"How is that possible? He just took over your body, spoke the words you were thinking." Shocked, he whispered, "Can you make sure he can't connect again?"

She gave a broken laugh. "I didn't expect to connect now. … How can I stop him if he tries again?"

"Did you learn to protect yourself at all?" he asked. "You always talked about needing to do more of that."

"Yes," she said. "I've done a lot of work in that area. You're right. The next time he tries, maybe I'll stop him, now that I know he's there."

"Next time?" he asked, his heart sinking. "How do you know there will be a next time?"

"He's not done," she whispered, her eyes huge wells of grief. "He's a killer himself. And he'll kill again. But now that he knows I'm here, he wants to show me what he can do."

HE SOBBED GENTLY in his bed in his dark little room in the basement. His tiny body shook with pain. There was blood on his face, his hands. ... He wanted to leave, ... but the door was locked. It was always locked now. He'd wanted, begged, to go to school, but Daddy said it wasn't going to happen.

That made him all the sadder.

One of the big spiders walked across the boy's pillow.

He whispered, "Please help me. Please ... find someone to help me ..."

The spider walked closer. Then a second one and a third one.

"Please," he cried brokenly. "There has to be someone who can help."

Now dozens of spiders appeared. He watched with a happy smile as they waded through his blood to get to him, then over him and the bed to the wall, where they climbed up and out the crack in the window, like soldiers of the night.

"Find her, ... please."

WELL, AS A contact went, she hadn't been receptive. But she

hadn't been scared. Interesting how she'd connected to one of his subjects. He hadn't seen that coming. She'd tried to shut down her defenses on him. But she wasn't very skilled at that. She was one of those bleeding hearts, always open to helping others but not really capable of helping herself. She didn't understand danger when it was there inside her already. And that was the fun part. All of this, all of her efforts to shut him out were for naught. He could step inside any time because, of course, he already was inside.

What he wanted to do was watch her, keep an eye on her, see what was happening.

He zapped out of that space, back over to the little family he'd been following for a few weeks now. He watched as the wife packed up her husband's sandwiches. Her husband would go to work again, though he was sick, sick, sick. But he would keep trying. He had to do the right thing.

The Watcher grimaced. "These bleeding hearts." The world was full of them, and they were all useless.

As the wife went to fill the coffee thermos, the Watcher made the wife's hand reach for the white powder in the tub beside the coffee. She put another healthy spoonful inside the coffee and stirred it. Then she quickly closed the container with the white stuff and put it back on the shelf.

The Watcher smiled. "Just like a good little wife." He watched as she packed up the rest of the food and carried it out to her husband. "Sweetheart, you be careful today. And please, if you start to feel sick at all, come home."

Her husband leaned over, kissed her on the forehead and said, "I promise."

The Watcher looked on as the two of them hugged briefly and then separated. The little girl at Mommy's side, tugging at her hands, said, "Daddy is sick, isn't he?"

The woman smiled down and nodded. "Yes, he is."

"The doctor says they can't fix him, right?"

The mother nodded. "But we can't lose hope. We love him very much. We have to stay positive."

At that, the intruder just laughed. The man was dying. Still, he'd die from shock if he understood what had happened to him in the first place. And by whom.

The intruder wasn't putting his own career in danger. He watched the woman gather up her child in her arms, the two of them crying gently. That was perfect. The Watcher really did love a good sob story.

CHAPTER 4

Sunday, Noon …

QUEENIE WANTED KIRK to leave. She wanted to sort out what just happened to her. Who was this Watcher? What was he really doing? She didn't even know how to explain this vision to Kirk, but it was like she'd been crushed into somebody's embrace, an embrace she didn't want, an embrace she couldn't see but could only feel. It hadn't been painful as much as an icy chill grabbing on and holding her tight. Forcing her to see what the Watcher wanted her to see. She didn't know what it was, who it was, but somehow somebody had caught sight of her abilities. And had latched on—opening some communication channel without her permission.

"Go away," she whispered. "Please just go away."

"How am I supposed to do that?" Kirk cried out. "Look at you. You're a wreck."

Slowly using every ounce of her energy, she utilized her outrage to stand and glare at him. "I am *not* your problem."

But, instead of backing away, he leaned over the table until they were nose to nose. "Why can't I be a decent human being and worry about you? Why do you have to look at me as if I'm taking pity on you or some other stupid emotion? Why are you always pushing me away?"

"Because you don't give a damn." Her voice was more of

a snarl than anything. "You didn't then and don't now, so don't try to fake it."

He stepped back as if she'd smacked him hard. He stared at her in bewilderment. "What are you talking about?"

She sagged into her chair and waved her hand. "It's all water under the bridge. Just leave." She pointed at the tent opening behind her. "I'm supposed to be here making money, not making your arrest record look prettier." Inside, she was breaking into pieces. She hadn't meant to bring up all the old pain.

"I'm not going anywhere, not until you explain yourself."

To his credit he did sound completely bewildered. Just then somebody poked their head through the tent door and asked, "Is it our turn yet?"

She smiled. "Yes, absolutely it is. He's just leaving." She glared at Kirk. "I have to make a living."

He stood off to the side.

She shook her head. "These sessions are private. Stand outside please."

He moved outside a little way from the door.

She watched his back recede through the tent flaps with relief. Pulling all her resources together, she summoned up a smile for the child standing in front of her who must have been maybe twelve or thirteen. "What is it you would like to know?"

Eagerly he stepped forward.

Queenie worked her way through the line that had gathered outside while she'd been arguing with Kirk. Her coffee had long since gone cold. She thought she'd eaten the hot dog but even now wasn't sure.

When the little girl came in, her hair in rosy ringlets,

Queenie smiled down at her. Queenie was so damn tired, but she could always give them something to look forward to. "What's your name?"

"Kirsten," replied the child.

"What would you like to know?" she asked Kirsten. She'd only given the mother half a glance. Her interest was solely on the little one.

"I want to know if my daddy's going to live."

And just like a sock to the gut, the breath rushed out of her mouth, and she sagged in her chair. She desperately tried to pull herself back together again. From the look on the mother's face, the tears in her eyes, her trembling lips, Queenie understood the mother already knew the answer. There wasn't much anybody could say to Kirsten to change this outcome. Unfortunately a whisper of the Watcher's energy was still here. She deliberately cloaked her mind, pulling Kirsten and her mother into Queenie's protective circle. She looked down at Kirsten and said, "Do you want him to live?"

Kirsten's head bobbed up and down. "Of course I do. He's my daddy, and I love him. He wants to see Maddy because she's a miracle worker," Kirsten said as if repeating phrases she'd heard.

"I've heard that. Has he tried to get onto Maddy's Floor?"

"He has," Kirsten announced as if she knew all about the intricacies involved.

Queenie turned to look at the mother. "Is this true? Is Dr. Maddy taking your husband's case?"

The woman shook her head. "No. We've been trying to get Dr. Maddy to help. But there's no room on the floor," she said sadly, adding, "And her schedule is booked months in advance."

"Have you contacted her personally?"

The woman nodded. "I've tried, but it's hard to get through."

Queenie thrummed her fingers on the table. "I don't know her myself," she said, "but I have heard about the marvelous work she does."

"That's why we had thought, if we could just get on Maddy's Floor, maybe there would be hope."

"There's always hope," Queenie said. "But sometimes it's just not meant to be. Sometimes we're here for a short time. Sometimes we're here for a long time. And sometimes our journey includes a debilitating disease or injury." Her smile was gentle as she added calmly, "We can't always know the ways."

The woman smiled, but there were still tears in her eyes. "Maybe if you have some message of hope for Kirsten?"

Queenie glanced at Kirsten. "Do you believe in miracles?"

Kirsten nodded. "And angels and unicorns and rainbows," she announced, doing a little happy dance.

"Then you keep hoping and asking for a miracle, okay?"

With another head bob afterward, she dashed out to the front of the tent, calling back, "Mommy, Mommy, ice cream time."

The mother looked at Queenie and whispered, "Thank you."

As the woman walked outside, Queenie knew she had to say something. "Wait. What's your husband's name?"

She turned back in surprise and said, "Brian Callahan."

Queenie nodded. "Thanks."

The woman looked at her with a question in her eyes. "Why?"

Queenie didn't quite know what to say because she didn't know why she needed to know the name. But it was important. "I'll put out a prayer for him." She spoke quietly, hoping she hadn't insulted the woman.

Religion was one of those topics so very difficult to discuss, particularly when you were a psychic. It seemed that what she did flew in the face of religious beliefs, and she ended up in more trouble than anything.

The woman smiled and quietly said, "Thank you." And then she walked through the tent flaps.

Queenie sat at the table for a long moment, figuring out what the hell she was supposed to do now. She had the name of this person who needed Maddy's help, but Maddy was obviously completely overwhelmed with so many other patients. Somebody needed to set up some angel service, where people in need could get the help they required from these people without having to go through the normal institutionalized channels. Because Dr. Maddy certainly wasn't a traditional healing specialist. That she was a doctor was one thing but that she was incredibly psychic and a strong healer was what made her so very special.

But this Brian Callahan and his daughter, Kirsten, … and the Watcher, … was there a connection? Not that she understood how … Maybe it was the odd lingering energy that made her think of him? That it seemed to be lingering here after the woman and her daughter left? Or was it odder that it was here while those two were here? Maybe she was trying to make something out of nothing.

She still thrummed her fingers on the table, lost in thought, when Kirk strode back inside. "Why are you still here?" she asked, but no strong feelings were behind her words. Her mind was still on this Brian person. "Do you have any connection to Maddy's Floor?"

Kirk stared at her at the complete change of conversation. "Not really. I've met her partner, Drew, once or twice, but that's all."

She leaned forward eagerly. "You have?"

He shoved his hands in his pockets. "You have too."

"I have? When?"

He snorted. "Trust you to not even remember. It was years ago. There was a child you had found who needed help. Drew was part of the FBI team there. At his direction the child was whisked away, taken to Maddy's Floor so his own Maddy could handle the child's recovery."

"*His own Maddy?*" she repeated, vaguely remembering the incident. But, if she'd been involved in tracking down the missing child, she was often so exhausted at the end that she didn't recognize anything around her. At times like that, she had leaned heavily on Kirk's presence, not seeing him as much as feeling him, sensing him. They were linked in a way he didn't understand, and, because he didn't understand it, he didn't acknowledge it. And, because he didn't acknowledge it, in many ways it just didn't exist.

He shrugged. "I have no idea where their relationship is right now," he said drily. "I have way too much on my plate to worry about things like that."

"Still, if I've met him, then maybe I can contact him."

"Why?"

She sighed. "Because a little girl needs her father to be healed."

Kirk shook his head. "You can't do that. You know millions of fathers are dying out there, leaving children behind. You can't help them all."

"I know that," she said, "but, when they cross my path, I feel like I must do something. We can't all be blind to the world around us. I'd like to believe the right people are there at the right time, and those are the ones I'm capable of helping." She groaned. "Besides, something's very odd about this one …"

He stared at her in disbelief. "Look at you. You're already a wreck. How can you take on something else like this?"

"It could be just a phone call." She didn't really believe it herself. "Is it that hard to make a phone call?"

"I don't know. *Is it?*" There was a challenge in his voice. "You called me. How hard was that?"

She pursed her lips together. Because, of course, the answer was *almost impossible.* She'd waited years to call again. But then who could blame her? She rubbed her temples, realizing she still had on the stupid headdress. She lifted it off her head and placed it on the table. For some reason her clarity had been really strong today. Then her abilities were very odd since yesterday. Since the woman in the lake.

"Maybe I can send an email instead," she announced. "I'm not sure I can do it on my phone." She pulled out her phone, but she felt this odd sense of disconnection. She glanced around at the room, frowning.

"What's wrong?"

She shook her head. "I don't know. I feel like I'm being watched." She cast a half glance at him. He had never believed her when she said things like that before.

He stared at her, then looked around the tent. "Is it him again? The Watcher?"

"I'm afraid it is," she said with an uneasy glance above her. "I wish I knew how he did that."

"Can you feel his presence?"

"Maybe. I don't know. I don't understand this."

He spun in a slow circle. "How can anybody who isn't involved in this shit understand?"

She stared at him. "Do you really want to?"

He frowned. "I always tried to understand."

She raised both hands, palms up. "Place your hands on mine."

He stared at her suspiciously.

She gave a broken laugh and dropped her hands. "So you don't really want to learn."

"You never asked me to hold out both hands before."

"You never said you wanted to understand either," she countered. "With one hand, I can see into your world. With two hands, I can allow you to see something in mine."

He stared at her. "Why did you never give me that offer before?"

"I'm stronger now. I have better control. It's hardly a one-way street."

At that he pinched his lips together; then slowly he held out both hands, palms down. She put her hands under his and slowly they connected.

Instantly he straightened. "What's that buzz? Voices?" he asked. "Have you got a radio on?"

"Those are the people calling out to me. Those are the ones I haven't been able to completely shut down. I do have most of them shut down. Otherwise you would be screaming at the noise level."

He stared at her. "All the time?"

"All the time."

"When did you learn to put in those blocks?"

"After I almost died," she said. "Because of those voices that I refused to listen to, I got as ill as I did. When I got pregnant, I promised myself and my son a better life, so I walked away from that work. Shut down my ability, but I couldn't shut out the voices. I tried to block them out, tried to ignore them, but it didn't work. It burned out my energy levels, wore me down …" She gave a tiny shrug. "I got sick and almost died …"

He took a step back, breaking the contact. "Are you saying you weren't physically ill but just worn down from listening to all that?"

"At the time that each one of those people were pulling on me, each one wanted a piece of me. And I couldn't keep feeding them. They were taking all my energy, and it took everything I had to stay alive and to stay well. So, yes, my defenses went down, and I got ill. I didn't have enough energy to heal, and I was burning up and out. … So it really had only one ending …"

"How is that possible?" He stared at her in disbelief.

"You didn't used to be so disbelieving," she said.

"No, that's quite true," he said, running his fingers through his hair. "It's like I lived in a completely different world when I was with you. Then, just like that, it all changed, and it's like I'm only living half a life. Living in a gray world, not one full of color. Our life was busy," he admitted. "Okay, crazy busy, but it was a good crazy. It was a good life. We were doing good things. Now it's simpler, … colder, less chaotic. And not as rewarding."

"I think that's a self-defense mechanism." She stood, put the money jar underneath the counter and walked to the tent entrance.

"Explain," he demanded.

"When you were with me, you were wide open. You were learning. You were becoming so much more than you are. You were my grounding rod. You kept me stable through all that craziness." She spoke quietly. "When we split up, you stopped, closed off that avenue to you, and I didn't have that to count on. So I started on a slow slide down on my own. But, for you, you built a new life, a saner one."

The noise of the amusement park was always there in the background—the crazy music, the chimes, the men calling out for the games, the laughter, the cheerfulness. But the thing that she loved the most was the smell. Cotton candy, hot dogs, popcorn. When she'd first come here, she'd laughed and thought it was great; now there was a solid rightness to it all.

Kirk grabbed her shoulders roughly.

She spun to take a look at the anger in Kirk's face. She smiled. "You don't really understand, do you? I was a wreck then. I needed space. I needed to heal. So I pushed you away. And you left."

"Oh, no you don't. We're not making this all about you again."

She stared at him and laughed. "Absolutely. Let's make it all about you." She poked him in the chest, forcing him back a step. "You, there one day and then not the next. You had all these cases you were trying to solve, and you kept bringing them home, asking for my help. I felt I *had* to help, that I had no choice. You …" But she saw, at every poke, at every backward step he took, that he really hadn't understood.

He grabbed both her wrists and said, "Why did you never tell me about this?"

She snorted. "Tell you what? Tell you I was afraid that, if you no longer needed me, you would walk away from me? That, when you got your shiny new promotions and raises and the accolades and admiration from everyone around you, you would no longer need me? That I worked harder and harder to keep giving you more and more? Sure, I wanted to help all those people too. But it was you I was trying to help the most. And why? Because I felt like, without me doing that, you didn't love me. That your love was conditional on me helping you close all those cases." She shook her head and backed away. "And you proved it when I was washed up and sent you away. You left. Never to return. I was more the fool, right? Because I am the one who sent you away. You must have been waiting for that chance. Walk away as the good guy, free and clear ..." She gave a half laugh. "And, when you walked away, I crashed."

"What do you mean, *you crashed*?"

She snorted again. "What do you care?"

"How did you go from a crash to being pregnant, then in the hospital with your son all of a sudden?"

"I hit rock bottom," she said simply. "Finding out I was pregnant was my miracle. I learned to take better care of myself—for him. I finally had another reason for living. My son."

She smiled, although tears were in her eyes. "At least I thought so. But raising him alone, without any employable skills, was brutal. I'd spent so many years helping the police and doing small private jobs that I didn't know how to make a living any other way. I tried and failed as I became so sick from overwork and stress that I ended up hospitalized, and we all know what happened after that, don't we?" she said bitterly.

"I'm so sorry," Kirk said. "I had no idea that's how you felt in our relationship."

"It doesn't matter." Fatigue plagued her voice. "Like you said, it was a long time ago."

"I feel like we were young," he said quietly. "Maybe too young."

"You mean, young and stupid? Young and ambitious? Both selfish? Both worried about our futures instead of trying to enjoy the now?"

She didn't even worry about his reaction. She turned and walked to the front entrance of her tent. She pulled open the curtain, pinned it back so it stayed open and said, "You need to leave. There's absolutely no benefit to having you here, and, right now, just enough is going wrong that I don't want you around. You're a distraction I can't afford."

"I said I'm sorry."

She looked at him in surprise. "Yeah, you did. And?"

"I would like us to be friends."

She studied him, amusement filtering through her. "We're as much friends as we can ever be," she said sadly. "You have no idea what we are, what we had, what we could have had."

"I know you made me crazy," he said as if in explanation. "You always knew everything. I'd bring you home files, and you'd immediately pick up the salient points I had been struggling to find. I always felt insecure, *less than* when I was around you," he said suddenly. "Stupid. Missing things that seemed so obvious when you pointed them out."

She stared at him. "What?"

He shrugged. "You 'got' it. I never seemed to. I'd have these files all laid out, and I'd be pouring over them, making notes. … You'd walk up, and, within seconds, you'd pinpoint the sentences in each of the reports that made sense, the ones that pulled together as clues, forensic evidence. I'm much better at it now. But, at the time, I was so insecure and felt like I had nothing to offer."

"Nothing to offer us?"

He shrugged uncomfortably. "Maybe. I don't know. I certainly didn't do a ton of soul-searching back then. I know I walked away after you told me it was over. You'd become something I didn't recognize. The police, all my friends, peers, bosses, they were all talking behind my back. It made it very hard for me. Plus you wanted nothing more to do with me—with my world." He straightened. "You were adamant, if you remember."

She stared at him. "Right. I made it hard for you. Then I made it easy for you." She shook her head, motioned toward the outside. "And now I'm asking you again, please leave."

He walked toward the front and stopped. "How will you protect yourself from this Watcher guy?"

"No idea," she snapped. "But I will survive. I always have."

"Life isn't just about surviving," he said quietly. "You need to work on thriving."

Her lips twitched, but only sadness was inside her heart. "It's hard to thrive when you've loved and lost."

And then, as he stepped through the gate, she whispered, "Twice."

HE WASN'T SURE he'd heard the last part of her comment correctly. Kirk turned around to ask her about it, but the curtain dropped in his face. As a message, it was hard to argue with. She'd always been like that, always clear about how she felt. So that was why her words today stunned him. They didn't make sense. None of it made sense. To think she'd felt so insecure about their relationship, about how he felt about her.

It blew him away that she thought he wouldn't love her if she didn't continue to solve all those cases. He'd hated what those cases had done to her. But he knew she needed them, she thrived on them. He'd firmly believed she was doing her soul's work. He couldn't imagine her not doing it.

How was he supposed to deal with that now?

A lot had been wrong with their relationship way back then. Also a hell of a lot had been right. And maybe the stuff that had been so right had scared him. Because the stuff that had been so wrong had terrified him. He hated to look back and see the young man he'd been, both insecure and needy. Things he never would have expected himself to be.

They had been through so much together that it was like living ten years in one. It had been exhausting. He didn't know how much of that was his fault. The cases that never seemed to end had opened up this big antenna and sent out a message: if you need her help, call us. Because they had cases upon cases, people upon people, coming to them for help. She'd never said no. But then neither had he.

Maybe she was right in the sense he had loved the fact they were closing so many cases, that people were getting their loved ones back—or at least exposure of the never-ending deaths. They had done a ton of good. But it had also taken its toll on them. They had been partners in all ways. And yet, somewhere along the line, they'd forgotten to look at all the good things they had, the reasons why they were doing what they were doing. It was hard to consider how much he'd been to blame.

But there was no doubt he had been. Maybe not all the blame but more than he'd ever allowed himself to acknowledge before. And that was tough. He considered himself a fair shooter, but the years without her had been even more difficult than he could have imagined. He hated that he felt drawn back to her. Absolutely hated it. No way he wanted to return to the nightmare circumstances of their previous relationship.

And he knew there was no way he could. What they'd

had, had been good while it lasted, but he'd moved on. He was really sad that she hadn't. Was she still caught up in her grief? Or was she doing much better? There'd been nothing he could do to help her back then. Could he now?

"INTERESTING, INTERESTING. QUEENIE'S talents are wasted here."

The Watcher stared at the woman in the amusement park tent. Every time she'd given a reading, there was this burst of light. He'd watched for the last forty minutes. Like clockwork, almost every five minutes, somebody came and went. That burst of light which flashed every time she gave a reading meant she had used her abilities to give the answers.

"But, if that's the case, why is she doing this here? Somebody with that level of talent could be doing this work anywhere." He was alone so felt free to talk to himself out loud. He had to have someone to talk to about this, right?

He watched for another few minutes.

"Obviously she's no good at business if she's here taking five dollars for each message."

He chuckled. Not everyone was blessed to be in his position. The fact that he had learned to do what he was now doing, staring down into her world, attracted by these flashes of light, was amazing. But, of course, he already had a connection with her. A connection she didn't know about.

He'd been having fun with people for a long time. He could make them do all kinds of things. But not her. Not Queenie. And he had tried. He had tried very hard. And then he'd gotten bored. He'd walked away. He had found other things, other games, other people to torment.

But then she'd crossed his path again. Now he was plain

fascinated. She used to work with the cops, and here she was, doling out advice at an amusement park. There was another flash. Followed by another flash. He watched in amazement. If she knew how much energy she was losing every time she let it flash like that, she would stop. Because nobody could afford that much energy depletion. It was way too much. It would drain her. It would take her home at the end of the day, exhausted.

But he wouldn't tell her. That was for her to figure out. And, if she didn't, well, that was the same as psychics all over the world. They had talent and ability but no brains. Whereas he had both. He led a blessed life with respect; he was highly thought of and had talent in abundance. In many ways.

He smiled. "Look at her. There she goes again." There was so much focus and determination as she went through that line of people. He could feel the window into her world closing. He tried to force it back open again. It was almost an instinctive reaction. He didn't want to let go of this connection. There was so much she could see, and yet she hadn't seen him. Why?

Of course he was good. He knew that. He had deliberately kept his tracks hidden, and he had certainly led a convoluted past, just in case another psychic like him was out here on the ethers who could do what he did. And, as long as he kept shifting, he figured nobody could find him.

Who wouldn't want to look through a window into somebody's life and watch them, knowing they didn't know you were there? And they had no way to stop you from coming and going. As long as he stayed secret and silent, then he could do that. Still, it was lonely on this side of life. And would it really hurt if she knew he was here?

CHAPTER 5

Tuesday ...

QUEENIE HAD GONE through the next few days in an almost numb state. She'd gone happily for years without having any contact with Kirk.

But every year at this time, the memories overwhelmed her. Today was the day she'd woken up to be told her son had been taken from her and had already been cremated. It was bittersweet that Kirk had divulged the news to her.

Having him show up again in her life had brought the memories from the past to the surface. Painful memories. She knew, in another few days, weeks, months, it would all fade again. Yet something was different this time. That voice in her mind, for one. She hadn't heard it in these recent years, but she hadn't gotten rid of its presence. And that spider with a message to share. Spiders didn't talk. But she was psychic enough to realize the spider had given her a message of some kind. She just didn't know what. And she was desperate to learn how and why. Did it have anything to do with that little boy being dragged along with the murderer? Should she ask Kirk about the missing boys' cases?

He'd told her to call him anytime. That he'd make time for her. Even after she had kicked him out of her life. Again.

It was early for her to be up, much less already at her tent. Yet, for some reason, she couldn't sleep again last night.

Not that she needed to look too closely at the reasons why. But here she was, before eight in the morning, coffee in hand, standing in the dark shadows of her tent. She could still feel Kirk's presence, the disturbing energy from the Watcher, even the energy from the man who had killed for property gain. Her heart wanted to grieve for the woman in the lake, wishing Queenie could help more. She wanted to cleanse the tent from all that energy too. There was no power in here. She turned toward the entrance, tied up the tent opening to let in as much light as she could, went to the back and rolled up what passed for a window covering. A large mesh area at least would allow some light in.

Carlos wanted her tent to be in darkness, adding to the spooky, mystical element. But, for somebody who loved light, being in the dark all day was depressing. She had a wooden floor and a broom in the corner; again Carlos had thought it was appropriate, one of those big old straw witchy-looking things. She grabbed it and gave the small space a quick sweep.

As she did so, she kept a close eye out for any sign of that spider. She knew perfectly well everybody would say it was her imagination, and a spider was a spider, and hopefully it had died somewhere along its way.

But something had been different about that one.

After she gave the floor a good sweeping, she lifted the cloth off the table, took it outside and gave it a good hard snap to remove the dust that had collected. Then she went back and did the same with that little stand she kept beside her. It held her water bottle and a couple books underneath it, in case she got too bored waiting for customers.

Things once again cleaned and dusted, she sat at her table without its covering because she had a good forty minutes before the amusement park opened. She pulled out her books and took a look at what she kept here. One was on mediumship, which she'd intended to read, but her interests had waned in the last few months. She flipped through it.

Her eye caught on the acknowledgment page. She never read pages like that. But this one gave credence to somebody named Stefan Kronos for his assistance and training. She frowned, remembering hearing that name from way back when, while she worked in the police department, but, just like so much of everything back then, she'd blocked it out.

She brought her prepaid phone up to refresh her memory, and, as soon as she typed the name into Google, she was amazed at how many pages came up with information on Stefan. The man had a vast and checkered career. Everything she read was either about cases he had worked on or his artwork hung in galleries all over the world. Mostly in private collections, from what the articles said. As she devoured the information, she realized many people credited him for finding their lost ones and for helping them deal with a certain issue.

His name was often linked with Dr. Maddy's as well. There was no website; there was no contact information. She couldn't blame him. Anybody who had talents like hers—or, in this case, like his, which were way beyond hers—the last thing they wanted was an outlet where the public could reach over and say, "Hey." There was just way too many of the rest of the world and only one of them. Those knocks on their psychic doorways had to be monitored very closely.

She sent out a quick message, saying, "Universe, if you want me to have any contact with Stefan, show me the way."

A weird buzz sounded in her mind. She laughed, knocked on the wooden table in front of her and said, "Hey, if that's you, Stefan, let me in."

A voice boomed in her head. "Why the hell should I?"

She froze. Then jumped to her feet and spun around. "Who are you?" Normally she only had contact with entities through people. Rarely through the dead ... So she had to assume it was somebody alive and probably somebody with very strong psychic abilities.

"You know who I am," came the voice in exasperation.

She stepped back, and the bond was broken.

She stood there for a long moment, wondering what and who, and then realized she had felt no negativity in that message; there'd been no darkness in the contact. Instead a lightness has infused it, with a positive, almost loving aspect to it, and she'd called out to Stefan herself.

She just hadn't expected an answer.

He didn't know her, and she didn't know him. She closed her eyes, opened her mind and asked telepathically, *Stefan, is that you?*

This time there was almost a rumbling of thunder in her mind, as if she had disturbed him. Instantly she withdrew and winced. "Sorry," she called out.

For what? a male voice snapped in her ear. *For disturbing me twice? Make that three times now.*

She smirked, marveling that the connection was so clear and crisp. Almost as if talking in person. Not in her head. Yet that was exactly what he was doing. "How can I be disturbing you? The only ones who can even hear this are you and me, and everybody would say I was crazy."

And you know that's not true. So let's not beat around the bush. You called me. What do you want?

His response was so breathtakingly honest and direct that she was charmed.

You know that makes you odd, right? But this time there was a note of humor in his voice.

She belatedly realized that, not only was he talking to her but he was essentially reading her thoughts. That was so not cool.

Then stop making them so obvious and out there.

"Obvious and out there?" she said in wonder. "And here I thought they were in my mind."

And everything that's in your mind, you telegraph outward.

There was a fatigue in his voice, as if he was tired of having to say the same thing over and over again. She wondered if he was some beacon of energy that attracted this kind of conversation.

Somewhat, he said. *But that's not why you called me.*

"Are you a medium?"

And?

He gave nothing away. His voice was direct, smooth, and yet there was almost a container around it. As if he had some sort of a defense mechanism.

Don't you think I would have one, given the type of work I do?

"How do you get that?" she asked urgently. "I need better defenses myself."

Only silence followed.

She winced. "Please? I'm not sure how to unlock this ability."

It's not a case of unlocking the ability. You already have plenty of abilities, he said. *What you don't have is a constructive path for them. And what you do have is in many ways confused.*

She sagged in her chair. "Well, that's one way to put it. The shrinks would say I was crazy."

You've done enough work with the police to realize you're

not, that your abilities have value, and you've helped a lot of people because of them.

Her chest squeezed tight. "Do you know who I am?"

Do you know who I am?

She was left gasping at the speed of their conversation. She was speaking out loud, but he was talking in her head.

It doesn't have to be that way. Close your mouth and speak to me the other way. You'll do it more effectively and, with time, less effort.

Knowing it was almost a turning point in this conversation, and, if she wanted anything else to do with him, she needed to do this, she obediently closed her eyes, not sure why that was important, and said, *Like this?*

Yes, just like that.

She opened her eyes and realized she stood in a massive cave. Beside her was a glowing arc. *Are you this ball of light beside me?*

I could be, if that's what you're seeing.

She frowned. *Meaning, I'm projecting something onto you, not that you are projecting this yourself?*

Correct. Now that you're speaking to me this way, tell me why you contacted me?

For several reasons, but the most important is to help build up my defenses. It came out in a rush, but she hadn't intended that.

Interesting.

What's interesting?

The bloody amusement park would open soon, and she'd be inundated with people asking questions. And not that she meant to mock them—they were her bread and butter—but this was so much more important for her.

You're hiding, he said thoughtfully. *Most people don't hide in plain sight.*

Nobody would think to find me here, she said to him.

And yet you're still helping people? Still using your abilities to help others?

I'm hoping that whoever needs my assistance comes to me. Besides, I learned at a huge cost what happens if I don't use my abilities.

That's the way it works, but you were doing bigger things before.

Bigger, yes. Better, I'm not sure about that. All things come at a cost.

There was silence, and she could feel a surge of energy rippling through her. She frowned. It was almost like files flipping around her head, images, videos playing. She turned in a slow circle as if inside some massive memory bank. It took a moment for her to realize it was her own memory bank.

Are you searching my memories? She was completely awestruck and horrified at his temerity.

Yes, feel free to stop me at any time, he said smoothly. *But, if you're asking for my help, I have to understand what it is you've gone sideways on.*

Who says I've gone sideways? she asked, her hackles starting to rise.

Good. Get angry. I'm taking advantage of you right now. You don't even know how to say stop. *You don't even understand how to close the doors in my face.*

She glared.

He said, *Well, you're getting there, but you still haven't figured out how to do the rest of it yet.*

She reached out and swatted a door. It was a mental door, but she slammed it tight, pissed off at him and at herself. She'd asked for help, not to be taken advantage of. It was a simple-enough request; he could have said yes, or he could have said no.

Yes, he said, chuckling.

She gasped and bounced off her chair, realizing she was back in her small tent again. *You're still talking to me, even after I slammed the door in your face?*

I had to know if you were there or not or whether you were so far gone that you were past being able to use simple tools.

She frowned, not quite understanding. *Meaning, if I can't manage a door to let people in or out, how will I defend against somebody insistent on getting in?*

Oh, somebody is already in, Stefan said softly, too softly.

She gasped. "Can you see him?" she cried out fearfully.

I can see his energy.

Can you track it backward? Can you find out who it belongs to? This guy watching me is a killer. And he somehow connected to me, having fun in the fact I can't stop him. But he can share what he's done with me.

Stefan's lackadaisical attitude dropped away. *How do you know he's a killer?*

I don't know for sure. She rubbed her face, then explained what had happened. Her shoulders sagged, and she added, *Is there anything you can do to help me? Show me what direction to go in next?*

He sighed. *If you have a killer attached to you, that makes you a very important connection to him.*

"I don't want to be an important connection to him," she whispered painfully. "I helped the police for years. It didn't do me any good, except leave me broken and alone."

I can see that, he said cautiously. *I myself went down that path. Now I selectively pick and choose those I can help who won't destroy my hard-earned peace.*

I don't know how to pick and choose, she whispered in her mind.

And what was that about your son? he asked.

She smiled. *I was hoping you'd ask.* She gave him what she knew. *He's all I could think about when I woke up in the hospital and found out he was gone. I tried so hard to contact him, and it took weeks, months even, but, even though I'm not a medium, I managed to connect. Although something is there, I only see energy and hear laughter. It's the only way I found peace with his death, knowing a part of him lived on.* She laughed at that. *There's always beautiful cascading colored energy accompanying his presence. And he doesn't come often but enough to bring me comfort. But I wondered how to deepen the connection.*

There was a gentle disapproving tone to Stefan's silence.

She winced and stepped out of her tent. The morning sunshine hit her in the face. She backed up into the gloom of the tent. She wasn't ready to step out there into the sunshine. She didn't know why, she didn't know how, but she needed to be inside the tent. *And then there's a spider.*

This time Stefan's voice took on an odd note. *What do you mean by a spider?*

And she could sense she was losing him; something inside of him was withdrawing.

"Please don't go," she said urgently, out loud.

What about the spider?

She winced, knowing it would sound beyond stupid. But she told him what she'd sensed when the spider had been here with her. *After hearing the spider, I heard the little boy crying out for his mommy.* She took a deep breath. *I have to tell you, that hurt.*

She could hear Stefan sucking in his breath, but she didn't know what that meant. *I need to connect to him again. If he's in trouble, I need information to give to the police, so they can help him,* she said, tears pouring down her cheeks. She knew she had a note of desperation in her voice. She knew it, but she couldn't control it. *Please help me.*

Having said that, tears clogged her throat, had her sobbing quietly. She clamped hard on her control, or lack of control, and tried to pull her strength together. *I'm sorry. I'm so sorry,* she said urgently. *I don't want to be desperate. I don't want to be clingy. I just don't know what to do next.* And then she heard voices. She groaned. *The amusement park is about to open, and it'll get busy in here today.*

You can do so much more. Don't give up. We'll talk later. And with that he disappeared.

She didn't know what to think. She stood in the middle of her gloomy tent, watching as people came gushing through the amusement park. She knew a half dozen were heading her way. She didn't need to know how she knew; she just knew it was a fact.

She walked back to her table, pulled out a Kleenex from her little set of shelves and blotted her eyes. Stefan hadn't said no, but he hadn't said yes either.

She closed her eyes, took several deep breaths, reached for her silly headdress and put it on her head. She walked around the table, covered it once again with the cloth and pulled out her crystal ball, putting it on the tabletop. Then she sat behind it with her empty money jar and waited for the crowd to rush in.

She sent one last thought to Stefan. *Please help me.*

Then she closed the door quietly this time, not slamming it shut but gently, and she didn't lock it. If he wanted to come in, maybe he could knock, and she'd hear him. And, if not, well, she was a survivor. She'd always been a survivor. That wouldn't change. But, with his help, maybe she could be so much more.

KIRK SAT AT his desk. It was hard to write these emails. He had basically nothing to say, and they were going into his draft folder anyway. They were more of a journaling form. They were notes regarding Queenie's messages, her psychic insights. He had hundreds by now, just not any in the last few years.

Before, she'd been able to give him a lot more information than a dead body in a lake floating just beneath the surface. What the hell did that mean? The woman could be two feet deep or twenty feet deep. It would be almost impossible to see her unless they went right over her. Was that a sign of Queenie's abilities deteriorating, or was it the chaos in her own world?

He hit Save on the draft email and let it slide into his Drafts folder. Other people laughed at such a system, but it worked for him.

His mind glommed onto that damn spider thing again and the little boy. Of course it being a boy had triggered Queenie's protective instincts. It wasn't that Queenie was interested in spiders.

But she'd now associate spiders with this little boy. Kirk had checked but found no active missing-boy cases in the area. Yet the little boy didn't have to be missing to be in trouble.

Still, why would Queenie pick a spider in this instance? That made no sense. He thought about the description she'd given of the man who'd come into the tent, then thought about her being caught by some other psychic force to view what the Watcher wanted her to see. "No way," he said sourly. "My belief system will go only so far."

"If you're muttering about Queenie again," Peter said, "you know your belief system can go a hell of a long way."

Kirk groaned. "I've been to hell and back over Queenie and the stuff she tells me. I'm not going there anymore."

"Sounds like it's too late already," Peter joked.

Kirk stood, grabbed his jacket from the back of his chair and said, "Damn well better not be." He picked up his keys and his cell phone, slid them into his pockets and started to walk out of the office.

"What are you doing?" Peter asked from the far side of the room. "Going to visit Queenie again?"

He froze, turned to look at Peter and said, "What do you mean, *again?*"

Peter chuckled. "Walking past the amusement park entrance a few days ago, I saw you leaving the park."

"Are you following me, Peter?" Kirk asked.

Peter shrugged. "I figured Queenie had to be there."

"Why the hell would you think Queenie was there?" Kirk asked, his voice suspicious. He hadn't warmed to Peter since the first day the guy had arrived. But five of them worked closely together, and, to work well, they had to get along. So he did, but it was harder with Peter than anyone else.

Peter shrugged his shoulders. "I saw her on the amusement park website. Queenie's Spooky Truths, ask the Queen Seer," he said in a mocking voice. "Like, good God, how far has she fallen?"

There was silence in the rest of the room as everybody

else understood what was happening. Kirk shoved his fists into his pockets instead of Peter. "I don't know. How far has she fallen? Seems like you know better than I do."

"Jesus, dude, you almost married that witch."

"Hardly a witch," he said, his voice deceptively mild.

"Well, given the shit she was doing, I'd say *witch* is just about the right term." Peter's voice was getting obstinate. "Kirk, look at her. She's reading crystal balls." He shook his head and chuckled. "I suppose she's got some of those little fancy tarot cards in there too. Does she tell you who to sleep with next?" There was a twitter of amusement running through the office.

"No clue. But apparently you need to get a reading done," Kirk said. "Your love life hasn't been doing so well, has it?" On that parting shot, hearing the laughter explode behind him, he headed outside, mildly satisfied with the last part of their exchange.

Something about that guy always got to him. The trouble was, the reason Peter upset him was because Kirk saw himself in Peter. Years ago, when he'd been with Queenie, it seemed like he was Peter—upwardly mobile, everybody loved him. Kirk was the topic of every conversation as he was the one closing the cases.

Behind his back they all whispered about him sleeping with the psychic. But he didn't care because he was bringing closure to so many people. His superiors loved him. As long as he didn't broadcast where the information was coming from, everybody was happy. And then everything blew up. Nobody spoke Queenie's name again.

Until she was hospitalized, and several men told Kirk where she was.

She'd been distraught, completely overwhelmed at the loss of her child. When a couple of the guys had questioned

Kirk about whose child it was, he'd snapped back and said it was the wrong age. Eventually the talk had died down, but his suspicions hadn't. He had always wondered in the back of his mind whose child she'd had. She had never said anything to him, and he'd always trusted her, but then they hadn't left on the best of terms. Maybe she thought he wouldn't want anything to do with a child of hers. He wasn't sure if he was angrier at the thought she'd think that and then do what she did or if she'd gone and slept with somebody else and had another man's child.

If it had been his, he'd have wanted to be there, to help in some way. Back then he'd had several raises, several honors awarded. Queenie hadn't been given anything. And now, when he considered that, he thought how damned unfair that was.

When she walked through the office, people would always say hi and be friendly, but they wouldn't want to be friends. They were afraid she could read their mind or she'd know something about what they were doing in their lives. At one point, after shaking one of her bosses' hands, when Kirk and Queenie got home that night, she'd told him what she knew about that boss.

"You know he's got a mistress on the side, right?"

He remembered saying, "Hell, no. He loves Helena. He's been with her for like twenty years."

"No, he doesn't love Helena. He loves Helena's money. His mistress is Louisa. And Louisa has two of his children already."

Kirk had hated hearing that. It was none of his business. It wasn't a criminal matter, but he did like Helena, and anything negative and upsetting, like this, that would affect Helena was just plain shitty. He had blamed Queenie because she'd brought up something he didn't want to know, something that put him on the spot, something about somebody he admired, and he didn't know what to do about it. So he did nothing.

He wondered if he should tell Helena even now. If there was a way to get an anonymous message to her, he might have done it. But, if Kirk's boss found out that the news came from Kirk, he'd be fired for sure, and that was unfair. But that was the way it was. He might not get fired today; he might not get fired this week, but it would be soon. And that wasn't something he was ready for. He didn't want to put his job in jeopardy because some man couldn't keep his dick in his pants. But he no longer respected his boss because of it.

Outside, he stopped and took several deep breaths. It seemed like life had slowed since he had separated from Queenie, but he wasn't sure it was a good thing. He'd had several relationships—some weeks long, others months long—but out of loneliness, … not caring. Lorraine had been the longest, mostly due to her. He wasn't sure he could care anymore. He'd loved Queenie completely. Living with her had been intense, her focus 100 percent, so his had been too. It was one thing when it was directed at him, but it was another when it was on some of the most gruesome murders in the world …

Several deep breaths later, he hopped into his Acura and headed to the grocery store. For months after the breakup he did takeout, and then he decided that had been enough of that. He needed to settle down, learn to cook and eat a little better. Just as he eased back the crazy caseload at work, he tried to ease back the crazy stress on his system. He'd even taken up yoga. But that wasn't easy. His body wasn't meant to be compressed into the positions he asked of it. But he was getting better. He'd also taken up swimming.

He'd rather swim in a lake or a river or any natural body

of water. He hated the chlorinated water, but the pool was the only thing available to him.

His phone rang as he walked to the car. He stared down at the number and frowned. He didn't recognize it. He lifted his phone to his ear and said, "Hello?"

"Hi, you don't know me," a woman said. "My name is Erin. Erin Callahan. But I wanted to thank you for getting my husband in to see Maddy on Maddy's Floor."

He shook his head. "I'm sorry. I don't have a clue who you're talking about."

"Queenie said you'd say that. Anyway she said I should call you and say thank-you. I just wanted to let you know that, no matter what happens, I'm grateful." And Erin hung up.

Kirk stared down at the number in surprise. He'd shot off an email to Drew but hadn't heard back. It didn't make any sense. Inside his car, he checked his recent calls, found Queenie's number and called her. "I just got a weird call from some woman who said she got her husband in to see Maddy on Maddy's Floor."

"Oh, good. I'm glad she called."

"She said you told her to send her thanks to me."

"Well, I don't need thanks. You know that. But it looked like you were suffering, so I told her to send it to you. Maybe the good vibes would help you out."

He stared out the window. "You're weird sometimes. You know that?"

She chuckled. "*Always* weird. Remember that." And she hung up.

He was grinning now as he tossed the phone on the seat beside him.

At the grocery store he picked up the phone again, pocketed it and headed inside. He grabbed a cart as he went in.

He picked up a few apples, some fresh grapes and then headed to the veggies. By the time he had four days' worth of meals and had picked up some granola for breakfast, he was ready to pay. He got through and headed back out.

As soon as he reached his car, his phone buzzed again. He looked at the number, not recognizing this one either. "Hello? … Hello?" A weird crackling noise filled the phone, and then it went dead. Shrugging, he pocketed his cell, got in the car and drove home.

While putting away the groceries, setting up to make himself a large salad for dinner, marinating a steak to barbecue, his phone rang again. This time he jotted down the number and answered. "Hello?"

No answer.

Frowning, he shut off the call and hit Redial. It rang and rang, but nobody picked up. He put his phone on the counter beside him and seasoned his salad. And his phone rang again. Getting pissed, he looked at it again. Same number. He clicked on Talk and said, "Hello?"

A weird static filled the air, but nobody was there.

He disconnected the call and laid it back down again, went out and lit the barbecue. When it was the perfect temperature, he tossed on the steak and set the timer. He liked his steak medium rare, and it was too damn easy to overcook it and not have any pink left in the center. He waited beside the barbecue until it was ready, then brought it back in, slapped it onto a plate and filled the other half with fresh salad.

He walked back outside with a steak knife and a fork, his plate full, and a cold beer to drink. He sat down on his chair. He thought he'd have owned his own house by now, but he was still renting. Mostly because he didn't want to deal with the problem of finding a new place. It seemed stupid to buy a whole house just for him, although he knew lots of people who did. He'd thought about it when he was with Queenie. He had been so sure that's what they would be doing at this stage of life, but it hadn't worked out that way.

He attacked his steak and carved up several good-size bites. With the first bite popped into his mouth, he sat back and relaxed, chewing happily. The steak was cooked perfectly. He washed it down with a slug of beer and kept eating.

Sure enough his phone rang again. He looked at the number, shrugged and set it down without answering it. But it kept ringing. He frowned. His voice mail didn't even pick up. Finally he hit Talk. "Who is this?"

Instead of a voice, instead of the same crackle, a weird mocking laughter came from the other end.

"Hey," he snapped. "Who is this? What do you want?"

And again more laughter. And then the call ended.

He stared at his phone uneasily and set it off at the far corner of the table. He continued to eat, but he kept glancing at it. His phone's voice mail should've kicked in after eight rings, and it had rung fourteen times, and still voice mail hadn't taken over. He would have to check it. But he knew, in his heart of hearts, nothing was wrong with his phone. The voice mail worked just fine. This call had all the earmarks of more woo-woo stuff.

Thankfully the phone didn't ring again for the rest of his meal. When he was done with the dishes, he picked up a second beer and walked back out on the deck. He had the whole evening to himself, and yet he was out of sorts. He couldn't get Queenie off his mind—or Peter's comments for that matter.

Kirk walked inside to grab his laptop and returned to the deck. He logged onto the police database to see what cases had drownings. There was a chance Lee-Anne Jenkins's mother, Bonnie Jenkins, had been found. Just because Queenie said Bonnie was in the lake didn't mean she was there today. There had been other cases where Queenie's timeline had been off. And it added to the confusion and undermined her validity with her information. But eventually they'd sorted it out.

At the time, she had shrugged her shoulders and said, "There's only so much I can be accurate about. It's not like I have a full and complete timeline. I get what information comes to me in bits and pieces."

He hadn't understood that. He still didn't understand that.

As he meandered through the cases, looking for drowning victims, he thought about Lee-Anne who had come in wanting help looking for her mother. He'd sent an email to the sheriff's office, asking if somebody would go to the property to check but hadn't heard back. He looked up their office number, grabbed his phone and called the sheriff. Of course the sheriff wouldn't be there at this hour, but a deputy should still be on duty, depending on how big the office was. It could be just a dispatcher. But then it wasn't all that late.

By chance the sheriff answered the phone. He sounded frazzled.

"Sorry to bother you, Sheriff. This is Detective Kirk Sanders," he identified himself. "I sent a request to have Bonnie Jenkins's property checked to see if she was in residence. Have you had a chance to do that?"

"Two of my boys went out there today," the sheriff said. "We didn't see any sign of her. Bonnie is a bit of a loner. But the couple times we've been by and stopped in to see her, she's been home. This time they got no answer, and the door was slightly ajar, so they walked through. Found no sign anybody's been there for at least a couple days."

"What do you mean ajar? What did your men find?"

"The door was slightly open. Dishes on the counter with food dried or baked on them, milk going sour in the fridge. Opened package of cinnamon buns left on the counter that were hard as a rock."

"So potentially she could have been missing for at least a week."

"Honestly it could've been longer. The milk was dated four days ago, according to my boys."

"So it could have been ten days before that too."

"Exactly."

"Did they walk the property?"

"They did. They went down to the lake, walked along the shore, crisscrossed, calling out, but found no sign of her."

"She had dogs, didn't she?"

"She did, and again we found no sign of them. Her vehicle wasn't there either."

"So what's your take on it?" Kirk leaned forward. This could be Queenie's drowning victim.

"If it wasn't for the food sitting on the table, I'd have said she had gone off for a few days. But, because the milk was going bad, and food was on the counter, I'm not sure what to think."

"She wasn't the kind to leave food around?" Kirk asked. He knew from the daughter that the mother didn't have any money, so wasting food was generally not something people did who were broke.

"No. She was always very generous with tea and cookies, or some treat, if she had them the couple times I've been there. But I also know she doesn't have much in the way of income, and the place is in poor repair. I don't think she ever had much. So to waste food like that is not really in keeping with who she was."

"What about the neighbors?"

"The boys knocked on a couple doors but didn't get anybody at home. They're up there again right now."

"Good. Thank you very much for checking, Sheriff. Her daughter is looking for her, and there hasn't been any contact now in a few weeks."

"That's not good. It's possible she went for a walk with the dogs and had an accident. I've certainly seen dogs sit down and die beside their owner in some cases."

Kirk winced at the thought. "Let's hope that's not what this is about. How many dogs were there, and what breeds were they?"

"Two beagles," he said. "Don't know their names. Only that they were brown, and one was spotted."

"Thanks so much. Let's keep in contact, in case anybody has an update." Kirk rang off, did a search and came up with the closest animal rescue center. When he got somebody at the other end, he identified himself and asked, "Any chance two beagles were turned in over the last couple weeks?"

The woman was surprised at the request. "I do have two beagles here," she said cautiously. "But I'm not sure when they came in."

"Could you check please?"

"Certainly. Just give me a minute."

He could hear papers rustling as she searched through intake forms. She came back on the line a few moments later and said, "They came in eight days ago."

"Do they have name tags?"

"Daisy and Dolly," she said. "A neighbor found them wandering the roads. They took them home but didn't find anybody there, so they brought them to us."

Kirk frowned at that. "Wouldn't the neighbor have tried again, kept the animals for a day or two?"

"He said he did. But he has his own dogs, and he couldn't keep them as well."

"Do you have his name and number?"

She gave that information to him.

He thanked her and rang off and called the sheriff back. He gave him an update on the dogs.

"That's really not good," the sheriff said in alarm. "Are you going to call the neighbor, or do you want me to?"

"I suggest you give him a call. Let your deputies know and have them stop in and talk to him."

"Will do."

Kirk hung up again and sat there with his laptop open, thinking about a missing mother who had disappeared and finding her two dogs. Did the daughter know what happened to the dogs?

He brought up her file and called her. "What are the names of your mother's dogs?"

"Daisy and Dolly," the daughter said. "What about them?"

"They were turned in to an animal shelter eight days ago," he said.

She cried out, "My mother would never give away those dogs."

"A neighbor apparently found them wandering around on the road. He tried to return them to your mother, but nobody was there. He kept them for another day or two and tried again. Then he took them to the shelter. The shelter has not heard from your mother or anybody trying to claim them."

"I'll get them myself," the daughter said. "As soon as we

get my mother back, I'll make sure she gets them. She would be devastated if she doesn't have them."

"Here's the number."

She was almost in tears when she finally got it written down correctly.

"We're still looking for your mother. The sheriff's deputies were up there the other day and again today, walking the property, calling for her. There is sour milk in the fridge and old food on the table."

"That's not like my mother," she said. "She never wastes food."

"That's what I thought. But it does give credence to the theory that something is wrong, that maybe she's fallen on a walk, or maybe she had a medical emergency and was alone."

By now the daughter was crying full force.

"I can't tell you any more than that yet," he said. "The deputies are out talking to the neighbors. Hopefully they can connect. Otherwise they'll try again tomorrow. Maybe somebody has seen her. Maybe somebody knows something about her."

"And her truck?"

"It's missing," Kirk said. "Another reason to wonder if maybe she headed to town for the day and had an accident."

"She took those dogs everywhere," Lee-Anne said. "She'd never have left without them. And, if she was coming to see me, she always brought them too."

Leaving the young woman sobbing but promising she'd contact the shelter about the dogs, he rang off and sat there wondering what the hell would cause a woman to run away and leave her dogs behind. Of course the answer was, if she was alone, and those dogs were everything in her life, the only reason she would have left them behind was if they would have been safer. But that didn't mean very good things in terms of her own safety. More than likely, something happened to her, and somebody else took her vehicle.

And that brought him right back around to a woman in a lake drowned several feet beneath the surface. And then to Queenie. Damn her.

IT WAS COLD in his room. But it was better to be here and alone. Daddy had hurt him again. He sniffled. Pulling up his blanket around his neck, he shifted uncomfortably on the bed.

The spiders were gone.

He kept looking for more, but they'd left him. Alone.

Another scream erupted upstairs, followed by a heavy *thud*, then whimpers.

He scrunched down in his bed, his throat choking back his own cries. He had to stay quiet. He sniffled again. *Please don't let Daddy come down here again.* The little boy was so cold; he just wanted this all to go away.

He'd heard them talking. He was adopted. He didn't know what that meant except he had a real mommy out there.

Silence settled upstairs. And no footsteps. He sighed and whispered into the darkness, "Mommy, are you there?"

He wanted the spiders to come home. He missed them. But they couldn't come yet. They were doing important work, he knew. They were helping him. They were going to find his real mommy so she could rescue him. He just wanted to leave here. He wanted to be with his mother. He wanted to be safe.

Someplace where Daddy couldn't find him.

CHAPTER 6

Wednesday Morning …

"Excuse me," asked the plaintive voice of the little boy.

Queenie stopped her words tumbling freely after the woman's question on a second husband. Queenie looked at the little boy, smiled at him and said, "What's the matter, little one?"

He pointed at the side of her desk. "Will he bite me?"

She leaned over to take a closer look, not sure what he was talking about, but still couldn't see anything. She got up from her chair, walked around to crouch down in front of him, and, sure enough, there was the spider she'd been looking for. At least it looked like the same one.

With excitement surging through her belly, she shook her head. "I don't know. Maybe it's best not to touch him."

The little boy looked like he really wanted to, but his mom tugged him backward. She smiled at Queenie and quickly rushed the little boy out of the tent. Queenie stared at the spider. A line of people still remained outside, but she didn't want the spider to disappear. At the same time, she wasn't sure she wanted to touch him either. But, if somebody else was going to hurt him, he had to be protected. He was Queenie's only connection to that little boy.

The pinkish color around the spider was similar to the

color she saw when her son was close by. Then she heard it. Her son's laugh. She sent a big happy smile to the ethers.

As always, hearing his laugh brought a smile to her face. He'd always loved nature. Bugs, birds, any animals used to make him laugh. She'd take him to the park just to hear him chortle with joy.

She lifted the cover on the table and nudged the spider onto the tabletop. That was an improvement, but now anybody else coming in would see him right away. She walked around to where she normally sat and pulled out her lunch container. She'd brought some grapes with her. She took the lid off of the now-empty container and upended it over the spider. Then she gently lifted the cloth until she could turn over the container and set the lid on it just enough to deter the spider from climbing out, yet giving him an air supply.

Just then people entered her tent. She slid the container on the shelf beside her, whispering to the spider, "Sorry."

Instantly an almost angry rumble echoed through her mind. She shot a surprised look at the spider and frowned, but several boys and girls already stood before her. It was a group of teens, maybe thirteen, fourteen years old. They were laughing and giggling. With a quick glance to see if her son's pinkish-lavender energy was still around, Queenie straightened, smiled and prepared to deal with questions about boyfriends and girlfriends and schools. They were easy answers to give. Unless they were answers they didn't want to hear.

It took about thirty minutes to get through all their questions, but they all cheerfully paid. One even left a large tip before they raced out, still laughing and giggling among themselves.

As soon as they were gone, she sighed in relief and turned to look at the spider. She lifted up the container, and, feeling guilty, lifted the lid ever-so-slightly to give him more air. The container glowed pink.

Her son's gasp and light joyous laughter filled the room.

"I don't want to do this," she cried softly but could already sense her son was gone. He never spoke but he laughed all the time. The most joyous sound in the world.

Feeling like a fool, she said directly to the spider, "Sorry for doing this. But there weren't many options. Do you have a message for me?"

Unfortunately there was no answer. She wanted so desperately for the spider to have some psychic speaking ability, yet why would it? Since her son liked spiders, she'd do her best to keep this one safe. She knew she was making a fool of herself. But desperate times called for desperate actions, and, if anything would assist her in relation to her son, she'd do it.

In the back of her mind, she had that weird sense of being watched. She got up, walked around the damn tent again, figuring out what she felt. Then she recognized the energy, … the weird crackling in the air. How did he do that? She frowned and called out, "Why are you here again?"

There was a shocked silence, and then the sense of being watched disappeared, and peaceful silence reigned again in her tent. She smirked. "I do know you're there, asshole."

Static crackled.

A building anger floated around her. It was such a weird feeling. She realized—belatedly—that pricking the Watcher's temper wasn't a smart move. She might have been a decent psychic herself, but she never fooled herself into believing she was the best.

A deadly menacing voice whispered through her. *Good thing*. And then the Watcher was gone.

Chills ran up and down her arms as she realized she might have made an enemy of the wrong person. In a muted voice she called out, "Sorry."

But there was an emptiness, as if either he didn't hear or he didn't care. She suspected it was the latter. He was the kind of guy who, the minute you did something wrong, wiped you off the face of the planet to never be forgiven.

She'd met people like that. They usually had a lot of psychological problems and were often criminals. When she touched these characters' lives—as she had done many times while working with the police—the energy was wrong, poisoned in some way. Touching the energy used to make her sick, as in almost vomiting sick.

She wasn't doing the touching with the Watcher—he was. It was unpleasant to be in the reverse situation. And unnerving too but she hadn't a clue how to change the status quo. Apparently he could check in on her at any time, yet she couldn't even figure out who he was.

Some psychic she was.

Frowning, she wondered how much he could do. And how much could he get others to do? Which was a scarier thought.

She hadn't heard back from Stefan, but then she hadn't tried to contact him again either. She sat back down, staring at the spider trying unsuccessfully to crawl up the side of her plastic container. She felt bad. She upended the container and released him on the tabletop.

"I'm sorry," she said quietly. "I know what it is to be a prisoner. Maybe not in the same way as you, but a prisoner of circumstances, a prisoner of everybody's disbelief and mockery. I didn't mean to hurt you."

When a tinkle of laughter whispered through her, she knew her son approved. She laughed, joy in her heart as she watched the spider. How she'd changed these last few years. She'd never have given this critter another thought before. Even at first sight, her instinctive reaction was to scream and back away. Not now.

Still not a fan, she was more accepting. Besides, she didn't want to let her son down, and, if she hurt the spider, she'd disappoint Reese. That she didn't want to do. That connection with Reese was everything to her.

The spider stared at her for the longest time; then it walked over to her crystal ball and raised a leg to touch it. Instantly inside her ball, which was just a prop, swirled a mist. She cried out in excitement, "It *is* you!"

The spider didn't say anything, and no little boy's voice rippled through her mind. But, in the midst of the white cloud, a little boy's face shone bright. Tears came to her eyes, and her heart squeezed tight. It was Reese, her little boy. Even as her heart recognized him, her mind recognized the picture was one she had taken about a month before they'd both ended up in the hospital. It wasn't a current picture; it wasn't an updated picture. It was one from her memory banks. She shook herself free of the spell, anger curling inside her.

"I don't know what you're doing or why you're doing it," she said to the spider, an edge to her voice. "I know Reese is gone. If there's another little boy out there who needs help, then show him to me, but don't torment me," she warned. "Does that other little boy need help? If he does, show me something useful ..."

Maybe it was the tone of her voice, or maybe it was a

complete coincidence, but the spider scurried around to the other side of her crystal ball. Instantly the inside of the globe cleared, and the image of her son disappeared.

Sadness filled her. Yet a warm energy surrounded her, making her feel better. Her son again. She got up and looked for the spider. But found no sign of him. Why had he come? What did he want? She sat back down, her hand instinctively reaching for the crystal ball and the image she wanted to connect with. Her fingers gently stroked the ball, the overwhelming pain of loss once again in her heart. She needed to protect herself even more. She'd learned a lot on her own but had more to learn. And with the Watcher playing with her, it needed to be fast.

That meant contacting Stefan. She closed her eyes, reaching for the door she'd closed the last time, and opened it. There was a door on the other side.

She snorted. "Of course there is. What did you expect? That he was open to everyone all the time?" She knocked on the door. Instantly it dissolved. On the other side was this glowing orb. And she smiled. *Do you appear in any other form?*

I don't know, do I? he asked laconically.

Of course he'd answered her question with a question. Not wanting to go down that road, she said, *That's not why I'm here.*

Why are you here then?

He's watching me, she said baldly. *He was just here a few minutes ago.* She relayed the conversation they'd had. *I pissed him off, but I didn't mean to. I knew better. I wasn't thinking. I was reacting.*

Of course you were. But having somebody like that as an enemy is not cool, Stefan's voice said quietly. *Sit down for a moment.*

She did as he asked and felt a weird sensation as if he'd crawled into her mind. She gasped as weird icy shards slipped in and out of her brain in her consciousness. *Are you searching for him?* she asked as she finally understood something of what he was doing.

Yes, he said. There was silence, and a few more slices of weird energy, and then he sighed and said, *He's very good. He hid his tracks.*

She stared blankly around the tent. *But he wasn't inside my head, was he?*

He put an anchor into your system, giving him a deep connection to you. It's hard to say where that could have come from, Stefan explained. *But, once inside your energy, with an anchor in place, he could access it anytime.*

Would he have had to be with me physically?

No, not if he's very good, Stefan said. *He could have been originally but not necessarily. At a particular point in time, when your defenses were down, it would have been the easiest thing in the world to do. But you either allowed it or were completely out of it and didn't notice.* He paused for a long moment. *Has there been such an instance?*

She laughed, but it was a twisted, angry laugh. *When I had a breakdown after a case blew up, absolutely. When I was sick with pneumonia, feverish and in a coma, undeniably. When I was beside myself with grief over the loss of my son, more so than ever.*

In other words, there's no end of opportunities for somebody to have done that.

If I had known that was even possible, I would have taken steps to protect myself. She was still shaking her head in disbelief. *How is it that somebody could do this, and I didn't know?*

Often it's a friend, or it could be a family member, and those are the best-case scenarios. It could just as easily be an enemy, Stefan said. *We accept hooks from all kinds of people. But, in a case like this, it's somebody who probably just wanted to touch base with you. Either loved your ability, appreciated it, admired it, respected it even, and wanted to be connected. It's almost impossible to know at this point.* His voice deepened, saddened. *What we do is very lonely. And, if you don't have a supportive group around you who understands you, you often end up at odds with society.*

Yeah, that's me. At odds with society, she said in a brittle tone. *So many predators are out there in the physical form, yet I've never came across one in a psychic form.*

Interesting, Stefan said. *Because, for somebody who's done the kind of work you did, it often attracts predators from the other side too.*

There was silence for a moment as she thought about that. *It's never been an issue as far as I know.*

How did you get started doing this?

It happened when I was quite young. I was eight when the little girl next door went missing. I tried to get the cops to listen to me, but they wouldn't. And then I showed them where she was, and they found her. But then they turned their suspicions on me. It took a little longer for me to figure out that it was her uncle who had stolen her away. Once I got them to see that, and they confronted the uncle, he confessed. After that they listened to me a little more. If anything came to me during my teen years, I would call one of the two cops who had worked the original case. They usually gave me the benefit of the doubt, and most of the time I was able to help. Of course nobody is ever 100 percent, and that's always a problem. I did a lot of work for years with them, but they didn't always listen either, she said with a half laugh.

Nobody's ever 100 percent, Stefan said. *And getting the authorities to understand that we're serious can also be a problem.*

You're not kidding. There was a puppy missing, and I was bound and determined to save its life, but I couldn't see anything more than its immediate surroundings, so I didn't know where it was. I kept calling them, telling them they had to help the puppy. I think I was about thirteen at the time.

Did you save the puppy? he asked, a note of amusement in his voice.

Oh, I did. They didn't appreciate all the phone calls to get there, but we did rescue the puppy that'd fallen down a well.

He chuckled. *What are you doing for defense now?*

The usual stuff I read on the internet, she said calmly. *White circle of protection. I do a cleansing before and a cleansing afterward.*

Prayer? he asked curiously.

No, I can't say I have believed in anything worth praying to in a long time. When you see what man does to man, it's a little hard to believe somebody's above, smiling benevolently down on us.

I believe that takes us back to free will, he said. *Anything else?*

No, she said, frowning. She bounced off her chair and paced her small tent. She knew her grace window of no customers coming would end soon. *That's why I'm asking for help.*

But you're not telling me the whole truth, are you?

She froze. *What are you talking about?*

He sighed. *I can see a lot. Maybe more than you would like me to see. But the thing is, I can't work with you if you won't tell me the full truth.* And he disappeared.

Shaking, she went back to her chair and sat down again. Outside she could hear voices coming closer, which meant she was about to get more clients. But it was the last thing she wanted.

It had felt so weird to have him inside her mind earlier, searching for information on this guy tracking her. What she really wanted was a way to stop the Watcher from gaining access—or finding her in any way. She wasn't sure if she was looking for a defense system, per se. She was definitely looking to keep him out or to just hide from him so she could function, knowing he was around but unable to see her.

Just then Stefan's mind spoke to hers. *And once you do find a way to create a shield to hide yourself from him, you also can't move out of the shield unless you drop it. It poses its own barriers and its own dangers.* And he disappeared again.

A cough at the doorway of her tent brought her back to her surroundings as a young man walked inside nervously. He looked at her and gave her a boyish grin. "I understand you're really good at what you do," he said.

She smiled up at him, loving that innocence and hope in his eyes. "And where did you hear that?" she teased.

He flushed. "A girl I know came in to see you."

Queenie settled back and smiled. She held out her hand and said, "Place your hand on mine and ask me your questions."

He did so and talked about engineering, a big program he wanted to get into, and he didn't know how to make it happen.

She could certainly see him as an engineer. What she

couldn't see was if he was getting into that particular program. "You're certainly doing engineering work," she said, frowning. "Are you studying right now in that field?"

He shook his head. "But I have been accepted into the engineering school here locally."

"But that's not what you're asking about, right? Because you will be doing engineering."

He nodded. "That's what I would expect to do. But there's a specialty program afterward I want to go into."

She smiled. "You know the future is always open and available to you, right? And that you shouldn't be looking too far down the road. Do the best you can do today."

He nodded. "I was hoping you could tell me if it was worth doing."

Well, that was easy enough. She could certainly put him at ease there. "It's absolutely worth doing," she said gently. "I see you doing engineering work at a very high level for a long time."

His face lit up. He tossed ten dollars on the table and raced from the tent. She chuckled. It was always nice when she had something good to say in her message. She put the money away and sat back.

There was a weird sound in the tent, almost like a cackle, almost like a laugh. She looked around. "Stefan?"

Oh, no, not Stefan, although I'd be interested in knowing who that is, the Watcher said. *Why didn't you tell the young man about the rest of the message?*

She frowned, icicles sliding up and down her back. *Who are you?* she demanded. She got up and raced out of the tent, looking around all its sides, but nobody was there. She stepped back inside. *Who are you?* she repeated.

Doesn't matter who I am. That's not important. You're

important because I can see into your world. I never knew I could do that, he said thoughtfully. *I'll count this as a success.*

What's nice about it? she cried out. *You're a Peeping Tom into somebody else's mind.*

Not likely, he snorted. *But you see? We're connected. I've never been connected to anybody before like this. It's fun.*

Her world was just full of wonderful human beings. Not. *What do you mean about the rest of the message?* she asked curiously. *I told him what I saw.*

There was a snort in the air around her. *Then you didn't look deep enough,* he said. *The kid ends up dying from an engineering accident. A crane explodes on a site, and he gets taken out.*

She stared into the blankness. *I didn't see that,* she cried out. *I often don't see that far down the road.*

You could. You're too scared though. You only want to give people the pretty messages. I'm not interested in pretty messages. I like the ugly ones. And he disappeared.

Immediately she called to Stefan, *Did you hear that?*

No, I didn't hear that came the exasperated voice. *And could you at least knock? I have a life too, you know.*

She winced. *Look. I'm sorry, but that asshole was just here. I gave a message to a young boy, and the Watcher came afterward, asking why I didn't give the boy the full message.* She relayed the other bit of conversation. *I didn't recognize him.*

You're obviously linked if he could see what you were seeing when you touched that young man, Stefan said. *Hmm.*

"*Hmm?* What does *hmm* mean?" she yelled out loud, ready to shriek in frustration. *This has never happened before.*

Once you head down this path, it doesn't matter if it's happened before or not, Stefan said. *Every day is something new in my world.*

She walked around to the table and laid her hands on top, trembling like a leaf. *I can't keep doing this*, she said brokenly. *I already feel like I'm coming apart at the seams.*

Well, buck up, Stefan said in a snappy voice. *There're things you need to learn.*

You think? she grumbled. *Remember? I'm the one who came to you for help.*

And I said I wouldn't deal with you unless you were honest with me.

"What the hell are you talking about?" she hollered out loud. "I've told you everything I know."

Not really. You didn't tell me about the case that blew up in your face, did you?

Instantly her mind shut down. *That was a terrible time. I can't go there again.* She shook her head. *That hurts too much.*

If you can't tell me, I can't work with you came Stefan's steadfast response. And then he disappeared.

She stared out of the tent, wondering how her world had gotten so stupidly crazy and what the hell she would do about it.

MADDY, YOU THERE?

For you, Stefan, always came Maddy's laughing voice. *I do have another patient in a few minutes. What's up?*

I just need to check in with reality, Stefan said. *I've another young psychic who is incredibly powerful that's hooked into a killer—or at least we think he's a killer. I'm not sure I can even work with her.*

For you to say you can't work with her says a lot, Maddy said. *But it would be very sad if we lost one. We can't help them all, I know. If they come to us, you know we're bound and determined to do the best we can.*

I know. I know. Stefan groaned. He didn't know how he felt about Queenie. There was something desperate about her energy. He couldn't see beyond the layers of it because, although he'd gone searching through her mind, looking for information on this killer, she had so many steel trap doors that she kept locked that he didn't understand what was going on. She had defense mechanisms she had no idea she had put into place. Yet she was asking him to help her build more, as if she didn't know about the ones she did have. But that a killer was getting through to her was something very strange. She obviously was open on some level. And this killer had stepped in and was using her.

He explained what he understood. *I know it sounds bizarre, and I wish there was something I could do to help her.*

Send her some healing energy, Maddy said. *Obviously she's stressed out to the max. Something's bothering her tremendously. Her energy is fractured, and a lot of stuff is going on in her world, so of course she's struggling.*

I'm trying to give her energy. It gets rebuffed.

What? Maddy said. *In what way?*

Like an umbrella is around her all the way to the ground, and she's locked inside this sealed egg. And yet she's the one asking me for help setting up a defense system, something to keep this asshole away from her.

She doesn't have a clue what she's doing?

No, I don't think she does. She's in protective mode, hanging on by a thread. I've done a lot of research into her since she first contacted me. Apparently she's very gifted, and the police had no problem using her until she broke apart at the seams. There was one case, the Handkerchief Killer, involving several women. Some of her information was wrong, and the last woman they tried to save ... died. Queenie had a breakdown shortly afterward.

That's not all that unusual unfortunately, Maddy said sadly. *We're not perfect.*

I know. I know that, Stefan said. *There's just something about her ...*

What do you want from me? Maddy asked.

I don't know, Stefan said, shaking his head. *I really don't know. She also mentioned something about a spider.*

Well, that's a new one, Maddy said. *Maybe you should be talking to Tabitha and her animal connection then.*

Stefan groaned. *I think Tabitha is more than ready for me to stay away for a bit after we had that owl case she was heavily involved with. She needs time to just be Tabitha.*

Tabitha's like the rest of us. She steps up to serve when called, Maddy said gently. *I can send this Queenie some healing energy, but, if she has bounced back your energy, then I doubt she would accept any of mine.*

I wonder, Stefan said thoughtfully. *We might have to get a little tricky.*

Maddy chuckled. *That's always a dangerous thing with you. I could do some spirit work with her. But again, if I have an unwilling person, it's takes a lot of my energy to deal with them.*

I don't know if she'd be unwilling if she knew what was happening, Stefan said. *This guy got to her somewhere. She was hospitalized with a major illness at some point. I wonder what it would take to get her in to see you.*

On her side or my side? Maddy said drily. *I'm booked up for weeks and weeks.*

Right. I'm sorry, Stefan said. *Things are getting so much more involved these days. We have more and more people working with us and for us, but we're also finding more and more people we need to work with.*

I had a patient in this morning, Maddy said. *His wife said she was at the amusement park, and they spoke to Queenie, and that's how they got to me. Drew had mentioned it the night before. Anyway I had a cancellation, and, for whatever reason, one of my girls let them come in.*

We know that often happens for the right reason.

Yes, but it was definitely the name Queenie, Maddy said thoughtfully. *I'll call the patient's wife back and ask her to clarify.*

Or you could take a spirit walk and check the energy to see if it came from that source, Stefan said. *It's not like you're in your body all the time these days.*

I'm out so much these days, Drew is afraid I'm not coming back, Maddy said with a bright laugh. *But you're right. I can check it out.*

What did the patient present?

It's an interesting case, Dr. Maddy said. *The little girl, Kirsten, got to me. She said she spoke to the fortune-teller who said I could help. The thing is, I do believe I can help. It's just I don't have any beds.* Dr. Maddy sighed heavily. *I'm over-whelmed with patients between Maddy's Floor, the children's hospital, and then I've got two more hospitals going up across England.*

And all that traveling takes its toll too.

It's gotten better now, Dr. Maddy said, *because I can do most of my work from here.*

Can you work on this man from there?

That's possible. I told him I'd have to run some tests, and they've gone home for the moment. I needed to think about what I could do. She gave a light laugh. *I'll do the same with*

Queenie.

Stefan disconnected the call, which was mentally anyway, and turned to see his beloved sitting beside him with a tea service waiting.

She smiled and said, "You can't save everyone. Remember that. Tell me about this Queenie."

"The trouble is, she's too much like I used to be," Stefan said with a sad smile. "I can't ignore her. Otherwise I'm ignoring who and what I was."

"Tell me more," she said, leaning forward. She reached out a hand instinctively.

He reached back. As soon as their fingers connected, his own energy became centered and grounded, like it always did. He lifted his gaze and smiled deep into her eyes. "Have I told you lately I love you?"

She kissed his fingers and whispered, "Just this morning."

But her gaze was twinkling, and then he remembered just how he had said he loved her. He chuckled and said, "Well, I still mean it."

DR. MADDY SAT in her chair, a folder in front of her, wondering at the turn of events. Brian Callahan was the patient who had come in to see her. She had his medical records. They hadn't been able to pinpoint the bleeding, and he was getting more and more fatigued. The doctors would stop it, and it would start again. They'd run X-rays; they'd done MRIs, and they hadn't found anything. But she had a better idea of things that could go on at an energy level.

He'd gone home, and she had the address. On a spirit-walker system, she could certainly hop over to his house and take a look at him, but she'd rather have him in a more controlled environment.

She placed his file off to the side, but her fingers thrummed atop it, and she kept looking back at it. Finally she snatched up the folder and called Brian himself. "Mr. Callahan, I have a bed in one of my day-patient rooms here. Can you come in tomorrow so I can run some tests?"

Brian was tired. But there was excitement in his voice as he agreed.

Smiling, she closed the folder and stuck it off to the side. At the same time, Queenie just wouldn't leave Maddy alone. She would talk to the couple when they got here in the morning. Maybe that would help clarify her thoughts.

She looked up as Gemma walked in.

"Dr. McIntosh from the children's hospital has a problem with a young boy. He wants to know if you have a bed available."

"How serious is it?"

"The doctor says seven out of ten."

Maddy's eyebrows rose. "In that case, we have the bed. Call Sherry down at the children's hospital, have her take a look at the beds and see if we have room available now or if we need to make room for this little boy and get him transferred immediately." She looked at her watch. "I'm due to be there in about an hour. Is he already at the main hospital?"

"The doctor did mention that, if you had a bed, he could get him there within the next hour."

Maddy sighed, stood and grabbed her purse. "Make it happen." And she turned and walked out.

She had just enough time to pick up a coffee, something to eat—a little more than a salad, according to her beloved

Drew who was constantly on the lookout for her, saying she wasn't eating enough. As she took the elevator down, she assessed her form; it was long and lean. She was in fighting form still but maybe a little on the skinny side. That was a little disconcerting. She had bouts where she overworked herself but managed to keep on a little bit more weight than she currently had.

With that thought in mind, she picked up several muffins at the coffee shop and a lovely sandwich that looked to be full of vegetables. With those packed up, she caught a cab to the children's hospital. That was much faster and easier than trying to drive.

Once there, she walked inside to her office and sat down. She brought up her computer records to see what was happening with the kids on the ward while she ate. Not ten minutes later Dr. McIntosh walked in, a big smile on his face.

"I really appreciate you doing this," he said. "I've brought Timmy. He's the little boy whose case we can't figure out. We thought he'd been bitten by a snake or something, but there's no sign of any venom. Yet he's comatose, and we can't get him back up again."

She stared at him, her mouth full of food. She chewed and swallowed before asking him, "What did all the test results show?"

He shook his head. "Nothing. Absolutely nothing. Nothing in the blood. Nothing in the urine. We've run MRIs, and we did every test imaginable. We can't come up with anything. He's like the walking dead."

Interested in spite of herself, she polished off her sandwich, unwrapped the muffin, snagged her coffee and said, "Show me."

"HOW INTERESTING. I can connect to Queenie, but she can't connect to me." The Watcher chuckled to himself. "This stuff is fascinating. Who knew I could be so strong and so good at something nobody else does?"

He hadn't even begun to test the limits of his abilities yet. He'd always been a good manipulator when he was younger. He loved making people do what they didn't want to do. As a young child, he'd been a bully. As an older child, he'd become a master manipulator.

Once he'd learned the psychology behind all this stuff, it was so easy to get people to do what he wanted them to do. He understood what buttons to push, what pressure to apply, what leverage to use, and they always buckled. Even the big tough guys buckled. He thought that was pretty funny.

But this, this was something else again. He'd only found out by accident years ago. He was pretty sure that's when he'd first connected with this woman. Who the hell called themselves Queenie anyway? If she was *queenly*, maybe. But that would imply she had an arrogance and a presence. Instead, this woman was a basket case. She was two steps from being homeless, worked in an amusement park, ate the most god-awful food and was turning psychic tricks in a bloody circus tent for five bucks.

He laughed, got up, and poured himself an espresso. The espresso machine had been a gift from somebody who hadn't wanted to gift it. He laughed. "Best gift ever."

He took his cup out to the deck and surveyed the pool area. He frowned at the long grass. Surely the lawn care company should have been here yesterday. But he had strict instructions. He didn't want to be bothered on Wednesdays.

That was one of his days for strategy. He was big on strategy. He had a job, like everybody else, but he was wondering how quickly he could ditch that too.

"Definitely a strategy day." He turned and walked back to his big whiteboard. He had a list of names he was working with. Some would be a little harder work than others, and some would be nothing more than practice runs. None of these cases would benefit him in any monetary way, so he would need to find a couple cases that would. It was the only way he could ditch his day job.

There was Brendan, one of his earlier victims. He put a little checkmark beside his name. There was the dead woman in the lake. With that mention, he put a straight line through her name. He considered that one of his best successes. Bonnie's case had gone off like a dream. Hardly any work at all. It was all about finding the right victim. Timmy was an interesting case too. He'd been easy to sicken, … almost too easy. But how long before someone figured it out?

He looked at the next name on his list and brooded. "I don't know if I'm ready to talk to you yet." He considered that one of the most important things about being a strategist: understanding his own weakness. To allow ego to interfere in his job would get him caught.

"Although how anybody will catch me, I don't know." He let out a belly laugh, walked over and turned on his stereo system. Every good strategist needed a symphony orchestra to accompany them.

As the beautiful sounds of Mozart filled the room, he picked a name on his board and walked to his computer to start researching. Who knew what he would find? But the chase was almost as good as the end result.

KIRK WALKED INTO the office late. He updated his notes on the case of the missing mother at the lake. And he checked his messages to find already several emails from the sheriff. He frowned. "Sheriff, you are in early." He read the messages, then picked up his phone and called him. "I just read your emails."

"Yeah, we're up with the birds here." The sheriff chuckled. "It's only you city folk who get up after the best part of the day is gone already."

Privately Kirk agreed. But he wasn't willing to argue about it. "Still no sign of an accident along the road into town?"

"No. We've got vehicles up there, a couple deputies walking the area, looking to see if anybody ran off the road and into a ravine," the sheriff said. "We've gone back to the address, checked out the house and walked the property again, and we've looked along the edge of the lake. She had a dock, and we checked out all along there but didn't find a body floating in the water. By now it's possible she already sank."

"Is that the most likely scenario, do you think?"

"Except for the vehicle, yes," the sheriff said. "That's what I'm concerned about. That would put her behind the wheel, and most likely a medical emergency took her off the road somewhere. But, so far, we haven't found out where."

"I spoke to the daughter," Kirk said. "She's going to run to the shelter and pick up the dogs. Apparently her mom never went anywhere without them."

"That would take us back to it being a drowning. But then what happened to the vehicle?" the sheriff wondered aloud. "I do like a good puzzle, but not when there's a bad ending on the table."

"How big is the lake we're talking about?"

"Not huge," the sheriff said. "But too big to dredge and would take a big slice of our budget if divers have to search the whole thing. It is full throughout summer. It's a popular swimming spot. If she drowned, unfortunately we'll probably get a phone call when somebody finds the body."

"On the other hand, that's also a good thing because then it's closure for the family."

"True enough. So is the daughter coming up here then?"

Kirk frowned. "I didn't ask her. But maybe she should." He checked his watch. "I imagine she's already gone to get the dogs though. She didn't have a vehicle and was trying to borrow one, I think, or get a friend to drive her up."

"Then I imagine she'll head to her mother's house too. I wouldn't mind her talking to a deputy while she's up there, to see if anything's missing."

"I'll send her an email or try calling her phone, and let her know that's what you would like. And here's her phone number." He read off the number and gave her name to the sheriff.

"Good enough. We can call her too, if she comes into range."

"Right." Kirk ended the call, then quickly called the daughter. By luck she answered.

"A friend is driving me up," she explained.

"Good enough. The sheriff wants you to meet at deputy at your mother's house to see if anything's missing, in case there was a burglary or if she packed a suitcase or something." He heard the daughter catch her breath.

Weakly, she said, "That is probably a good idea, but I can't say I'm looking forward to it."

"No, but it needs to be done. He also wants to get a little more information from you, if he can. They're checking the highway right now to see if a vehicle might have run off the road. That would be one of the most viable reasons neither your mother nor her car are around."

"Right. Maybe I'll call you when I get to the house," she said hopefully.

Understanding that she needed this connection to him right now, he agreed.

When he hung up, he entered his notes into the case and then shut down the file. There wasn't anything he could do from here, and, as much as he wouldn't mind taking a run out there, the sheriff was already working the area. If it ended up being foul play, that was a different story. Kirk could always take a look at the evidence himself. There was nothing like being at the scene to see how much damage was done and what forensic evidence might be available to collect. The sheriff wouldn't have access to the teams Kirk had at his disposal.

Thinking about that, he called the sheriff back. "Did anybody see signs of blood? Any furniture overturned? Anything along that line?"

"I don't believe so," the sheriff said. "My deputies are looking on the road still. I can give them a call and confirm, but they didn't mention it."

"If there is, I might take a trip and have a look myself."

"If you got any free time, then fly at it. Most of the time all I ever hear is how you guys are too busy to visit."

Kirk chuckled. "And I do have cases stacked up high on the side, but that doesn't mean her case is any less im-portant."

"Glad to hear that," the sheriff said. "If you decide to

come, stop on by." This time it was the sheriff who hung up.

Kirk got up and walked over to the coffeemaker, just down the hall. Several officers were hanging around. They made way for him so he could grab a cup. He filled it to the brim, and, as he left, one of the guys asked if he'd seen Queenie again.

"Nope, I haven't. Any reason why you're asking?" He didn't even bother turning around, just kept on walking.

The one guy said, "Wouldn't mind her assistance."

The others just laughed. "Queenie was good while she had it, but then she lost it, remember?"

One of the guys hushed the other one up. But Kirk had heard it all before. Even worse, his sister would just repeat their same warning. She'd hated Queenie. And never gave him a reason why. But then, as Queenie would have said, she was a bitch. His sister kept telling him for years to drop her. And he hadn't listened. Once they broke up, she did nothing but crow about how right she'd been the whole time.

He hated to say it, but Queenie was right. His sister *was* a bitch.

"She doesn't do that anymore." The men were still chuckling as Kirk left them behind.

The trouble was, if Queenie didn't do it anymore, then she wouldn't have emailed him. Why she'd emailed him, he didn't know. But it certainly put him in a tough spot. Although it might have led to something, it wouldn't be something easy to close.

Back at his desk he sorted through the three big cases there, multiple rapes where they suspected it was one guy. Another was a rash of break-ins that were getting more and more violent. That one really concerned him. There were no rapes, attacks or murders associated with the break-ins, but the perp *was* escalating. He had killed the dog in the last house, and he had interrupted the young couple making out on the couch. He'd taken off, but there was a good chance that the next time he wouldn't. When anything like this escalated, things just got ugly. Which was what worried him about Queenie—this was bad and would only get uglier.

CHAPTER 7

Thursday …

QUEENIE WAS GRATEFUL when she reached the last person standing in line. She didn't know if people had spread the word about her or if it was just the craziness of the world around her, but people were coming in asking for answers to everything—if they should buy stocks, ditch their boyfriends, try again for another pregnancy. And one guy even asked her if he should eat his lunch because it had dairy in it. She'd never seen the likes of this before. And, because of it, she was exhausted just dealing with all the different energies.

She didn't know if Carlos had done new advertising, but, if he had, he was off the mark. Sure it was bringing in money, but money wasn't everything. At least not to her. What it seemed like Carlos was doing was sending everybody her way with a silly question. She figured next he'd want her to raise the price so people would still come but pay more. He was doing just fine with her abilities as it was, but it was exhausting to her. She might have to change her own agreement. If he kept bringing in as many people as he was, she would need more downtime, which ultimately meant less money. Carlos just didn't get that.

Speaking of which, as she sat here in her chair, enjoying the peace and quiet of the room, even now filled with the energies she hadn't had a chance to cleanse the space, Carlos walked in. His cries were immediate.

"What? Nobody here?"

"Thank God, nobody's here." She made no attempt to hide the fatigue in her voice. "I don't know what you're doing, but you're making my life crazy. I can't do as much as you're trying to get me to do."

He stared at her in surprise, but a crafty gleam was in his eye. "What are you talking about?"

She shook her head. "Don't pull that. I know what you're up to. You've been running all kinds of ads, trying to bring in more and more people. Well, today it's been nuts. I've had more people than ever, but what you're forgetting is, I'm only one person. If you want to bring in a shyster or somebody else to take my place, who can do what you want them to do, great. But if you expect me to handle the influx of extra people, then no. I'm done."

The crafty look disappeared. "No, no," he wailed, his hands waving in front of him. "I didn't think it would work that well."

"What would work that well?"

"The Facebook marketing I've been doing."

She stared at him. "Really? You're pouring money into Facebook again? I thought those ads stopped being effective?"

"I made some changes," he said, rubbing his hands together. "They are doing well again."

She thought about her afternoon and nodded. "If it sent all those people in, then it certainly is more effective. But again, it's still just me here. You have to give me more downtime and less people. You don't understand how draining it is." But of course he didn't—he believed she was a fake anyway.

"So, don't make such a big deal out of it. Make the shit up," he cried out, as if hating the idea of losing any money because she was tired.

"If I weren't the real thing," she said sadly, "I'd have no problem making shit up. But I am the real thing, and I have a level of integrity that obviously you don't give a damn about."

He was almost at the edge of the tent when he heard her words. He stopped, twisted and rolled his eyes at her before ducking his head.

She leaned back in her chair and looked around the room. She'd called this place home for a couple years now. And even now she didn't quite know that she was ready to leave. But maybe something showed on her face, so he took a more conciliatory stance.

"I'm sorry. I didn't think you'd be so tired."

"Of course I'm tired," she said. "Already too tired to even argue with you. I've told you before how it wears me down."

"At least you're making more money," he said hopefully.

"Not enough," she said quietly. "Definitely not enough." She pushed herself from the chair, grabbing her wallet and cell phone. "I'm going home. Put somebody else in here or close it down. I don't care."

He looked around as if to find something to say that would make her stay.

She shook her head. "Don't bother. There isn't anything you could say right now that would keep me here. I'm too damn tired."

He nodded. "That's what you should do. Go home and just rest. We'll see you in the morning." And he bolted.

She groaned. Because tomorrow would be the same as today. She understood his eagerness, but there was only so much she could do. She walked to the tent opening only to turn and stare behind her again. She wondered what the draw was. She had her cell phone and wallet, but she couldn't help thinking she was forgetting something. She walked back inside and realized she'd left the lunch container.

She reached down to pick it up. As she lifted it, she stopped and stared. Inside the container was the same spider she'd released before. At least it looked like the same spider. She carefully upended it onto the table. Instead of moving, it just sat there.

"Have you been inside there all day?" she asked, worried for his sake, which was stupid because she had no clue as to what spiders even needed on a daily basis.

The spider didn't appear to do anything or to give a damn about what she said; it just sat there as if uncertain of its new reality.

"Sorry," she whispered, again backing away.

Almost instantly a weird sound vibrated through her mind. She wasn't sure what it was. She turned back toward the spider, and the sound stopped. Frowning, she slowly pivoted ninety degrees away from the spider. The farther away she went, the more the noise sounded. Not sure what was going on and feeling foolish for the thoughts rippling through her head, she took a step closer to the spider. The sound stopped. From that position she did a full circle around, but there was nothing. When she tested it by moving a foot farther away, immediately there was that weird vibration.

She glanced at the spider, took a step closer and said,

"Are you sending out messages, and that's your limit?"

It just stared at her.

She looked at it from where she was, wondering if it was even alive. Had it moved since she placed it on the table? Or had she somehow killed the thing? Maybe it was sending out a distress call. That was unsettling to consider. Although she'd heard of people being amplifiers and others being reducers, and some who could transmit and some who could receive, there were some who could do both. She didn't have a clue if spiders came into the same categories of abilities.

But then what did man actually know about spiders? There were probably a billion of them in the world, but, with so many different species, who knew what their actual abilities were? And did they have abilities beyond the physical that the doctors and scientists couldn't see and feel or measure? That was the question that always stumped her. It wasn't like she could be tested for the stuff she did. Sure, if somebody could sit in another room and hold a card, and if her abilities felt like cooperating, they might tell her what that card was, but chances were also good she'd be wrong.

She walked closer and of course couldn't hear anything. "So are you sending now?"

From behind her, she heard a voice call out, "What are you doing?"

She turned to see a boy somewhere around eight, maybe ten years old. Feeling foolish, she shrugged and said, "Not a whole lot. What are you doing?"

He stared at her like she was an insect herself, and then he spun away and disappeared.

She didn't know why his attitude should bother her. It wasn't like she hadn't seen hundreds of the same type of glances before. Her whole life had been as one of the outcasts of the world. She turned back to the spider only to realize it was gone now. Relieved it wasn't dead, she hurried back toward the tent entrance. When she reached the same spot as before, again the weird crackling filled her mind. She froze and turned, but found no sign of the spider. She didn't know what to think of this.

As she took one more step toward the tent opening, she felt something weird on her foot. She looked down, and, sure enough, the spider raced up her leg. She danced around, trying to shake it off. But it wouldn't be. In the process she dropped her lunch container. And damn if the spider didn't do a flying leap off her pant leg to land inside the container.

Still not sure what the hell was going on, she backed away from the spider. "You want the container? You can have the container," she cried out.

And of course it didn't say anything. What was it supposed to say? Or was she really expecting to hear a child's voice in her mind again? It was the last thing she should want to hear. Yet that was what she'd heard the first time, and that was what had sent her to call Kirk.

Hearty condescending laughter filled the air.

The Watcher. She glared into the room. *Can you see me?*

Sure. Not all the time unfortunately, just at moments when you're the weakest. And apparently that spider has got your number.

She gave a mock shudder. *I hate spiders.* It was a standard answer. This spider was special, but she didn't want anyone to know. Especially the Watcher.

Do you? I wonder why. They're really harmless, you know.

In the back of her head she was busy throwing up walls, finding out where this guy was seeing her and how he was talking to her. And she had been talking to the spider in the tent, so he could hear her as well then. Similar to Stefan but … different.

Definitely different, Stefan said in a dry tone in the back of her mind.

She froze, afraid the other guy could see or hear Stefan and know he was here. But the Watcher was talking now.

You know? Spiders are really a scientific marvel. So I don't know what this spider's problem is, the asshole said, *because he seems to be attached to you for some reason, which I don't understand. Not sure why anything would be attached to you.*

Not sure what the hell Stefan's presence meant but grateful he was here and could hear, she cautiously asked the Watcher, *So do you know me, or are you judging me based on this little glimpse into my world you can see right now?*

He gave a bark of laughter. *Oh, good question. Glad to see you got your brains on. Not that you have too many of them, if your life is anything to go by. You're a mess, aren't you? I mean, look at the stupid questions you're answering for people. You're wearing your life force down at a level that's dangerously low too. You should fix that.* And then, almost as if with a casual wave of his hand, he disappeared.

At least she thought he had disappeared. She walked the room with her eyes closed, desperately trying to figure out where he'd come from and how she would know before he arrived next time and also how to make sure he'd left.

In the back of her mind, Stefan said, his voice low and calming, *He's gone.*

She spun to look at him, and yet he wasn't here. She reached up, wanting to pull her hair out of her head in frustration but instead massaged her temples. *How can I be sure of that?* she asked, but she could sense the emptiness.

Get a sense of what it felt like, what his energy looked like, what it smelled like, if there was a taste or color associated with it, Stefan said. *What you're looking for is that tingling that says he's on his way or for the absence of that tingling to tell you that he's gone.*

Did you hear him?

No, Stefan said. *But I could sense him. I couldn't see him either, which is also unusual.*

She snorted. *Unusual? How is any of this normal?*

Well, as you've already been working in this field for a long time, you know perfectly well nothing is normal about our lives or the things we can do.

Can you tell me if there's anything special about that spider? It's almost like he wants me to take him with me, or he wants my lunch container for himself.

Did you ever consider maybe you should take him with you?

You did get that part about it being a spider, right? She walked closer to the lunch container to see the spider curled up inside. *I can't imagine that a spider would want my lunch container,* she murmured. *There's also a weird buzz when I get too far away from it.*

What kind of a weird buzz? Stefan asked sharply.

She straightened. *Well, that question made you wake up and take notice.*

Anything that has a buzz is something that makes me stand up and take notice, he said. *Now stop playing games and talk to me.*

She raised her hands in mock surrender. *When I'm about ten feet away, I get a weird crackling in my head. But the minute I step back toward the spider again, it goes away. The closer I am, the less buzz. The farther away, around that ten-foot mark, there's a really strong buzz.*

Interesting, Stefan said.

I don't know about interesting, she said, *but it's definitely irritating.*

When you talk to it, do you hear anything?

She wanted to smack her forehead. *No, but there's a weird buzz. Do you know what it is? Have you heard anything like it?* This conversation was beyond ridiculous. She waited, desperate to hear his answer.

No, he said. *I never have. But that doesn't mean they can't project that noise as some sort of communication.*

Well, I highly doubt it. It's one thing if it were some animal that everybody loves, like a dog or a cat talking back to you. But to have a spider? I don't think so.

I don't think we get to make that judgment. I've seen some pretty amazing connections between animals and people, birds and people, he said softly. *I imagine it takes the right person to connect with our arachnid friends.*

I'm so not the right person, she snapped. *I don't like spiders, nor do I like snakes and beetles. As much as I can tolerate them, I'd prefer not to have them anywhere around me.*

He chuckled softly. *Do you know if that buzz had anything to do with your visitor?*

She frowned. *How could that be?*

I don't know. I'm asking you. Stranger things have happened in our world.

I noticed a crackling well before he came. At the same time, it seemed to me it happened well before he arrived, but it was probably only minutes.

What if that spider was letting you know of this visitor's arrival? Stefan said thoughtfully. *I know that's pretty far out there, even for me.*

You think? She shook her head, reached down and picked up the plastic container. *It's barely alive.*

Maybe, but, if it was sending you a message or setting off some alarm system, then it would need time to recover, right?

I have no clue, she snapped again. *This is just crazy.*

Maybe. Are you ready to tell me the truth yet? He waited a split second; then he said, *Right. I'm gone.* And he disappeared from her mind.

She picked up the lid of the container, and, holding both carefully, she walked out of the tent, refusing to look back inside again. She headed to her car. She'd had more than enough for today.

KIRK SAT AT his desk, wondering if he should check out Bonnie Jenkins's property. In the back of his mind he couldn't forget what Queenie had said. But he had no concrete proof. He had no boat either, and it was damn hard to get money from the chief to justify renting a boat. Now, if the sheriff had one available, that would be a different story.

Reaching across the desk to his phone, he picked it up and called him. "Sheriff, this is Detective Kirk Sanders. Do you have any news?"

"Not yet," he said. "Starting to think she might be gone."

"Yeah, me too. You don't happen to have a boat available up there, do you? To take a trip around the lake?"

"Yep, got one here at the office. You want to come on up? If you can spend half a day here, we can search the lake."

"I'm thinking about it," Kirk said. "Hardly have the time for it, with all the other cases, but I can't let it go."

"I hear you. Pick a day this week. I'll make time. We'll take a run around the lake. It's big, but it's not huge."

"We can pretty well only check the shores, as the water

will be too dark to see her unless we get lucky," he said, "It's not like we have money to drag the lake or to get divers in. We need to have a whole lot more reason to believe she's in there than what we have so far."

"Exactly. Don't have much budget money for things like that," the sheriff said.

Kirk made a quick decision. "How about tomorrow?"

"Yeah, Friday? What time?"

"How about I be there elevenish?"

"Okay, I'll see you then." The sheriff hung up.

It was late in the afternoon, and he wondered whether Queenie was still at the amusement park or not. He checked his watch to find it was dinnertime.

He had to admire a sheriff who answered the phone even though it was well past business hours. It said much about who the man was.

He called Queenie, but the phone went to voice mail. She could be driving; she could be sleeping. He didn't know. He didn't have a current address for her either. He could run by the amusement park; chances were somebody there might have seen her or would know where she was. But would they tell him? For all intents and purposes, he still looked like a cop, and some people could smell that a mile away.

He closed down for the day, grabbed his jacket, picked up his cell phone, sliding it into his pocket, and left. He didn't say a word to the others. They'd just bug him about seeing Queenie again. As he walked out, Peter walked in.

Kirk stopped and said, "What? Did you forget some-thing?"

Peter chuckled. "Nah. I had to run by the hospital and talk to a doc."

Kirk nodded. He didn't really give a shit what Peter was

up to. The guy was obnoxious at the best of times. Kirk walked out to his car, hopped in and got to the intersection, only to find he was in the turn lane. That lane would take him to the amusement park. Swearing softly to himself, he took the corner. Ten minutes later, he drove into the parking lot at the amusement park. He hopped out, navigated through the crowds, all the events and the man calling out for the games to find Queenie's tent with the drapes down and a sign reading Closed. He frowned, pulled back the drapes and stepped inside. It was empty.

He stepped back out again and saw no sign of her. He looked around for somebody to ask and realized he should have asked at the ticket counter at the entrance. He still had the stub. He checked it to see that the park was open for another three hours. Beside him was a woman making doughnuts. He stopped in front and asked, "Do you know if the psychic is coming back again today?"

The massive woman fisted her hands on her ample hips. "And what do you want to know for?"

He held up his ticket stub. "I paid the entrance fee so I could ask her a question." It wasn't a lie, but it wasn't the kind of question she expected either.

"That's what they all do." She snorted. "What's the matter? Can't figure out your own love life?"

It was on the tip of his tongue to say hell no. But he held back the words.

She stared at him, as if trying to get his measure, and then she nodded. "I think Queenie is gone for the day. She wasn't looking so hot."

Interesting. He managed to keep the frown off his face, nodded politely and said, "Thank you." He turned and walked away when she called out behind him.

"But you didn't want her for that, did you?"

He turned and said, "For what?"

"The same questions everyone in that long line outside her tent was asking today?"

He shrugged, not knowing what she was talking about.

"It's personal, isn't it?"

He smiled. "Absolutely it's personal." He turned on his heels and started to walk out. But he hadn't gotten more than ten feet before a massive man stepped in front of him, his arms crossed.

"Why is it personal? What's your business with Queenie?" he barked.

Surprised to see she had friends, maybe even defenders of her, in the park, Kirk stopped. "I'm an old friend."

The big man shook his head. "Not sure *friend* qualifies," he said. "Queenie doesn't have any contact with anybody from before."

"Before what?"

"Before she joined us," the woman called from behind him. "We're her friends. And, if you're such a friend, why the hell haven't you been around to help her out these last few years?"

Feeling cornered and not having any decent answer, he said, "I didn't know where she was these last few years. She just called me a few days ago, and we reconnected."

He watched the two of them look at each other as if assessing his answer and trying to figure out if they believed him or not before the big guy stepped off to the side.

"If you're really a friend, then don't be such a stranger. And, if you're not a friend, stay the fuck away from her."

Kirk walked away, happy for Queenie that she had a champion but sad she apparently had no friends. At least friends from before, the ones she should have had. That would have been him and his cop buddies. There hadn't been time for a whole lot more. There had been a couple doctors she dealt with, but, other than that, she knew few people. One shrink had enjoyed spending time with her. When Kirk saw her at the hospital, there had been nobody. Everybody had already scattered from her life and weren't particularly interested in collecting around her again.

But then Queenie would have been the first to say they wouldn't be around her now because she couldn't do anything for them. She'd always upheld that the cops were only her friends because of the cases she could close for them. And, when that last case blew up in their face, there was an immediate backlash, and they had turned on her.

Well, it was pretty easy to understand why. She had such a negative view of them all. And, as he looked back, he admitted their behavior had been less than friendly, more like she was a tool to be used. She worked for them for free, but she did the work especially for the families of the deceased or the injured or the kidnapped. She'd always been about helping others.

But so many people didn't give a shit. Maybe he'd been in that camp. When he realized just how much damage it had caused her, he'd wanted her to stop. But, at that point, she'd been so focused on getting through all these cases that she couldn't hear what he was saying. This was his fault too as he was the one who had sent her down that path.

Still, years had passed. What he needed now was to confirm any slight details about this woman in the lake, so, when he went up there with the sheriff, they didn't waste the slice of time they had to possibly find Bonnie. He had no way to know that Queenie's dead woman in the lake was the missing Bonnie Jenkins, but it sounded like she might be. But he had to find Queenie first. He pulled out his phone and called her again. This time she answered.

A sleepy voice said, "Hello?"

"Queenie, it's Kirk."

She sighed, but there was sadness to it. "What do you want, Kirk?"

He winced because, of course, that was what she'd always figured. People only contacted her when they wanted something. And here he was, once again proving her right.

"The woman in the lake," he said abruptly. "I'm going out late tomorrow morning with the sheriff. He's got a boat, and we'll go out on the lake. I was wondering if you could give me any pointers as to where she is."

"Across the lake from her property," Queenie said. "If you're at the top looking down, you'll see her. She's about two feet down, floating, but caught in the plants close to shore."

"Directly across from the property? Like if we put in the boat at her dock and go straight across?"

"As much as I can tell. It's almost like the woman's head is pointing directly at the property. But, of course, there's a lot of leeway within that."

"Any idea what she's wearing?"

"Blue jean capris and a pink blouse," Queenie said. Then her voice changed. "I don't know if you'll find her though."

"Why is that?"

"Feels like something's over her face now."

"Seaweed?"

"I don't know. It's hard to see. Maybe." But her voice sounded puzzled.

"We should see the pink top though."

"Maybe," Queenie said. "But again I can't help you with that. I really don't know anything more to tell you."

He tried to hear if there was a note of apology in her voice. He hoped there wasn't, but of course there was. "You've helped," he said warmly. "I didn't want to have to question you about the details, but you're the one who told me about her in the first place."

"True enough," she said, her voice quiet.

"Are you okay?" he asked sharply.

"Sure, just tired," she said.

But something more than tiredness hung in her voice. He frowned. "Did you eat today?"

"Yes," she said, her voice a little stronger. "I do know how to look after myself, you know."

He let that one slide because, of course, a lot of times when they were together, she did forget meals, lots of them in fact. "Are you at dinner now?"

"No, I haven't cooked anything yet."

And instinctively he knew she didn't have any food around to cook. "I'll pick up something and drop it off," he said without thinking. "As a thank-you for giving me the information on the woman."

There was an odd silence at her end of the phone. Then she said, "Are you sure you don't want to wait? You might not find her now."

"True enough. But at least there's a file open on her, and her daughter knows we're doing something for her now."

"Don't bother about food," she said. "I'm just going to go to bed."

"Oh, no you don't. I know this is a one-way path. You need to eat. You need to eat healthy."

She gave a broken laugh. "Why bother? Everything else inside my world is a disaster. What difference will a little bit of nutrition today make?"

"A lot," he said, forcing a cheerful note into his voice. "I need your address."

And again there was that hesitation.

"I'll get the delivery man to bring it right to you, and I won't even come by, okay?" He almost heard a mental shrug. He didn't know what that could be, but it was like he felt her acceptance.

She gave him her address.

He wrote it down and said, "What do you want? Greek or Chinese?"

"Greek," she said. "And make it lots." And she hung up.

He chuckled. Queenie was feast or famine. She didn't eat, and then she couldn't stop eating. And he had no doubt that she hadn't eaten enough in days. He checked out the location of her address and shook his head.

She was at the edge of the seedy part of town. If she was lucky, she'd found a place to live that wasn't rent by the hour. But knowing her, she wouldn't give a damn. She'd feel right at home. Her self-esteem and self-care had dropped to almost nil after the one case had blown up in her face.

Queenie had gone through hell and back losing a child. He'd gone to her address at the time to see if she had any pets in need of care, and that was when he found toys and little people clothing in her apartment. Not that it was much of an apartment, more like a one-bedroom studio, a sign of how poorly she'd been doing. It had been heartbreaking. He knew it wasn't his problem, but, at the same time, it hurt to see her struggle so much. There also hadn't been any sign a partner lived with her.

That had made him both mad and happy. *Stupid.*

He pulled up his Contacts list, found the Greek restaurant and called them, only to find out they wouldn't deliver to her address. Swearing softly, he placed an order anyway and said he'd be there in thirty minutes to pick it up. He would have to change his plans and take the meal to her. He didn't blame the lack of delivery service to her area. He imagined he would have the same problem with a lot of different restaurants.

By the time he got back to his car and crossed town to where his favorite Greek restaurant was, he only had to wait another ten minutes for the order. He paid for it and then drove past the amusement park to where Queenie currently lived. He parked in the motel's parking lot and got out, the smell of Greek food filling his nostrils. He didn't think she'd share at this point. He expected to have the door slammed in his face. After all, he had told her that he would just have a delivery man take it to her.

She might suspect a trick if he delivered it. He walked to the outdoor hallways, realizing it was more of a motel that probably rented by the week or by the month. He could see her room number on the second floor at the far end of the building. There was an outdoor staircase. He climbed the stairs and rapped on the door. When it opened, she took one look, and her mouth dropped.

He held up the bag in his hand. "I didn't have a choice," he said. "They wouldn't deliver here."

She frowned as if assessing his answer and then gave a quick nod. She pulled the door open, and he stepped inside. It was clean but painfully empty. She had a single old couch and chair and a low coffee table in the living room. There was no TV, nothing but a laptop. He followed her into the kitchen area where she had a folding table and two lawn chairs, more evidence of her lifestyle.

She snatched the bag from his hand, placed it on the table and opened it up. She carefully lifted out the four dishes he'd ordered, then cast him a glance. "Is this supposed to be enough for you too?"

He snorted. "I know how you eat. So I guess not."

She smiled. Her voice was soft, when she said, "I don't eat quite the same anymore. When I'm not doing that same kind of work, I don't need the same number of calories."

"Don't you do that kind of work at the amusement park?"

She glanced at the food. "Well, today I did, so who knows? Maybe I will eat lots." She opened up the dishes and smiled. "But, since you delivered it, I'll be nice and share."

He had half a mind to say, *Don't bother*, and then he thought, *To hell with it*. He nodded. "Thank you."

She went to the small cabinet to get two plates. They were mismatched, and one had a small chip. But she didn't seem to notice. He pulled out one of the lawn chairs and sat down. She got two forks and a couple serving spoons, and proceeded to split up the food, half and half. Some was still left in the containers, which was good because, if she had had the kind of day she used to have, she would need it.

She took the first couple bites and then sighed happily, sitting back. "I'd forgotten."

"How good Greco's was?" he asked, not sure what she meant.

"About good food," she said with a laugh. "I haven't had Greco's since we were together. But I also haven't enjoyed much good food. The amusement park hot dogs are cheap."

"There was a time you wouldn't eat hot dogs."

"There was a time when I could afford to be picky," she said, calmly eating another big bite of lemony potatoes.

He had to admit that, when one was broke, perspectives changed. He ate slower than she did, wondering if he could give her half of his plate because she was working through the contents of hers at an alarming rate. He got up and poured himself a glass of water. After asking her, he poured her one too. When he returned, her plate was almost empty.

She sat back with a happy sigh and said, "That was wonderful."

"So maybe you had a rougher day today after all?"

"Not really. Just my boss has been doing ads, driving a lot of business into my tent. Apparently the word is spreading. But it's exhausting. Even if it's only five bucks a question, that's still a dozen questions in an hour, if not twice that. He wants them to get the question, get the answer and move on so I can do many more an hour. But it's too much."

He stared at her in alarm, seeing the fatigue and the pallor on her face. "That many?"

She nodded. "And today it was hours upon hours. I haven't even counted the money. I don't have a clue how many people went through there."

"And how much of that money do you get?"

"Half," she said. "But I can't keep this craziness up. Carlos came in upset because the tent was empty, thinking he had to up the ads. And I told him that he had to stop them—or at least decrease them—or hire somebody else."

"What did he say?" But Kirk knew the answer. When they had an attraction that made money, they tried to scale it up in a big way. Because nothing ever lasted forever.

"He told me to just make up the answers," she said disgustedly.

"Ouch." He knew one thing. That was something she couldn't do. Queenie was as honest as the day was long. "I'm sure you told him that wasn't possible."

"I did," she said, running a hand through her hair, upsetting the curls riding across her face. She blew out of breath and tossed a tendril back up in the air. She reached up impatiently and brushed it back off her face, tucking it behind her ear. "He didn't want to hear that either."

"No, but, for you, you have to give the truth."

"And most of the time I can do that, or at least hedge it so it's more of a positive answer. But sometime I can't do anything about it, as you well know."

"Like the lady in the lake?"

She nodded. "A little boy came to see me a couple days ago. The same day as the murdering man. And the little boy had a cone over his head."

"That must have been tough." Kirk laid down his fork. "How did you handle that?"

"I didn't have to say anything to him thankfully. But of course it affected me. It always affects me."

"Especially when it's a little boy."

She nodded but didn't say anything, just continued to pick away at the last of the food on her plate.

He stared at his food and thought what it must be like when you looked at a person and could tell they were going to live or die. Or when someone walked toward you with the cone over their head, something he'd never understand. Do you tell him? Or do you stay silent? In Queenie's case she usually stayed silent, wanting to believe there was a chance to change that fate.

He didn't know if she ever followed up on the people

with cones. It wasn't something she could really ask them about. But it had to be tough seeing that over a young boy, particularly after losing her own. And, if she hadn't been in a coma, would she have seen the cone over her son's head? How many days had she been in that coma? He frowned, wondering about that. But it was hardly something he could ask her about.

MADDY COLLAPSED AT her desk. What a day. She kicked off her heels, got up, walked to the corner of her office and sat down on the big floor cushion. She leaned against the wall, her back straight, her hands palms up on her knees and started deep breathing. She needed to do this for herself, no matter her patients. She was due to see Brian next. Here at her office, in the one room they had available for treatment. She had no clue what she would find, but it seemed important that he come. At the same time, something disturbed her floor. Energy floated there that she didn't like. Something was off.

She rubbed at her temples. *Stefan, any idea what's going on with my floor?*

Sorry, I've been painting all day. What's the problem?

I'm not sure. Just felt it in the last half hour or so. But something's moving.

Can you do an assessment?

It's this man who came via Kirk and Queenie that I'm about to see next.

Did the disturbance start when he arrived? Stefan asked sharply.

She froze, opening her gaze to look around her office and frowned. *I have no idea.*

I'm not sure it makes any difference, but it could be that whatever is going on with him is causing the problem.

She chuckled. *So some guy finds out he's got cancer, comes to see me and decides everybody else in the world has to suffer?*

No, but we've seen a lot of weird things.

I know. I know.

Just then her intercom buzzed, letting her know Brian had arrived.

I'll let you know what I find out afterward. She disconnected from Stefan. He wouldn't be upset. She'd had to do it many times over the years.

She dropped herself into a deep meditation and stepped up and out of her body. Brian could wait five minutes. She slipped out to the hallway and studied the energy from the entrance to all the patients. Everything looked normal. But there was definitely a ripple, like a frayed edge somewhere. She headed toward Brian. His wife was here, as was his child. Maddy studied the wife and then the child. All the energy was normal—hopeful, scared, looking for good news, terrified it wasn't coming.

Then she studied Brian. She hadn't seen him on this level before. But a ton of darkness was in his system, darkness she didn't like the look of.

Stefan's voice whispered in her head. *No, I don't like it either. That's not* his *energy.*

If it isn't his energy, who the hell's is it, and why does Brian have it?

She approached, knowing the others wouldn't see she was here, at least not likely to notice. It was always possible she was up against a strong psychic, or the child might have more awareness than the parents understood. But at the moment Kirsten sat, playing with her mom's cell phone.

Games presumably. Maddy approached the chair where Brian sat talking to his wife, studying the blackness deep inside his muscles and bones. But it wasn't the black of a disease. Stefan was right; it was somebody else's black. Maddy wanted to look beneath it. She reached out a hand. As she did so, Brian winced and shuddered.

Instantly his wife asked, "Are you okay, Brian?"

He gasped and nodded. "Just a sudden sharp pain." He squeezed his wife's hand. "We have to face the fact my time is almost over."

But Maddy wasn't so sure about that. As a matter of fact, she was pretty damn sure what was going on wasn't anything quite so simple. The end result would be the same. Brian would die if Maddy didn't do something fast, if she was capable of doing something that would stop this. From what she could see right now, the only thing clear was that somebody was doing this to Brian. He had been slowly and systematically poisoned.

This knowledge slammed her back into her office, and she entered her body. She sat there, gasping for breath, as she tried to sort through her impressions. Chances were he was being fed something or was lying on the poison somehow. It was coming either through his skin or stomach—those were the two easiest ways to poison somebody. But what if it was something else? Like through the air?

She hopped to her feet and walked out. Tammy caught her in the hall. "Your next appointment is ready."

Maddy smiled. "Thank you. I did a quick energy scan of his system. I'll talk to him now." She knocked on the door, picked up the folder from the wall pocket file holder outside on the door and stepped in. Brian sat still, holding his wife's hand.

The wife popped to her feet and cried out, "Thank you so much for seeing him."

Maddy smiled. "You're welcome. But I can't make any promises. I don't know what's going on yet, and I don't know if I can do anything to help him."

Kirsten jumped up and ran over to Maddy. She wrapped her arms around her legs and squeezed.

Maddy dropped her hand to her crown, gently pulsing some loving healing energy into the girl's traumatized system.

Almost immediately Kirsten gave a happy sigh, looked up at her and smiled. "You're the angel lady, aren't you?"

Maddy laughed. "I'm not sure what that means," she said, "but what I need you to do is sit on the chair beside your mom and let me work on your dad, okay?"

She nodded and raced back to the chair, where she scrambled into it and grabbed her mother's hand.

Maddy stepped up beside Brian and said, "Lie down. Let me take a look."

Obediently he lay down.

She ran through the standard tests, checking his blood pressure, listening to his heart, but all the time she was studying the different layers. "How long has this been going on?"

"About six months," he said, gasping for breath.

"Are you allergic to anything?"

Surprised, he said, "No, not that I know of."

"What kind of work do you do?"

"I'm a carpenter."

The questions went on and on as she tried to figure out not so much who was doing this but how somebody was doing this to him.

Finally she turned back to the wife and daughter and said, "I need to spend a few minutes alone with him. Please return to the waiting room and wait there for me."

The wife looked down at Brian. He smiled and said, "Go. We came here to see her. You know she's my last hope."

Nervous but willing, the wife grabbed her daughter's hand, and the two of them walked out. She glanced back at Maddy and said, "Please help him."

Maddy smiled, waiting until the door was closed, and then she focused on Brian. "So, Brian, you've got a big problem. And it has absolutely nothing to do with your body dwindling away. Yes, if this keeps up, you'll die. There might be a chance I can help you, but what we have to do is stop the cause."

Confused, he looked at her. "Well, I'd be happy to if I knew what the hell was going on. The other doctors don't have a clue. But they said I was dying, and I have to admit that I'm half the size I was. My muscles have wasted away. I can't eat anything. I can't hold food down. It's all I can do to drink enough water. I don't sleep anymore."

"Is your hair falling out?"

He looked at her and frowned. "Yes. How did you know?"

"I'll run a few tests on you. They're not tests that you've ever had run before. I want you to close your eyes, and absolutely, under no circumstances, do you open them. Do you hear me?"

He nodded and obediently closed his eyes.

"I want you to stay where you are. Try to relax, but, no matter what you feel, don't open your eyes, okay?"

"Okay, no problem," he said in surprise.

She sat down on her chair and jumped out of her body. It was easier for her to access what was going on in him if she didn't have to deal with the physical restraints of her own body. She placed a hand on his abdomen and pushed deep inside. He groaned. "It's all right," she whispered. "Rest, relax. I want you to accept that that this temporary pain is good for you. I don't want you to fight me."

She pulled the black from his system, taking it out and tossing it away, scooping it out. Pools of it filled his abdomen, filled his heart, filled his lungs. She didn't even know where it came from. If on an energy level, she really wanted to know. But she suspected it was a combination. It was something poisonous. It had been diffused in a way she'd never seen before. But poisons were like that. She suspected arsenic, but then it should have showed up in the tests, if they'd done any tests for poisons. She pulled. She cleaned. She waved. She wafted. She wasn't able to get it all, not at least this first time. But what he had to do now was get healing energy.

In her mind she called out, *Stefan, have you got five minutes?*

His warm and loving voice answered, *For you, of course.*

We need to fill his system with good healing energy. He's been poisoned, but I don't know by what or how. I'm trying to save him, but the damage is pretty extensive.

You cleaned out all the old black?

Mostly. But now we have to fill his system with good energy. You take the crown. I'll take his feet.

They separated to each end of Brian's body. Placing their hands on his feet and his head like a warm blanket, they sent healing energy forward through his body to meet in the middle, to blend and to pass to the other end.

Brian groaned several times, his legs moving restlessly. He cried out once, as if feeling life coming back to his body, or maybe taking so much of the black out and putting the healing energy back in was just too much of a shock for his system. "I don't know what's happening," he cried out nervously.

But she didn't let up. Stefan poured as much energy as he could through Brian's crown chakra, filling the man's head, shoulders, chest. Stefan said, *I think it's in the blood.*

I agree, she told to him. *But any poison that's been in his system a long time would have already permeated every cell in his body.*

Then he has to stop whatever he's doing and get away from whoever it is who's doing it. Do you have any suspicions if his wife is involved?

I hope not, she said. *There's a lot of love there. If she is doing it, I'm not sure she's aware of it.*

Can you deliberately poison somebody and not be aware of it? Stefan asked.

I don't know if you sensed it or not, Maddy said, *but look closer.*

There was silence as Stefan delved deeper between the layers, the different energy motivations, past, present and future. *It's not his energy, right?*

No, it's not. Somebody else is involved, two people actually, but with different levels of involvement. But I'm not seeing it as having a male or female energy to it. And I don't know if that's because Brian's energy is already so low or if it's because of the way the poison has been given to him.

So anybody in his family could be giving him the poison and maybe doesn't even know it? Stefan hazarded a guess.

And I don't know if that's even possible either, she said. *It could very well be somebody at work or somebody he sees on a regular basis. Brian and his family need to step back long enough from his usual daily routine for him to heal and to get strong enough to fight back, and then take on who and what did this to him.*

And, in order to find out who did it to him, we have to find out who benefits.

I know, but there's only so much we can do. My job is what I'm doing.

Who will you get to help with the rest?

The same person who sent him to me. Kirk.

Interesting, Stefan said. *Because I'm now involved with Queenie on several levels.*

Is she okay? Maddy asked. *I haven't had a chance to check her out yet.*

She's not okay as she seems to have attracted another psychic into her space. And not in a good way. Somebody is watching what she's doing, seeing what she's doing and potentially twisting what she's doing.

Maddy froze, realizing she was slowing the energy. She refocused and sent the healing energy, now no longer great big waves of it, but a gentle rumble throughout Brian's system. He no longer struggled but lay there with a smile on his face. She knew how he felt—a gentle warmth and tingling as nerves came alive again and as wasting-away muscles sprung to life. But this wasn't a cure. This was a hell of a big improvement, but it would take some time to get him fully back to normal. And, for that, he couldn't be allowed to be given any more poison.

When I'm done here, she said, *I'll call Kirk.*

You do that.

Stefan, do we have another one? He'd know what she

meant. They'd survived many traumatizing events with psychics who had more abilities and little kindness.

Stefan's voice came as a sad whisper. *I'm afraid so.* And he disappeared.

Dr. Maddy stepped back and sat down, taking a deep breath as she reawakened inside her physical body, then stood and stretched. She patted Brian's hand and said, "Open your eyes."

He opened his eyes and stared at her in wonder. "I don't know what that just was," he whispered.

"It's not something you'll find in very many places," she whispered back. "I have some difficult requests for you now."

She helped him sit up. He smiled at her. "I feel so much better. What happened?"

"In order for this to continue to work, you need to stay away from your normal routine. You can take your wife and daughter, but you need to go away from everything and everyone else. You're not to go to your mother's, your brother's, and you are not to go to work. Do you hear me?"

He looked at her in complete puzzlement.

"For a minimum of three weeks," she said. "I won't see you again if you don't follow these instructions. I'll explain after the three weeks."

He looked at her, still puzzled. "We have a cabin on a lake. It's been in the family forever. We could go there for a couple weeks."

She nodded. "Perfect. The thing is, I want you to leave today."

His jaw dropped. He looked at the time, and she nodded.

"You can stay at a hotel tonight. I don't want you sleeping in your own bed. I don't want you in your own apartment for a long time. Do you hear me?"

He nodded.

She turned to leave.

The urgency must have filtered through his brain as he asked, "Am I in any danger?"

She was about to step out of the room. She turned and looked at him. "If you follow my instructions, no. But, if you return to your routine, to what has been killing you, then yes. You need three weeks to assimilate. Then we'll talk again."

"Do I come back here then?" he asked.

She nodded. "And don't worry. I'll keep an eye on you over the next three weeks." As she motioned to his wife and daughter, he called out to her again. "But how?"

She laughed. "Don't worry. I know how."

CHAPTER 8

Friday, Before Dawn …

MOMMY, … MOMMY …

Reese's voice woke Queenie from a restless sleep. Staring up at the yellowed ceiling tiles, she lay shuddering, trying to shake off the vestiges of the nightmare. Rubbing her eyes, she sat up slowly and looked around. She'd had nightmares for years after losing Reese, but things had been relatively peaceful lately. Until tonight. … His voice still whispered through her heart, leaving a deep wrenching ache.

Why the nightmare tonight?

But she knew. The arrival of the spider and the lady in the lake. She switched on the light beside her, her gaze quickly searching for any spiders lurking around. But she couldn't see any.

Still faint in the distance were sounds of a little boy crying. Frowning, she got out of bed only to shriek and jump back. Her floor was alive with spiders. *"Eww!"*

"Why are there so many?" She involuntarily shook all over. "One or two I can manage but dozens?" she wailed.

Instead of crawling up the corner of the duvet lying on the floor, they mingled like they were having a damn tea party. Pushing back her revulsion, she calmed down enough to study their movements.

And heard a tinkling laugh.

It never failed to put a smile on her face. "Did you have something to do with this? Or are you enjoying these creatures and their antics?" she demanded. How like a little boy. Still it made her relax that much more.

The laugh came again, lightening her heart, making her chuckle.

"If you'd lived, you'd have loved these guys, wouldn't you?"

She only ever saw the pinkish-lavender ball of energy and usually out of the corner of her eye. When she tried to look closer, it dissipated. No matter what she did, she couldn't get a face or words or even a stronger image of him.

Actually it was so much more. For the longest time she'd hoped seeing his spirit meant that maybe, … just maybe, … he was alive. She'd spent countless hours trying to confirm it, only her research had confirmed the opposite. It had taken time, but finally she'd accepted it. This was what she had, and it was so much better than nothing.

For so many, death was so damn final. But not for her. She was blessed.

And she'd do anything to keep that communication line open.

Even putting up with the damn spiders.

Still, she needed to know what they wanted. "Do you know why they are here?"

The laugh whispered again, but it was fainter.

She frowned. "Don't go—not so fast." But, as she watched, the pinkish-lavender glow faded. "Wait …" she cried out. She didn't like the neediness inside her. She normally didn't have a problem when her son's spirit came and went. It was such a joy to feel his presence. Since seeing the lady-in-the-lake vision, her life was off balance. Nothing seemed the same nor felt the same.

And the spiders were sending her around the bend.

"Tell me what you want," she whispered to them. Of course there was no answer, but she crouched closer. There was a pinkish-lavender tinge to them too. Was that Reese's idea?

Still, if she could see pink, then she was seeing something special. Not that she needed more proof; the dozens of spiders on the floor already said something was going on. But what? And how?

Groaning, she knew she needed to touch them. That was how her gift of sight worked. Her features curling into a grimace, she placed her palm on the floor. The spiders raced toward her. She closed her eyes and shivered at the thought of all those spiders crawling on her.

The first one ran onto the back of her hand, followed immediately by a second and then a third. With her lips pinched together, she lifted her hand gingerly with the three spiders perched thereon, and she eased into a cross-legged position and slowly opened her mind to the visions racing toward her.

The first thing she saw was the same little boy sitting on his bed, playing with a scratched and dented toy.

"*Vroom*," he muttered, moving the car along the edge of the bed.

The vision appeared to be a happy one. It was daylight, but his room seemed belowground, with one window high up. No curtains, a crack in the glass. The blanket was threadbare, but the room had a mattress and a night table. No carpet. Just a cement floor. Like in a basement.

Still, nothing was unpleasant about it. The boy was healthy as far as she could see.

But his face was downcast, looking at the floor. She couldn't see his features clearly, and, outside of being thin, dressed in old striped PJs, she had no way to identify him.

She whispered to the spiders, hoping the vision would stay around long enough to give her additional meaning.

The little boy suddenly clapped his hands over his ears, his face scrunching in fear.

Queenie's heart wept for him.

Just as suddenly, the boy dropped his hands, bolted from his bed and raced to the far side and disappeared from sight.

Then the vision faded.

"No," she cried out. "Don't go. I don't have enough details to find him." She leaned forward, as if that would help, but, of course, it didn't. The vision slowly faded to a light-pink fog and finally dispersed completely.

She sagged back on her bed, desperate to retain the bits she'd seen.

Gently flicking off the spiders, she reached for her notebook and wrote down the details she could remember. But it wasn't enough to give to Kirk. He couldn't help if he didn't know more. She hopped off her bed, and the spiders scattered out of her way, as if happy to see her in action after their message had been delivered. She strode with purpose to her laptop. Bringing up a new email, she quickly noted everything she'd seen. Then hit Send.

When finished, she returned to her bedroom. With the lights on, she searched to ensure no more spiders hid in the bedcovers before she crawled in and closed her eyes.

Her last thought was of her son. She whispered to the pinkish-lavender energy, "Thanks, baby. I'm trying to help him."

FRIDAY MORNING KIRK pulled up outside the sheriff's office and parked. He hopped out and stretched. It was a decent drive, but it had been hectic at the police station before he'd left. He told his coworkers where he was going; they were a team after all. There'd been some raised eyebrows as he explained what he was doing. That was hardly within the parameters of his current list of priority cases, not when a sheriff was willing to go out on his own search. But, after hearing the bits and pieces from Queenie, Kirk wanted to see for himself.

He walked into the sheriff's office and stood, looking around. It was like taking a step back in time. Everything was made of wood, the floor scuffed and faded from years of wear. Of course there was only so much money to spend on small departments, and things like refinishing floors wouldn't have a very high priority on the list.

As he stood there, a woman seated at a desk on the left side of the room smiled and asked, "May I help you?"

He nodded. "I'm here to see Sheriff McArthur."

She picked up the phone and presumably called the sheriff. Within seconds a door opened in front of Kirk, and a big burly man came out, wearing a cowboy hat. His face was plump. His barrel chest stuck out well over his belt, but he didn't look to be all that fat. In fact, he looked like an aging linebacker who had had a tad too much beer and comfort food.

The sheriff walked toward Kirk, holding out his hand. "James McArthur."

Kirk introduced himself and smiled. "Are you ready to hit the lake?"

"I am. Are *you*?"

The two men chuckled.

"We've already got the boat loaded," the sheriff informed Kirk. "We were just waiting for you to show up. We do have a bit of a drive, although it's not too bad." The sheriff led the way to his truck, the boat hitched on a trailer behind it.

It was a nice Zodiac with some decent horsepower on the back end. Kirk didn't question what they would do if they found a body because that probably would necessitate bringing in a dive team.

Because of Queenie's touch, he knew a body would be there, but that didn't mean he'd have any luck in finding it himself. It also didn't mean she had the exact location. As he knew from the heavy cost each of them had paid in the last case they had worked together. He thought back on the strange email from her waiting for him when he got up. The tone had been a little chaotic, but then a nightmare had woken her up, so that was to be expected. She'd seen the little boy again. She'd also made a point of mentioning it wasn't her son, and she wasn't losing her marbles.

On that note he'd filed her latest email into his special Drafts folder and had carried on.

Now he and the sheriff headed out of the small town—barely a blip on the radar, as far as Kirk was concerned, particularly when compared to Seattle, which had sprawled so far inland. He couldn't imagine where Seattle's growth would be in another fifty years. "What's the population here?"

"Twenty thousand roughly," the sheriff said. "Swells to about thirty, thirty-five in the heat of summer."

"Tourists. Gotta love 'em, and, at the same time, gotta hate 'em." Kirk laughed. "I'd be one of the tourists myself. But I could certainly see retiring here."

The sheriff gave a sage nod. "Absolutely. That's why most of us are here. We did our time in the big city, Seattle or wherever, and we couldn't stand it anymore. You wake up one day and say, *I'm done*. At least that's what happened to me."

And the funny thing was, Kirk could see the exact same thing happening to him. "You still have to have a job and an income though, unless you happen to wake up rich one day," he joked.

"I was lucky enough to get elected sheriff. It'll do me until I retire."

It was just the two of them heading up to the lake. "Anybody else still looking for Bonnie?"

"No. I had to pull them off for a couple accidents we had overnight. Bunch of drunk yahoos—some superwealthy punks out of the Seattle area—were racing and crashed a couple sports cars on the highway."

"Street-racing on the highway?"

The sheriff nodded. "They get the idea into their heads, *We want to avoid the cops*. So they come up here, thinking they can do it on a couple flat stretches we got. But what they forget is, some really dangerous corners are here. And, going the speed they're going, those corners hit hard and fast. Mother Nature is incredibly unforgiving when it comes to stupidity."

"Any fatalities?"

"No, at least not yet." The sheriff's tone was full of frustration yet sad at the same time. "But it's possible. One's in serious condition. He was airlifted to Seattle last night. We've got another in the local medical clinic with a broken leg, and the female passenger—it's hard to say how she's doing. There was talk of shipping her to the big hospital too, but I'm not sure if that ever happened."

"It's tough when you're young, and you have more money than God, and you don't know what to do with yourself."

"Never had that problem," the sheriff said. "I always worked for my dollars. And worked damn hard."

Kirk understood. He'd been the same. No money to inherit from family. What he had, he'd worked for. But it wasn't the same for so much of the world, with millionaires popping up between YouTube and Bitcoins. Of course Seattle itself was well known for its moneymaking tech sector, some incredibly large amounts made without even thinking about it. Seattle had similar problems as what the sheriff had talked about. Street-racing was a bad deal in a lot of cities.

They drove in companionable silence for another few minutes, and then the sheriff took a turn-off. A brown public park sign showed them the way. "Is this a popular camping spot?"

"It is. Bonnie has the property right beside it. When she went missing, I wondered if there had been some foul play. But I couldn't find anybody staying at the campsite right now."

"And would you consider that normal for this time of year?"

The sheriff frowned, giving it some serious thought. "Well, I'd have expected it to be pretty damn full with the long weekend coming up, but it is just May and isn't as popular as it will become in June, July and August. Kids are still in school. Families are still waiting for the summer holidays to hit."

"Makes sense. If you found no sign anybody has been

staying there, I presume there's also no sign anybody went missing from there."

At that, the sheriff turned and gave him a sharp glance. "Meaning, there might be somebody out on a rampage?"

"Not necessarily but it's quite possible that maybe Bonnie saw something she shouldn't have and had to be taken care of, so to speak. Or happened to be in the wrong place at the wrong time."

The sheriff nodded. "I hadn't considered that," he announced. "Hate to as well."

"I hear you," Kirk said. "But, when people go missing, particularly a female in her age group who lives alone, you have to wonder just what went wrong."

They drove up the road, and Kirk saw a large turn-off to the campsite. But the sheriff kept going. Another driveway appeared after one more mile. The sheriff pulled onto that and drove one hundred yards to a small old clapboard cabin and one of the most incredible views of a lake that Kirk had ever seen.

He stared. "Wow!"

The sheriff nodded. "Right? I'd buy her place just for the view."

"And that's something to keep in mind too."

"What's that?"

"Her daughter told me that Bonnie refused to sell the place, even with a million-dollar offer," he said. Then remembering Queenie's words, he added, "Maybe … somebody decided they had to have it anyway."

MADDY SAT AT the little boy's bedside. She'd done what she knew to do, but that black energy wouldn't shift. She'd tugged. She'd pulled. She'd wrapped it up in love. And still the black energy persisted. The boy's energy had surprised her, but, even with his energy paired with hers, she hadn't been able to make the black energy shift.

She'd worked on the little boy physically and in spiritual form. She didn't understand. But she needed to. Otherwise Timmy would die.

No luck? Stefan murmured.

No, she whispered back, her tiredness echoing in the one word. *I don't understand.*

I might.

She straightened. *What? What am I missing?*

The energy is being masked.

How? I can't see a foreign energy.

Yes, but I can from farther away. He's masking the funnel and feeding the energy as you take it away.

Shocked, she jumped out of her body. *Show me.*

But he didn't need to. As they pulled farther back, she could see where the cord disappeared into the air. Only now, even farther back, she could see where that masking energy was inside the little boy—integrated so deep into the boy's system as if they were one.

She severed the cord at the point where it disappeared. Then she dove inside the child and poured love into his system, filling his bones, his muscles, his veins with healing energy.

When she pulled back, drained, yet more exhilarated than she could believe, and settled into her physical form, she heard the little boy asking, *Mommy, where am I?*

"WHAT THE HELL is she up to?" the Watcher said to himself.

He stared at Queenie as she headed out of the tent after yelling at her boss. The carnival boss appeared to be the one person Queenie didn't get along with. The Watcher didn't know how he felt about her having the friends she did. While everybody needed somebody, these guys were really more caricatures than real people. Some of them were downright ugly. And Queenie, with her stupid fake hat over her head, looked pretty ridiculous herself. Of course she only wore it when she was giving out messages.

Now she looked like a lost young woman, as if the world had been too hard, too tough, and she was done. He could see from her energy that she was down in some way, just not sure what exactly was happening.

Even going about his own day, doing his own job, he'd always been drawn back to Queenie, wondering what she was up to. He knew who she was and what she was to him, but she didn't know who he was and what he was to her. That was really disappointing. He wondered if he could leave her little clues. He'd left her one in the lake, but she wasn't getting the message. He might have to do it again.

He thought about all the other cases he'd worked on, wondering if he should imitate one or find a new unique way. He prided himself on his creativity. He wasn't much for following other people's ideas or methodologies. But he wanted her to know who he was. And yet, somehow he had to do that without letting the cat out of the bag. Because the only thing more dangerous than playing the game was getting caught.

Just then a vacuum-like suction hit his energy, one of the many threads he'd been playing with. The pressure was intense. He fought to control it, only to suddenly be released, his energy cut, the thread disconnected.

With a precision-like skill, his victim had been freed, and there was nothing he could do to stop it.

Pissed, he dove in to reconnect, only to slam into the equivalent of a stone wall in ether form. He couldn't see in that direction nor could he move in that direction.

And that just pissed him off more.

He'd finally found someone with better skills than he had.

And that made him seriously angry. That was not allowed.

CHAPTER 9

Friday, Midafternoon …

QUEENIE WALKED AROUND the amusement park. The day was over as far as she was concerned. After her crappy night, she'd struggled to get through her heavy line of customers. She was exhausted and chilled to the bone, even though it was the hot, sunny day the weatherman had promised. Clouds had covered the sun for most of the day; then, late in the afternoon, it rained. Most of the time that would have been fine by her.

But her tent developed a leak, and dampness had set in. She attempted contacting Carlos several times, but he hadn't been too bothered about coming to rescue her. She'd taken the opportunity, after she'd finished a long line of people, to put up the Closed sign and escape. She sent Carlos one last text message, saying, **Fine. I'm now closed for the day**. And she bolted from the tent before he had a chance to stop her.

The only thing that mattered to Carlos, it seemed, was money. And, if she shut down her tent, then he wasn't making money from her.

Now she was on the far side of the park, where he wasn't likely to find her. The only good thing was, no uninvited spiders had showed up at the tent today. Perversely she found herself missing them. Maybe after their early morning message to her at her apartment, they didn't need her anymore. They hadn't been visible when she got up this morning. And she'd looked. Boy, had she looked. Did spirits connect to other spirits? Had her son connected to this little boy as she thought? And, if so, why?

She was still musing when she reached her destination. One of her favorite hot dog vendors was here. She picked her way around a puddle and came up on his blind side. "Did you save me one?" she asked hopefully.

Lugar spun around, caught sight of her and grinned. He manned the stand and could work the machines like a pro. He was one of those invaluable assistants, a jack-of-all-trades kind of guy. He bent down, pulled out a tray from the open-ended warming shelf, lifted a plate from inside and held it out for her.

She clapped her hands in delight. "Oh, it's pierogi day," she cried out. "I forgot."

"How could you possibly forget?" he joked. "It's your favorite."

The pierogies were massive. Three were on the plate, but she knew she'd be lucky if she could even eat two.

He motioned toward a stool and said, "Sit down and eat."

She did. The pierogies were barely warm. He'd wrapped them in tin foil, but that had probably been a couple hours ago. She was famished and exhausted, and she knew it must have shown on her face.

Lugar took one look, shook his head and said, "What's wrong with you, girlie?"

She made a face at him. "Carlos has been running Facebook ads, of all things. Drumming up business for me. And it's been working too well."

He stared at her, his mouth dropping open. "He's been what?"

She nodded. "Who knew he was such a businessman?"

"And, even if he did, then what?"

She shrugged. "I've had lines outside the tent for days now. Not too sure how much longer I can keep going at this pace. I told him that he had to cut it back, but he said I should make up answers." She scoffed. "And he wants me to run through the people faster, with less effort."

Lugar looked at her sorrowfully. "And, of course, an answer like that would just piss you off."

She chuckled. But she took another bite of the pierogi, moaning in delight. It was better not to answer questions like that.

"I should've saved you an extra one," Lugar said. He nodded toward the plate she'd already half emptied. "You do need extra food when you're so exhausted."

"The trouble is, my stomach won't handle any more right now." She finished most of the second pierogi and just sat quietly.

A man came up beside her, looked at her plate, turned to Lugar with a frown and said, "Hey, I was just here asking for those, and you said there weren't any."

Lugar nodded. "She bought and paid for those earlier and asked me to hold them until she was done with her shift."

The man puffed up like he would lunge at Lugar, but Lugar was no small man to take on. He just crossed his arms over his chest and waited for the man to decide what he would do. Spluttering angrily, he stormed off to a different stall.

She smiled at Lugar. "Thanks for saving me these."

"No problem. What are you gonna do about Carlos?"

She sighed. "Is there anything anybody can do? Money drives him. It doesn't matter if I fall over dead from the work he's piling on me. The only thing he'll care about is, if I stop, how he won't make any more money." She snorted. "Oh, wait. He'll just hire somebody else to sit in there with that silly headdress and make him money. They'll probably make him a ton more because they'll be charlatans and will say whatever everybody wants to hear."

"You really do have the sight, don't you?" Lugar asked.

She tossed him a glance and nodded. "But, like anybody with the sight, there's no guarantee it will cooperate and give you the answers when you need them."

The two sat quietly as she nibbled away on the third pierogi. She had planned to take it home, but her stomach kept telling her it was still empty. She slowed down, hoping it would fill up, plus giving more time for her brain to get the message from her stomach. But evidently two pierogies weren't enough. She continued to plow through the third pierogi until it too was gone.

She sat back, patting her tummy. "Now it's feeling better."

"Good." Lugar nodded behind her. "Because Carlos just found you."

She stiffened and glared at Lugar. He held up his hands and said, "I just caught sight of him myself. But it's too late to run now."

Her shoulders slumped, she pushed the empty plate toward him. "Any of that coffee left?"

He turned to look. "Yeah, you might as well have what you want. It's lukewarm."

"It's still coffee," she muttered.

He poured her a cup, and she'd just wrapped her hands around it, warming up her fingers and the palms of her hands, when Carlos snapped like a turtle at her. She let his tirade blow over her head and turned to look at him.

"Unless you want me to quit right now, you'll back up five paces, and you'll shut the hell up."

Both Lugar and Carlos stared at her in surprise.

Her glare upped in wattage. "And that should tell you how exhausted I am. Because normally it would take a hell of a lot for me to start swearing at you, but right now I am so done."

As if Carlos finally saw how exhausted she was, he frowned and said, "How many people did you have through there today?"

"Well, I'm sure you'll tell me when you start counting the money," she said, "but it was well over a hundred."

He clapped his hands in joy.

She stopped it right there with her hand up in the air. "And don't forget half of that's mine."

He nodded. "Of course it is. Of course it is." But then he couldn't resist doing a little jig.

"I presume you have my replacement ready," she said, the fatigue evident in her voice.

He stopped and stepped forward. "Why would I replace you?"

"Because you haven't done what I asked. You know I can't handle that many people."

"I told you how to handle them," he cried out.

She just glared at him. "If you don't want me to start broadcasting the color of your underwear all around this amusement park, plus who you slept with last night, then I suggest you shut up about asking me to fake it."

Ever-so-slowly his jaw closed, and he pinched his lips tight. He stared down at her, drawing himself up to his full height, which was still only shoulder height for Lugar, and said, "You'd be making it up, and nobody would believe you."

"Everybody here would believe me," she snapped. "Because everybody who works here already knows I'm the real deal."

Carlos hemmed and hawed but was obviously a little more conciliatory.

She wondered if she'd have to prove it to him. She knew he wore purple underwear. She didn't give a damn. The fact that he slept with Jimbo the Giant was something he probably didn't want the rest of the world to know. Jimbo was a teddy bear. But he could sure do with somebody a whole lot nicer than Carlos.

Carlos stepped back and said, "You're bluffing."

"Sure. I'll go tell Jimbo that."

He gave a horrified gasp and dashed forward. In a harsh whisper he said, "You can't know that."

"I know it. Now so does Lugar."

Lugar stared at Carlos. And then over at Queenie. She held up a finger, wanting him to be quiet.

But Carlos was dancing in fury. "It's not true. It's not true. You can't go telling lies like that."

"I won't tell anybody else, providing you cut back on those ads and give me more time off."

He nodded. "Why don't you take off two days a week? I'll get somebody else in to take your place on Tuesday and Thursday."

She slowly raised her eyebrows at him. "Somebody who can just make up the answers people want to hear?"

"Why not?" he wailed. "They want answers."

"They want the truth," she corrected. But inside her own mind she realized she wasn't quite telling the whole truth. People wanted answers, but they didn't necessarily want the answer she gave. They wanted the answers they wanted to hear. And that was a different story. She didn't know how she felt about Carlos bringing in a replacement for two days. Could she afford to take two days off a week? In a way she could because she was making so much more money on the other five days, but she'd been wondering if he'd been cheating her from her half as it was. Now she wanted to see if he would give her the full amount of money.

"We'll try it this week," she announced. "But I need my pay today."

He shook his head.

"You didn't pay me yesterday either," she snapped. "That was our deal. At the end of the day, you would pay me."

"You left early yesterday," he slid in smoothly.

"That's fine. Now you owe me for two days."

He glared at her.

She crossed her arms over her chest and said, "And no cheating me."

In front of Lugar, he straightened and glared at her. "I never cheat."

"You don't like getting caught cheating, but, like everybody else, you fudge the line."

His face went red.

And she got a vision of him sliding some money into his pocket before handing out a wage. It hadn't been hers, or she'd have taken him to the cleaners for it. "I don't particularly trust the person who's so busy counting out money that he doesn't care about the people making it for him."

She *must* be tired. She never talked to him like this. Her filter was gone. It was also a sign she was getting ready to leave. Because she didn't give a damn. And, when she didn't give a damn, she shouldn't be here. The trouble was, she didn't really know what else she would do. This wasn't an easy job to replace. Yet, she could do something else full-time. She wondered about opening up her own shop, having a website, something along that line, but it still took money to do that. Maybe if she did this gig for another few months, she could get enough money to set that up. She could do readings over the phone potentially too.

She sat here, contemplating what her options were, when Carlos said in a stiff voice, "Let's go to the tent and check it ourselves."

She nodded and then froze because she saw a vision in her head of Carlos going through her tent, taking money out of the jar and stuffing it willy-nilly into his right-hand pocket. And she hadn't needed to touch him to get that vision. *Interesting.* Also a sign of her growing skills. A change that both intrigued her and worried her. She needed to learn to control her skills now before they grew any bigger. Catching Carlos right now would do a lot for her self-confidence—and would allow her to walk from here. She didn't know to what exactly, … but time to let go of her past.

"Only if right now you empty that right-hand pocket on the counter and show me that ten, twenty and a bunch of fives."

He cried out as if she'd injured him.

She shook her head. "No, while Lugar is here to watch, I want you to do that for me."

He shook his head. "I will not."

"Then I quit," she said. "And the money in that jar is mine. What money you've left there. Because you just walked through my tent, picked a handful out of the money jar and stuffed it in your pocket." She called out to the rest of the employees gathering around them, "Did you know Carlos here is cheating you from your full pay?"

He cried out, "No, no, no, no. You can't say that."

"I can say that," she snapped. "Oh, but that's okay. You'll hire a charlatan to take my place and to make more money for you. If you do that, you do it without me. Because right now you're cheating me, and I want my pay for yesterday and today."

He glared at her.

But she wouldn't let up. "And you empty that damn pocket of yours so everybody can see I'm telling the truth and you're lying."

"Hey, I picked up some money earlier today," he protested. "No way to prove that money came from your jar."

She closed her eyes for a brief second and saw the mess of fives. There was one twenty and possibly a ten in there. She opened her gaze, looked at Lugar and said, "It's full of fives. There's one twenty and one ten in there. They all came from my tent."

Jimbo, standing behind his lover, stepped forward and said, "Carlos?"

Carlos was so furious he stomped his feet.

She glared at him. "Empty your pockets right now, or I'll get Jimbo to help."

Carlos scoffed. "Jimbo does what I say, not what you say."

"Jimbo, do you realize why he doesn't want anybody to

know about your relationship?"

Jimbo looked at her, his huge brown eyes staring at her, but dread was in them.

"Any time you want to know," she said, "I'll break it to you gently. But right now you need to help me. He's cheating all of us. And, if we don't stop him, he'll continue to do so."

Jimbo slapped his palms on top of Carlos's shoulders, his hands so huge they pretty well wrapped around the ball joints. "Carlos?" Jimbo said, his voice stern. "Empty your pockets."

Carlos glared at her, and now she knew she'd made an enemy. But she didn't give a damn apparently. She'd go wait tables before she worked for him again. Ever-so-slowly he put his fist into his pocket and pulled out money, dropping the paper bills on Lugar's counter. And sure enough it was all fives, a twenty and a ten.

She looked at the crowd gathered around. "He walked through my tent and took a handful out of my jar so he didn't have to split it with me."

Angry murmurs now rose in an ugly crowd growing around him. Everybody here might have some problems, might be antisocial, might just want to be carnies, but they were all honest in their own way. Being part of this team, they were honest with each other. To think Carlos was stealing from them was about the worst thing he could ever do.

She turned her gaze back to Lugar. "Can you count that please?"

Lugar counted it out. "There's a hundred forty-five here."

"Take out seventy-five please, for me." He did so. She

held out her hand.

Carlos snapped. "That's not half."

"No, it's not. It's two dollars and fifty cents more," she said. "But you owe me that and more for trying to cheat me. And now, Jimbo, if you would please hold the other seventy dollars for Carlos, while we go to my tent. Jimbo and anybody else who wants to come can see what's left in the money jar in my tent. Out of your half, Carlos, I'll take the money you owe me for yesterday." And she marched away.

She could hear heavy footsteps behind her as Jimbo and the rest followed her. It was a good seven-minute walk across the amusement park, but she was in a steaming hot mood, and she didn't give a damn. She was so done with this. She stepped into her tent, picked up her jar and dumped it on the table.

As everybody watched, she counted it into two piles. The five dollars extra she put in Carlos's pile so things had evened up. She pocketed her half and then looked at his. "And you owe me for yesterday. I had a hundred and thirty-two people through here, times five dollars each." She quickly did the math, divided by two. "Jimbo, give me the money we allocated for Carlos earlier."

Jimbo, who held the money in his hand, handed it over and she counted out the balance due to her.

She picked up what was hers, pocketed it, grabbed her lunch container, cell phone and purse, and said, "I'd say it's been a pleasure, Carlos, but finding out you've been cheating me makes this a hell of a bad deal." She turned to face the crowd of her friends and coworkers. "He's not only cheated me for the last three months," she snapped as visions kept rolling on like an endless feature movie in her mind, "he's cheated Jimbo, Lugar and at least Betty. For the rest, I haven't seen visions. But, if Carlos cheated the four of us, you know he's cheated all of us. I bet he owes all of you at least a thousand dollars apiece in back pay." Instantly numbers slammed into her mind. She winced. "No. It's more than that."

She turned to face Carlos. "I'll come collect mine on Saturday. That's tomorrow, asshole." She leaned toward him and said, "Do you hear me?"

At this point, Carlos turned to say to them all, "I don't have the money. The amusement park is losing money. It's the only way I could pay the bills."

"Not true," Queenie snapped. "Yeah, you ran through a bad patch." She easily read it on his energy. "But you haven't been in that bad patch for the last month and a half. Once you made money off everybody, you decided to keep doing the same damn thing. So you had a little extra money in your own pocket. You fool. Every one of us would have helped. Every one of us would have pitched in if we'd known the amusement park was in trouble. But you didn't give us that chance."

By now a fury rode her. She wanted to smack him silly. And, just as quickly, all the fire went out of her.

She shrugged, looked at the others and said, "I'm so sorry. I thought I had a place here. I thought Carlos was decent." She turned to look at him and spat on the ground in front of him. "But I was wrong." And she marched from the tent. "Jimbo, I hope you'll be here tomorrow morning when I come back to get the rest of my money."

Jimbo's voice was hard as he called out, "I'll be here. Whatever money we can find, we'll be splitting with everybody."

"Good idea," she said. "I'm not the only victim. We all

are."

Word had already traveled by the time she hit the ticket gate. Chuckie leaned forward as Queenie walked up and asked, "Did that really happen?"

She nodded. "He's been cheating you too, kiddo. I'm sorry."

Chuckie's face fell. "Why did he do that? We had a good thing going here."

"You're right. We did. But once again, it's greed. We've all worked for him, done extra hours, long days, taken all kinds of shit from him, and most of that only happened once he started cheating us. His attitude went downhill about six, maybe eight weeks ago."

Chuckie nodded thoughtfully. "You're right."

"And that's when he got back out of the red and took our money to keep for himself. He got greedy. He got arrogant. He got egotistical, and he thought he'd get away with it." She gave him a sad smile. "Have a good life, Chuckie."

And she walked away.

"WOW, I DIDN'T see that coming," the Watcher said. He tried peering deeper into his vision, but he couldn't. "She's quite a spitfire."

He chuckled, rubbing his hands together. She provided no end of amusement for him. It still bothered him that she couldn't see him the same way he could see into her world. There had to be a way to make that more of a two-way mirror, not just his one-way version he had now. Yet, this way, he had the upper hand.

It still smarted that he'd been bested over his other victim; that little boy had been a great trial. The Watcher had gone back and tried again with the little boy but had no luck reaching his intended victim. He did find faint traces of two trails, meaning two individuals had been there recently. He'd admit defeat with Timmy, realizing there was a lesson in all this: two people out there knew something he didn't. At first he thought it was only one, then felt the difference in the energy and realized there were two who had bested him ...

That grated. As long as the pair didn't know about his other victims, the Watcher was okay with it. But they bore watching ... He could learn much from them.

He wanted to find them. Get that information. It ate at him. The balm to his soul was to play with those below him. Like Queenie. Her life was such a mess that it made him feel so much better about his. And that was a hell of a display he'd just watched. What an asshole Carlos was. Like, *really?*

The Watcher shook his head and thought about it. Maybe he'd have to do something about Carlos. It really wasn't fair for him to cheat everybody in the park like that. And they were all working for peanuts anyway. When you took away the peanuts, what did they have? Nothing but the damn shells. And they couldn't subsist on that.

The Watcher imagined there'd be a hell of a rampage at the amusement park in the next couple days. If they didn't all just walk out today. Carlos would have a hell of a time keeping anybody on staff.

The Watcher chuckled, backed out of Queenie's view and returned to Timmy's view. The Watcher glanced over at the clock in the hospital hallway outside Timmy's room. The Watcher still had another couple hours of work himself to do. But at his day job, not here. And not on Timmy. That sucked. But this hospital was one hell of a feeding ground.

He really enjoyed applying his new skills in this place. People were dying here anyway. And the doctors weren't looking for any unusual causes of death.

Still the Watcher had to be careful.

It was almost euphoric to take so many lives. Of course, it wasn't him taking them. That was the beauty of it. He could never be charged with murder. Although he might make an exception with Carlos. That man was damn irritating. The Watcher couldn't believe Carlos had treated Queenie like that. She did work damn hard; the Watcher had seen several of the answers she'd given people. He wasn't sure he could sit there all day and do that.

He tried to calculate her earnings as she just had, then gave it up, chuckling. "I always sucked at math. Guess that's why I'm not an engineer." He drew in a big breath, exhaled and brought his focus back, centered on himself now.

He walked up the hallway, his arms full of files, and plunked them down at the receptionist's desk, gave the girl a bright breezy smile and kept going. His coworkers had no clue either. Just the way he liked it. It was one thing to let Queenie know. But that was because she had the ability to see. Queenie, the one who had tapped into him first. She couldn't really be upset with him. He had just followed the same energy back home again.

But then he already knew about her energy. He'd been watching her work for years.

He swept his way through the double doors and marched to the cafeteria. He still had a few hours. He would need coffee and a snack. She might manage her whole day without food, but he couldn't.

KIRK STARED INTO the water. He was leaning over the bow of the boat, had been for the last two hours. But they'd been out at least five hours already. They were across from Bonnie's place, going slowly through the weeds. The problem was, the motor would get caught up in those same weeds if they got any closer. They had already stopped twice, shutting down the engine to clean out the props on the motor. Also sunken logs hid just beneath the surface, and that was never a good thing. But he didn't want to give up yet. He let the boat direct itself along the shoreline. He had no reason to go one way or the other.

He grabbed his phone and called Queenie. "I know you're busy, but if you could possibly give me a little more direction."

"I can't see," she said in exasperation.

He heard the temper and the frustration in her voice. "Bad day?"

"The worst."

"Well, brighten mine by helping me find this poor woman."

"Just a minute."

There was silence. He glanced back at the sheriff, who was staring down at the lake himself. It was just the two of them in the Zodiac, and, if it wasn't for the job they were doing, it would be a stunningly beautiful event. It was only about four o'clock in the afternoon, maybe even an hour or two later. He'd lost track of time being in the water. He should have thought about that. "Are you still at work?"

"No, I'm not," she snapped. "That has changed."

"Where are you?"

"In my car," she said, the fatigue evident in her voice. "Never mind. Right now you've got a dead body out there."

"Can we do hot and cold?"

That was a game they'd played when she'd been in a deep trance, and he had men out searching for a child buried underground. "You're getting cold," she whispered. "And colder."

He pointed his arm in the opposite direction, and the sheriff turned the boat around, gently nudging it that way.

"Better," she said, "but it's still just tepid."

"Any idea how much farther?"

"At least a mile," she said.

He turned to the sheriff and said, "I suggest we ignore this section as we've already searched it."

He nodded and picked up speed, sending the Zodiac faster in the direction he wanted to go.

After five minutes Kirk said, "Queenie, now?"

"Warm," she said, but her voice was fading.

He frowned. "I wish you were at home."

"So do I," she said. "I might not be able to drive home."

"Take the bus," he said, urgently getting a horrible sense she was in danger in some way.

"Can't. It takes forever." And then, as if giving herself a mental shrug, she said, "I'm leaving now. I'll be fine."

"No, I need help still."

There was silence, and then she said, her voice sad, "She's up about forty-five feet in front of you on the right."

Pocketing his phone, Kirk motioned to the sheriff to cut down the speed and do a very slow idle. Kirk leaned over the bow and studied the left side, then the right side of the boat. No way to know if Queenie was 100 percent. Sometimes rights and lefts got mixed up, depending on her viewpoint. He remained leaning over the keel, trying to watch both sides, until something pink caught his eye. He held up a hand. "Stop."

He grabbed an oar from inside the boat and plunked it down, slowing their progress. With the engine killed, he paddled toward the gleam of pink in the water. He came up against a tree and peered over the side of the boat. What was that? Using the paddle, he brought the Zodiac ever-so-slightly closer and then turned a grim face back toward the sheriff. "I think we've got her."

The sheriff clambered forward with the other oar. Together the two men came alongside the female body just a few feet under the surface of the water. And, indeed, she had on a pink shirt.

"Wow, you must have caught a flash of that pink. No way we would have found her without it."

"I did," he lied. "But look at her face. It's almost completely covered."

"Like a scarf or something is over it." The sheriff frowned. "Like a bandanna."

They studied the body, now bloated and distorted. "We can't even ID her face because of it."

"No," the sheriff said. "I have to get a team out here. If there's any forensic evidence, we need it."

As it was now the sheriff's domain, Kirk sat back and thought about how far away the body was from the property. "It's almost like whoever it was took the same path we did directly across the lake and just dumped her."

"Too early to tell. I understand you come from the big city and all, and chances are, in your mind, this is a murder. But I can't be too sure of that."

He nodded. "True enough. But it's pretty hard to come up with very many scenarios that explain why she's fully dressed but miles away from her property in the water."

"Aye, that it is," the sheriff said. "That it is."

THE LITTLE BOY once again sat on his bed, the blankets tugged around his shoulders. Today had been a good day. He got to play, and he had ice cream. But, when Daddy came home, he yelled and screamed at Mommy and had hit her hard. The little boy had made himself scarce, knowing the next blow was for him. He'd run down here, shut the door and curled up on his bed. He'd heard his father laugh and shout, telling him to run away like the little scaredy-cat he was. But then it had gone quiet. Now he just lay here, not wanting to go anywhere.

"Mommy, find me soon please," he whispered into the night. "Please, Mommy."

One lone spider crawled on the bedpost. He looked at it and smiled and reached out a hand. The spider hopped onto the back of his fingers and raced up his arm. As it crawled up his neck, the little boy chuckled because it tickled so much. He gently moved it onto the back of his other hand.

"Did you stay to keep me company?" he whispered. He didn't know if the little spider understood him or not. But, when he leaned forward to take another look, it rose up on his back legs and reached out a front leg to touch him on the nose. He whispered, "Thank you. I didn't want to be alone anymore."

Feeling much better, he curled up on the side of the bed, careful of the spider on his hand, pulling the blanket up around him, almost closing his eyes.

The spider appeared to settle down right there on the back of his hand and to fall asleep.

CHAPTER 10

Friday, Late Afternoon …

I T WAS ALL Queenie could do to keep her eyes open and her hands on the steering wheel as she navigated slowly through town. Vehicles honked at her because she was going so slow, but she didn't dare go any faster. Her reflexes were not normal. For whatever reason, something was draining the hell out of her. She understood her temper tantrum and her long day, but right now it seemed like something so much more, something else, was pulling at her energy stores.

With her instincts kicking in, she called out, "If that's you—piss off."

There was a surprised silence, and then her Watcher said in an aggrieved voice, *Maybe I'm trying to help you.*

If you were helping me, she snapped, *I wouldn't feel like I'm walking through molasses, that I can hardly keep my eyes open. You'd be giving me healing energy.*

Well, that's an interesting description, he said cheerfully. *And you're right. I haven't been helping you. I've been watching you.*

And I'm wondering if that isn't draining my energy too.

Don't know why it would. It's effort on my part, not your part.

She thought, *Well, it should be on my part too.* She considered that and realized he was effortlessly accessing her energy when she couldn't even keep him out. She was burning through her energy trying to.

Oh, you can't keep me out, he said. *I'm much too evolved for that.*

Evolved? she said sarcastically. She pulled onto the block just one away from hers. She wasn't at all sure it was safe to let him see where she lived.

I haven't seen the address, but I've seen the inside of your place. Tsk, tsk. That's pretty disgusting.

It's home, she said. She drove past her place and wondered what her options were. In the background she thought she heard someone call a name. *Oh, look at that? David, you're being called,* she said cheerfully.

Silence followed for a long moment. *How did you hear that?*

She grinned at the anger in his voice. *I have no idea. But I just heard you being called.*

No, you couldn't have, he said angrily. *Nobody can hear that.*

Somebody called you David.

Instantly he disappeared from her mind.

David. ... That made him sound much more normal. More human. Less like an exalted all-powerful being with abilities she couldn't combat. Because *human* meant he made mistakes. Buoyed by the thought that she had a weapon to turn against him, she quickly pulled around the block and parked outside her place. She got out, went into her apartment before he could see her traveling. Inside she locked the door, tossed down her purse, emptied her pockets of the money and threw herself onto the bed.

The phone call from Kirk had probably killed her limited energy reserves as well. "The least he could do was repay me for the prepaid minutes he used up on my cell," she muttered out loud. And then she didn't give a damn because she was already drifting off to sleep. But it wasn't to be. A knock came at her door. She froze, petrified it was her voyeur. But, when she glanced around, she found it dark outside. Frowning, she sat up, rubbing her forehead. Her throat felt thick, her tongue swollen.

The knocking came again. "Queenie, answer the door."

She groaned. "Kirk, what are you doing here?"

"If you open the door, I'll tell you," he said, his voice exasperated and angry.

Not sure she was up for him but feeling marginally better, she walked to the front door and opened it.

He stormed inside.

She looked at him and said, "You found her. Why are you so angry?"

"You didn't know?"

She stared at him, seeing the banked rage in his gaze. She stood her ground. "What are you talking about?"

"Her face was covered with a cowboy-style handkerchief."

Her hand went to cover her mouth, and slowly she shook her head. "No, no. That's not possible."

"You never saw the scarf before either, did you?"

She was still shaking her head as she stumbled into the living room, where she collapsed on her couch. "No. That's not possible." She started to hyperventilate, having trouble catching her breath.

Kirk grabbed her neck, bending her over to lower her face between her knees. "Breathe," he ordered.

"I am breathing," she whispered. *But not enough.* She took a deep breath, slowly returning to herself, her panic down to just an alarm setting. Finally, she sat back against the couch, curled her knees up to her chest, wrapped them tight with her arms and stared at him. "Was it the same knot?"

He sat down beside her. "I don't know," he whispered. "It's possible. They were bringing in a forensic team to retrieve the body. But it would've been a couple hours yet before they were done, and I couldn't stay."

"But surely you would know."

"I couldn't see the knot."

She stared at him. "Was it the same kind of handker-chief?"

Ever-so-slowly, he gave the answer she did not want to hear. He nodded. "Yes, it was."

The shaking set in. She tried to squeeze her knees tighter against her chest, but now her whole body rattled. Within seconds her teeth chattered.

He gave a harsh exclamation and picked her up, pulling her into his arms. "I'm sorry. I didn't … I was afraid you knew and hadn't told me. I knew you wouldn't have withheld that information, but … then I didn't know if I should tell you or not."

She gave a broken cry. "Of course you had to tell me."

"Why?" he whispered, holding her tight. "It can only bring you more pain."

"How is it even possible that the Handkerchief Killer did this?" She searched his gaze. "Is he still in prison?"

"I don't know. I haven't had a chance to check."

"Or it's a copycat," she said slowly. Her mind kicked into gear. "It would have to be a copycat."

"Possibly or he's training somebody."

She grimaced. "I never understood that."

"How can anybody understand any of these people?" He was trying to interject a note of humor. "That guy killed four women."

"And now somebody has killed a fifth." She shook her head. "Maybe my visions were all wrong. Maybe the guy in my tent with the little boy had nothing to do with the murder."

"That guy in your tent is another reason I'm here. Now that we found the body, we have to find her killer. You met him once. It would be helpful if you could connect again."

She snorted. "What did you do without me all these years? Did you close any cases?" She pulled out of his arms, tumbled to her feet and walked into the kitchen.

He followed her, watching her every move like a hawk.

She hated that sensation, as if she was too frail, too childlike, too incapable of looking after herself, and so he would have to step in and take over. Granted, for part of their relationship, she had been like that. She'd driven herself so hard that she'd gotten sucked into the cases, and the world had dropped away. Kirk had looked after her as if she were a child.

Not a memory she wanted to examine closely.

She filled the teakettle and plugged it in. Her arms bracing her weight on the kitchen counter, she stared out the window. "It has to be a copycat," she whispered. "Nothing else makes sense."

But, regardless, she knew this would get ugly yet again.

"Any chance of you remembering the man in your tent? Any way to track who came and who went? Cameras? Sign-in sheets?"

She shook her head. "It's not like we have memberships where people get their pictures taken and can use their card every time they come in. People buy tickets at the front entrance, but I get paid in cash for each transaction. That's all. And I don't even know if cameras are on the corner streets."

"Can you remember his face?"

She waved a hand. "I can't even remember the description I gave you originally at this point."

"Why not?"

She turned to glare at him. "Because I've seen hundreds, *literally hundreds*, of people since then," she snapped. "Don't you get that?"

He took a step back and nodded. "I'm sorry. Of course you have. I gather you had a shitty day at work?"

She gave a broken laugh. "It's not every day you find out your boss has been cheating you for the last few months, taking part of your money. But I caught him redhanded today, in front of everybody. And after telling everybody what he'd done, I walked. So I don't have a job anymore. I'm missing half of my wages for the last few months, and I'm too damn tired to give a shit."

"Good," he said quietly. "That's not where you should be working anyway."

She gave a mocking laugh. "Says the person with a regular paycheck, a place to live and food on the table every day." She shook her head.

When the teakettle whistled, she made herself a cup of tea. She didn't even bother offering him one. He wasn't a tea drinker anyway. She took her teacup onto the small balcony and sat down.

"I mean it," he said. "Your talents are wasted there."

"Well, that depends. That father got in to see Dr. Maddy. So then it wasn't wasted, was it?"

"You know what I mean. You could be helping a lot more people."

"Yeah, but people are willing to pay five dollars, and that's about it for that kind of help." Then she gave a broken laugh and said, "But I was thinking I could do a website, maybe do readings by email and even an online chat system."

"You could," he said, sitting down heavily. "Or you could come back and work for the police again."

With a studied glare, she turned to face him. "What did you just say?"

He sighed heavily. "You know what I said. And I meant it."

She snorted. "*You* might have, but I bet your boss doesn't have a clue that you just said what you said."

KIRK STARED AT her. "Okay, so I haven't talked to them yet."

"Of course you haven't. You know perfectly well what they'll say," she said in disgust. "Besides, I worked my heart out for them but never got paid."

"Okay, I don't know what they'll say," he said firmly. "I wouldn't have you necessarily work for the department but be a contractor. Get paid this time. I'm sure other psychics out there do similar work. For a long time, your reputation held you in good stead. It's not tarnished. You've been gone over five years. You could come back and do the same work again."

"Contractor? That just takes me back to my website."

"I don't know that a website is necessarily a good idea," he said cautiously. Visions of crystal balls flashing on a screen with *Call me in the next five minutes to get the truth about your next love life* came to him. He tried to block it out. "What I mean is, something classy and discreet would be good. Run it like a legitimate business, and I'm pretty sure you would find people all over the world looking for help."

"People all over the world *are* looking for help," she said quietly. "That's what I was doing at the amusement park."

"And now that you're not there, what do you think will happen?" he asked curiously.

She shrugged. "I'm not sure. Except I do think Carlos will put somebody in who'll just lie."

"And how long before people don't bother going back?"

She shook her head. "I don't have answers for you."

"What if, on your website, you said that's who you were, but you're now running your business independently?"

She frowned. "I don't know how people would pay me if it was over a website."

He waved his hand. "That's minor. Set it up as a business with an online shopping cart. Set it up properly. Let everybody know you were at the amusement park, and now you're on your own, and you also consult for police and detective agencies all across the country."

"Across the globe," she said absentmindedly. "It's not just this country that I can help. It can be anywhere."

He looked at her. "You know you've got a ready-made business right here."

"I still have to pay for rent and food in the meantime, until I get it up and running," she said, "and that's not easy."

"How much did he cheat you out of?"

"I can't be sure." But the figure $2,795 flashed through her head. Her lips turned down. "A number just flashed in my head that's a hair under twenty-eight hundred."

He whistled. "If you can get your money back, that

would make all the difference in the world."

"It would pay for a website and a month or two of living," she admitted. "But I doubt he'll give me my money back."

"WOULD IT HELP if I paid him a visit?"

She looked at Kirk in surprise. "Why would you do that?"

It was his turn to be surprised. Did she have such a low opinion of him? "If you make him think you've gone to the police and are likely to make an official case out of this, he might be quite willing to pay you back what he owes you."

She thrummed the tabletop for a long moment. And then she shrugged. "It can't hurt. I'm going tomorrow, as is everybody else, to get our money back. I gave him four hours' notice to get to the bank before it closed for the day and get enough to cover what he's figured out he owes us all."

"And what makes you think he won't skip town with the money?"

She stared at him. "I don't think he can do that."

"Why not?"

"He owns the machines and leases the land."

"How much money do you think he's cheated you all out of?"

"I really don't like where you're going with this," she said, her voice barely above a whisper. "From my visions, I know he's taken at least twenty grand from people. For all I know, it could be much more."

"Well, if it's almost twenty-eight hundred from just you, how many people work at the park? Forty?"

She nodded slowly. "So it could easily be a hundred grand."

"Why would he stay and give that all back? It'd take him forever to make that kind of money. His other choice is to just grab the money and run, and leave you all sitting there, holding the empty bag as it were." He watched as she slumped in the chair.

"I *really* don't like where you're going with that," she said. "He wouldn't do that, would he?"

Kirk stared at her steadily. "You're the one with the psychic abilities, and I'm the one with human knowledge of what people will and will not do."

She bolted to her feet. "Then come with me now. We'll go back there and talk to him."

Kirk slowly stood. "I can't say it is the best time for it. I'm pretty tired myself."

"But, if he's taking off, he'll be gone tonight. That means we have to go now."

"Then let's go for a drive."

She said, "I'll drive."

"No," he said. "You're too tired. I remember talking to you earlier today, and you were barely able to get home."

"Yeah, but the thought of him running away with everybody's money is enough to make me sick."

In his car, he headed toward the amusement park. It was open until nine, and it was almost that time now.

Once parked, they hopped out, and she strode toward the offices. Several employees raised a hand in greeting and watched her progress, her determined step. Not to mention the set of her shoulders, the jut of her chin.

Kirk smiled at the others as he followed behind.

She rapped hard on the office door. There was no answer. She tried the knob and pulled it open, stepped inside. She came back out seconds later and asked one of the men running the Ferris wheel, "Where's Carlos?"

The guy shrugged. "He was at the other side of the fairgrounds. One of the bumper cars is having trouble."

She nodded and headed toward the bumper cars.

Kirk looked around with interest. He'd never really spent much time here, not as a kid nor as an adult. It was pretty fascinating with a lot of activity. He thought about trying to keep the park running and wondered when it stopped being a passion and ended up just being a nasty headache.

At the bumper cars Queenie looked around, then spoke to a tall skinny man. Kirk watched her shake her head and turn to the left of the Ferris wheel and wondered if Carlos hadn't already disappeared.

She walked back to him. "He saw Carlos about an hour ago but not since."

"Inside the office, what did it look like?"

"Empty," she said curtly.

"What about a vehicle?" he asked. "Does Carlos drive?"

She nodded and then headed around the back of the Ferris wheel. "Staff vehicles are over here, for those who live around here and live in their own trailers."

She walked around another corner, and a dozen vehicles of various ages were parked haphazardly. And then she picked up her feet and ran. "Carlos," she called out.

A man ahead of her jumped into a vehicle and turned on the engine. She ran after him.

Assessing the situation, Kirk, instead of going after Carlos, headed to the exit. There wasn't much in the way of room for the vehicle to get out. He grabbed several planks of wood used to hold up truck canopies and made himself a blockade.

Carlos revved the engine, glaring at Kirk.

Kirk stood, pulling his shield out of his pocket and raising it so Carlos would understand, if he tried to run Kirk over, Carlos was attacking a police officer. Kirk watched as Carlos pounded the steering wheel. Queenie wrenched open the door and shouted at him.

As Carlos hopped out of the vehicle, Kirk reached in and pulled out the keys, shutting off the engine. He listened as Carlos yelled at Queenie.

"What the hell are you doing here? We said tomorrow."

"And then I figured how maybe you'd run out of town on us," she yelled back.

While they argued, Kirk popped the trunk of Carlos's car. Kirk had already seen multiple bags in the back seat. But what he wanted to know was whether Carlos was leaving for good or if he was just making deliveries of some kind. As Kirk opened the trunk, he whistled.

Carlos turned. "Hey, get out of there. That's my stuff."

"I don't think it is now," Kirk said. "Queenie, come take a look at this."

She came around, and he watched the look of shock on her face as she eyed the bags full of money. She turned to Carlos. "You piece of shit. That's everybody's wages. We work from morning until night for you, and then you steal from us?" She pulled out her phone and made a call.

Kirk didn't have a clue who she was talking to, but then he caught the name *Jimbo* and realized she was calling the rest of the staff.

Within seconds, they heard running footsteps. Kirk turned to see a half-dozen men coming toward them. They stopped at the trunk and stared. As their anger rose, Kirk could feel a bloodbath building. He stepped in front of Carlos and addressed the crowd. "Now stop. I get that you're angry. I get that this is your money. But you don't get to tear him limb from limb."

Carlos whined behind Kirk. "You have to protect me," he said. "You have to."

Kirk hated being in this position. But, in a way, the answer was *Yes, he did*. Because he couldn't afford to have all these people do something that would ruin their lives.

Jimbo, the biggest of the lot, said, "We won't touch him as long as we get our money."

Carlos snapped. "Don't touch that money. It's mine."

"I wonder about that," Queenie said. "What are you doing? Money-laundering, drug-trafficking through the place? Or are you just stealing everybody's wages?"

"Nothing like that," Carlos said. "I've done really well gambling."

She sneered. "No, you haven't. The only gambling you've done is with our paychecks." She studied him, then reached out a hand. "Place your hand on mine."

He backed up.

She laughed. "I thought you said I was a fraud anyway. If I'm such a fake, put your hand on mine, and I'll see where the hell that money came from."

He pulled up behind Kirk again and said, "Keep her away from me. You gotta keep her away from me. She's dangerous."

She turned to look at Jimbo. "You want to do the honors?"

With a grin Jimbo walked around to Carlos, and, even though he was kicking and screaming, Jimbo grabbed

Carlos's hand and pulled him forward. And then, under duress, he slapped Carlos's hand on top of Queenie's.

Kirk watched her face as the visions hit and kept hitting. She turned and let her hand fall away, giving it a good shake, as if something nasty was stuck to it. "It is more than just our money," she said quietly to everyone. "He's been stealing from other people too." Turning to address Kirk, she asked, "Have you had a rash of break-ins in this area?"

Kirk looked at her in surprise. "Yes we certainly have. Are they his jobs?"

"Yes. He got lucky at one place. He found one of the bags full of cash in a house. He grabbed it and ran." She walked around to the car, pointed to the black leather bag. "That one. He doesn't even know how much he got. But, when we came after our money, he decided to run."

In the meantime Kirk had already snapped handcuffs on Carlos's wrists and said to Jimbo, "Make sure he doesn't move, but you don't get to hurt him."

Jimbo smiled. "I don't need to hurt him. And he ain't going nowhere."

At that, Kirk walked over to Carlos's car and did a quick search. "His luggage is in here. He's got a box of paperwork, a laptop, some other electronics, like hard drives, but the money is in the trunk." He opened a second bag to see it was not as full but also held cash in smaller denominations.

Queenie said, "That's ours. We take in a lot of cash money in small denominations, and he pays us out the same way. I presume he banks the rest. And he owes us all a ton of money."

"This isn't a free-for-all," Kirk said. "We need a commonsense way to figure out who gets what."

"He has a ledger in this box," she said, "of how much he

has systematically been stealing."

Kirk spun and looked at her.

She nodded. "I saw it in my vision."

At that, Kirk walked to the back seat of the car, pulled out the box, lifted the lid again, moved the laptop and, sure enough, there was a ledger book. He pulled it out and read off names. "Jimbo, $2,140 as of"—he looked at his watch—"today." But it was hard for Kirk to know how accurate these figures were until he came to Queenie's name. He turned to look at her. "What was that figure you said you saw earlier?"

"He owes me $2,795."

Kirk tapped the ledger and said, "Bingo. This ledger is the actual money owed to everyone."

They all surged forward. "Can we get it?"

He looked over at Carlos. "How do you want to play this?"

Carlos shook his head and muttered, "You can pay them. I shouldn't have taken their money in the first place."

"No, you sure as hell shouldn't have," Kirk snapped. He went back to the trunk and grabbed the bag Queenie had said was from the amusement park, pulled it forward and using the light from the trunk, started counting.

Based on the ledger, there were a lot of people to pay out.

After he paid Jimbo, Kirk said, "Can you round up the rest of the employees? The park should be closed now anyway, shouldn't it?" He put a checkmark beside Jimbo's entry and went through the list. He was amazed at how much money Carlos felt he could get away with. "So you were going to run, taking everybody's money, trying to hide afterward?" he asked in a conversational tone. "You realize that wouldn't have worked, right?"

"Sure it would have," he snapped. "Who would have known?"

Kirk laughed. "Seriously?"

Carlos looked at him in confusion. "Yes, seriously. Who would have known?"

Kirk looked over at Queenie, who was giggling. "You really don't understand you got the real deal with Queenie, do you? Because *she* would have known. She's the one who sent me back here. She's the one who came with me because she figured out that, once I mentioned you might run, you'd be disappearing tonight." He glanced over at Queenie. "Any idea where he was running to?"

She turned to Carlos and said, "California. He was heading to see his mother in California."

At that, Carlos's jaw dropped. He sagged to the ground.

Jimbo looked over at Kirk as if to ask if it was okay to leave Carlos unattended.

Kirk nodded and said, "He's not going anywhere, Jimbo, especially not now that we have the money he stole." He glanced over at Queenie as he counted out the money due her and handed it to her. "Now do something about that damn website."

She gave him a cheeky grin, pocketed the money and said, "Maybe I will, and maybe I won't."

He groaned. She was just as irritating as ever. But, for the first time in a long time, he didn't feel that was a problem.

CHAPTER 11

Saturday Morning ...

QUEENIE AWOKE THE next morning for the first time feeling a sense of renewal. Some new beginning was occurring. She wasn't sure what it was, but she'd take it. She would miss the people at the amusement park, but she was on a whole new trajectory.

The fact that she was back to being friendly with Kirk was a new adventure as well. She knew it wouldn't go anywhere, and that was fine. She wasn't ready for anything else either.

But to consider they could be friends, well, that put a smile on her face. She hopped out of bed, got a shower and walked over to her laptop. She had sent an email last night before going to bed to Nick, the webmaster who had run Carlos's website, asking him for a price and/or suggestions. She could only hope he'd answered and that his price was doable.

While her laptop booted up, she put on coffee. She stepped outside on the balcony, but the sky looked dismally gray. She wouldn't let it get her down though.

With coffee dripping, she checked her email to find that Nick had gotten back to her. She read his reply and crowed with delight. He would give her a deal: set her up a simple website, but one that would allow her to hook up for payments online with a secure email delivery system for sending her readings. He also gave her suggestions on how to do readings over Skype and similar programs, like Voom. She was enthralled at the idea.

He could have her up and running in three days. She'd have to write up some material to put on the website and needed to put up a pricing scale. He suggested starting at fifty for a reading. She sat back in awe.

"I've been doing readings for five bucks. Would people pay fifty?" she wondered, but it was hard to imagine such a thing. At that new rate, she wouldn't need very many in a day to more than cover her business and living expenses. To start off with, one a day would be absolutely huge for her. At least this way, it was under her control. She could do however many readings she deemed possible and would push off the others for another day. She would book them over the next few days, or, if they felt wrong, not do them at all.

She responded with a big thank-you and a bunch of questions as to what materials he'd need and whether she should have recommendations or references.

As she waited for his response, hoping he would respond immediately, she got up and poured herself a cup of coffee. She checked her fridge, but a whole lot wasn't there. She found some bread. She popped it in the toaster, and, while she waited for it, she sat back down again. Thankfully Nick had already answered her.

He suggested references, preferably if she had some from reputable people with real names, not names like Jimbo.

She laughed out loud at that. "I can probably get some," she said thoughtfully. She'd worked for a lot of detectives over the years. Then she read the rest of his email out loud.

"You should also have a set of prices for difficult clients, for clients who want readings in a rush, for people who want over and above a simple reading, and your readings should have a certain time frame. No more than ten minutes, or make it, say, fifty dollars for one question, for example, and possibly a hundred for three."

He'd given her a lot to think about. She told him to go ahead and get started. She'd send him a deposit, and she'd start working on what to put on her website. He responded by saying he'd send her some mockups later in the day. Did she want a particular color scheme?

She thought about that. The typical purples and lavenders were such psychic colors that she knew she needed to include those as people would expect them. Still, it should be colors that made her smile. She sent him some suggestions, then researched other psychics' websites.

Most were tacky and perpetrated the charlatan feel. That wasn't what she wanted. She sent him a couple links with a note saying she didn't want hers to look like this. The emails went back and forth as she had toast and coffee. He sent her a couple websites he thought would be nicer, and she fell in love with one. They were akin to some of the horoscope websites, and there was a vast difference between those. But this one was something simple, and he promised it was easy to change themes and colors down the road and how the text could always be changed. So she left it to him.

And then she had to sit down and do some initial accounting. She pulled out all the cash she'd collected the previous day and set up a budget. When she took off the internet fees, hosting fees and shopping cart fees, she then looked at how many days she could last with the money she had, like how much she'd need for food and was there a cheaper way to keep herself for the next month? But, as she sat back and took a closer look, she realized she wasn't in bad shape.

The money Kirk had rescued for her yesterday was the most she'd had in a long time. She had always been frugal, but now she had enough to relax for at least sixty days plus the rest of this current month, which made it close to eight weeks without having to worry about money coming in daily.

She'd have put aside more from her years of hard work, but she'd spent so much on private detectives to make sure her son truly was dead—until the money ran out. Still, the process had served its purpose. She'd finally accepted that her son was dead, and that had allowed her to move forward.

She had another month's buffer that she'd scrimped and saved for as her warning before panicking about money. So, with more than a three-month cushion between her and destitution, she could sit back and feel a whole lot better about her decision to go out on her own.

She smiled, wondering how else she could use her skills to draw attention to what she could do for people. She thought about the local newspaper, wondering if they had done a lot of coverage on the amusement park itself. She went to the newspaper's website, noting a couple of the articles Carlos had tagged. She contacted one of the reporters.

Queenie explained how she was going independent and asked about getting an article regarding her new website.

The reporter laughed and said, "Sure, but then I'd be putting my name to something that is probably a crooked deal from the beginning."

"It's only a crooked deal if your wife's new business is a crooked deal," she said coolly. "Not too many people are out there doing piano-tuning."

There was a shocked silence on the other end of the phone. "How did you know about my wife's piano-tuning?" he blasted at her.

"The same way I know you're wearing one red sock and one blue sock," she said drily. "I'm the real deal."

A heavy sigh could be heard on the other end as he must be considering her words. "Shit. Are they really those colors?"

"You're color-blind, aren't you?"

He groaned. "I so am."

She chuckled. "That's all right for your business. I don't think it matters."

"Nope, it doesn't. Okay, I'm convinced, so I'll write an article. I can't do it this weekend though. How about Tuesday next week?"

"Sure. Will we just talk over the phone?"

"Why don't we meet at a coffee shop?" he suggested. "I'll write it and submit it to my editor. I can't guarantee they'll run it, but there's no real reason to consider they won't."

"Good enough," she said. "Thanks." She ended the call with a warm fuzzy feeling inside. She'd gotten her first promotional event set up. She sent a text to Nick. **I hope the website will be live by Tuesday. I'm meeting a reporter to do an article on my services now that I've left the amusement park.**

It will. Now I have a deadline, Nick replied.

She laughed, closed her laptop and walked out onto the balcony. She was restless, keyed up with energy but no outlet. She wasn't sure what the hell to do right now. It was only ten o'clock in the morning, and she'd already set so much in motion. She needed to take the money to the bank, and she probably should do a bit of shopping.

With that in mind, she grabbed a notepad, a second cup of coffee, sat out on the small balcony and considered her budget for food for the next couple weeks and wrote down a tentative menu. If she followed the budget and her menu planning, it would help her save money. She listed a few of her favorites, and, by the time she was down to next Wednesday's meal, her phone rang. She glanced at it and saw it was Kirk. "Good morning," she said gaily.

Silence ensued.

"What's the matter? Am I not allowed to be happy?"

"If I knew quitting your job would make you this happy, I would have suggested it a long time ago."

"But you didn't know what I was doing a long time ago," she said, her voice calmer, quieter. "And I wouldn't have listened to your advice anyway."

"Now that is very true," he snapped. "Besides, I did know what you were doing. I was worried about you, so I kept an eye out to make sure you were okay—at least for a little while."

"Do you have a reason for calling?" Some of her good mood was falling away.

"I do. They brought up the woman's body. Her name is Bonnie Jenkins. Her daughter contacted me a few days ago about her mother. I've talked to the sheriff about the knot. He sent me some pictures."

"*Great.*" She shook her head as reality came smashing down. "Are you sending me the photos?"

"I can. Or can you tell me what it looks like?"

"If this is another test, I wouldn't bother," she said, "because I'm deliberately not looking. I don't want this to be the same guy, remember?"

"I don't think it can be the same guy because I checked, and he's still in prison."

Relief swept through her. "Oh, my God. I'm so grateful for that bit of information."

"Why? It just means you're right. It's a copycat."

"Sure, and true the devil you know is better than the one you don't. But that was one hell of a nasty-ass devil."

"It was, but that doesn't mean his copycat is any nicer. What kind of guy wants to kill in the same method somebody else did?"

"I don't know. Someone lacking self-confidence? Have you done a search yet to see if any other bodies with that handkerchief trademark pop up?"

"No. I just got off the phone with the sheriff. I'll start on the databases in the next hour or so."

"Good," she said, her voice drifting away as images of all the other murdered women's cases she'd been involved in came to her mind. "What color was it?"

"Blue."

"Already one difference."

"I know. But maybe he couldn't get red ones."

"No, I think it's more about making it his mark. Making it *his* kill."

There was a thoughtful silence on the other end. "You're probably right," he said finally. "You usually are."

"Not often enough to count," she said sadly. "That woman still died."

"That's not your fault. I tried to tell you that before, but you just weren't hearing me."

"I was connected to them. I was so plugged into that case. I swear she was alive and thought we'd keep her that way. But the Handkerchief Killer got ahead of me somehow."

"We've been over this before," he said gently. "You have to let it go."

"I thought I had," she said, feeling her throat clog up with tears. "I thought I had."

"Your involvement with the police was well publicized in the press at the time."

"I remember," she said, anger evident in her voice. "It's one of the reasons I was so off my game. Every time I turned around, a microphone was shoved in my face. People were touching me all the time, and you know what my rule was about not being touched."

"And yet you don't seem to be too bothered by it now," he said curiously.

"Maybe," she said quietly. "It depends. I've learned to put in a few defense mechanisms. At least when somebody casually touches me on my shoulder now, I don't freak out and see who he slept with the night before or what he might have done on a weekend ten years ago."

"Still no more control over the visions? During these last years?"

"Yes, some, but I need more control yet."

"Sorry? What do you mean?"

To clarify, she said, "I didn't have any visions for a long time. I deliberately shut down that part of my life. I was house-cleaning and waitressing, doing odd jobs, anything I could, running errands, mowing lawns, to keep Reese and me safe. But, after I lost Reese, I went berserk for a while. In the hospital, when I was under, I was caught up in what seemed like never-ending unsolvable cases. The same women were being killed, the same kids tortured. As if not seeing them enough while working them, I was forced to live them over and over again. When I woke up, I didn't have any abilities. It seemed like I had burnt out for a while. When I asked the doctor about it afterward, he said it was just the medication."

"And so that coma burned you out?" he asked.

"Or the grief. I don't know about *burned out* but maybe *overwhelmed*. At the time I didn't care." She reached up and rubbed her temple. There were so many sad memories from that time … "When I recovered enough to access my abilities, all I wanted was to contact my son. I wasn't a medium, but I'd have done anything to communicate with him. It's bad enough he died while I wasn't conscious, but to wake up and know his little body had already been cremated and buried without me seeing him …" She stared at the railing in front of her, wordless for a long moment. Skipping part of the story, she added, "Then I realized that, by not using my abilities, I'd been out of practice. And I needed to use them to keep them. So I worked at the amusement park. Unfortunately it seemed like my abilities came back with a vengeance. And some things I saw I'd have preferred not to know."

"What do you mean?"

"I saw a cone over a woman walking across a street."

"That means death. That would be a hard way to jump back into the reality of that world."

"It so was," she said. "I came home and screamed and railed at life, saying, if that's what I'm supposed to see, I didn't want anything to do with it."

"Did it help?"

"It made me feel better, but it didn't help with the visions. If anything, that break had the visions coming faster, clearer and more detailed."

"Oh."

She could hear his interest, almost a *how can I use this type of thing* interest. She shook her head. "And, no, it's not something you can use."

"So you read minds now too?" he asked, but there was only mild astonishment, not any anger that she might have read his mind.

"No. But I get intuitive feelings."

"Have you talked to Stefan again?"

"Several times but not recently," she said. "I haven't exactly had time. Not with the amusement park last night, and you and your damn floating woman."

"Well, you might want to remember that floating woman," he said. "The fact that we found her was huge. But, of course, it just brings up a ton more questions."

"I know, but I don't have any more answers." She thought about hanging up on him.

He called out, "Wait."

She waited, wondering if he wasn't a bit psychic himself.

"Did you have breakfast?"

"I just finished toast, and I'm having my second cup of coffee now. Why?"

"I'd like to take you out for lunch," he said quietly. "Just for old time's sake."

She stared blindly across the parking lot. She hadn't expected this. She'd been delighted to have him back as a friend again, particularly as it seemed right now she didn't have anybody in her personal world, but she knew how dangerous it was to depend on him. "Where?" she asked cautiously.

"How about Merinos?"

One of her favorite restaurants. Her breath caught in the

back of her throat as memories hit her. Memories of the two of them sitting down to candlelight dinners, being so into each other, getting their eat-in dinners to-go before rushing home to make love, often in the living room, often on the stairs. Every once in a while they made it to their bed.

"They've changed their lunch menu," he said in a persuasive tone. "I think you'd like it."

"I'm sure I would," she said, faintly giving her head a hard shake. "What time?"

"Twelve," he said promptly. "I'll pick you up." And then he hung up.

She laid her phone down slowly. "Is this a mistake?" she asked no one in particular. "Why does he want to go out to lunch with me?"

Of course, after years of living the way she had, she'd also learned to be a whole lot less than trusting. She didn't want to read his mind, and she certainly had no intention of accessing any visions about him. She didn't want to see him with other women. ... He'd been free; she'd been free too but not ready. Of course he'd had other relationships. No way he hadn't. He was a very sexual animal. Then she'd been one too. But, after her son's birth, she focused only on Reese. He'd been her miracle, pulling her back from the brink. She did everything for him and really had no time for a relationship. In the last few years at the amusement park, there had been a few gestures in that direction, but she'd shut them down. The men had been otherwise protective, as if realizing she needed that the most.

But where did that leave her now?

Her mind shifted to the men around her. They all worked at the amusement park. Most lived on the grounds as well. And what would happen to them now? She thought about it for a long moment and then picked up her phone, calling Betty.

Betty answered, calling out, "Thank you, thank you, thank you."

Queenie laughed. "Hey, we also have to thank the cop I brought with me. At least everyone should have gotten their money back by now."

"Yeah, we did, and Carlos is in jail. For fraud and God only knows how many other crimes."

"But what about the amusement park?" Queenie asked anxiously. "I was afraid it would shut down, and you guys would have no place to go."

"We have a meeting tomorrow afternoon. We'll discuss what our options are," Betty said. "Do you want to come?"

"No, I think my time there is done," Queenie said sadly. "I'm getting a new website, and I'll start an online business with my psychic readings."

"Oh, my goodness. That's perfect. Then you have better control over who you deal with. And, with your abilities, you should be able to filter out most of the nasties in the world."

Queenie chuckled. "That's what I'm hoping."

"If you want to come, it'll be at two o'clock," Betty said. "No commitment, just come and see us. Maybe you'll have some ideas about what we should do."

"We'll see," Queenie said. She hung up and went back to her laptop to check her emails. Found a couple from Nick. It took him a little longer to answer them than she'd thought it would. By the time she was done, she checked her watch. She only had an hour until Kirk arrived.

Just as she considered cleaning house or doing something else, Stefan popped into her head. *Or you could tell me the truth.*

She winced, walked back outside to the balcony and sat heavily in her chair. *Tell you the truth about what?*

For now, the case that destroyed you.

Slowly she told him about the four murdered women. And how she'd been so certain the last one was still alive that she'd motivated all the local policemen to look in one specific direction because she was absolutely positive the woman was being held there. The Handkerchief Killer wasn't going to kill her before they got there. *But I was wrong,* she whispered. *Finding no one, the cops had returned, and they were more than pissed. Only a few hours later the woman was delivered to their station's doorstep—dead, her throat cut, her body still warm. They turned on me.* Still, even under those conditions at that time, she'd given them enough information to go after the killer, and they had caught him. But they couldn't get over their rage that they hadn't been able to save the woman.

And you think that's your fault? Stefan asked thoughtfully.

Yes. I was so sure of what I'd seen, she said tearfully. *No way I wouldn't do everything I could to save her.*

You're not alone in making a mistake. Our abilities are not infallible. I wish they were. But we can only give our best guess at the time.

I know. I knew that then too, she said. *I have no excuse. But I was exhausted. I'd been running on this case and several others for days. I wasn't sleeping. I was hungry, not eating. It was the accumulation of months and months of working for them over and over again as I tried to do my best for all these victims. But I couldn't. I couldn't see clearly on this one. Then, when I got a flash of insight, I figured that's what had happened. Even now I don't know.*

Don't know if it was the wrong vision? Don't know if you

just interpreted it wrong?

All of the above, she said sadly. *And it's too late to do anything about it. But it's one of those cases I'll never forget. It was also a major turning point in my life. I had a full-on breakdown right after that, and my life unraveled.*

It was not your fault. It was the killer's fault and the killer only.

She gave a broken laugh. *That's easy to say, but it's not so easy to deal with every day.*

True enough.

There was silence in her mind, but she knew he was still there, thinking. *Is that what you wanted to know?*

That will do for now. You're hiding other things, but I'm not sensing barriers to them.

What do you mean by barriers?

This Handkerchief Killer case. You have it all wrapped up in your mind, locked up under a very tight defense system. So I wasn't sure if it was something that, when you opened it, would explode and send you off the deep end.

Meaning, like commit suicide or go off my rocker and kill someone?

I've seen that much more often than you'd think, he said. *Psychics are notoriously unstable. I had to know what was behind it.*

And the other areas?

You have some interesting defense systems in place now. Which is why I'm curious about this other psychic who appears to see into your world and can get past your defenses.

The thing is, I've learned to take some preventive measures, you know? Like the white light in the cleansing of my aura and all that stuff.

All that stuff, he said with amusement, *is very important. The fact that you have such an attitude means you don't really understand how important it is.*

I was looking for something much more secure, something much more powerful, she said, searching for the right words but coming up blank. *I guess I was looking for something foolproof.*

And, in our business, there is no such thing. Sometimes, when you are under attack, the best thing you can do is join it, he explained. *Then you can follow it back to the source and get a perspective of who it is and what is involved.*

She listened in fascination. *It never even occurred to me to do that with David.*

I know, and that's an interesting thing. It's almost as if you accepted his presence. As if maybe he's been here either for a long time and you haven't noticed, or, for some reason, you trust him.

That makes no sense, she said, jumping to her feet, she went back inside and started pacing the living room. *Why would I have trusted him?*

It's hard to say. His voice was once again pensive. *But generally we trust religious leaders and medical professionals and law enforcement and other such uniformed service people. Along with family and close friends. By that I mean, partners and the occasional best friend.*

She froze, staring out the front window. But her mind didn't see the physical things. She was thinking of all the cops she'd had dealings with. *I've dealt with a lot of law enforcement,* she said. *Many of them didn't like me. But I can't imagine any of them murdering this woman.*

Can you access that vision and see if his energy is there?

She frowned and looked around. But, of course, Stefan wasn't here. He was in her head. Her still-small living room stared back at her. *What do you mean?*

If you sit quietly and think about the vision that was strong enough for you to contact Kirk in the first place, go a layer deeper and see if you can access energy surrounding that vision.

But it would be my energy, she said in confusion. *Because it's my vision.*

He chuckled. *Every time we do anything with another person, tidbits of our energy are left behind.*

Yes, I know that. That's also sometimes why I get confused readings because I'm reading more than one person's energy in the same space.

Exactly, Stefan said triumphantly. *And that could very well have been what happened when you saw that last woman in your last case.*

No, that makes no sense, she said. *And you're talking about different visions here. I can't remember those visions now. But I do remember the lady in the lake.*

Okay, why is it so strong?

Because I didn't like the man who asked me the question in the amusement park.

And why didn't you like him?

He was loud, bossy and arrogant, she snapped. *Three qualities I can't stand in a man.*

Stefan chuckled. *Good reasons. But, when you saw that vision, how did it appear to you?*

She thought about it and said, *All my visions show up in this window in a cloud.*

What color is the cloud?

White.

Was this cloud white?

She frowned as she thought about it. *No, it wasn't.* She shook her head. *No, it must have been. I think I only ever see white.*

But you don't really know, do you?

She tossed her hands up in frustration and plunged herself down on the couch. *You're making me doubt myself.*

The next time you get a vision, I want you to look at it in detail. Not just feeling that emotion but I want you to look at the vision. I want you to frame it so you can see where and how it's presented.

I don't generally get that much time, she said slowly. *The visions come. I get the answers to the questions. Simple.*

You need to draw it out, so you have a little longer to look. Do the visions disappear right away?

She thought about it, then shrugged. *I honestly don't know.*

Well then, you need to practice, he said. *I have to leave. I want you to practice on that vision, see if you can pick up the energy of the killer left behind.*

But she was in the water, she protested. *How can I possibly see that kind of thing? And now that she's been found, I might not see the vision again.*

You might, and you might not. Try, because you're not talking about forensic evidence here, he said quietly. *You're looking for psychic energy.* And with that he disappeared.

She sat for a long moment, feeling dazed. It had never occurred to her that anybody could track energy backward nor had it occurred to her to look at how her visions were framed. But both were damn good ideas.

She got up, walked to her notepad and wrote down what Stefan had told her.

So what are you going to do with your life now?

The Watcher, … David, … had he heard her talking to Stefan? She wondered if the voice was in her head or in the room. *So you are visiting me telepathically, David?* she asked, trying to play dumb. *Or talking to the room at large?*

Is that how you're hearing me? David asked with interest. *You're the only person I can talk to, you know? It's really unique. I'm quite fascinated by the whole process.* Delight was in his voice, almost glee.

She sat back and nodded. *You're the first person I've ever met who could talk to me this way too.*

But you don't talk to me, per se, he said. *You respond to me, but you don't reach out and call me.*

I don't know how, she exclaimed. *Why don't you teach me?*

He chuckled. *No, that's not happening,* he said in a patronizing tone. *I've worked too hard to get here.*

She thought about that and then shrugged and moved back to writing on her notepad.

You didn't answer the question, he said.

That's because I don't know what I'm going to do now, she said in a brisk tone, trying to ignore him. The more she succeeded, the more she sensed his frustration. As she wrote, she thought about Stefan and what he'd told her. So she wrote down *frustration, patronizing, won't give information.*

You'll figure it out, I'm sure. Otherwise there's got to be some other little five buck jobs somewhere.

Her back stiffened at that, but she refused to rise to David's baiting. *I'm sure I'll get a job somehow.*

Sure you will.

What kind of work do you do?

I work in a … Then he stopped. *Oh, no you don't.* And he disappeared.

She sat back and blew a loose strand of hair off her face. "So he can be caught out," she said thoughtfully.

She thought about the energy it had taken for him to talk to her in this way. Stefan had said something about following David backward, but she couldn't even see the energy to follow, so how did that work?

Shrugging, she returned to writing down her notes, putting down the time and the date, realizing she probably needed to keep track of this guy. She certainly needed to stop him from coming into her world, saying and seeing whatever he wanted. That would be the first thing she'd get Stefan to teach her. And she knew instinctively Stefan would say something about the energy around David, but she hadn't seen any. Just that weird feeling of being watched.

Frustrated, she got up. She had time to change before Kirk arrived. She rushed to put on prettier clothes, added a touch of makeup for the first time in a long time, then walked out her front door.

Sure enough, Kirk was walking along the sidewalk.

He stopped and smiled at her. "Ready?"

She nodded. "I'm ready."

He looked at her carefully. "Are you okay?"

"I'm fine," she said, aiming for a bright cheerful smile.

He shook his head. "Don't even try to lie. You've forgotten that never worked on me. Spiders? Kids? The perv watching you?"

"You could let it work on you just once." She sent him a resentful smile. "And not spiders or little boys. And the Watcher's name is David."

His eyebrows shot up. "What? He told you his name?"

"It was weird. I heard someone calling him. I asked him about it. Then today I called him by that name, and he answered. Maybe he's letting me believe that's his name. And, no, before you ask, I didn't get a last name or anything else helpful."

He chuckled, holding out his arm. "As long as you tell me if you do."

"Deal. And why are you being so nice to me?" She tucked her hand through the crook of his elbow, and they walked to his car. She was loving the easy camaraderie between them.

"I care," he said simply. "We have a lot of history, and we're different people now, but I'm happy we reconnected."

"Really?"

He stopped and looked at her. "Yeah, really. I missed you."

Her eyes searched his face. "You ignored our connection for a long time," she said. "So what's changed now?"

He looked at her, his lips kicking up in the corners. "You. You've changed."

THE SHOCK ON her face made Kirk chuckle.

She shook her head. "You don't know what you're talking about," she said, but her tone was sharp, as if she wasn't used to having anyone close or keeping watch.

"Yes, I do."

And he realized sadly that, as he had tried to move on, she probably hadn't. She had been well on her way, but, after the loss of her son, her world had come to a screeching halt. In a way he was jealous of her having a son. Someone to love like that—a connection with a blood relative. Of course, her loss was all that more terrible. He'd not found love in any way since. His stellar career had stalled out as he no longer closed his cases at the same rate without her help. Not that he cared about his career aspects as reflected on some spreadsheet. He'd always been quick to give her credit for all the assistance she'd given him, but the police department higher-ups had never wanted the media to know. They also had never paid her. As if giving her a paycheck for her services was an endorsement of her psychic gifts or something.

And that hadn't helped his relationship with Queenie. It wasn't that he didn't have enough money for both of them, but there was never a ton of it, not when they were looking to buy a house, not when she was working full-time and not getting compensated. She was working for the dead or for the lost or for the missing. And she'd be the first one to do it for free. Her heart had been incredibly large.

But over time it had been harder for her. She kept saying something about needing defenses, finding ways to let go of all these people pulling on her, and she'd been working on it but definitely not fast enough. The real killing blow was when all the cops had turned on her when she'd given them the wrong information.

They'd been devastated and had needed a target.

That was when everything fell to pieces in their relationship. He himself hadn't turned on her, but he had been so frustrated and angry that he was just as guilty because he'd snapped at her several times, asking how she hadn't seen it. And, of course, the answer was, *She hadn't seen it because she hadn't seen it.* She could only tell him what she saw, and he understood that. But, in the heat of the moment, the frustration and grief had overwhelmed him.

After their breakup, his record of closing cases had dropped down to some pretty small numbers. And he realized that was what the other detectives dealt with on a regular basis. Because Kirk had had an inside line to somebody who had access to so much more information, he'd been stellar in the office. But, of course, the other guys had hated him for it.

He'd never once considered his success rate from their point of view. He had offered her assistance for their cases, but a lot of the guys didn't want anything to do with her. If she did come up with something, she would talk to them quietly on the lowdown, knowing they didn't want others to know. Every once in a while they'd get so frustrated they'd ask her. And often she had something that would send them off in a new direction, leading them to close the cases. But there was a lot of distrust. There was a lot of skepticism.

"You're not saying anything," she said. "So it was just words you didn't mean?"

Startled, he looked back at her. "I'm sorry. Did you say something?"

"I asked you, in what way you thought I'd changed," she repeated slowly, her gaze searching his as if trying to figure out where he'd been.

He didn't know himself. He'd been caught up in a world still impacting his present day but was long gone.

"You're calmer," he said quietly. "Less driven."

She gave a self-conscious shrug. "I'm not sure that's a good thing."

"It's good. You were down to skin and bone, and so close to the wire. I was afraid you would snap at any time."

"And of course I did," she said bitterly. "I have been trying to not end up in the same condition again." She acted as if she would say something else, and then pinched her lips shut.

"You know you can tell me anything, right?"

She just stared at him.

But her face gave nothing away. He could sense the secrets inside, and that bothered him. He also knew he didn't have any right to be bothered. When she'd sent him away, they'd gone their own directions. He'd lived his life; she'd lived hers. But he never forgot her, never forgot how she'd given her all to everything she did. Whether that was making love or closing cases, she dove in with both feet. It was all or nothing. She went after killers with the ferocity of a bulldog, and she wouldn't let them go until she had them cornered and caught.

The thing was, because of her abilities, the criminals never understood how they got caught, how they slipped up, how the cops managed to nail them.

"I haven't changed at all," she said quietly. "Not really." Then she thought about it and shook her head. "What am I saying? Of course I have. I'm not the same person." She chuckled. "And that's a good thing. I was a nervous wreck, constantly trying to overachieve, to gain acceptance. After a lot of hardship I finally came to the conclusion *acceptance be damned.* I am who I am, and, if that's not enough, then you can get the hell out of my life."

She said it with such conviction that he realized she really believed it. He wondered what it had taken for her to come to that point. And then her earlier words hit him. "What do you mean, *acceptance?*"

She waved her hand. "Don't give me that. You know how hard it was for me to deal with the cops … the distrust, the disbelief, all the time. And yet, at the same time, all of them wanting answers. And I gave them everything. That first chance they got to turn on me, they did. Not only was I trying to find the victims and to help them but I was always looking for approval from them, from you, from myself. And, of course, I could never do enough," she said sadly. "Because life still kicks you in the ass, and it's up to you to get back up again and carry on, whether you like it or not."

He winced. "You've had a rough few years."

"Maybe a few ..." she said, her stare bland. "But it's for the best. You've had an easy few years," she said. "At least that's how you make it look."

"At least easier than I really deserved," he admitted. "But I didn't rock the boat. I didn't go for very intense relationships. I did nothing but stay at my job and close the cases I could without your assistance. And I realized just how much you had given us over the years. I only closed one-tenth of the cases without you. And, of course, that's what the other detectives were closing all the time. But we worked in teams a lot, so we had the numbers cracking down pretty good when you were there working with us."

He wrapped an arm around her. "Honestly I missed you. I missed us. It's not been the same since we broke up. I get that we're different now. That you've been to hell and back, but I like what I see. And ..." He took a deep breath, staring down into her midnight blue eyes, seeing the surprise, the shock and maybe some heat inside.

"I'd like to get to know you again."

CHAPTER 12

Sunday Morning …

THE NEXT DAY Queenie woke to a cloudy sky. Memories of the previous afternoon visiting with Kirk over lunch filled her mind. It had been nice, pleasant. More than pleasant if she were honest. Almost like when they'd been dating. Even better now as they were both different people—older, wiser. Yet the connection was still there. A happy sigh escaped. It was nice.

As she lay here, something caught her attention from the corner of her eye. She jerked back to see a spider on her bedspread. "Uh-oh, it's you again," she said, sneaking out from under the covers. "What do you want? Why couldn't you have been a butterfly or something a lot easier to deal with? Why a spider?"

But as the spider sat on her blanket and stared at her, she looked a little closer, studying its body and realizing it looked very similar to the one from her amusement park tent. Could it be the same one? Surely not. She'd seen dozens the other morning. She glanced around nervously. "Where are the rest of your friends?"

It was one thing to deal with them when you saw them first, but having them come out of dark corners really got her.

She knew after her previous encounters she should be

more used to them, but somehow they still unnerved her.

"Just stay there until I get back," she whispered, walking backward to the bathroom. Inside she gave her teeth a good brushing before stepping out of her pajamas and into a hot shower.

As soon as she scrubbed down and shampooed her hair several times, she turned off the water and stepped out, wrapping herself in a towel. She usually avoided looking in a mirror. For some reason, seeing her reflection, or maybe the lack of her reflection, bothered her. She knew it had something to do with her abilities. But the outline always looked blurred to her. She didn't know what the hell anybody would say to that. She'd mentioned it once to the law enforcement mandatory doctor, more as a joke than anything. Dr. Hutchinson hadn't taken it as a joke, and she'd apologized and then shut up. He'd monitored her mental health seasonally for all the years she'd been an advisor, and she'd seen him a couple times after that last case blew up, then once after Reese's death.

At that point, she'd decided she was better off on her own. Not that the good doctor had done anything but try to help her, but, if she were honest, what she did was outside the parameters of his reality, and, therefore, any help he had to offer didn't really apply.

What she wanted was to have a group of peers. Wouldn't it be lovely to have a circle of people with abilities like hers, or similar to hers, to discuss the challenges? Because, damn, there were a lot of them.

She braided her hair, then headed back to the bedroom. Her gaze zinged to the bedspread, only to find the spider had disappeared.

She pulled on a pair of shorts and a T-shirt and walked

out to the kitchen. There she put on her habitual pot of coffee and booted up her laptop. While both were doing their jobs, she headed out on the balcony and took several deep breaths of the fresh air. It smelled like rain, but it felt like something else, darker, like some ugliness brewed on the horizon. She frowned and stood there for a moment, checking in with her senses to see if anything was coming to her, looking for her own vision. It was much harder to view her own world.

When she couldn't pick up anything unusual, she stepped inside and poured herself a cup of coffee, then went to the table to check the laptop. Just about to sit down, she saw the spider on the kitchen table. She glared at it. "How the hell did you get out here?"

Of course it was a foolish question. As she walked to the sink, she saw the spider again. She glanced over at the table and groaned. "Now there are two of you? So where is the rest of your army?"

She filled a glass with water only to see a third spider. She stepped back against the fridge, her gaze going from one spider to the other to the other. "If you guys have a convention at my place, just let me know ahead of time, and I'll happily vacate," she called out in an effort at light humor.

Maybe you should look at why they're there instead, Stefan said quietly, his voice resonating through her head.

"You're just as freaky, dropping in like that," she called out. Then remembering Stefan's earlier instructions, she spoke through her mind connection with Stefan. *Can you see them?*

No, I'm not in your room. I'm just telecommuting with you.

Is there a whole group of you? I would really love to connect with other psychics.

Haven't you before? Only curiosity could be heard in his tone.

She shook her head as she stepped lightly, getting closer to the coffeepot. Watching the nearest spider, she moved her hand forward until it lifted a leg at her. She bounced back. *No, I haven't been so lucky. Is there one who deals with spiders?*

You've asked me that before. The answer is still no. I don't know anybody who connects with spiders.

Too bad, she snapped. *If somebody does out there, I'd really like to know why the spiders are haunting me. I see visions of the little boy, but nothing I can use. Two nights ago I touched several spiders to see if they had a message for me.* She quickly explained the vision she saw. *But there's been nothing since. Only this morning I'm seeing them again.*

How many do you see now? he asked curiously.

Three. And then she caught herself. *Unless there's a fourth one still on my bed. I don't know if it's one of these guys or not.*

But you had more before? Interesting.

She walked to her laptop, grabbed it with her free hand and strode into the living room. She searched the area, looking for a spider, but there didn't appear to be any. *Yeah, that about sums it up. The other night there were dozens of them. I don't understand why they are here or what they want. That they might have been sent by someone is another curious possibility because I can't for the life of me understand why.* She sank down in her chair, placed the coffee on the floor beside her and opened up her laptop. *I need a spider specialist.*

I don't know one, but I did come for a specific reason.

Yeah? What's that? She sifted through her emails, not seeing anything of interest, though there were a couple about the website. Eagerly she went to click on one.

I need your help.

She froze. *What do you mean, my help?*

Remember the patient you sent to Dr. Maddy?

Yeah, of course. Do you have a progress report? She bounced to her feet and paced her living room. *Because that would be freaking awesome if she could help.*

Well then, be prepared to be awesomized, Stefan said humorously. *She did, indeed, see him. And that's one of the reason's I'm contacting you. She found something … odd.* There was a pause, as if he were collecting his thoughts.

She brightened. *Is it a good odd? Is there anything she can do for him?*

What did you see when you saw his little girl?

I'm not sure I saw anything. I did get the answer to their question, but it was basically that they needed to see Dr. Maddy.

Dr. Maddy thinks he's being poisoned.

She gasped in horror. *Oh, my God! Will he be okay?*

It depends whether we can find out who's poisoning him.

Queenie frowned. *Usually there's a certain amount of energy when I see murderous intent like that, but I'd normally have to have a connection to him, like touching him.*

True. I would normally see that too. But I'm not seeing it in this case. Neither is Dr. Maddy.

So other people see it the same way I do?

I don't know. We all see things differently. And then some people have the ability to mask what they are doing.

But, if it's evil energy, then I generally see something.

Right, that's what I was thinking too. So how is somebody poisoning him if it's not done on purpose?

Chances are it's accidental, she said cautiously. *As in, giving him something they think is good for him, but it's hurting him instead. Or maybe eating food that's doing it? Other than that, no clue.*

We haven't found anything either. He paused. *So back to the spiders. Do you have anything you can give to the police to find the little boy?*

The first time I saw the spider, I thought I heard a little boy crying for his mommy. This time the boy was scared as someone approached, but he was okay in the vision. What came afterward, I can't say as the vision stopped there. Honestly I don't know that I want to see. I can't handle anything bad happening to little kids.

Stefan was quiet. *Are you sure you heard and saw this?* His voice was very gentle.

She nodded and choked back the tears ever threatening to fill her eyes at the thought of that little boy. *Yes, I'm certain. But I didn't recognize the voice. I'm not crazy,* she said firmly. *And I'm not thinking it was my son or anything else like that, but obviously any cases involving terrified little boys will trigger a strong response from me.* Too strong if the truth be told. What could she do to help him?

Back when you helped the police, were there any cases with missing children?

Lots, she said bluntly.

One that would be close to that age, maybe a baby back then?

She frowned and cast her mind back to the multitudes of cases she'd worked on. *I don't think there were any that weren't solved,* she said slowly. *I mean, it's possible. We certainly had enough, and I know I didn't work on all of them by any means.*

No, but for you to have heard that voice, you'd think there would need to be a connection.

But what kind of a connection? she asked. *I don't remember having had physical contact with this boy, although my abilities are changing, and I don't always need to touch.*

It might not need to be that at all. It could be a boy that you, at one time, held his hand. Maybe he was kidnapped afterward.

She made a startled sound. *If you're talking about a boy from one of the cases I knew of or worked on, that could involve any number of possibilities.*

Exactly, Stefan said. *How are you doing with the reframing?*

She shook her head. *I haven't had much time to practice. Things at the amusement park blew up. It's dominated my thoughts.* Although Stefan was silent, she almost heard him hum. *Are you reading my thoughts?*

Your energy, he said calmly, as if unaware or uncaring that he might be intruding. *And I'm not intruding. If you don't cloak your thoughts, they're open for anyone to read.*

Is that how that asshole is watching me, or stepping into my world, seeing what I'm doing?

No, Stefan said slowly. *That has to be something else.*
Why?

Because you have a unique defense system that I'm not even sure you're aware of.

I didn't think I had much of any defense system, she cried out. *Isn't that why David could get closer to me? I always struggled to get rid of all these memories and the people crying out to me.*

Explain.

She was coming to realize that direct curtness was just Stefan's way. It wasn't an order but not exactly a request. It was somewhere in between yet given in a way he knew she would answer. *When I do readings for people, it's like I'm collecting bits and pieces of them,* she said, slowly trying to formulate what the problem was. *So, when I wake up in the middle of the night, it's often the messages I gave them that are running through my mind.*

As if the message was wrong? Or as if you wanted to change something?

No, not like that, she said. *It's just not being able to forget them. Not being able to move on. Having them sit there in my thoughts and drag me down.*

After you let go of somebody's hand, what do you usually do?

Bewildered, she said, *I give them their message. I usually give my hand a shake because it always buzzes.*

So then you need to make sure, when you give your hand a shake, you're mentally shaking off their energy too.

I do that too, she protested. *But it doesn't always seem to work.*

Does it not work with any particular people?

She frowned, not quite understanding.

Is it always children for example?

She thought about that. *It's mostly children. But I don't think it's always children.*

So maybe just the ones that touch you a little more?

She nodded. *I think so. Like the little boy with the cone over his head. I'm sure he's passed into the realm after this by now,* she said sadly. *But he was so full of life.*

But death is not an end. We have to remember that. How often have you seen the cones?

She shrugged. *Maybe a half dozen times?*

He nodded. *Interesting. Not very many people see those.*

Why not?

That's seeing the actual life force around a person. It's one thing to give a message, and it's another to see auras, but seeing that death cone is deeper than both.

Maybe, but it's what I see, she said. *I don't have any training in this stuff. I just see what I see.*

You've trained yourself. The more you use these abilities, the more abilities you have. They grow. They develop. They change over time, over distance.

That last one was a concept she almost grasped but struggled with. *Over distance?*

The time spectrum. In the energy world, time is of little consequence, as is distance. There are spaces between spaces, physical worlds related to nothing but more energy.

So you're talking about the in-between?

What do you know about in-between?

Not much. A couple times I had some really bizarre experiences, and I wondered what the hell was going on, but I didn't really stay long enough to see anything.

What was it like?

It was gray, almost a silvery light. I thought it was the dead zone, if there is such a thing, she said with a shallow laugh. *And I know that makes no sense.*

Interesting, because, if you can cross into that, there's an awful lot you can do that you probably aren't doing yet.

But what I am doing is already very confusing, she said. *I've never pretended to be anybody other than somebody who could get messages.*

Yet you say messages as if somebody is talking to you. Is that how it is for you?

She shook her head. *No. I guess I don't get messages. I get pictures, and I interpret those pictures into messages.*

And how do you interpret the pictures into messages?

I just do, she said. *It's instinctive.*

There was silence again. Then she became aware of a crawling sensation on her foot.

Don't move, Stefan urged. *See what it wants.*

She stared in fascination as the spider slowly crept up her pant leg. *It's the same as the others.*

It will be one of the others, he corrected. *A little braver, it's on a mission.*

Could you at least tell me if it's poisonous or not?

I don't see any energy around it to confirm that, but every animal has a defense mechanism.

Well, I don't really want to find out the hard way, she said. She felt herself tensing, everything inside her too. *It's one thing to see them at a distance, but it's another thing for them to catch you unaware. Even after touching several of them. I'd really rather the messages came in the form of something less yucky.*

But you've been seeing them for a long time, haven't you?

She shook her head. *No, I haven't.*

Remember the truth?

She frowned, her gaze never leaving the spider creeping slowly up to her knee. *Of course I've seen spiders around, but I can't say I recognize this spider.*

This spider? Interesting. You're picking up on this particular one?

I think you're making too much of my words. I'm not saying anything exactly when I say that.

Of course you are, he said smoothly. *Every word you say has meaning. And you know it.*

Well, what is the meaning of every step this spider takes? She stretched out her leg, wishing the damn thing would fall off.

What are you really afraid of?

I don't know, she said. *It's a creepy-crawly thing. I can't stand it.*

And yet you're getting more perturbed with every one that you find. Why?

I don't know, she cried out, her knee jiggling, instinctively trying to shake it off.

Don't, Stefan ordered.

She sagged back on the couch and stared. *Why not?*

Push through the fear, he ordered. *This spider is on a mission. We need to hear what it has to say. Don't forget the little boy you saw. This spider could have another piece of the puzzle.*

So you can see it?

If you would lift your eyes from the spider, you would see me too.

Hating to, but curious, and feeling compelled to follow his instructions, she lifted her gaze to stare at a glowing form in front of her. She frowned. *Stefan?*

He nodded, sending sparks flying off with the movement. *Yes, it's me.* He motioned at the spider, little gold sparks flying toward it. *There's an energy about it. And the energy isn't necessarily his.*

What do you mean by that? she asked, her gaze returning to the spider. *Do you think somebody is sending it to hurt me?*

No, that's your fear speaking. Look at it intently. What color is the aura?

She studied the spider, trying to separate from the fear choking her, looking at the color around a small ball. It was spotty. *White, but it glows pink or lavender. The same as the others I saw.*

Not quite. Take another look.

She peered a bit closer. Which was a little too easy to do because this thing was now midthigh. She could feel her heart slamming against her chest. *I'm getting more terrified the longer I stay here,* she said suddenly. It made no sense. She'd touched them several times now, and, although not her favorite activity, it didn't make sense to be as afraid as she was now.

Focus on that energy, Stefan ordered.

She could feel her energies easing back, almost as if he'd done something to calm her down. As she looked at the pink around the spider, it seemed to glow brighter and brighter. She stared in awe. *Why is it glowing?* To her amazement the spider was no longer driving her fear higher and higher. *What did you do to me so that I lost that panic?*

Trying to help calm you down so you can see the purpose behind this spider's visit.

And if I can't?

You'll get dozens and dozens more spiders until you do hear and understand why this is happening.

The thought of her walls crawling with these spiders was enough to make her cringe again. Instantly a calming wave rode down her spine. She sagged against her couch. *That's you, isn't it?*

Yes, it is. This is too important to not sort though.

There are layers of pink, she announced. *And it completely surrounds the spider, despite every step he takes. There's pink energy flying off.*

And what about the eyes? Do you see anything in the eyes?

I don't want to look that close, she said, shuddering. *Besides, spiders have too damn many eyes.*

Look in the general direction, he said in exasperation. *Did you ever think somebody is using a spider to call for help?*

You mean, that little boy is using the spiders? She shook her head. *No idea. I was thinking it might be someone else, showing me the boy's plight so I could help—because they weren't in a position to.* Realizing Stefan would want more explanation than that, she hastily added, *Maybe so I could help him.*

Mommy?

She froze, and, on the heels of his first cry, the little boy cried out again in her head, *"Mommy, Mommy. Where are you?*

She didn't think it was possible to sink any deeper into the couch, but it was as if everything inside her drained out her big toe, and she was completely weak as she heard that voice over and over again. Finally she couldn't stand it, and her maternal instinct kicked in. *Mommy is here. It's okay. Mommy is here.*

She could feel Stefan's sudden silence as everything inside him strained to hear what she heard. She wanted him to; she wanted Stefan's take on what was happening. She held out her hand and said, *I don't know if this will help.*

Stefan placed his hand on hers. Energy bolted up her arm, to her shoulder, across her chest and split, going up and down throughout her body.

The little boy's voice morphed into a vision. The same little boy was lying on his bed, playing with what looked like little trucks and cars. His bed was rumpled. There was a window with a curtain. For all intents and purposes, he looked well fed and more or less okay—as in he wasn't tied up or chained.

What's the matter, little one?

He kept his head down as if not wanting to admit what the problem was.

Are you scared?

The little boy's head nodded up and down. *I am scared.*

Why is that? she asked.

I wanted to find my mommy, and they got mad.

Her heart ached. *How do you know your mommy is missing?*

He gave a tiny shrug, the T-shirt over his small body barely rippled at the movement. *I know she's missing because she's not here. She's supposed to be here with me.*

She could feel Stefan urging her to stay calm and to keep talking. She wondered if he could see the same vision. She felt a squeeze on her shoulders, realizing he could, indeed, see. She released a gentle breath and asked, *What have you done to find her?*

The little boy's face scrunched up. He wiped his cheek, but his face was still downcast, so she couldn't see who he was.

She searched the vision, looking for something that would give her a location for this little guy. *Can you tell me what you did?*

You'll laugh, he whispered.

She whispered right back, *My name is Queenie, and I will believe you.*

There was silence for a moment, and then he said, *I asked the spiders to find her.*

Queenie froze, feeling the spiders. The one on her leg had somehow crawled up her arm, and she hadn't even noticed. It sat on her elbow and stared at her. She couldn't watch it and the vision of the little boy at the same time, so she kept her eyes on the boy. *How would the spiders know how to find her?*

I gave them some of my blood and told them to go find my mommy.

Do the spiders always listen?

Most of the time, he whispered, his voice getting fainter and fainter. *But it's hard for them.*

Did you tell anyone else what you did?

His head bobbed up and down.

And what did they do?

They laughed, he said, his voice barely audible. *Then they locked my door.*

She could see the vision starting to fade. *Do you know where you live?* she asked urgently.

The little boy shook his head. *No. It's just a house.*

Do you know what city? Do you know what town? Do you know what block you live on? Do you know your phone number?

The vision got fainter and fainter.

Look at me, she cried gently. *Look at me.*

Slowly, ever-so-slowly, he raised his face so he could look at her, his lips moving as he tried to speak, … but no words came out, … and then he was gone.

But it had been long enough. It had been long enough for her to see his face and to know her nightmare had just gotten so much worse.

She could feel Stefan wrapping her in his arms, but she was past moving; she was frozen, locked in place, because that little boy's face was a mirror image of his father's. *Kirk.* That little boy, locked in a bedroom, who'd spoken to spiders, was her own son. *Reese.*

The world closed down to the one solid fact she couldn't let go of. Her son was alive. And that meant everything for the last three and a half years had been a lie. A lie somebody had perpetrated on her.

And what about the pinkish-lavender energy she'd believed in her innermost being was the spirit of her dead son?

She could feel her world closing in, everything becoming this black pinpoint of total darkness. That circle came ever closer and closer, and she knew, when it closed over her head, she would be out cold.

Her energy already so depleted, in her mind she whispered, *Stefan, protect the spiders. They lead back to my son.* And she fell unconscious.

MADDY? I NEED your help, Stefan ordered.

Maddy landed in the living room beside him. *Can't get a decent night's sleep anyhow, can I?* she said humorously. Her eyes landed on an illuminated figure in front of them. She dropped down beside Queenie and whispered, *Oh, my goodness, what happened?*

He explained the vision she'd seen, the truth that had been unlocked and how the spiders, even now, crawled into the room. And that he knew she'd lost a child several years ago.

Maddy looked around. *My God! I've never seen this many spiders in one place.*

Stefan continued. *I had thought they would leave, not needed here once she got their message. But instead it's like that connection and her request to me to protect the spiders has sent them all coming in at a run.* He stared at the walls, even now turning black with spiders.

I've never really been one to love spiders, Maddy whispered, *but I can see the energy within them. I can see the pink aura around them. Why? Is that energy coming from the spiders?*

The little boy in the vision said he gave the spiders his blood so they could find his mother—so through his DNA, I presume, he said, his tone confused and yet exhilarated. *Do you understand how powerful this little boy is? Of course it's possible she's not his mother but is simply receptive to his energy*, he said, worried, as he stared down at the unconscious Queenie. *In that case this will be incredibly hard on her.*

What you mean is, how driven he is, Maddy corrected. *He's after his mother. And nothing on the face of this earth will stop him from achieving his goal. He can't come to her himself, so he sent his soldiers to find her.*

And he picked a hell of a soldier, Stefan whispered in awe. *Spiders travel miles. They communicate on wavelengths we have no idea about. They understand things we can't begin to. Somehow they found her. Does that mean the little boy is close by? I don't know,* he said, shaking his head. *I was attached to her, trying to see the vision as she saw it. I saw more of a slice, a paler version of it. But there's definitely a little boy in a room with a window and curtains. He was playing with trucks, but I detected his energy, weak and frail in his body.*

And that could be because he's pouring the bulk of his energy outward to his mother, Maddy said quietly. *It doesn't mean the little boy is in any danger or that he's ill.*

No. But, if Queenie is his mother, we have to wonder what happened to separate him from her.

Do you know her story?

No, not entirely. But I know somebody who does.

Well, you need to contact him, and we must get the details because I don't know how to pull her out of this.

As they watched, spiders slowly crawled all over Queenie, almost like a blanket wrapping around her.

They aren't going to bite her, are they? Maddy asked with a frown.

Stefan chuckled. *Take a closer look.*

She leaned in and then gasped softly. *They are snuggled up, body against body, as if protecting her,* she cried out in amazement.

I think that's what they're doing, now that they found their target. But they're probably not sure what to do at this point. And that little boy won't know either.

Her energy is very faint, Maddy whispered. *How the hell did she hold that vision for so long?*

I think the question is more about, how is it that she accesses these visions? Her methodology is one I haven't seen before.

Maddy turned to study his face.

He smiled at her. *It's like she opens a corridor. Just a quick in and out. She sees something in somebody's psyche, and then she's out again.*

So they're not visions?

I think she taps into their memories or their current position or possibly even their future. Maybe all three. Who really knows?

So that's how she understands the answers to their questions? Then Maddy's features paled with shock. *She doesn't open a worm hole, does she?* Maddy asked in fascination. *If she's this talented to tap into somebody's future and into their past, no wonder the little boy is as strong as he is—if he's hers.* She stared at Stefan. *If he is, that's incredible. But, if he isn't, that'll be a terrible shock for her.*

Oh, I'm pretty sure he's hers. The spiders alone prove that. He pulled Maddy back ever-so-slightly. It was a good thing they weren't in physical form because the entire floor was covered in spiders.

They're wrapping around her like a protective suit of armor, she said in awe. *I've never seen anything like this.*

I don't think we ever will again. This is the son's love for his mother. This is a mother's love for her son. A bond that was denied and broken, or attempted to be broken, he said, correcting himself. *And this just proves that love does beat everything else.*

We have to help them, Maddy cried out.

I know. Can you boost her energy? Give her a dose of something?

Maddy studied the woman on the couch. *Oh my, I don't think it's necessary*, she said, her voice enthralled. *Her energy is already strengthening, as if the spiders are giving their energy to her.*

Or giving her the little bit of her son's that they each have. Queenie was broken over the loss of her son. Which is to be expected. But that loss affected her abilities, so, when she tried to connect with his spirit, they'd changed. She not only opened up to her abilities, but she forged new pathways. She'd always had that communication with her son. She always kept that tunnel open, and, once the tunnel was cut with his separation from her, his supposed death, she took that energy and fired it off on many neural paths that we've never seen the likes of before.

Well, she's definitely one of us then, Maddy said softly. *We certainly collect the odd ducks.*

And the incredibly talented ones.

Maddy stepped back. *The spiders are doing for her something I can't,* she said. *She's in good hands at the moment.*

Okay, I'll contact Kirk. He should have more information on what's happening.

Right, he contacted me regarding the patient being poisoned.

He's also involved in another way.

What way is that?

Stefan sighed. *He's the little boy's father.*

KIRK WOKE SLOWLY. He didn't know why he was so tired. It had taken him a long time to go to sleep, but he thought he'd slept well once he finally got there. When he woke, finding a stranger at the end of his bed, he bolted out of it, reaching for his holster that held his weapon. "Who the fuck are you?" he roared.

"My name is Stefan," the man in front of him said calmly. He crossed his arms over his chest. "I suggest you look closer."

Kirk tried to wipe away the cobwebs of sleep to deal with the fact a man stood in his bedroom. A man he'd heard of but hadn't met. "Look closer at what?" he said.

"At me."

Cautious, realizing the man had made no threatening moves toward him, even if he had somehow gotten into his bedroom, Kirk stepped forward, his gaze locking on the man's features, then frowned. "What the hell?"

"What do you see?" Stefan asked curiously.

"The dresser in the mirror behind you." He shook his head. "Am I still dreaming?"

"You, who have spent years working with Queenie, are asking that? Have you not learned anything?"

Kirk stiffened. "How do you know Queenie?"

"I just came from her place," Stefan said. "That's why I'm here. You need to get over there right now."

Kirk was already pulling on his jeans from yesterday. He walked around Stefan, whose translucent body allowed him to see everything in the room through him. "Are you a ghost?" A lot of things in life had terrified him, but they were usually related to crazy men holding weapons on innocent women and children. He never imagined he'd have a ghost in his room.

"No," Stefan said. "I'm as alive as you and Queenie are."

"Is Queenie okay?" He pulled out a clean white T-shirt from his drawer, yanked it over his head, grabbed a pair of socks and tugged them on while he waited for this entity to answer.

"No," Stefan said thoughtfully. "Although she is healing now."

Kirk was in the process of grabbing his holster, putting it on. He spun and asked, "What are you talking about?"

"She saw another vision. I was there too."

Kirk shook his head. "What are you talking about? How could you be there too? You mean, you both saw the same vision? I didn't think that was possible."

"We both saw the same vision. But the only reason I saw her vision was because I had joined my energy to her."

Kirk couldn't help himself from stiffening. *That seems oddly intimate.*

"Oh, it's intimate," Stefan said, "but not on a sexual level."

Hating the heat of the flush that must be rising on his cheeks, and ignoring for the moment that this guy read his thoughts, Kirk shrugged it away. "And what was this vision about?"

"Spiders," Stefan said gently. "Lots and lots of spiders."

"She's been completely obsessed with spiders lately," Kirk snapped. "It doesn't make any sense."

"Well, prepare yourself for when you get there."

Kirk grabbed his wallet and keys. He stopped and turned back to Stefan. "Prepare myself for what? Just exactly what happened during this visit and this vision?" he asked.

"If you give me two minutes, I'll explain as best I can."

Stefan proceeded to fill his head with something he never even thought was possible. "Her son? Are you sure she said it was her son?"

Stefan's form nodded, bit of flashes happening at his

every move.

Kirk was fascinated. He'd never seen anything like this man in front of him or his abilities. "You know it's not possible, right?" And then he thought about what he'd said. "Or maybe her son is a ghost? Because he's dead. We all know that for sure."

Stefan smiled. "The longer I spend in this world, the more I realize I know nothing for sure."

"Are you saying her child is alive?" Kirk barked, his heart shaking at the thought. "It almost destroyed her to lose that little boy. We can't fill her head with hope and have her lose him again." Then he realized what he was saying. "And, if he is alive, I want to know what the hell happened …"

"And again I can't say anything for sure at this point," Stefan said. "But, with the best of my ability, and hers, I'm going to say that little boy, whoever he is, is alive. Is he her son? I can't say for sure." Then he said, "And there's one other thing you need to know."

Kirk headed to the front door. He'd heard enough. The thought of her being covered in spiders was enough to make his stomach churn. He had no problem with spiders, but he knew she was terrified of them. For all he knew, she was unconscious, in shock.

"No, I said she's fine. She's not in shock. The spiders are helping her. What you cannot do is disturb her when you get there."

Kirk flung open the door and turned to look at him. "Then what the hell is it that you want me to do?"

"Be there for her," Stefan said quietly, following Kirk to the front door.

It was so bizarre for Kirk to look at this man whose form seemed to be fading. The hallway and kitchen were coming through him stronger and stronger. "And why should I do that?"

Stefan sighed. "It shouldn't be me who tells you this. But I feel like I have no choice."

When he didn't say anything else, Kirk shrugged and said, "So are you going to tell me? I have to get to Queenie."

"Yes, you do have to go to Queenie. You have to look after her. And you have to find that little boy," Stefan ordered.

"I'll do my best obviously," Kirk said. "But you haven't said why?"

"Because that little boy is wearing your face." And, with that, Stefan disappeared.

CHAPTER 13

Sunday, Late Morning ...

QUEENIE WATCHED THE images float past her as if she were in some dream state. It wasn't like the visions she normally had, not that much was normal about those either, but she didn't recognize these pictures. They floated, not like a film, coming in order, but were bits and pieces popping in and out of her psyche.

She couldn't grasp much here, and the effort it took was so damn much. She just wanted to float, wanted to make it all go away. So much stress had been in her life, so much pain, that escaping felt perfect right now. If she was dying, she knew nobody would be around to stop her, and, if she was living, and going to stay alive, she'd wake up from this fugue at some point. Maybe. She sighed happily as pictures of her son, pulled from the deep recesses of her mind, drifted through her vision.

And yet, pinkish-lavender–tinged energy flowed in and around the visions, bringing tears to her eyes. Reese? Could it be that the pinkish-lavender energy and this little boy were one and the same? She'd never been able to get the lavender energy to talk—was it too young? Too undeveloped?

She should have asked Stefan. She desperately wanted the little boy to be hers, but she knew Reese was dead, ... and she'd only had one child. It was all too possible that, being a strong psychic, she had picked up on the little boy's energy. *His* pinkish-lavender energy. And that meant her dream of finding Reese would never come true. … Yet another mother was struggling with her loss of this little boy out there somewhere.

Then a sad thought flitted through her mind. What if the little boy had been given up for adoption? What if his mother wasn't alive anymore?

Reese had been such a cute boy, so happy, so talented. … She couldn't imagine not wanting him. But then she thought every mother would care this deeply. Every mother would have thought her child was the best, the most perfect. Of course they couldn't all be perfect. But Queenie was damn sure her son was. She smiled at that, because, of course, Reese had cried at odd times, and she hadn't always been able to sort out why.

Sometimes he'd reach out, and, like a little zap of energy, that brought tears to her eyes as she realized the perfection she had created. She knew his father had played a major role in that creation, but he hadn't known she was pregnant. … She should have told him. She had tried at one time. She had called him up, but a woman had answered. A woman who called Kirk *darling*. That had been enough for Queenie to hang up the phone and to sit, quaking, with a very rotund belly, realizing Kirk had moved on and most likely wouldn't want a reminder of what they'd had together—and definitely not a child to support. She didn't know how he felt about children. She couldn't pull up a conversation on this topic from her brain. Had they ever had one?

Their life together had been so busy, full of killers and horrible criminals. She'd been so proud of him when his own abilities had sparked. It happened that way. He'd been her ground, even though he hadn't recognized his role.

He had helped her find normalcy in an often ugly world.

More pictures of Reese floated in her mind. Of Reese laughing, him in the bathtub, him in her arms. Cell phones had created a moment-by-moment, day-by-day history of her life with her son.

More pinkish-lavender energy caressed her.

Surely an answer was in here somewhere for her. With that came the name *Stefan*, and she slowly remembered the last time she'd spoken to him. And the spiders. She could feel her body tensing.

A weird crawling sensation could be felt all over her skin, but, rather than terrifying her this time, she found a certain comfort in it. Almost like a blanket shifting. She sighed, a deep heavy breath that worked up from her toes past her knees, her hips and up through her chest, releasing through her throat. That exhalation of pain and frustration and anger was old energy, long-dead energy. Releasing it felt so good. She took several more long, slow deep breaths.

"Just take it easy. Your body has been under a lot of stress. You need to wake up slowly."

She murmured in protest. She didn't want to wake up. She knew that to return to awareness was to greet pain again, to greet loss, to face her grief, and she so didn't want to do that. She deliberately floated toward the clouds, hoping for more fog, more quiet, and not that voice becoming more and more insistent.

"But I want you to wake up," the man said. "It's not an option."

She could feel her body twitching in protest.

"I don't want you to move when you wake up. Open your eyes and just be still," he urged.

And she caught something odd in his tone. What was that? She slowly opened her eyes to see Kirk. He smiled down at her. "There you are. What's the last thing you remember?"

She gave him a small smile. "What are you doing here?" she whispered.

"Looking after you," he said gently. "Stefan called me—or came to me. Whatever you want to call it." There was a note of humor in his voice. "And what I found … Wow."

Her eyes drifted closed again, and she just lay peacefully. "What did you find?"

"You."

"Who else would you expect to find here? It's my place. If I'm still at home."

"You are, and it is your place," he said. "But you remember all those spiders you kept seeing?"

Her mind drifted from one spider image to the next, and she remembered a good half dozen were in her apartment. "Spiders," she whispered. "Stefan wanted me to communicate with them, to find out why they were here."

"What did the spiders tell you?"

Still floating gently, she thought about the spiders, their message and her vision. Just as she went to rise, he placed a hand on her forehead and held her down firmly.

"Don't move," he said.

Her eyes were open and locked on his face. "*Reese*. The spiders were talking about Reese."

"Well, I'm not so sure about that," he said quietly. "But apparently you saw a vision of a little boy, correct?"

She frowned, hating how the cobwebs in her brain wouldn't go away, even now that she wanted them gone. "Yes. He was calling for his mommy."

"Right, and you took that to mean it was your lost son."

She studied his features, trying to pinpoint what was wrong with what he just said. "He wasn't a ghost," she said, thankfully latching on to that odd note. "The little boy wasn't dead."

"So, if he wasn't a ghost, then he wasn't Reese, correct?"

She closed her eyes again, hating that he pulled her back to the more-accepted reality that her son was dead. "He was talking to me through the spiders," she said. "I remember he gave the spiders his blood to find his mother."

"I don't know how any of this works," Kirk said, his voice urgent, "but do you hear what you're saying?"

Gathering strength, she opened her eyes and said, "I'm saying the exact same thing I've been saying all these years. It's possible my son is alive." She glared at him. "If so, everybody else has been lying to me. That little boy has abilities like I have abilities. And he used them to communicate with spiders. And me."

Kirk sat back on his heels.

She lay on the dilapidated couch in her living room, and he was crouched in front of her. Worry was on his face—and sadness.

"And there's something else about that little boy you haven't told me, isn't there?"

Instantly she tried to retreat. "No. I don't remember anything," she said vaguely. But inside she wondered. Of course with Stefan involved, there was no way to keep Reese's heritage a secret.

"Who's the father of your child?" Kirk asked boldly.

"What difference does it make? You think he's dead anyway."

"Unless the father missed an opportunity to know and to

be there for his son," Kirk said, his voice turning hard and accusing.

Inside she groaned. This wasn't how she wanted to tell him. And this wasn't the time for a confrontation. But then there would never be a good time at this point. And she stayed silent, hoping he'd let it drop, yet knowing he wouldn't. She waited, her heart sinking, knowing this day would always come. Just how sad that it was a day when Reese wasn't here to be with them.

"Who was Reese's father?" Kirk repeated. But instead of accusing, he just sounded defeated. "It's me, isn't it?"

She remained silent.

"Why didn't you tell me?" he cried out. "Why wasn't I given a chance to know my son?"

He got up, pacing the living room while she lay there, staring through her lashes at him. She didn't have a good answer. She'd been petrified he'd take her son away from her. She knew in her heart of hearts he wasn't that kind of man, but it had just been her and Reese for so long that she'd been terrified she'd lose him. And then, of course, she had … for a totally different reason. And the loss had crippled her as she'd known it would.

"You know I would have loved him," Kirk snapped. He squatted down in front of her, frustration all over his face. "I would have loved to have known him."

She opened her eyes. "I know," she whispered. "You would have. And I did call. A woman answered the phone the one time I finally got up the courage to call you, and she called you *darling*. And the thought of how you'd feel if a child from a past relationship intruded into your current happiness, how you'd feel if you were caught up in child support for eighteen years …" She winced, then admitted,

"And it gave me an excuse to keep Reese to myself. If you had someone already, you didn't need him. But I did."

He shook his head in bewilderment. "I'm sorry, but your lack of a relationship or my temporary one have no bearing on me finding out I have a son. I would have loved to have known him. I would have helped you, so you didn't have to be at the end of your wits, trying to make ends meet …"

Tears rolled down her cheeks. "You might have. And you might not have." She took a deep breath, then another one, releasing all her pain, all her torment. "At the time I couldn't deal with the thought you might take him away. You might have said I was an unfit mother. You'd hurled a few insults at me along those lines before you left. About me having a breakdown, that I needed help. If you thought I was pregnant and maybe your son would be in any danger, you would have done everything you could have to save him. And it would have killed me."

This time the silence was on his part. He sat down in front of her, his fingers reaching out and hesitantly stroking her cheeks. "Maybe," he admitted. "You were in very rough shape then. I don't think you understand how bad it was. You hadn't eaten for days. You wouldn't drink anything. You were a basket of nerves, so you couldn't sleep, and you paced all night, and you cried all day. Dr. Hutchinson was really concerned. He spoke to me several times, even suggesting you might need to spend a few days in a special ward so you didn't hurt yourself. What was I supposed to do? You wouldn't let me get close. You were so racked with guilt because of the Handkerchief Killer case that you sent me away."

"That poor woman died because of me," she said, her voice stronger. "How was I supposed to react? Just close the file and say, *Oh, well, win some, lose some?* You know I gave my all to every case. I still don't understand how that went so wrong."

"No. Of course I didn't expect that. But you grieve and then you move on. We couldn't help her anymore. But there were other cases."

"I hit a wall," she whispered. "I was of no value to you or the department at that point. I needed time to heal, time to regroup, time to rebuild my energy and my faith in humanity. I wasn't given that."

"What do you mean?"

"The department told me that they no longer needed my services. The media was hounding me. I was broken and thought you were better off without me. I found out a couple months after you left that I was pregnant. But, in those months, you'd moved out and hadn't said a word to me." She watched the pain and the regret cross his face.

He nodded. "I get that it was a tough time for you. But it was also a tough time for me. That's no excuse. I tried hard to get you to look after yourself, but you wouldn't listen, and you kept shutting doors in my face. Then you said it was over. *We were over.*"

"Instead I found myself pregnant, joyously pregnant," she murmured. Her lips twitched into a smile. "I had a psychic connection to the child. I knew him intimately before he was born. We were always bonded, even before his birth. When I woke up from that coma, that bond was not broken. I knew it was still there. And everybody kept telling me how I was wrong, that he was dead. And slowly, a bit at a time, I shut it down, thinking I was so crazy, so grief stricken that maybe you were all right. So I reawakened my abilities in order to find him, … and I did," she said so faintly he had to lean in to hear her. "But now I feel like I don't know anything." A broken laugh escaped. "Then the spiders came ..."

"Why spiders?" he interjected.

She opened her gaze wider. "As far as I can tell, they were his pets. I think he overheard his parents fighting about his birth mother, and, when he asked about her, they got really angry and locked him up." She tried to tap into the same energy that had been giving her the information, but there was so little there.

"That's harsh," he said.

She nodded, and that spider blanket wiggled around her shoulders. She opened her eyes and stared at him. But he wasn't looking at her face, he was studying her body, a look of fascination in his expression. Then she knew. "It's spiders, isn't it?"

His gaze zinged toward her. "Pardon?"

"This blanket covering me, it's spiders, isn't it?"

He took a deep breath and then slowly nodded. "Yes. There are a thousand, if not more, all over you."

She waited for that sense of revulsion, but it wasn't there. Just a warmth, a caring. "They came looking for me," she whispered, closing her eyes, mentally sending out a thank-you and a warm glow of energy to them. She was hoping that, when she saw them, she wouldn't be terrified. But she knew it was one thing to know they were there, but it was another thing entirely to see them.

"They came to you, but that doesn't mean you are the boy's mother. They might be answering his request but could only come to someone strong enough to help. You are not the only psychic out there. You know that. But these spiders, ... they are covering you like a blanket all over," he said. "Their hard backs are bumped up against each other. Their arms, I swear to God, they're almost locked around each other to hold their position."

"I don't know why they're doing this," she said.

"Stefan said they received instructions from the little boy to find you, and, now that they have, they probably don't know what to do."

She considered that. "It makes a weird kind of sense. Are more still coming?"

"Since I've been here, dozens more have arrived."

KIRK COULDN'T BELIEVE what he saw. From the minute he'd walked in the door of her small place, the spiders had done nothing but make kind of a shivering movement, as if tightening their ranks to protect Queenie. He'd stared at her, taking pictures, stunned at the spiders coming together in one act like that. It was freaking amazing. It also opened his eyes to something he hadn't even considered before—how men and animals came together in such a way to help each other. But this was beyond his comprehension.

He couldn't believe what Stefan had said, about the little boy involved being his son, Reese, but as Kirk stared at the spiders in front of him, he had to wonder if it was possible. Other considerations rose to the surface. If he accepted that Queenie's son—their son—was dead, and this other boy had similar features to his, then had Kirk fathered another son? One he also didn't know about? He had no brothers to have produced offspring that looked like him, and, although his bitch of a sister would quite likely have handed over any child of hers for adoption. Yet, Kirk had not known of her ever conceiving. She'd most likely have aborted it first. So whose child was it that looked like Kirk?

He'd already suspected Reese was his and Queenie's. The timing had been so damn close. Or she had had an affair within weeks of their breakup. And he knew she hadn't been in any shape mentally or emotionally back then.

At the hospital three and a half years ago, he hadn't said anything because what was the point when the boy was already gone? And she'd been destroyed by the news. He didn't want to add any more stress on her at that point. But now, as he sat here, the truth pounded into him by Stefan was overshadowed by this amazing spider teamwork.

Still, he didn't understand why they were covering her. Could they do nothing but cling to her? Were they or were they not helping her?

Kirk studied her as she lay there. "I don't know what will happen when you move," he said. "It's quite possible the spiders will run away, or they won't shift enough to allow you to move."

She stared at him in surprise. "They're all pretty small, aren't they?"

He nodded. "They are, but they've all banded together to do this."

She smiled. "I guess I don't have any good reason for being afraid of them anymore, huh?"

"You never were really afraid of them though, I think. Just their fast movements always startled you. Like so many women, it's more about the movement and the creepy-crawliness of them than an actual fear."

"I want to move."

"I'm not sure you should," he cautioned. "If they're helping you, then you should accept their help."

"Well, I can't just lie here forever," she said.

"What else do you need to do right now?"

She was silent for a long moment and then gave a tiny shrug. "Nothing. How late is it?"

Kirk checked his watch. "Almost noon."

He heard her soft gasp. "That means I've been out for hours. The meeting with everyone from the amusement park is at two today."

"I wouldn't worry about the meeting," he said. "That's hardly your priority right now."

She narrowed her gaze at him. "No, it isn't necessarily a priority, but that doesn't mean I can ignore all those people trying to figure out how to solve their current problem. Do you have an update on Carlos?"

He shook his head. "No, but I can get one for you, if you want."

She shook her head. "It doesn't really matter. As long as the cops won't let him go. My friends are trying to find a solution, and I don't know that I can do anything but be there for moral support."

He nodded, pulled out his phone, stood and walked slightly away.

CHAPTER 14

Sunday, Noon …

SHE STARED DOWN at her hand and couldn't see flesh. It was literally covered in small black, almost metallic-looking things. She understood in theory these were all spiders, and her heart still shuddered at the thought, but she was overcome by her fascination that they had worked together to accomplish this.

"How?" she whispered. "How did you find me? And what is it you want from me now?" She tried to shift upward, only to cry out in surprise, as if the spiders had tightened their net around her. Not a spiderweb in the normal sense but as if she were bound and wrapped. She was covered all the way to her toes. The casing stopped at her neck, for which she was grateful. But, when she tried to move, the spider blanket tightened around her.

She fell back on the couch, stunned. "What do you want from me?" she cried out. Of course they didn't answer her.

But, in the background, she heard Stefan say, *Ask them directly.*

You mean, I didn't?

Of course not. You just cried out to the universe, as if looking for somebody to give you the details of what you're missing. The spiders found you. They are the ones with the answers.

She sank back into the couch, understanding—in theory—what he had said. She closed her eyes and whispered in her mind, *What do you want?*

There weren't any words, but there was a rumble, as if an answer of some kind. An answer she didn't understand because she didn't understand the language.

You found me. I don't know what I'm supposed to do now.

Another rumble, slightly louder. As if more spiders were responding.

Do you have a spokesperson? she asked, feeling foolish.

Don't look for words, Stefan said. *Look for emotions, look for images. Whatever is your usual methodology for getting answers. Just think how not only are they there for you but you're touching them. What is it you're getting visions of?*

With her eyes closed, she reached out and wiggled a finger, letting her mind acknowledge she was, indeed, touching a spider and could pick up its visions. All she saw was a dirt pathway as the spiders had moved a long distance.

Show me where you've come from, she ordered.

The vision sped up, the pathway racing ahead faster and faster. She followed it, not quite understanding, like she was in some tunnel. She followed the spiders' path, seeing more and more spiders converging, coming in from different avenues. All headed for the same place.

It's never been like this before, she whispered.

Nothing will ever be the same again either, Stefan said with certainty.

The assurance in his voice made her realize just how much he had seen in his life and how much he knew about this.

Don't get distracted, he warned. *Stay with the spiders. Follow them to the source. See if you can find a location where this boy is.*

Eagerly she dove deeper, faster, flying through the air as she fast-tracked back through the spiders' route. She slammed to a stop on a street. Several dilapidated houses were on the left of her, and another one looked more like a junkyard on the right. Vehicles were all over the property of the one on the right. The other two houses on the left had busted toys and an old junkyard-type car—but only the one—whereas the one on the right had dozens.

Not knowing which way to go, she closed her eyes and whispered, *Show me.*

Instantly she was sucked into that same vortex at the spiders' level, racing backward until she squeezed through a crack in the cement and inside a dark and dank basement. She followed it closer and closer until she came to a bedroom. The spider slipped underneath the doorframe.

She could see the little boy tucked on the bed, blankets up to his chin. He slept. But tear tracks marked his cheeks. Her heart broke as she studied his face; she knew he could be none other than her son. She reached out a hand, knowing it was only an ethereal energy but so full of love that she hoped she could touch him. She stroked his cheek gently.

He opened his eyes and stared at her. Ever-so-slowly he sat up. She didn't know what he could see, but obviously he saw something. He wasn't shocked. He wasn't afraid. He reached out a hand and whispered, *Mommy?*

She could feel her energy splinter in shock, in pain, and yet slam back together again in joy. She knew he was her son but had no proof. And regardless if he was or not, he was someone's son, and he needed hope. She whispered, *Yes.*

He didn't appear to hear her. He leaned forward, his gaze narrowed. *Mommy, is that you?*

She reached out with both arms and wrapped them

around him. Yet, she was nothing but a wispy cloud and had to be very faint at that. She mentally sent him a message of love and whispered, *Yes, it's me.*

He frowned and looked around, shrugging, and curled back up on the bed.

Her heart breaking with disappointment, she lay down beside him, wrapped her arms around him, so scared to leave and to not find him again. At least this way she was with him, which made everything else in her life worthwhile.

But the pull to return to her body was so strong that she could feel something dragging her back. As if her energy waned and her own physical form was in danger.

She'd heard about things like that but had never experienced them. Still, she was desperate to stay with her son. She studied the room around her, but there was nothing to say where he was. Then she was dragged outside of his house.

She was desperate to catch a glimpse of something to identify this location, but the speed which jerked her back blurred her vision and had her head spinning. She thought she saw the color blue with black trim, but that was all before she was pulled back through the tunnel, twisting and turning her like some drill boring in reverse.

When she slammed into her body, she jerked physically, and then the net of spiders tightened down once again. She opened her eyes, gasping.

Kirk bounded to her side. "Are you okay?"

"I saw him. I saw Reese."

He shook his head. "What do you mean?"

She told Kirk what she saw, what had happened. "He's out there, and he's alive."

"My son, you mean?" he said, his voice hard. "*My* son is alive?"

He sounded more incredulous than ever, but there was also a faint note of hope. Of course it was completely wrapped up in disbelief, but that was normal. She'd certainly dealt with that from many nonbelievers over the years.

She nodded slowly. That was something else to consider. The little boy looked like Kirk. Had he produced another son? Another one he didn't know about? "Maybe he is. The other thing is, the spiders won't let me go."

His eyebrows shot up toward his hairline, and he stared at her body, at the spiders obviously meshed around her. "Why not?" he asked.

"I don't know. Stefan wanted me to communicate with them. But, when I tried to do that, I saw the boy."

"Well, try to move again," he said promptly. "You can't lie here completely surrounded by spiders forever."

She glared his way. "I know that."

He shrugged, looked toward the kitchen and said, "I'll put on coffee. I'd like a hell of a lot more than that, but it's too damn early in the day."

She watched him until he moved out of her sight. She closed her eyes and whispered to the spiders. *I saw him. I don't know how to find him though.*

Again that weird murmuring mumbled in her head. She tried to ask other questions in different ways, but the responses never came back any different. Always this weird mumble. But she was touching them, and they were touching her. She reached out a hand and placed the pad of her finger against a spider's back. The energy was different, humming, *connected.* The spider was coming from a whole different place. She watched the pathway which existed between her and the spiders and realized that, as one spider had gotten the message, he'd passed on the message to the others. So, although a lot of the spiders knew about the little boy in the basement, not every spider did. So not all of them drank the boy's blood, but somehow they communicated with each other, and they were all here helping in the same mission.

What is it you want from me?

Again that weird mumble but also a weird sensation of connection.

I want to find him too, she whispered. *Why won't you let me go?*

Instead of answering her, they tightened down.

She tried to struggle, but it seemed even worse.

Stefan whispered in her mind, *Don't struggle. They can only respond to one thing.*

Love, she said, understanding the pinkish energy around them. She slammed her eyes closed. Instead of fighting the spiders, she blended with them. She let her energy soften, let the spiders sink deeper and deeper into her soul. They were just more of God's creatures, not ones she'd ever been particularly interested in meeting on this level, but there was no reason not to. They were coded in love, and that was something she could respect.

She reached out mentally and touched every spider on her body in a wave of a loving pink blanket, washing it over herself from head to toe and slowly encompassing every spider here. She didn't want them staying out of fear because surely she would be strong enough to break their grip, or at least Kirk would be, but she didn't want them hurt either.

I got the message, she whispered over and over again. *I'm going to help him. I'm going to find him. If you can show me where he is, that would help.*

She had to wonder at her son, who had connected with

these spiders at such a level that the spiders were willing to do what he asked of them. And she was here with all the spiders. How did she get them to send her back to her son? It seemed like a one-way street at the moment. Maybe her son hadn't figured how to get the message out any clearer.

As she lay here, the spider blanket stirred and trembled and relaxed its grip on her. She slowly sat up, and the spiders broke and reformed, covering the back of the couch in another blanket. She watched as they all clung together in this long vertical metallic-looking beadwork.

Kirk stepped forward. "How did you get them to let go?"

"I covered them with love," she said softly.

He stared at her. "You sent the spiders love?"

She shrugged. "What can I say? They were covered in pink, and they were coming from a little boy. I desperately want to confirm that he's my son, but I just don't know." She was so confused. She needed Stefan's help to sort this out.

"*Our* son," Kirk said, his voice curt.

She knew they would have a heavy discussion about it at some point. But she was willing to tell him now. "You need to find the answers," she said abruptly. "If he's Reese, how could this have come about? If he's your son by another woman—which woman is that? And, again, how did this come about?"

"I have no children," he said. "At least as far as I know."

Moving slowly so as not to disturb the spiders, that remained on the back of her couch but showed no sign of leaving her apartment, she stood and stretched. "If that is our son, we need to know how he disappeared from that hospital. And if he's not ours, he's still a lost little boy, and we need to help him."

He looked at her hesitantly. "You said you found him."

Frozen, she looked at him. What could she say that wouldn't make her sound crazy? She opted for the truth. "When I reawakened to my abilities, I found him. This faint lavender-hued energy and with laughter identical to my son's laughter. And yesterday I'd have sworn it was Reese. Today I can't explain any of it. Are these two different boys? I don't know. I do know if I can't handle it, if I lose my son all over again …"

The look in his eyes had her turning away. "I know I sound crazy." Then she turned and poked his chest. "Finding the truth is your domain. If that is your son out there, somebody in that hospital lied. Somebody forged the death certificate and the cremation certificate, then walked out of that hospital with Reese in their arms. That's not only criminal, it was vindictive and mean. But did they kidnap him to hurt me or because they wanted my beautiful son as their own?"

"I don't know," he said cautiously. "I will find out though."

She nodded. "It takes a lot of hate to do something like that to someone."

"If it's Reese, and if he was stolen, there are a lot of reasons for it. You're assuming *you* were targeted," he said. "There is still me. What if somebody knew I was the father?"

Startled, she stared at him. "I hadn't considered that."

"So you admit it?"

"Admit what? You're Reese's father? Yes, you're his father. I can't believe you would suspect I'd had a relationship so soon after you walked away." She shook her head. "I was so incapable of having another relationship after you left. No way you did not know."

"I think I knew when I found out what happened at the hospital, but what could I say? I hid my grief under a blanket of denial." His voice hardened. "I would have very much liked to have known about Reese before he was born. I only left because you pushed me away."

"Except you stayed away," she snapped. At the uncomfortable silence that followed, she added in a softer tone, "Well, that time has come and gone, but, if we find Reese, we can both have him back."

He looked at her for a long moment, then nodded. "I'll start delving into that."

"Don't start," she said. "Get that damn investigation ended. That little boy is in danger. Whether he's ours or someone else's doesn't matter. He needs our help."

"I could use some assistance," he said, holding out his hand.

Something much more significant than just asking for her help was in that extended hand. She wasn't sure what it meant, but she'd do anything to get her son back, and, if Kirk needed her hand, then she was all his.

She reached out and clasped his hand. "Just find him," she urged. "And find the asshole who did this to us."

He nodded. "As long as you remember it might not be Reese. I don't want to raise too many alarms at this point. Not only does everybody think I'm much better off without you beside me, I don't want them thinking I've gone down the same mental path you traveled all those years ago."

"You mean, the one where I thought my son was alive, and yet all the rest of you were busy telling me how he was dead, and I needed to stop being so unbalanced about it?" she asked drily.

He had the grace to flush. But he gave a quick nod and

said, "I still trust you. But I can't guarantee, at the end of the day, that the little boy you're talking about is our blood. Neither can I guarantee that whoever it is you were talking to was not a ghost."

She smiled. "Haven't you realized there are no guarantees in anything?"

"SPIDERS MAKING A blanket," David said to himself in wonder as he studied her world.

He really enjoyed this opening into her life. It had become a huge source of amusement for him. It had also helped develop his hobby further. It was almost too boring now. It was pretty easy to make anyone do what he wanted them to do. It used to be exciting and thrilling but not any longer. There was just something freeing about it all.

But watching her, seeing those spiders, that amazed him. It was like she'd gone into some sort of psychic trance. He'd watched her body jerk as she did something. Then he saw energy around her, but he couldn't see what had happened.

"I'll do some research on that spider thing," he said, "because that's beyond cool."

It also amazed him that it was something she was involved in. Didn't all women hate spiders?

"Obviously she's different," he said.

He sat back and thought about what her weird jerking meant.

"Was she getting visions from them? Were they healing her? What the hell's going on there?"

The longer he thought about it, the more it bothered him. He wasn't the kind of person to leave any rock unturned. And, as far as this woman—Queenie—was concerned, she was the first person he could actually communicate with. The first one he could talk to and brag to. His work was very stressful, but he was very good at it. But the reason he was good was because this hobby of his allowed him to connect to other people on a very different level. It put him back in control. And that was something so many people didn't have anymore.

He returned to studying Queenie, but the curtains into her life were closed. He stared and tried to rip the curtains wide open. But instead they snapped shut again. Getting angry, he tried harder, but there was no help for it. She had erected some wall between them. And all it did was make him madder. He closed his eyes, reached out with his mind and firmly pulled the curtains back. And this time it gave. He crowed. "See? I'm a hell of a lot stronger than you are."

And then he stared. Because, although his curtains had opened, she had closed curtains on her side. And he knew, even as he tried over and over again, that somehow she had found a way to block him out of her life.

Well, she might have won this one. But no way in hell would she win the next one. He'd make damn sure of that.

STEFAN, DID YOU find anything more about the poisoner? Maddy asked.

Isn't that a question for you? he said humorously.

You were going to talk to Kirk about it.

Things have blown up in Kirk's world. I haven't had a chance to mention the poison to him, Stefan admitted. *And I should have, but I didn't even think of it.*

Tell me, she demanded.

He quickly updated Dr. Maddy.

Maddy gave a soft cluck of sympathy. *I don't think there could be any nightmare more horrifying for a mother.*

I did try to reinforce her umbrella. She's letting me add energy to it. But I haven't been able to get through. And that's why I'm trying to figure out just what this guy does to see into her world, whether she likes it or not.

It's got to be somebody close to her, Maddy insisted. *You know as well as I do that somebody with that ability is generally a close friend or lover.*

Unless it's one of the people she's helped, remember? Stefan said. *She's dealt with hundreds and hundreds of people in the last few years alone. And that's saying something. But any one of them could have used that as an entranceway into her space. As she's getting flashes of insight into their world, they could have opened a door into hers.*

But to keep something like that open, to keep the connection so strong, Maddy said, *takes more than just a passing touch.*

Stefan nodded. *We haven't figured it all out yet, but we will.*

Of course you will, Dr. Maddy said, chuckling. *But how about we get to it before all hell breaks loose, and people end up dead or dying?*

Stefan's voice was light, but an undercurrent of worry was beneath it. *I think it's already too late. I think this guy is not only a killer but has been doing this for a very long time.*

Then we need to catch him, don't we? Maddy said lightly. *After all, it's what we do.*

At that, Stefan could only nod. As much as it wasn't what he had planned to do with his life, it was what he'd ended up doing. And when the world gave you a job to do, you stepped up, and you did the best you could. In this case, he was scared it wouldn't be enough.

CHAPTER 15

Sunday, Afternoon …

THEY WALKED INTO the meeting about the amusement park ten minutes late. Queenie was tired, yet energized. And, as much as she wanted to look for the little boy, she felt she needed to be here for her friends. She was greeted with a round of cheers, and, when they saw Kirk, there were even more cheers. Kirk and Queenie automatically stepped to the front of the crowd, where Kirk gave them an update on Carlos.

"He's being held for fraud, embezzlement and we're looking into the multiple B&Es," Kirk said. "Chances are he won't be back anytime soon."

"Can we talk to him?" Brutus asked. "We don't know anything about his agreement with the amusement park."

Kirk nodded. "It's possible you might be allowed to see him. We could take one or two of you, but that would be about all."

Everybody turned to Brutus. He shoved his hands in his pockets and nodded. "I think it should be me and Queenie."

There was a murmur from the crowd as they all agreed.

Queenie shrugged. "I don't think Carlos will be happy to see me," she warned. "That might make him very uncooperative."

"But you're the one who blew this all up in his face, and

you might have a solution to our problem."

She shook her head. "I'm not at all sure I understand what the problem is."

"We don't want the amusement park to close." Jimbo's voice was loud and rumbled across the crowd.

She studied him. "Then run it yourselves. I'm sure there's paperwork in his office as to an agreement. Talk to the person who owns the property and see what kind of a deal they might make."

There was head nodding and a round of clapping. She held up a hand. "This still isn't for me to do though. I'm not staying. I'm setting up my own business with a nice website, the whole works. But I will help you guys any way I can."

"The first place to start would be to find the paperwork in his office," Kirk said. "Carlos would have had a lease on the land, and that's what you're looking for. Find out when it renews, what the payments are due, and then get your rides and booths back up and running."

"But what about payments of the lease and other expenses, plus the profits? How do we split that?"

Kirk suggested they hire a business consultant to make sure they had an agreement everybody was happy with. "You don't have to get fancy. You don't have to keep paying somebody to do that for you. You just have to find a way that's fair. Something like, a certain amount of money goes into a pot to run the machinery and to pay for the lease, and a certain amount of money goes to payroll. You set aside money for regular maintenance. But, other than that, you should be pulling your regular wages and enough money to keep the place going. Because if it isn't working like that, then what the hell has Carlos been doing for these last few years, and who's been paying the bills?"

Betty spoke up. "I don't know what arrangement the property owners might want, but if they give us even a year's trial, I think we can make a good deal out of this."

"I have no doubt you can," Queenie said warmly. "You're very business oriented too. Maybe you should take over the books, make them transparent so everybody can come in at any time and ask you just what the expenditures are. If you've got them online, then you can put them in a cloud storage to make sure everyone buying into this program sees what they need to see. Stop this secretive stuff. I don't know all the crap that Carlos pulled on us," Queenie said. "But, if you're upfront and honest, I think you can all make a really good go of it."

Cheers broke out again.

KIRK WAS AMAZED and delighted with the way everybody stood up and cheered Queenie on. As they walked out over an hour later, he said, "You've really created a family for yourself there, haven't you?"

She chuckled. "It was a rough couple years. I was a bit of an orphan at the time I joined in. They were the ones who welcomed me into their homes. I have a lot to be grateful for."

"Are you still leaving?"

She nodded. "Oh, yes. My time here is done." She laughed. "Listen to me. I sound like some odd-ball psychic reader."

"And is it your abilities telling you that you're done here?"

She shook her head. "I almost never get any information about myself. You know that."

"I always wondered about that. Because there certainly is a lot you could benefit from with your own skills. What kind of a curse is it that you can help others but not yourself?"

She chuckled. "I often wondered that myself."

"You're stuck on doing your website?"

At his phrasing, she turned to look at him. "I'm not stuck on it. I think it's a way forward."

He stayed quiet, a little perturbed at the idea of somebody with her talents selling herself on a website, but then it was the way of the world today. "At least it might help get the word out so you can charge decently," he muttered.

"I should have been charging the police department the whole time," she said. "At least then I would have had a job, and I would have had something of my own when you left."

He winced. "I didn't fully leave, you know?"

"Yes, you did," she said smoothly. "Mentally, emotionally and physically. That means you left."

"Not energetically."

She turned to look at him. "So you're aware of that tunnel between us?"

"Of course. We talked about it before."

"Until you closed the doors on your end."

"I did that a lot anyway. Sometimes, when you're having a hard time, or when you're on a case, I would get this really weird buzz in my head. I had to mentally close the door in order to keep doing what I was doing."

She nodded thoughtfully. "So how do you think it felt to know that door was permanently closed?"

"I didn't say anything was permanent," he protested.

"No, maybe not," she said, "but, at the same time, you never opened it again."

"I tried," he admitted. "But every time I did, it didn't

seem to make any difference."

She stayed quiet for a long moment. "I guess it would depend on when you tried," she said. "After Reese was born, I kept the door locked."

He gave a groan. "Of course you did. Anything to keep me away from my son."

"You'd moved on," she said. "My life had changed. I couldn't give you what you wanted anymore, and I had what I wanted, which was my son."

He could feel the same anger boil up inside him. "He was my son too."

"He was," she said smoothly. "And, when we get him back, we can both spend some time with him."

"Or you'll try to take him away from me again. And re-member, we can't know for sure who this little boy is," he snapped. "You're making me crazy."

"I never moved anywhere," she said. "I'm still in the same part of town."

"I paid the lease on the house for the rest of that year."

"But you moved out with all your furniture."

"No, I didn't." He stopped at the car and turned to look at her. "I left everything. I just took my personal belong-ings."

She frowned. "What do you mean, you paid the lease? I was told I had until the end of the month. It was the twenty-fifth as it was. I had days to vacate."

He stared at her. "No, I paid for the rest of that year." He frowned, trying to figure out what could have gone wrong. "It's been a long time," he admitted. "I'm pretty damn sure I gave you six months with a paid roof over your head."

"Well, I got a letter in the mailbox the next day, saying I

had less than a week to get out."

He shook his head slowly. "That's not right."

"That's what I said at the time too." She gave an angry laugh. "I found out about a couple months after we split up that I was pregnant. And that's when I realized I'd been working for the police department and for you for all those years with no money to my name. How much of our money should have been mine?"

He stared at her in surprise. "What money?"

She frowned. "You had a savings account. I didn't."

He nodded. "And I left you half of it."

She stared at him, completely blindsided apparently.

"Did you even try to access the bank account?"

She nodded. "Of course I did."

"I left you twenty grand in there. I figured you walked away with it, not wanting anything more to do with me," he cried out. "How do you think I felt when I came back to the house only to find you'd moved out right away? And when I went to access the bank account, it had been changed. I figured you had the money, but I didn't know why you were living the way you were living. I really didn't know how you were living until I saw you at the hospital."

"I was living the way I was living because I didn't have access to any money, much less twenty grand. And I was told to get out of the apartment within five days of your leaving." She couldn't keep the shock off her face or out of her voice. Just the thought of what that money could have done for her and Reese …

He shook his head. "Something is definitely wrong. And, if you didn't take that money, where is it?"

She stared at him. "Who handled your banking?"

He shoved his fists into his pockets. "I did. You know

that."

"Not all the time. When we were buried on a case, or if you had to go away, which was often, you got other people to take care of some things. Your family, for instance."

"Sure, my family sometimes might have had access. But I haven't let them have access in a long time."

"But back then you did." She gave a bitter smile. "Your sister?"

"My sister would never do that." But a note of doubt was in his voice.

"Your sister is a bitch. You and I both know that. If she had a chance to screw me over, she would have in a heartbeat."

"But not to steal from me," he said. "She'd never do that."

"Maybe she would. Maybe she wouldn't. I don't know," Queenie said. "But when I think back to what that twenty grand would have done for keeping me healthy and keeping your son healthy …" She shook her head. "That just pisses me right off."

"Not to mention, where is that twenty grand now?" He tried to think back five, six years, but it was such a jumble. There had been so much pain at the time. "I'll have to check my records," he said quietly, "and see what happened."

"It doesn't matter what happened. As far as I'm concerned, your family is behind it."

"That was always your answer," he said. "But it doesn't mean it's the truth."

She waved her hand at him. "Can I get you to drive me back home please?"

He nodded, unlocked the door so she could get into his car. When they were inside, buckled up, he said, "What are you doing this afternoon?"

"A thousand-plus spiders are in my living room. My priority right now is finding my son. All my friends at the amusement park have a path forward. I need to research these spiders and figure out where they came from."

"And I need to visit the hospital and figure out what happened when you were admitted."

"That would be nice," she said bitterly. "Because I sure as hell didn't do anything wrong. We have to find Reese."

"You can't get any images from here? Do you want to speak with your doctor?"

She thought about it for a long moment, her head tilted to the side as she studied him. "I think that's probably a good idea. But not yet. I need to know what questions to ask him first. If I go in there right now, he'll just see me as the same crazy woman so grief-stricken that she still doesn't make any sense. I can't have that happen again."

"Understood." He drove her to her apartment. "It sounds like we have a lot to make up for."

"No, we don't. Our history is over. You can't ever go back." Her voice was calm but very definite.

"True, but we're past that already. It's time to move forward."

"I wonder if we can," she said, her voice suddenly very, very tired.

Just when he was about to pull into her apartment parking lot, she bolted upright.

He glanced over at her. "What's wrong?"

"I'm not sure," she said quietly. "But something … something is off."

"In what way?"

She shook her head. As soon as he brought the vehicle to

a halt, she raced out and up to her apartment. He wasn't far behind. She unlocked the door and ran into her living room, Kirk still following. They both stopped.

Not only were the same spiders still here, but now there were one hundred times more.

He shut the door behind him and stared at the walls that were alive. He had to admit it was a pretty creepy feeling. He turned to look at her. Instead of being shocked or frightened, she was enthralled.

"They're still coming. He's sending out more and more for me."

"Well then, it's time you contact our son and figure out how to send signals back," he said. "Because these spiders can't just keep coming. At some point somebody will notice, and then the shit will hit the fan."

"They'll kill them, won't they?"

He nodded. "They so will."

She shook her head. "They can't be allowed to."

"Because each one might know a little bit about our son?" he said. "You have to get past that. You have to contact them and tell them to lead you back to him."

She stared at him for a long moment, then dropped to sit cross-legged on the floor. Before he could say anything, she cried out, "Stefan, help me."

STEFAN HEARD HER calling, but he was painting. He kept putting up a block to hold her back until he could finish the work. That was one thing about creativity in art; when he was in the mood, he had to release it fully and let it go. He couldn't paint when he wasn't in the mood. When he was in the mood, he had to honor it.

He stroked along the top of the canvas and over on the left. He wasn't sure what he was painting, but it was important. The strokes slashed and burned across his canvas. Reds, blacks, greens. His arm was in charge.

Wait a minute, he said firmly.

He could sense the waves of her emotions coming toward him. When people became so emotional that words failed them, their emotions came on stronger and stronger.

Finally his arm dropped to his side. With a heavy sigh he straightened his back, put down his palette, walked to the sink, rinsed his brush and then his hands. As soon as he had cleaned up, he stretched for a few moments and walked out of his studio without even looking at the painting. It wasn't going anywhere, and it wouldn't change until he came back and did more to it. He knew instinctively it wasn't done. He also had no clue what was happening with his painting.

He walked out in the kitchen, made himself a cup of tea, deliberately making Queenie wait. There wasn't a sense of urgency as much as there was anger and frustration. With his tea steeping, he walked to the center of his meditation room, placed his tray down on the small table and sank down on a cushion. *Now what is it?*

Thousands of spiders are in my apartment.

She was calmer, as if the extra few minutes he'd required had helped her to quiet down, knowing he was coming.

How do I stop them? Somebody will notice, and they will all be killed.

He thought about that for a long moment and said, *That's quite possible, yes. Maybe tell them all to go back to the little boy. At least that way we might have a chance of finding a house that's overwhelmed with spiders.*

But they could get killed that way too.

You aren't going to save them all, he said gently. *Tell them to return to the little boy and to protect him.*

That little boy is my son. Her voice was hard, determined.

Stefan worried on that for a long moment, then finally said, *Did you find a way to identify where he is?*

I couldn't see a street sign. I couldn't even see the outside of the house properly. I kept getting sucked back into the tunnel.

I know how that is, he said with feeling. *I've been there several times.*

There's got to be some way to track him down.

Is Kirk helping?

Yes, he dropped me off. I told him to leave. Then I tried to contact you.

I suggest you send out another wave of love and tell them all to go home, that you got the message.

I don't think it's enough. I think the second wave came with a new message.

What message? he asked sharply.

I think he's in trouble. I think he's in danger, she cried out. *I tried to open up the connection, but I can't.*

What kind of connection? Describe it.

Like a tunnel with a door at either end, she said. *There's just a wall on the other side. I figured that was proof he had died. But now I'm looking closer, and the wall is blocks, like somebody has bricked it up.*

Can you knock down the bricks?

I haven't tried. Will that hurt him? she asked hesitantly.

Stefan thought about it for a long moment. *I can't say definitively that it won't hurt him because I don't know how much of his energy is connected to that brick wall. But I think you have to get through it somehow. So maybe instead of trying to use force, use love.*

How do I do that?

Stefan reached up and pinched his nose. *It's different for everyone. What really matters is the space you're in when you attempt to do it. Come from a position of love and ask for the wall to disappear. For all you know, it will just dissolve in front of you.*

I won't be so lucky, she said sadly. *I've never been that lucky.*

Don't sell yourself short, he said. *You're very talented. And so is your son. If he understands you're on the other side, he's likely to blast through it himself.*

Could somebody else have put that wall there?

I haven't heard of it happening, but I'm not going to say no. If somebody understood you two were connected on a psychic wavelength, they would do anything they could to break it. Did you see any sign of his adoptive family?

No, I haven't.

You might want to revisit that house. Tell your son that you're coming for him. Give him some reassurance he's not alone and you're there for him. And tell him to open the door.

There was a sudden *snick* in the conversation. She'd shut it down. He sat there frowning for a long moment before he reached out and poured his tea. *Maddy, are you there?*

Her voice was hurried, busy, as she responded, *Always. What's up?*

He filled her in on Queenie's situation.

Interesting, she said. *I've got to tell you. I've also been checking on Brian Callahan. I feel there's something very bizarre going on.*

What do you mean?

He was definitely being poisoned. His health is improving now. I think we can pull him through it, as long as we keep the poison away.

Can you tell who poisoned him?

I thought for sure it'd be somebody at work. But, when I checked in on him this morning, the poison is back again.

But he is only there with his wife and daughter, right?

Exactly, Maddy said, her throat clogged with tears. *But I swear to God, I would have bet my reputation, everything I know, that it wasn't either of them.*

It's possible it isn't either of them, Stefan said slowly, not liking the direction of his thoughts.

I don't see how it can be anybody else.

I'll get back to you. He had a very good idea of how this was happening. But, if that were the case, how many others were involved in something like this?

Needing to know Queenie was okay, he opened a quick window into her world and stepped into her living room. He paused in amazement, seeing the thousands of spiders clinging to the walls, ceilings, furniture and floor. They were all over her apartment, moving, shifting, and yet she sat cross-legged in the middle of the floor. He could see her silver cord as she traveled a long way away.

Making an instant decision, he dove down into the sheath around her cord and followed it as far and as fast as he could. If she couldn't pick up something, maybe he could. There had to be one problem they could solve, and, for all he knew, maybe both problems were connected.

WHAT THE HELL was she up to now? David frowned, staring at the apartment. He hadn't been able to leave her alone. He'd been checking in on her constantly today. Something was moving in her world, and he didn't get it. He kept blinking as if something in his vision stopped him from seeing what he should be seeing. He didn't like it. He hated it when other people could do things he couldn't do. He stared as she sat on the living room floor, completely surrounded in something that shifted and moved, and he wondered what he'd done. Was he adapting his skills to seeing something *inside* her body? He couldn't figure it out. Getting a headache, he pulled back, until he thought he saw something else. He zoomed in to see her holding a small picture in her hand.

He twisted around to see what it was. When he recognized the image, he said, "Well, well, well. Now this will get very interesting."

And chuckling softly to himself, he pulled back into his world. He hadn't expected this to happen. But this was good. This was really good. Now to see if he could screw up a few more lives.

CHAPTER 16

Sunday, Late Afternoon …

QUEENIE WAS TRYING to hold her energy just outside the house. But every time she blinked and tried to focus, the house wavered in front of her. It was two stories tall with a peaked roof and had a veranda on the front of it. There were a million houses like this one all over the world. But this one she kept coming back to.

She turned to look behind her to see if either of the other houses were exceptional in any way. They both had the same dilapidated look to them. But this one, across the street, she swore was the one she'd been in before. Moving as slowly as she could, she drifted closer. She didn't even know what form she was in. She thought she was in the middle of a vision, yet she was directing this one, and that had never happened before. Normally she was carried by the vision instead. And she also had a sense of not being alone, and that was freaky. She wasn't sure if it was David, the Watcher guy, who could see into her world, because, if he could see into this, everything she knew was being blown right out of the water.

Was that because Reese was here? She slipped up to the edge of the wall. No house numbers were on the building, and that frustrated her. If she had an address, she could track him down. Knowing her time here was very short, she moved around the house, looking for anything to see if it was her son's prison.

The door opened suddenly, and a stranger stepped out. Big and blustery, but she'd never seen him before. "Maggie, come on. Let's go," he roared.

"I'm coming. I'm coming." A frumpy middle-aged woman stepped up beside him. "What about the boy?"

"Leave him. It'll do him some good."

Maggie chewed on her bottom lip. "He's been sickly," she argued. "I don't think we should leave him that long."

The big man grabbed her arm and tugged her toward the garage. "We aren't going to be long. Just a couple hours."

But the woman protested as he tried to drag her unhappily in the direction he wanted to go. "You said that last time, and we stayed out overnight."

"So what? The kid should grow up strong."

"He's just a baby," Maggie protested.

But the big man squeezed her arm until she cried out in pain. "I don't care how old he is," he growled. "The kid's a pain in the ass."

"He is not," Maggie said quietly.

"Ha. Don't you start turning all high and mighty on me now. You're responsible for that kid being as much of a loser as you are."

Queenie lost the sound of their voices as she stepped through the open door before Maggie had shut it behind her. Once inside, she drifted through the upstairs of the house, searching, and then she headed to the basement. She had to go under the crack in the door and downstairs, and, sure enough, there was the little boy. She had no proof, but she couldn't stop thinking it was Reese curled up on that bad. But he wasn't sleeping. She drifted toward him and wrapped her arms around him. Against his ear, she whispered, *It's me, honey. It's Mommy.*

He opened his eyes and looked around, sniffling slightly. *Are you here to save me?*

I'm here to find out where you are. Do you know your address? Do you know your phone number? Is there anything that will help me find you?

No. He sat up and looked around. *I can't see you.*

She squeezed him with all her might.

He smiled and laughed. *That tickles. I don't want to be here no more,* he said. *Can you take me home?*

We're working on it, she promised. *You stay positive and don't let them know anything about us, okay?*

He waved his hand. *I won't.*

Do you know what school you go to?

He shook his head unhappily. *They said I couldn't go to school yet.*

She looked around, frantic for any sign of where he was. *Do you know a doctor you've gone to see? Or a store you've been in? A mall?*

Milestone Mall, he called out happily.

She could feel her energy dissipating, sucking backward in time. She called out, *I'll be back, this time with help.*

He cried out, "Mommy." And then he burst into tears and collapsed back down.

That was the last sight she saw. She slammed back into her body. As soon as she opened her eyes to her living room, she burst into tears herself. She snatched her phone and called Kirk.

"Milestone Mall. He said he's been to Milestone Mall. I have an image of the house, but there's no house number, and I couldn't see a street sign. Somebody named Maggie lives there. Her husband or partner is a big blustery man, and he hurt her when she didn't want to leave Reese home alone."

She knew her rambling words were fast and atop themselves, but she couldn't help herself. As she shook all over, she realized the spiders were wrapping around her tighter and tighter again, holding her close. She took several deep breaths, trying to calm down. The more upset she became, the more agitated the spiders became.

To the empty room around her, she whispered, "I'm all right. Thank you. I'm all right."

A warm pinkish-lavender breeze wafted around her, bringing a smile to her heart and to her lips.

"Who are you talking to?" Kirk snapped in her ear.

She gave him a soft chuckle. "The spiders. They understood how upset I was. They've wrapped around me again like a blanket, but it's like a metal jacket, and I can hardly move."

"Jesus," he breathed out. "I'm doing a search for Milestone Mall. There's one just out of town."

She washed the spiders in a loving rain until they relaxed. Moving slowly she got to her feet, the spiders forming and reforming around her. "Where? Where is it?"

"Calm down. I'm figuring out what we've got here. We're also doing a house search for somebody named Maggie."

"That doesn't matter," she said. "Maggie could be Margaret. It could be any number of iterations, and, because of the type of guy he is, I wouldn't be at all surprised if her name wasn't even on the deed."

"Or they could be renting," he said. "It would take us days to drive up and down all those roads, looking for him.

Did you see the car?"

She thought about it. "No. When they went into the garage, I went down to see Reese."

"Milestone Mall is a small mall within Snohomish County," he said. "Just a little strip mall on the outskirts."

"Well, he's not very far away from that," she said in excitement. "There's got to be a way to find him."

"There will be, but that doesn't mean it'll be easy," he said.

"I don't care how easy it is. I'm leaving now, and I'll drive around the area. If I come across that house, I'm going in after him."

"Wait! I don't want you going alone."

She snorted. "You need to find out what happened to him at the hospital."

"No, stop. We can't know it's our son. We need to find this little boy now—no matter whose son he is. Sorting out what happened to him when he was little can be handled afterward. But we have to save him."

She took a deep breath. "You're right. I'm sorry. I'm not thinking clearly."

"I'll pick you up in ten." And he hung up.

She hugged the phone to her chest. Dear God, Reese was out there. He was actually alive …

Just then the Watcher's voice, David's voice, filled her living room. "What are you looking for?" He sounded almost like he was chewing gum and mocking her at the same time.

She stiffened. Since he was talking out loud to her, she would too. "David, how come you keep bothering me?" How could he still communicate with her? She swore she'd put up enough defenses to keep him out.

He chuckled.

She must have let her disgust show.

"Why do you keep blocking me? What are you hiding?"

"It's my personal life. I don't really feel comfortable with you coming in unannounced." She groaned. "And, if I did put up some defenses, it doesn't look like they worked."

"Nope, sure didn't," he said cheerfully. "But then, I'm way better at this than you are."

"Lots of practice, huh?"

"Lots and lots of practice. It got boring there for a while, so I had to switch it up. And it took a lot to even do that. But now it's amazing. I can do anything I want." His tone turned smug. "Of course that's not what you wanted to hear."

"Which is why you came because you know you can tell me anything, and, since I don't know who you are, I can't tattle."

He laughed, big rolling waves of laughter. "Exactly. But then I haven't even told you much, have I?"

"No. I know you had something to do with the lady in the lake, but I don't know how or in what way."

"That's too bad because honestly I'd hoped for more from you. Although I haven't killed any of these people, I've been responsible for about thirty different deaths."

Her heart froze. "Thirty of them," she whispered, trying to make it sound like she was in awe, whereas she was just plain in shock.

"Yep. And none of them died by my own hand. I've often wondered if I *could* kill on my own." The contemplative tone made her want to throw up.

She tried to sort out what he was saying, but it made no sense. "Anytime you want to tell me the details, I'd be willing to listen," she said, quietly wanting to vomit at the same time trying to shield her thoughts from David.

He laughed. "But then you might figure out what cases I'm talking about and learn who I am. I can't have that."

"I don't know any of these people, so I highly doubt I could track anything," she said. "But, if you're afraid, that's fine."

"I'm not afraid," he snapped, his surly tone giving her an idea about how short-tempered he was.

She'd raced around, going to the bathroom, tying up her hair, grabbing her sweater and purse, and now she was standing at the window, looking outside, waiting for Kirk. "Good. Besides, I don't have time. I have to leave right now," she said.

"Why is that?"

Immediately the temper seemed to be gone as if a new topic had changed his interest, almost like he was a child. "My boyfriend is picking me up."

There was silence on the other end. "Does your boyfriend have abilities?"

"No," she admitted. "He doesn't." Well, not exactly.

"Aren't you tired of always dealing with people who are less than you?"

She thought about that for a moment and how he obviously felt. "You've never found anybody, have you?"

"Not like me, no."

"I'm sorry," she said. "That must be very lonely."

"Yes, it is."

"But I know you don't want anything to do with me," she said on a laugh. "I'm a mess."

He chuckled. "Besides, you're not even close to my skill level," he said with a jeer. "Go off with your little humanoid pet and have fun. We'll talk again later." And just like that, he disappeared.

It was a weird session today with him. As if he could see her and yet couldn't see her. It didn't make any sense. But, with those thoughts, she watched as Kirk arrived at her place in his car. She stepped out, locked the door and realized something important had been divulged in that conversation she had just had with the asshole. But being so focused on her son, she hadn't caught what it was. Yet it was important.

THEY DROVE INTO Milestone Mall forty minutes later. He'd used his GPS to get there the fastest route possible, then had pushed the speed limit the whole way. There was a coffee shop, a Laundromat, a little corner store that looked like a five-and-dime. At the one end was a gas station.

Queenie hopped out and walked around the mall.

"What are you doing?"

She shrugged. "I'm trying to feel him. To see what direction to go."

"Okay. I'll stand here and make sure we don't look completely strange," he said drily.

"I don't give a shit how I look," she said. "Don't you understand this could mean our son is alive?"

He could feel the smile falling off his face. "I don't know what it means because we don't know anything. And I don't have a personality to remember, to hold close and to hope that this is him. Because I never had a chance to meet him, and, as soon as I did hear about him, it was to find out he'd died. *You* say he's here, but I don't have any physical proof of that."

She gave him a long assessing look and then nodded. "Fair enough." She walked to the corner by a tree, leaned against the trunk, bowed her head and closed her eyes.

He'd worked on over sixty cases with her, and yet he never found a level of comfort with her process as her methodology always changed. Sometimes she would open her hand. Sometimes she would lean against a tree. Sometimes she would touch something or someone. He never understood. Often he wished he could, but they were so busy all the time, he'd always pushed it off instead of trying to sort it out.

It was almost as if she were making things up as she went. Yet it always worked. Usually.

He watched and waited. It was late in the afternoon, but they still had hours of daylight. He had printed off a map of the area, but they had few details to go on. Finally she straightened and walked back to him. But there was no serene knowing on her face. There was nothing.

She pointed behind her and said, "My best guess would be out there."

"Why is that?"

She glanced at the pavement and kicked a rock. "I don't know."

"You didn't used to be so indecisive."

"I care too much," she said softly. Too softly. "Remember what happens when I care too much?"

His gut twisted because, of course, that's what had happened on their last case. She'd pointed in one direction, and the victim was in another.

"Then I suggest we take a look in that direction. One direction is as good as any other." He glanced at the stores. "Do you want to ask anyone?"

She shook her head. "I couldn't begin to describe the house any better than a normal, you know, standard house that I've seen time and time again."

"What about the partners?"

She frowned and then nodded. "Maybe I'll go into the Laundromat and see." She walked into the Laundromat ahead of him. He frowned and chose the corner store. There he stepped in and talked to the retail clerk, asking if he knew of a couple who lived close by, where the wife was more timid, possibly abused, with a big florid-faced man, who had a little boy, but the clerk might not see the little boy very often.

The clerk just looked at him as if he was nuts.

When Kirk flashed his badge, the kid calmed down and shrugged.

"No, I don't recognize anyone with that description."

"Do you know any little boys around here?"

The kid shook his head. "Nah. You could check at the school though."

Kirk nodded and walked over to the five-and-dime store. It was about ready to close. He stepped inside, pulled out his badge and asked the owner if he knew of any families with a little five-year-old boy and gave a brief description of what he had of the parents.

The older man looked at him and frowned. "I'm not sure. We got a couple like that. It's not a great area in some ways, at least not if you head to the north."

"Does that ring a bell at all?"

The man drummed his fingers on the table as if thinking. He nodded. "That almost describes Ben. I can't remember what his wife's name is though." He turned to the back room. "Hey, Flo. What's Ben's wife's name?"

"Maggie," Flo said, bustling toward him. She wore a huge apron over her dress, a big duster in her hand. She beamed up at Kirk. "Maggie's a lovely lady."

"Do they have a young boy?"

Flo nodded. "It's not theirs though. Maggie's sister adopted him. I don't know what happened, but Maggie ended up with custody."

Kirk wondered about the term *custody*. It was often used very loosely for people who had children but didn't have the rights to keep them. "Any idea where I could find her?"

"She lives up on Miles Road, maybe ten, twenty minutes out of town."

He nodded and smiled. "Thank you very much." As he turned to leave, so they could lock the door behind him, he said, "Do you know where either of them work?"

"Ben is a trucker, but he's out of work on account of his bad back," the man said. "Maggie, I'm not sure what she does." He turned to look at Flo.

Flo shrugged. "I think she cleans houses. At least she used to when she lived in the city, but now that she's here, I don't know that there's much call for it."

Kirk smiled, thanked them again and left.

Outside he watched as Queenie walked through a flower bed at the north end of the mall. A line of spiders headed out in front and behind her and turned toward the corner of the street.

He strode with purpose to her side. "It's okay. I know they live on Miles Road. About fifteen minutes up the way."

She turned to look at him and said, "Did somebody recognize the couple?"

He nodded with a smile and told her what the store clerks had said. Back in the car, he pulled out, taking the road the spiders had pointed out. "Are you talking to spiders now?"

"Not really. But it's like they seem to know Reese is out there."

He took the turn onto Miles Road and gave the car as much gas as he dared. The road was full of potholes and definitely not the liveliest of areas. They drove for a good five minutes, but they'd yet to pass any houses.

She frowned, but he kept going until they saw a couple houses up ahead. He pointed and said, "Do those look familiar?"

She shook her head.

They drove a little slower until he came to a few more houses.

"Wait! That one!" she cried out in excitement.

He was hard-pressed to bring the vehicle to a stop before she was already out the door. "Stop!" he said in a harsh whisper.

She did and turned to look at him.

"You can't just barrel into somebody else's house looking for a child you don't know."

Her frown was instant.

He shook his head. "Hell no. We do this properly."

She raised her eyebrows. "What the hell is *proper* in this instance?" Her words were bitter. "Nobody was there to help me when I was in the hospital, when somebody stole my child."

He didn't dare answer that. Instead he tucked her hand into his and said, "I'm the cop. You let me talk to them."

She stared the house. "They're not here."

He frowned at her. "We'll check."

They walked up to the front door and knocked. Sure enough, nobody answered. He walked to the garage to find the big door open and no vehicle inside. It was as she had said; they had left in the car. Possibly only gone for a few hours, which meant they could get back at any time. Or they could have come home and left again. Or they wouldn't be back for a while.

He turned and walked to the back of the house. He left Queenie on the front step to keep watch, but he couldn't count on her not bolting into the house, even though he'd warned her. He knocked on the rear kitchen door, and the door opened under his fingers. He stepped forward and called out, "Hello, anyone home?"

He thought he heard a faint voice. He walked through to the front door, still calling out. He opened it and let Queenie in. "We have no right to be here," he said.

"Sure we do," she said, heading for the stairs to the basement. "I heard a child screaming." She raced downstairs. He followed behind into a room. She stopped and cried out. He stepped in front of her, and there was the room she had described and the bed. But nobody was on it.

"The little boy is not here."

She shook her head in dismay.

He reached out and pulled her close. "That doesn't mean he's gone."

She continued to shake her head, but she seemed unable to speak.

He did a quick search of the rest of the house and then moved her back outside and seated her in the car with the door open while he thought about what their options were.

"You might not have seen them come back and pick up the little boy and leave again."

She nodded.

But he could see she wasn't convinced. "Any chance that vision happened a long time ago?"

She raised huge eyes to him. "Don't tell me that he's dead," she said. "I won't believe you."

"I know that, but are you sure the vision you saw today when you followed the spiders was current?"

She frowned. "I can't say anything for sure. But I wasn't alone. I know that."

"What do you mean, you weren't alone? Are you saying this asshole who looks into your world was there?"

She shook her head. "No, I'm not sure what I'm saying. All I can say is, I felt someone else was there."

"Who else would have the skill to keep track of what you were doing?"

"Stefan," she said. Mentally she called out to him but found only an emptiness.

"What do you want to do now?" Kirk asked.

"Wait here," she said.

"We can't just sit here all night."

"We hardly have a choice. I know he lives here."

"If we can be sure they live here, we can backtrack to see how they ended up with this little boy. I want you to stay here and keep watch. I'll look for something with their last name. Like a utility bill or something. Okay?"

She nodded.

He strode back inside, checked the kitchen table and in the junk drawers. Off to one side of the counters was a stack of papers. He pulled them toward him. Ben and Maggie Freeman.

So the little boy could have belonged to Maggie Freeman's sister. He used his phone and took a picture of both documents. Then, as he stepped out the door, a vehicle drove slowly toward them. He stepped back, away from view again, but it was too late. The car gunned past and ripped up the road.

Swearing softly, he raced to his car and said, "I didn't consider that." He jumped inside the vehicle and started it up.

Queenie buckled her seat belt as she said, "What's wrong? What's wrong?"

He hit the gas. "It never occurred to me Ben might have a good reason for not wanting to see a cop here. I was standing on the front porch when he pulled up. He took off as soon as he saw me."

"How many were in the vehicle?"

He shook his head. "I only saw two."

She gave a small cry and clasped her hand over her mouth.

He drove hard and fast for a good ten minutes as they looked for the car, checking each side road for it. But there was nothing. A half hour later, he was still swearing. "I don't know where they could have gone." He did a quick U-turn and drove the car back outside the house again. "I'm not sure what to do now," he admitted.

"I don't want to leave," she said. "It's the only connection I have to our son."

"I'll talk to the neighbors." He parked in front of a neighbor's house. "Again I want you to stay here."

She nodded. "There's nothing good about those people. That little boy has a terrible life."

He walked up to the first house but got no answer. At the second house, a little old lady answered. She smiled up at him, and he asked her about the neighbors across the street.

She shook her head. "We don't talk," she said. "That's the way I like it. He's trouble. Sometimes the shrieks from the house give me the chills."

"Did you ever call the cops?"

The old lady shook her head again. "No, not with a guy like that. Only a couple of us who would've heard. He would have known it was me."

Realizing how isolated they were, he could see her point. "If I give you my card, will you please call me when they get back?"

She looked at the card and frowned.

"It's the little boy we're trying to save," he pressed.

She nodded. "In that case, I will. But chances are, by the time you get here, they'd be gone again."

"I hope not," he said. "We've been tracking this little boy for a long time now."

She smiled and nodded. "He is the cutest thing."

CHAPTER 17

Sunday, Early Evening …

BACK IN THE vehicle he went to turn on the engine, and she stayed his hand. "I don't want to leave."

"We can't stay here. If he is avoiding us, he'll see us. And they won't come home."

Her hand fell away. "Reese is out here somewhere. I don't know what I'll do if they've taken him away again." Her tone was stark, no hiding the fear and panic rising within her.

"Can you reach out to him?"

She dropped her gaze to her hands. "If I wasn't so personally affected, maybe," she admitted.

"Why don't we head back into town, pick up a bite to eat and maybe find a place where we can watch this road and eat in the car. You can calm down and send him messages. Let him know it's okay, and that we're searching for him. I'll call Peter and get his help."

She nodded.

He started the engine, and this time it seemed like they were at the mall within seconds. They walked inside a convenience store, looking for anything that was food. They had hot dogs.

"You know how many hot dogs I have eaten in the last couple years?"

He gave a bark of laughter but ordered four hot dogs anyway. "There isn't a whole lot of choice here."

She nodded. "Add some coffee to that."

They also picked up some fruit. With their purchases they drove back toward the house and slowed down as they approached. No lights were on. There was no sign of a vehicle; the garage door was still open.

Kirk drove past the house to a little pull-out not far down the road and shut off the lights and the engine, and then they sat. "This is a pretty good position," he said, pointing at the house. "We can see if they come from here."

She nodded, opened the bag of goodies and handed him a hot dog. She took one for herself and munched away.

"How come you've eaten a lot of hot dogs in the last year?"

"They were cheap and readily available," she said. "Think about where I worked."

"How did you not get tired of them?"

"Because they were cheap and readily available," she said with a laugh. "Money wasn't easy to come by. By the time I paid for my cell phone, the rent, the vehicle, gas and insurance, there just never seemed to be quite enough left. And that was after paying for a private detective too."

"I'm sorry. I didn't realize how tough it was for you."

"If you had thought about it, you would have," she said. "But I find that's often the way with people who have an education or a skilled job. It never occurs to them how people struggle who work at menial jobs."

"Sure, but don't forget I thought I left you seed money and a roof over your head for at least six months. And most of us assume, if you don't like what you're doing, you'll do something about it."

"I liked what I used to do," she said. "But I hardly loved being at the amusement park." Then she thought about her words and slowly chewed the last part of her hot dog. "That's not quite true. Because I really like the people. They accepted me and brought me into their family, and I had friends again for the first time in a long time."

"Did you not feel that way about the police department?"

"No," she said curtly. "I was only there for them to use."

"I don't think that's quite true," he said.

"As long as I was giving them what they needed, they were friendly. But they weren't friends," she emphasized. "I was never invited out to lunch. I was never part of any of the groups or the coffee klatch, hanging around the coffee bar. When I came in, silence usually fell. There were friendly enough smiles, but sometimes I wondered if that was just to stop me from looking at them too closely."

He stopped chewing and turned slowly to her. "Is that really how you felt?"

"Of course. When was the last time I was invited out for lunch with the rest of you guys?" She watched the frown flit across his face.

"I never thought about it," he admitted.

"I didn't have their respect," she added. "Even when I did give them all the right information, they looked at it suspiciously. I think they admired what I could do, but they didn't trust it. And, of course, the one time I did mess up, I messed up bad. So then I lost whatever respect I had."

"I think it's a tough business, particularly when lives are at stake. The minute you mess up, and somebody dies, everybody's distraught and looking to lash out to deal with their own pain. Unfortunately you became the easy target."

"But it's all old stuff anyway," she said. "It doesn't matter anymore."

"I think it does matter," he said gently. "I asked the bank about the money. Apparently it's still sitting there. But the password was changed almost as soon as I left. I assumed it was you."

"And I assumed it was you," she said with spirit. "I wish I'd known. I might not even have gotten so sick trying to stay afloat then."

"No," he said softly. "Maybe you wouldn't have." He groaned. "As soon as we find the boy, I'll get to the hospital and check their records. I haven't had a chance yet."

"Can't you call them? Check their records that way?"

"The database on your file has photocopies of everything. I need to know who worked the shifts when Reese died."

"You mean, when he was *supposed* to have died," she corrected. "Don't kid yourself. The little boy I'm chasing right now is my son." At his stern look, she subsided. "Okay, he *might* be my son." He seemed to hesitate, and she cut right through the thick silence. "I don't give a shit if you believe me or not. But that connection between him and me is strong."

"If he's the one sending the spiders your way," Kirk said, "that would convince me as much as anything."

"You just need to see his face. That will convince you."

"Why?"

"Because he is the spitting image of you. You should have enough baby pictures still hanging around to see it."

"Maybe, Stefan certainly believed it as well," he said softly. He pulled out this phone. "Peter is looking for me."

"What did you tell him?"

He shrugged and answered the phone. "Peter, what's up?"

She could only hear Kirk's part of the conversation.

He glanced over at her and said, "I'm busy. Why?" There was a short pause. "No, I'm trying to help somebody." Kirk frowned, stared at the steering wheel and then at Queenie. "Look. I know you don't agree with this. But I have to do what I can do. And I need you to do something for me. Pull all the hospital records back from when Queenie was in the hospital."

Even she could hear Peter's roar on the other side.

"And what if she's been right all along? … She hasn't got her claws into me. I'm not completely over my head. I know what I'm doing," he insisted.

Queenie sat back and stared out the window. She knew nobody there wanted Kirk to be with her. When they were riding high, everybody cheered them on, but the minute she fell, they had all scattered and had pulled him away too. She fell into a deep dark pit of depression trying to figure out why her abilities had failed her. But there hadn't been very much she could do about it at the time. And she hadn't been there for him any more than he'd been there for her.

She tried to block out the rest of the phone conversation.

Finally he ended the call and turned to look at her. "I'm sorry about that."

"Why?" She shrugged. "They're all thinking it. Nobody wants you to hook up with me again. Nobody wants you even in the same room with me anymore."

"It was tough at the time for me too, you know?" he said in a conversational tone. He reached into the bag and grabbed his second hotdog. "For a long time they were jealous as hell. Jealous because I was with you, and you seemed to have the magic touch. Jealous because we were closing cases at a crazy rate. Jealous because the brass had noticed, and I was being fast-tracked upward. But, when everything blew up, it's like they turned on me, not just on you. They blamed you, but they also blamed me for pulling the department down, for tarnishing the shiny reputation I'd helped them build. They blamed me for not keeping you happy or not doing whatever you needed to make you work properly. And, as you got blamed, so much of that shifted onto my shoulders as well. I was raked over the coals by the brass, by my teammates, by everybody at the office. It was pretty rough for a while."

"I didn't know that," she said. "It's easy to get so caught up in your own shit that you don't see how much muck everybody else is wading through."

"The dead woman's husband," he said, his tone soft, "he cornered me in the hallway. He just railed at me for at least ten minutes before he burst into tears." Kirk stared out the car's window. "There was nothing I could do. We'd been so sure we could solve this, like we'd solved so many. And, when he lost his wife, he went to pieces. But not until after he verbally attacked me. The other men saw it, and nobody stepped in to help because they felt I deserved it. I was as guilty as you were."

"And yet I've finally come to see that neither of us were guilty," she said faintly. "Stefan said something weird about that. I'll have to ask him for clarification. He said something about it being ridiculous that law enforcement often wanted to only take credit for the good information and to blame us for the bad—instead of realizing it's a crapshoot all the time. We can only give what the visions tell us at that time. Sometimes it's great. Sometimes it's not. But to hold us responsible for bad information is not fair."

"And yet we were all high on the good information."

"You were," she said with half a smile. "I wasn't. I was glowing in the sense that I was doing something, that I was helping. But don't forget. I can see behind the words coming toward me. I could see that, while they said, *Good job, Queenie,* they were just shoveling more and more cases at me. I don't think it was because they wanted to help the victims as much as they wanted to clean off their desks, and they wanted to close all these cases for the commendations."

"We're a greedy lot, aren't we?"

As she reached for her second hot dog, she smiled. "I guess." She took a big bite. "Normally I only eat one of these."

"And that's why you're a bone rack," he said.

"No. I'm a bone rack because I woke up in the hospital without my son," she corrected. "And I spent years grieving for him."

He turned to her. "I'm sorry," he said quietly. "There were much better ways of handling what we went through, but the fact is, we were different people back then, and hopefully we're better and wiser now."

She swallowed the last of her hot dog, thinking about his words. "I can agree with that."

"Enough to forgive?"

Her nod was instinctive. "I never blamed you. I should have told you about your son. Maybe he'd be alive today if I had." Then realizing what she said, she added, "*If* he's dead."

Kirk chuckled, then, in a surprise move, tugged her into his arms and just held her.

Tears burned in the corner of her eyes. She slipped her arms around his waist and hugged him back. "I miss this," she whispered.

"Hugs? Human touch?"

"Being close to someone again. Being held by someone who cares."

His arms tightened; then he relaxed. "We were always good together."

"Then why were we suddenly not good together? I always wondered that. I know I pushed you away, but you stayed away when I honestly thought you would come back when you calmed down." Her whisper was so low but audible in the silence of the interior of the car.

"Dear God, I'm sorry. I'd give anything to return to that time and do it all differently." He swept her up close again.

She could feel his heartbeat pulsing against her ear and the regret in his voice. "I was such a mess. I didn't blame you for leaving."

"Don't say that. I blame me." He tilted her chin up. "You might forgive me, but I don't."

She looked him in the eye and put two fingers against his lips. "*Shh*. It's over and done with."

"Maybe for you."

There was one way to stop him as he prepared to launch in with more regrets. She stretched up and covered his mouth with hers.

As always their connection was immediate and deep.

He pulled back slightly, easing the pressure threatening to explode. Softly he stroked his lips across hers, and she whimpered in his arms. "Easy," he murmured, his arms holding her close, his hands smoothing up and down her back. He dropped kisses over her nose, cheeks, forehead. Every time he whispered, "It's all right. Take it easy."

"I'm fine." But was she? There'd been so much craziness

in these last few days; this was a piece of joy, happiness—and so unexpected that it slipped into the area of miracles. She heaved a heavy sigh and snuggled closer.

"It's nice to hold you again."

Lightness floated up inside her. "Ditto."

"Can we go back to what we had before?"

"No way." She looked into his eyes. "But I'd be happy to create something much better." There was just enough light to see the gleam in his gaze.

This time when he lowered his head, she reached up to meet him.

Until the flash of headlights lit up the inside of the car. Instantly they both twisted to watch the vehicle approach. The car slowed and, sure enough, made a turn into the open garage.

"Bingo," he whispered. "I want you to stay here. I'll see if the three of them came home. I can't be looking around to make sure you're staying out of trouble. So, like always, please follow instructions."

She nodded. "Just make sure you bring that boy back here."

He slipped out of the car, and, with the same magical touch he always had, he disappeared into the shadows. All she could do was watch and wait.

KIRK SLIPPED DOWN the road, coming around the back of the house. Just then his phone vibrated. In the trees behind the kitchen door, he answered it. "Kirk here."

"They just came home," came a whispery female voice. "I saw the car go into the garage."

"Good. Thank you," he said. "I'm not far away."

She hung up as if afraid somebody could trace the call back to her.

He put his phone on silent as the light went on in the kitchen and another one upstairs. He studied the room as the big man walked into the kitchen, opened the fridge and pulled out a beer. He popped the cap and tilted the bottle to take a big drink. And then he wandered into the living room.

Kirk checked his watch. It was almost eleven-thirty p.m. With no more activity in the kitchen, he crept closer to the house. Where was the little boy?

Upstairs a light went on in one of the bedrooms. Kirk sneaked around to the front of the house, but no more lights were on upstairs. So where was the little boy?

The man slumped into an easy chair in the living room and picked up the remote, turning on the TV.

Kirk frowned, slid around the back, checking out all the basement windows. But he couldn't see any lights on downstairs. Was the little boy upstairs? Or had they not brought him home? He stopped beside a slightly open window to the basement and tried to nudge it farther open. It opened just enough. He used his cell phone flashlight to shine in the room. It was the little boy's room, but it was empty. Swearing softly, he stepped back and considered the issue. Then the lady called down to her husband. "I still think we should go get him."

"Nah, he'll be fine for the night."

"He's just a little boy," Maggie cried, desperation in her voice.

"So what? He's not getting any older if he doesn't smarten up."

"It's dark. That's not fair."

"He never has a light on in his room anyway. What difference does it make?"

"We left him alone. Shouldn't do that to a little boy."

"We leave him alone in the basement all the time."

"But this isn't the basement."

"So what? It's just a cave. He's been there before."

Kirk's heart pounded. He whispered, "What the hell? *A cave?*"

"When will you get him?"

"Tomorrow. He shouldn't have thrown that scene in the parking lot."

"You didn't have to punish him like that."

"Shut the fuck up. Otherwise I'll drag you out and toss you into the cave with him."

Kirk could hear Maggie muttering away upstairs. What the hell? What cave? And where the hell was it?

He quickly backtracked to where he'd left the vehicle and Queenie. He slid inside and told her what had happened. She stared at him. "A cave. They left him all alone in a cave?"

He nodded. "And apparently it's not the first time."

Even in the half-light, he could see how big her eyes were, how pale her face was.

"What kind of monsters are these people?"

"See if you can reach him," Kirk said urgently. "I have no clue how to find a cave out here. We'll have to get a geological map and then figure out where they could have taken him."

He knew what he had to do. It didn't matter whose child it was. A little boy who'd been dumped in a cave for the night would galvanize a search-and-rescue team and the local police. He picked up his phone and called Peter.

CHAPTER 18

Sunday Night, Late …

QUEENIE COULD FEEL the shaking set in. She worked desperately to control it, but it was always a problem for her when she became too emotionally involved. As soon as she did, it was impossible to connect because she couldn't control her energy.

As Kirk called in for reinforcements from town, she needed to get reinforcement as well. Hearing the panic in her own voice, even with her best efforts to keep it under control, she cried out, "Stefan, I need your help. The little boy has been dumped in a cave somewhere within a couple hours of where I'm located. Apparently he needed to be taught a lesson." Tears choked in her throat.

The Watcher is behind this, I presume? Stefan asked.

It was a fair question. As somebody who saw personalities, spirits on multiple different layers, she knew that, in Stefan's case, there was no way to lie to him. *Yes,* she said. *I believe the little boy in the cave is the one who called the spiders to me.* She took a deep breath, and, her fingers clenching and unclenching, she added, *I believe he's my son.*

That would make sense, as he'd have tremendous abilities inherited just through his DNA. Give me the details, he said, his tone brisk. *We don't have much time.*

She relayed what had happened so far this evening.

And Kirk is sure that's what he heard?

She glanced over at Kirk, wondering if she could question his wording, but he was still talking to the police on his phone.

To the best that I can remember, yes, she said. *Why? What difference does that make?*

Probably none, he said. *I can potentially follow the adults' path backward a bit. I want you to connect with Reese as much as you can. Probably through the spiders.*

Spiders? She glanced around. *I'm inside Kirk's car. No spiders are here.*

Then step outside, call them to you and then send them off in the direction where the little boy is. Give us a north, east, south, west direction. Give us something. I'll contact you again in a few minutes. And he cut their connection.

She opened the vehicle door and hopped out.

Kirk called, "Hey, don't go anywhere."

But she heard somebody on the phone calling him back. She leaned down and said, "I'm just standing right here. I have to find spiders."

He looked at her in surprise and then nodded. He kept his gaze on her as she walked around to the front of the vehicle. She leaned against the hood of the car, crossed her arms over her belly and, in her mind, called out to the spiders. *Wherever you are, whatever you're doing, if you're between me and my boy, I want you to show me the way. From where I stand to where he is, give me a path.* She kept chanting various versions of her words. She heard the car door open and close behind her, and then a strangled exclamation. "What's the matter?" she asked.

"Have you looked?"

She opened her eyes to see the road covered in spiders.

As were her pants and shirt. "I hadn't even felt them," she whispered.

"Why did you call them?"

"Stefan asked me to call the spiders and to have them tell us in which direction Reese's cave lies."

"Have they told you anything?"

She sighed. "All I've done is bring them to me. Now I want them to go after Reese." She turned slightly, standing straight on her feet, and said, "Is my son in this direction?"

There was a rumble around her, but she couldn't tell if it was positive or negative. She turned ninety degrees, facing the woods, and asked the same question. Same answer came back. She turned again so she faced the car and asked again. And again no answer she could understand. She turned one more time, and this time the rumble was overwhelming. She pointed in that direction. "He's that way."

"Okay, good. That's west. We can at least look on a map and see where a cave might be close by."

And just like that, the spiders followed the direction of her arm. She took one step and then another.

"Whoa, whoa, whoa. You're not going anywhere." Kirk grabbed her hand.

"I have to," she said, her mind buzzing with some weird knowledge inside. "He's in this direction."

"But he's not likely to be close," Kirk urged. "Can't you go visit him in a vision, like you did last time?"

She gave her head a hard shake.

"Just because the spiders can cross that distance, doesn't mean you can."

She frowned, and then her mind cleared. She realized just how many miles away Reese could be. She nodded. "I'll try." She whispered to the spiders, *Show me where he is. Take me to him.*

She followed the path as the spiders swept across the countryside, meeting up with others ahead. She wasn't sure if she was still following the same spiders or if the message had been passed on, as more and more spiders followed a direct line forward. She knew Kirk held her physical body back because she could feel him, feel his energy touching hers, blending with hers. She was going to tell him to break the contact, but thought, no, she might need it. If she exhausted herself, she might be able to use his energy to help her.

She followed in her mind's eye as the spiders went across the meadow, through the woods, down a hill on the other side, across a gully. It was slow going this way. She needed to move faster. She hadn't asked Kirk what was going on with his side of the information, but she assumed, if she gave him a direction, the police would follow it.

So far all they'd done was cross open country. A road was up ahead, but the spiders crossed it, moving in a thick bulbous train as they raced to the other side.

There they met up with even more spiders. She didn't know there could be that many. And she would never look at a spider the same. If they helped her find Reese, she promised to always treat them with respect and to never hurt another one, even accidentally, if she could help it.

She also knew time was an issue, and she didn't know why. Maybe it was his adoptive parents arguing, the mother trying to coax the man to come and get him, or perhaps Reese was trapped and facing another danger, she didn't know. But she had to keep going faster and faster until she lost track of the countryside around her, just the wind whipping at her face, tearing at her hair, burning her skin.

And then, all of a sudden, she came to a dead stop. The

single line of spiders moved toward a hillside. It was more rock than actual grassy hill. And there was an outcropping. She tried to slip inside, but some impermeable barrier stopped her. *Hey, it's me*, she cried out softly. *I'm here, honey.*

Mommy?

Yes. The police are on the way. They're going to find you.

Stay, he cried out. *Please stay. I don't like this place.*

She tried to see where she was, but almost nothing here identified this spot. There was a grassy knoll above and more to the side, but the area was surrounded by hills and trees. This wasn't even a real cave. It was just a space among the rocks.

Stay calm, she whispered. *I'm here.*

Don't leave me, he cried. *You love me, right? He told me that my mommy didn't love me.*

He was so wrong, she whispered, her heart aching. *You have to believe me. I love you so very much.* She didn't know how or why, but this little boy was hers.

He sobbed quietly. She wrapped her energy around him as much as she could. No way would she leave him. Not now, not ever. In the dim background she could hear Kirk calling her. But she could not return. If she died, that was fine. No force on this earth could separate her from her son, not again.

Until a strange voice broke in. *Wow, now this is a pretty scene.*

She stiffened and refused to move. Did he know what she was doing? How was that possible?

This is very interesting. You have a lot more skill than I gave you credit for.

She deliberately stayed silent.

You think not talking to me will keep me out? That I'll

grow bored and leave? Or maybe you can't talk to me. Maybe talking to me is consorting with the enemy. He chuckled. *This is a very interesting little boy here. Maybe I need to do something about him. I could just, you know, steal him away, and nobody would ever know.*

Her son cried out, *Who are you?*

I'd like to say I'm your mommy's friend, but the truth is, I don't think she thinks I'm her friend at all.

She could feel her son shaking. But only being in energy form at the moment, she could do little here and now. She placed her hand on top of his head, sending as much calming and loving energy as she could into his little body.

Lavender energy wrapped around them both, adding healing energy to hers. She smiled, loving the togetherness.

Are you here to hurt me too?

Her heart damn near broke at Reese's words. Of course her son could hear David too.

No, no, no, no, David said. *I wouldn't do that. I don't beat up little boys.*

My father does, Reese said. *I don't like him. He leaves me here to teach me a lesson.*

I wouldn't be at all surprised if that's what he does. Chances are, he's on his way to see you right now. David laughed.

Queenie wanted to scream and rail at him because she knew somehow he was responsible for bringing the parents this way. That complication she didn't need. But then David wasn't about helping. He was all about hurting. She didn't know how he was doing what he was doing as it was.

I'm right, you know? I can make people do all kinds of things they don't want to do. Of course you don't know what I'm doing or how I'm doing it, but that's okay. Your parents will be here soon. David laughed and laughed, the hoarse sound of his voice echoing off the walls.

Reese's arms wrapped around his chest. He whispered, *Mommy, are you still here?*

She didn't dare speak, but she poured more and more energy into him, filling each and every chakra of his that she could, and, with every stroke, the lavender aura blended with it. And then she started from his toes and sent blue healing energy up his legs, through his knees, up his hips, anything she could do to make him feel safe and loved.

As she poured everything she had into her son, it was like pushing energy uphill. ... On the heels of that thought, the communication tunnel she'd always had with her son suddenly cleared, and energy poured from her heart chakra to her son's chakra.

The force was so strong as it flowed from mother to son. But her mind ... She was stunned to tears by the truth. It really was Reese.

Her son was alive ...

A fact so big, so wonderful ... and so devastating that she couldn't speak.

Mommy, I think you need to come here in your body now. Before those other people get here, he whispered. *Come back. Okay?*

She knew he was right, but she couldn't let him go.

But Reese stood, stepped back and said, *Mommy, go. You need to go.*

And, as if he had cut a line between them, she was sucked back into the vortex, her voice screaming, *Nooooooo*, into the ethers. But barely seconds later, she slammed into her body in front of Kirk's car. She turned a horrified face toward Kirk.

"That other man was there. David. The Watcher who

could see into my world," she cried out. "He said he was going to bring Reese's parents after him."

Kirk shook his head. "What? How could he have seen you there? You weren't even there."

"I know. I know. But obviously he's using energy to get into my world. Somehow he managed to see and to use energy to find me there."

Up ahead they could hear crying and yelling as Reese's adoptive parents got into the car and reversed out the driveway.

Queenie screamed, "Go, go, go. They'll lead us to Reese." She raced around and hopped into the passenger side.

Kirk already had the engine going, and, keeping the lights off, he drove a safe-enough distance behind the couple. "I have to stay close enough to find out where they're going, but I don't want them to know they're being followed." He looked at her. "Are you sure it's Reese?"

She nodded. "Oh, yes. I'm so sure."

"Any idea how David is getting this couple to go back after Reese?"

She shook her head. "No, I don't. Stefan might though."

Stefan spoke in her head. *No, I don't. But we need to find out.*

"DID REESE SAY anything helpful?" Kirk asked.

She shook her head. "No. He's the one who sent me away so I could bring back help," she said. "He was stronger than I thought. I just wanted to stay and hold him tight."

"I'm sure that's to be expected. Was he okay? Was he in good health? Was he hurt?"

"He was fine," she said. "Who could do that? Just take a child and dump him into an outcropping of rocks and leave him there all on his own. He's just a little boy."

"Was he dressed for it? Was he still in pajamas?"

"He had on jeans and a T-shirt and a sweater, like a hooded jacket," she said. And then she frowned. "Also a bandanna around his neck."

"Interesting. Maybe he had just been playing with it when they snatched him."

She shrugged. "I don't know." But inside she worried.

"What's bothering you?"

She turned to stare at him. "A horrible, horrible thought is what's bothering me."

"Tell me." He carefully took the intersection following a good distance behind the car ahead. But because he had no headlights, nobody else could see him coming. He crossed the intersection and slipped in a good quarter-mile behind the other vehicle. He turned to look at her. "Tell me."

"The bandanna."

"What about it?" He studied the car ahead. How far would they go?

"The way it was tied."

He damn near hit the brakes. He turned and stared at her. "What are you talking about?" he asked, his voice harsh.

She turned to stare back out the windshield. "Nothing. It has to be nothing."

"Queenie, for God's sake," he snapped. "Just spit it out."

She took a deep breath. "It was blue. That handkerchief around Reese's neck was blue."

Obviously he was focused on driving because he didn't get what the hell she was talking about. "And?"

"It was blue, like the woman in the lake."

His throat seized. "But it can't be the same surely?"

"I don't know," she said. "But I'm afraid it might be. I'm really afraid it might be."

"Can you tell? Can you see the energy? Can you check the knot?"

"I can't from here," she said. "But I felt something when I was there and when David talked to us."

"Do you think he's the one connected to all these cases?"

"I think so, yes," she whispered.

"But, if that's the case, what's his connection to Reese?"

"I don't know," she whispered. "Drive faster," she said urgently. "Because he's still there, and he's watching our boy."

"Why?"

"I don't know," she repeated. "But it won't be for anything good." She sank back and whispered, "I'm going back to Reese. Get there as fast as you can."

CHAPTER 19

Very Early Monday Morning …

MOMMY, WHO IS *he?* Reese whispered.

Queenie, back at Reese's side, struggled to maintain her energetic grasp of him while sitting in the car beside Kirk. She sent messages to Kirk to drive faster. And that somehow she'd tell him where they were going.

But, so far, he wasn't listening.

Stefan, help him please, she cried out in pain.

Mommy, are you hurt?

I'm fine, she reassured Reese. *Just trying to get to you as fast as I can.*

Is that what that man is doing too?

She frowned. *I hope not*, she whispered. She had no idea who this David person was. The fact that he could watch her in her world was scary, but the fact that he could see her son was downright terrifying. Because David showed absolutely no sign that he was willing to help. All he really wanted to do was watch and have fun, laughing at her expense. What kind of a man was that?

I don't like him, Reese whispered.

She poured more loving energy into the cocoon she'd wrapped around him. *Neither do I*, she whispered, feeling tears in the corner of her eyes at the sight of the lavender energy. She had been positive all this time that it had been

Reese's soul energy. Only that made no sense—not now.

He snuggled in deeper. A smile on his face, peace on his features. Her heart was so full of joy and, at the same time, so terrified they wouldn't get here in time to save him.

Well, of course, they won't. Or they'll think they got here just in time, David said.

What do you mean? she said quietly, trying not to disturb Reese.

He's going to die of course. That's the only way to make this a tragic comedy after all.

Her mind struggled to figure it out. *What are you talking about? There's nothing funny about this. It is a tragedy, yes, but it's not a funny one.*

He sighed. *I guess you're not a believer in the arts, are you? It's been a comedy up until now. A comedy of errors, a comedy of miscommunication and a comedy in the fact that you're also bloody stupid,* he said in disgust. *I figured when I could connect with you that maybe, just maybe, you would present me with some new knowledge or a challenge at least. I've had to do everything myself so far,* he said in a peevish voice. *Surely somebody is out there who knows more than I do.*

Her mind just couldn't quite fathom what the hell he was talking about. She had an inkling, but it was a little too nasty to even consider. *You want to learn from someone? Like from a mentor? What about Stefan?*

In the back of her thoughts, Stefan whispered, *Gee, thanks. And remember. My thoughts are masked from him, but you need to do the same with yours.*

She winced. She hadn't meant to throw him under the bus. But he was the only one she knew who had skills that would match this guy's.

Stefan's voice rumbled again in the back of her mind.

Not true. Yours skills are just as equal. Who is this man?

He's the one I've been telling you about, the man watching me. You know that.

Yes, of course I know that much, but who is he in physical form? And why can't we figure that out? What is he doing that I can't track him?

Does it matter? she asked, her tone weary. *He's just an asshole.*

He's masking his energy. Shit, Stefan said. *It's the same man who masked the energy to a little boy, Timmy, a patient of Dr. Maddy's. The little boy was slowly dying because of this asshole.*

Reese murmured.

Immediately Queenie refocused and poured energy back around her son. She thought about the times and places this asshole had been talking to her, around her, the words, the things he'd said. *Stefan, I think I've secured our connection. But can you bolster my shield to keep this asshole out of our exchanges?*

Done, Stefan acknowledged.

How many have you killed, did you say? she asked David in a conversational tone. *Are you looking for somebody to help you kill more?*

She had no idea where her bravado came from. But she could sense Stefan's approval. What she didn't want was to find the disapproval of this asshole. David had been fairly easygoing up until now. The only men she'd ever met so far like that were doctors. They tended to have that supercilious attitude. Of course she'd met an engineer once or twice who had been similar. But they weren't really the killing type of assholes.

Oh, you're finally getting it, are you? he crowed. *What do you want? A pat on the back for finally understanding what I do?*

But do you understand why you do it? she asked. *Motivation is everything.*

She'd learned that in all those years she had helped the cops. They were forever trying to figure out why somebody did something, as if that had more intrinsic value than the how of things. It'd taken her a long time to understand that it allowed them to second guess what the next step would be when they were dealing with killers.

Of course I know, David said. *Because it's fun. Because it's fascinating. It was too easy in the beginning, so I had to make it more challenging. After all, I wasn't about to get caught, so I had to make sure other people would get caught.*

People use other people as fall guys all the time, she said. *What's unique and different about that?*

Oh, dear, you still don't get it, he said, as if talking to a stupid child. *You see? It's not just that I make them the fall guy, but I get them to do the killing. Why should I get my hands dirty? I find the perfect victims, and I amplify their emotions. I can make anyone do anything. From giving me their brand-new laptops, TVs, paying for my lunch—whatever I want. I've gotten three raises the exact same way. But that's just everyday type things. Making people do bad things to those they love—or hate—is much more fun.*

She could feel Stefan's shock behind her. Inside, she was stunned. *So you find some asshole who's angry at his wife, and you amplify that emotion so he turns around and kills her?* she asked in disbelief.

Oh, look at that. Gold star for you, he said. *That's exactly what I do. Most of the time I don't even have to nudge them. I just take that ball of energy, usually red hot, sometimes black, always first-chakra stuff, sometimes into the heart chakra, but great rage, anger, frustration. See? And I pick up those. I can sense them. I can follow them back to where the people are. And I can watch the scenarios going on around them. Sometimes, not every time,* he said sadly, *but enough times I can add to their energy, build their rage and push them over the edge, so they release that anger burning up inside them. You know it's not healthy to hold that all in, right?*

And being the recipient of that rage, how healthy is that for the poor victim?

Well, I really don't care about the victim, do I? I can't connect with them. So obviously there's no feeling or caring. Just think about all the books you read. If you can't connect with the main character, you toss it, don't you?

Just because he was right didn't mean she had to admit it. But, from his smug chuckles, she figured he already knew. *So that's all you do?* she asked, trying to downplay his actions. *You find people pissed off at each other, amplify their natural inclination and force them to act?*

I don't force them to do anything, he said. *That's the joy of it all. I get to kill, but I don't get caught because, well, I'm not doing the killing, am I?*

She thought about all the people in the world who lived with a certain amount of rage or frustration, or those with quick-fire tempers that blew without any warning. *So it requires a heavy emotion for you to act? That's really interesting.*

And it was fascinating, but she wasn't at all sure how it would help Reese now.

Sure. I've been working on causing the emotions, so I can have them act, he said conversationally. *But it doesn't work that well. They have to have a reason to really care.*

A reason to really care about something? Like anger, frustra-

tion, love, hate?

Exactly, he said.

She could almost feel his benevolent nod as if to a favorite student. *So you can't make somebody kill who doesn't want to kill,* she said slowly. *But, if they have that murderous intent, or at least are close to that edge, then you push them over.*

Right. And I connect easier with some people than others obviously, he said thoughtfully. *I've been trying with those who I have a poor connection to, but that connection is everything.*

And what about people who want to do something but don't have the nerve to do it? Can you give them that extra courage?

I've tried a couple times. But I haven't been able to make that happen. I'll keep trying though because that'll open up a whole new level of entertainment for me.

Entertainment, wow. *Are you that bored in your normal life that you have to set about playing God with other people?*

Oh, I like that, he said. *That's a very nice way to put it. And, no, I'm not bored. I have a ton of challenges. But one can't always be the savior day in and day out. Everybody has two sides to their personality. I needed an outlet for the other side of mine.*

That makes sense. Too much of a good thing isn't good. In a secure partition of her mind, she was trying to figure out what the word *savior* meant to him. That meant he was a doctor? Or a priest?

Stefan whispered in her ear, *Keep asking questions like that.*

And how far away do you have to be? I mean, can you talk to people in Africa? Somebody in Norway, for example? Or does it have to be within the state or within even the town?

That's been one of the frustrating things, he said. *It really has to be somebody I've either seen or worked with before. I've tried with those I only know of, but I can't get the same result.*

But then, this is all trial and error, and I have to keep trying. Eventually I'll get better and better. I'd love to think that, if somebody was arguing in Norway, I could have somebody kill him just because I say so. Wouldn't that be fantastic?

I can see how, from your point of view, it would be. It would certainly gum up police investigations all over the world, she said, trying to interject more humor. Anything to keep him talking. And anything to keep his interest away from her son. *Stefan, where is Kirk? Is he not here yet?*

He's almost here. I'm protecting your body while we get you here. Normally we can't touch anybody when they're in this level of trance. If your silver cord is separated from your body, then there's no going back to it.

She remembered reading something about it but hadn't considered it in the light of what she was currently doing. But it made sense. *Thank you,* she said sincerely. *I don't care about my life. But Reese needs his chance to live.*

But David was spouting off again. *You know? That's been part of the fun. I haven't been able to kill dozens in a year, although that's my goal for next year, to actually take on a dozen. Last year it was only ten. It took me a couple years to make the first one happen,* he said, irritated. *Imagine if I could've done this a whole lot earlier. But I didn't even know it was something anybody could do.*

She mentally tallied up the number of murders he'd been involved in and shook her head. *What was your first killing?*

That was a while ago, he said still in a conversational time. *About the time I connected with you.*

She froze. *Sorry?*

Remember that case where all those women were murdered, and you were desperate to save the one? You did catch the right guy, by the way, but that last murder, he hadn't intended on killing the woman—he'd planned on letting her go. And I didn't know it at the time, but I was really responsible for him killing her.

She wanted to scream at him. *I worked so hard on that case. I was desperate to save her.*

Right, and I think that's when we first connected.

Hopefully thinking thoughts only to herself, she repeated *Connected? So how many doctors or clergy members do I remember interacting with?* More than she expected showed up at her readings, but she never got names, just flashes of a man with a collar or someone in a doctor's white coat. And, when dealing with them on police matters, it was surprising to have them pull her aside to ask her the odd question. *Is my wife cheating? Will my congregation grow?* She shook her head, back to the present.

David continued to speak, quite happy to hear his own voice. *You were screaming at the ethers, looking for help, looking for anyone, anything that could help you solve this case because you were desperate to keep her alive. You know? I think it's that desperation of yours that allowed me to funnel into the killer's frustration about how you were getting so close. But he really did not intend on killing her. I'm afraid I'm the one who hit that switch and threw him over so he crossed that line. Afterward, as I thought about it, I realized just what happened. Of course that was the perfect storm, that was the perfect set of circumstances, the perfect victim, the perfect killer. But I hadn't realized the connection with you. Maybe I tapped into your energy then, and that's what gave me the ability to kill, not so much with my own skill but with the addition of your skill.* His voice slowed as if pondering that thought. *No, that wouldn't make me happy.*

Her heart sank. That was so not what she wanted to hear. She'd tried desperately to save that poor woman. And to think she might have had a hand in killing her was more than she could bear.

Her son murmured in her arms. Instinctively she shielded him with more energy, more love. She could feel her own energy fading, but it didn't matter as long as she kept him safe. She could feel Stefan protesting behind her. But she wouldn't tolerate anyone hurting Reese, not again.

That's a daunting thought, she said faintly. *I must have been very strong back then.*

Of course you were. But completely off the wall. Sending out all kinds of pain and anger, he said cheerfully. *There was, of course, that connection. That kinship to you. And back then you just, you know, you didn't feel the same thing, and I can understand that because you were so focused. Still, I could use that desperation. I've been dabbling with my psychic abilities for a long time. But when you use them always to the good, and suddenly you're presented with that idea of using them for something other than good, well, it becomes a tantalizing thought you can't let go of. So I watched you for the whole case. Then your whole world fell apart. It was fascinating. I'm sure you don't appreciate it, but I decided to try something. You were in so much pain, more than I needed to feed on because—of course—your pain was my joy. But you had so much pain, I wondered if I could channel it—use it to affect the way people viewed you. In particular those you worked with at the station. Their actions, their attitudes, how they treated you. Especially Kirk. I mean, any real sane man would have no excuse for not standing by your side when you're going through such a bad patch. Not if he loved you. ... Did you never wonder why he left?*

She was reeling from the fact that David knew Kirk. *Of course I knew. I sent him away. I was a mess on a downward spiral, not suicidal, but not far off,* she admitted quietly. She knew Stefan was listening in, and of course that was part of the truth he was so intent on getting at.

I wondered about that. See? I probably could have made you flip that switch too. But I didn't really understand what I was doing. I would get one guy to treat you with a cold shoulder one day because that's all I could manage. The next time somebody would be spreading gossip because that's all I could manage. Kirk was kind of a triumph. But I picked him in a low spot. I picked him at a time when he was done. He was fed up, didn't know what to do anymore, and he just wanted a clean start. So I gave it to him.

She could feel her body shivering with the shocks as they came. She'd assumed Kirk had accepted her decision and left. Now she found out Kirk hadn't been following his own thoughts.

Stefan seemed to wrap his arms around her and give her a hug. He whispered, *Hold steady.*

Is that the truth? Or are you playing with me now?

Oh, wow. Now that's an interesting twist. No, it is the truth. I had a lot of fun with you back then, but then it got so damn boring. When you didn't do anything but mope around the place, I had to get rid of your place. So I managed to do that without any trouble. And once I had you completely isolated, I thought maybe we could have a stronger connection. But instead you just got weaker and weaker. It was really pathetic.

A trill laugh filled the room. *But you surprised me. After ignoring you for a few years, I saved you again. You were a real mess. Sick, sick, sick. Almost dying actually. You probably should thank me for keeping you alive.*

She could feel her heart hammering against her chest. This was what she needed. This was what she was after, the truth about what happened to her in the hospital. *Did you have something to do with keeping me in the coma?* she asked, deliberately avoiding the one question she wanted to ask.

No, no, no. Your body was already in shut-down mode at that point. I mean, how absolutely foolish of you not to go to Kirk. He was the father. I mean, the least he could have done was pay.

And then she remembered something else Kirk had said had happened. *So who did you use to change the password on Kirk's bank account so I couldn't access the money?*

Well, who does all his banking and stuff when he's too busy? Katherine. And she's so easy to deal with. She hates you. She really hates you. Made her an easy target. I got her to do all kinds of things, he said happily.

And why does Kirk's sister hate me so much?

She's jealous. Because, when Kirk is with you, she feels like he doesn't love her.

Queenie bowed her head, almost groaning because, of course, that was so very true. She'd told Kirk that many a time too. *Does she know what she did?*

I hope so. Because there's that hatred inside her. You play with it enough, and she's quite happy to do nasty little things. She's not a killer though. Killing takes that special threshold. Maybe if I could work with her long enough. But she doesn't really have anybody in her life worth killing. Unless I get her to kill Kirk. That would be quite a magnificent trip because she loves him so much. On the other hand, she hates you so much that it would be easier to have her kill you.

Instead you just decided to torment me, is that it?

That was her avenue of choice. All she could think about

was the fact you were in a coma, and Kirk was really worried about you, and she was afraid he would get sucked back into your life again.

So she targeted my son?

Well, she did, although I had to help her a little with that. You know how difficult it is to forge signatures?

It's very difficult. She almost choked on the thought.

But nobody really looks at signatures, do they? Not until something actually happens. But to find your signature on the cremation order, now that was an interesting twist. Because, of course, you had been awake off and on. It was possible you'd signed it. And you'd just blanked it all out. Grief will do that to you, you know? His tone was back to conversational. The teacher trying to teach his students about his great accomplishments.

And then how did you get my son to another family?

I'm pretty sure, if you'll track Kirk's sister's friends, you'll find that a couple friends removed is Maggie's sister. And Maggie really wanted a little boy.

So somehow you manipulated everybody to make that work?

When people have this passion inside, they'll do all kinds of things. When I said a little boy was desperately in need of a home, Maggie piped right up. Kirk's sister, Katherine, couldn't resist the chance to move him into somebody's warm loving arms.

Would she remember doing that? Does she know what she did?

Like a bad dream, he said. *Although I don't know. Maybe she does remember. Maybe it keeps her up at night in horror. That would be fun, wouldn't it?*

She didn't know what to say. To think of such a monster in her midst, yet only in ethereal form, didn't help her one little bit. *And the woman in the lake? Her name was Bonnie Jenkins by the way.*

Well, of course you know who killed her as you spoke to him already. His name is Paul Grogan if you want to look him up. He's not a nice person. That's what made it so easy to get him to do my bidding. But I thought the handkerchief would be a personal message. Connecting me to the Handkerchief Killer. Surely you could've connected me to those murders with that, but apparently I am way too subtle for you.

This is incredibly convoluted, she cried out. *How could anybody figure this out?*

You're quite right there, he said with a note of satisfaction. *And that's why I'm so accomplished. I'm just getting better and better. Once I realized how I could kill, well, that was a starting point. It took me a couple years to figure out how to get someone else to kill again. Very frustrating years, I'll have you know.* He sounded slightly put out. *But now that I've got it, I've got it. And that makes life so much more fun.*

Blue? she asked, still hung up on the handkerchief he'd used. *Why blue?*

Blue was my own twist on the case. I was sure you'd figure it out, but …

And the little boy? she asked, adding strength to her voice. *What did he do to deserve to die?*

What little boy? he asked, his tone suspiciously neutral.

You remember, she murmured. *Or at least maybe you remember the people who kicked you out of his space. And easily I might add.*

Stefan whispered in her ear, *Easy, you're prodding a tiger. The boy is doing fine now. And it took two of us to get to the bottom of the problem. I'll contact the police and get this Paul Grogan picked up.*

Good. She'd like to see that man pay for what he did. Although she struggled with David's participation in the case. Pushing him wasn't likely smart, but he was too arrogant and complacent for her liking. *The little boy is doing fine by the way. There are many excellent energy workers out there. You could learn a lot …*

His silence brewed with palpable anger.

Her words had to smart. But she'd do anything to stop him. Yet she had to be careful to not push it. At least until help arrived. *So what are your plans from here on out?* She desperately tried to figure out who could possibly have been around at the time of those cases who would have had such an influence on her.

I'm not really sure yet, he snapped, still perturbed by her comments it seemed.

Good. She had pricked his ego.

Playing God is one thing. But it gets a little lonely. I was hoping I could find, you know, other people like you. It's lonely up here. I'd like to share my accomplishments.

She nodded. *Did you have anything to do with what Carlos did?*

Carlos? Carlos? … Hmm. I don't think I know that name. Then he chuckled. *Your ex-boss? No, that was all his actions. But I should kill him—not a nice man at all.*

Almost with relief she tucked that tidbit away. At least Carlos had been Carlos when he'd stolen and cheated everyone. She didn't have to feel sorry for the slime ball. Kirk was an entirely different ball of wax. They had a lot to talk about when this was over.

So you used that same connection to me from way back when. But why didn't you step in and watch over me all these years? Why just in the last few months?

Well, it's an interesting thing. Once you connected with the killer I had worked on—Paul Grogan, the man who wanted that lady's lake property so bad it was worth killing for—your energetic connection to him was like an instant slap across my face. And I remembered all about you. You were just such a mess for so long. I knew it would take you years to recover. But there you were, all of a sudden, recovered. And that was fun because then I could take a step into your life any time, check out what you were up to.

In the far distance she could hear a vehicle racing toward them. But it didn't feel right. It didn't feel like the vehicle she wanted it to be. It wasn't Kirk …

Oh, this should be fun, David said.

Why's that? Queenie asked with dread.

Maggie called, "Reese? How are you, honey? I got Daddy to come back and get you."

Reese lay curled up in a ball on the floor. Queenie had completely nestled him into a cocoon of healing, loving energy. Lavender hues curled up deep inside. Another layer on top of that she recognized as being Stefan's.

And maybe another layer, but she didn't understand who it was.

Stefan whispered in her ear, *It's Dr. Maddy's energy.*

And that reminded her. She raised her head and asked David, *Did you have something to do with that man who was poisoned? His little girl—Kirsten, I think her name was—came in to talk to me. Her mother was with her.*

Yes, David said. *Brian Callahan. A coworker at his job was poisoning him—with a little help from me. Brian was promoted over him, so he fed him arsenic every day in his homemade fancy brownies at work. Then, when Brian was too sick, this caring worker sent a special health product to the wife to feed her husband. She loved him so much that she'd do anything for him.* His voice petered out. *I'm not sure what's happening with that case. I'll have to go revisit it.*

So why then are they coming to me? she cried out, puzzled.

You know? I was wondering that same thing. It's almost as if, now that our connection has been reopened, you're reconnecting with all my victims. It's really gratifying, he said.

Maggie's voice came closer and closer. "Reese? Answer me please. Reese?"

"Maggie, leave him," her husband called out. "He's a waste of time anyway."

Just behind them came another vehicle. Surely that was Kirk. In the distance she finally heard sirens too.

Oh, now this is really going to be fun. I wonder what I can make happen here? David cried out in joy.

She froze. *You don't need to do anything here. You've already done enough,* she snapped.

Yes, but you don't understand. This isn't finished, is it? This is just my chessboard pieces moving to different places on the board.

Queenie could feel Stefan ever silent behind her. Maggie stepped into the cave, her gaze going around the room. She ran back to the car, crying out, "He's not here. I told you that we shouldn't have left him."

"It's good if the little bugger ran off," the man snapped. "I told you that I didn't want him in the first place."

But Maggie wasn't listening. She sobbed quietly, calling out in a broken voice, "Reese? Mommy's here. Reese?"

But Reese couldn't even begin to answer. He was not only sound asleep but Queenie suspected in a much heavier state on the floor. What she didn't know was why Maggie hadn't seen him. Her flashlight had shone directly on him.

So Stefan must have had something to do with that.

Now why didn't she see him? David asked pensively, curiosity underlying his tone. *Oh, I do like a good mystery.*

Queenie heard raised voices outside as other vehicles arrived. Among them, Maggie screamed and cried, "You've got to help me find him. He's just a little boy."

Kirk called out, "Reese, where are you?"

The father yelled, "Hey, what the hell is going on here? Who called you into this?"

Kirk turned to him, his voice loud. "He's my son. And you and I will have a talk at the police station very soon."

Maggie gasped, and her husband started to bluster.

Queenie was afraid to step away and leave Reese alone. She reached out for Kirk. *Come inside,* she whispered. She could feel a sense of shock, that sense of awareness, her connection to Kirk reborn. But she was also afraid David would figure it out. She heard Kirk call back, "Keep them here. I'll take a look inside." He stepped into the small space, swearing as he saw where Reese had been hidden. "Stefan?"

And then it was as if a three-way conference call had opened up. Stefan said out loud for Kirk's benefit, "I'm here with Reese and Queenie."

Kirk froze and said, "Where is he? I can't see him."

"I've been using the masking energy," Stefan said. "I didn't want the adoptive parents to get hold of him." Stephan addressed Queenie. "We have to let him go."

She protested.

Kirk cried out, "Don't you understand? Your body is collapsed in the car. People will think I've killed you. Right now there's no life force left in your physical presence. I understand you're here to protect Reese, but you have to let him go. Let me pick him up and carry him outside. We'll get him to the hospital. We'll get him any attention he needs."

Stefan's warm caressing voice said, "Queenie, it's time."

She shook her head. "Don't you understand that so much danger is still here?"

But already Stefan's masking energy had been pulled away.

Kirk cried out, "Reese." He crouched down beside the little boy and picked him up. Nestling him close against his chest, he carried him outside to cries from Maggie and several of the cops.

Queenie, still attached to Reese, trailed out into the night. But she could also sense David close by. She nudged Stefan and realized he understood.

You'll have to put that umbrella defense system of yours back in place, Stefan said, his voice low but urgent.

She shook her head. *I don't know what you're talking about.*

Yes, what are you talking about? David asked. *Interesting to have a three-way conversation here. Fascinating actually. I'd give you my name but you'd probably recognize it, so I certainly can't tell you that. You can just call me God*, he said in a complacent voice.

My name is Stefan, Stefan said quietly. *Queenie, go back to your body.*

She struggled against the idea.

David laughed. *Go on. Go on. It's not like I can't get to your son anytime I want to.*

The trouble was, that was the truth. He'd never be stopped. He'd never be punished.

Why don't you come to my place and say that, she said. *You're nothing but a coward. Look at you. You won't go physically anywhere. You're using your abilities to harm and to torment people. You've already connected with my son so much that I wonder if that connection goes in reverse.*

She could feel Stefan behind her, willing her to try something. She just didn't know what.

You need to return to your body so I have access to your son, and David snapped his fingers.

But it didn't do any good. She stood there, strong in her ethereal body. *That doesn't work for me,* she said calmly. *Nobody will ever hurt my son again. You've already done more than enough damage. And, as you've said, you are connected to him.* She reached out a hand and placed it on Reese's chest. Then she felt Stefan grab hold of her hand, and then Stefan hung on to Dr. Maddy, who reached around and placed her hand on top of Queenie's over Reese's chest.

She whispered to Kirk, *Stay where you are. Keep everyone else back.*

And then, completely bolstered and fulfilled by Stefan and Maddy, she poured as much energy as she collectively could into her son's heart chakra. Then finding his tiny connection to her own body, she followed it back, searching for and finding that tiny energetic connection to David. As soon as she did, she smiled and zipped as fast forward as she could. She'd used this technique many times with criminals, finding little bits and pieces of their energy, tracking them backward. It was one of the reasons why she'd been so successful in closing cases. And likely the final secret Stefan had asked about. Then she pulled in all her years of experience, all the years she had of pain and grief and torment at knowing her son had been taken from her and not knowing by whom or why.

She could hear David calling out, *You can't do that. I'm too strong for you.* He kept putting up blocks, putting up barriers, and she blasted through them, flicking them away as if they were nothing but Styrofoam. Because on her side was the might of right and love and vengeance all in one. She knew she had to stay positive. She knew she had to say it all with love.

She followed that energy all the way back into town. The trees, the highways, the cars, the houses, everything whipping past in a blur. She didn't even know where she was. But, when she hovered over the hospital, she knew. She knew exactly who it was.

She whispered to Kirk. *It's Dr. David Hutchinson.*

The doctor who'd coached her through some of the worst times in her life, who had held her hand while she had bawled over the loss of her son. Who'd been available anytime she needed someone to talk to. Anytime she needed her sanity back from the craziness of the work she did.

A man who'd seen her at her most vulnerable …

A man who had taken advantage of her darkest moments for his own entertainment …

Shuddering, but knowing he had to be stopped, she dove ever forward, down through the building, through the floors, through the layers. His energy was ever present as she came to where he stood on the ward. He froze when he saw Queenie approach in her ethereal form. Shock and fear were both evident on his face. She reached out, picked up his hand and slapped it against his heart.

He cried out, clutching at his chest with both hands, but she had to make sure the crash cart couldn't bring him back. She kept her hand atop his chest, pouring energy in, more than his heart could ever possibly handle, funneling it forward, through it, around her, wrapping up his heart in so much combined energy until the damned thing exploded in her fingers.

Slowly the life force drained beneath her as the medical teams raced to him, crash cart coming, voices crying, as they tried to revive him. But she already knew it was too late. She had watched as his life force faded out of his toes. Right beside him on the hospital ward was something that should not have been here, but of course it was. A small spider. She smiled, leaned down and, with a scoop of energy, picked him up and carried him back with her through the towns, through the tunnels, through the mountains and the meadows and the roads until she slammed back into the vehicle where her body lay.

She sat inside Kirk's car, her eyes open, her body humming with energy she'd never felt before, a sense of connectedness she'd never experienced, had never performed. She was one with the vehicle. She was one with the air. She was one with the spider in her hand.

She opened the door, her body feeling odd because it was one with the grass; it was one with the rocks. It *was* the door. The physical world had become so solid that it was almost foreign feeling. Compared to being as light as air when in ethereal form, this human existence was like walking through molasses, trying to get an awkward and heavy body to do what she commanded it to do.

Carefully she moved from the vehicle to stand in the night. She walked to where her son lay in Kirk's arms. But Reese wasn't awake. Not only wasn't he awake but it seemed as if he were in a coma. She reached down and gently placed the spider on his cheek and whispered out loud, "Reese, wake up. It's Mommy."

Kirk watched her intently.

The little boy opened his eyes. He stared up at her and

whispered, "Hi, Mommy."

Queenie wrapped her arms around her son, around her lover and around the spider that had made everything so very possible. They all were as connected to each other as she was to both of them.

And still a pinkish-lavender energy surrounded them all.

She bowed her head and let the tears fall. It really would be okay now. She felt Kirk drop his head to rest against hers, the three of them tight in a world of their own.

"I don't know what the hell happened to us," he whispered, "but you know I've always loved you, right?"

She lifted her head ever so slowly, stared into his beautiful silver-blue eyes and opened the connecting door between them. This time she didn't just open it but she removed the door so he could feel her the same way he always had felt her before.

His gaze widened, and he smiled. "At least now you can see I mean what I say," he said gently.

She smiled, kissed him gently on the cheek, and then leaned down, kissed her son on his cheek. "I do indeed."

The only energy coming from Kirk was love. And she'd take all coming her way. She'd had a rough few years. But, as she gazed at her son, she knew it would all be okay from now on.

OVERWHELMED, EXHAUSTED AND seriously emotional, Kirk stood by Queenie and Reese throughout the following hours of chaos. They had to deal with the adoptive parents, the police, the paramedics who'd been called. A shift to the police station, listening to Maggie try to explain. And then Kirk's meeting with his own sister ... God, that had been painful.

"That child was mine, God damn you, Katherine," he yelled.

Queenie had stared in silent accusation as his sister broke down.

Katherine had been terrified and bawling the whole time.

Kirk found it hard to forgive her—even though he understood the damn doctor had a big hand in her actions, but she'd been the willing raw material. And, according to Stefan, people couldn't be forced to do something they didn't want to do. David had amplified the negative thoughts those people already harbored so they took action.

So was she responsible or David?

Both, Kirk decided.

The one thing he knew for sure was that his bitch of a sister appeared calmer, sadder—was that because David's influence was gone? Or because she'd confessed to her crimes? She'd dropped off the letter to make sure Queenie left the apartment. She'd changed the access to the bank account. But the money was still there. All Katherine's actions had been directed against Queenie. That didn't make it any better in his eyes. Katherine had still caused a world of hurt in Kirk's life.

But Kirk realized he was hardly innocent himself. David had taken Kirk's own pain and had amplified it, taking his need for a change and amplifying it, all so Kirk had walked away from Queenie and had stayed away.

When he thought about how David had manipulated Kirk's, Queenie's and Reese's lives, innocents who'd done nothing wrong—to suffer at David's hands on a whim—Kirk's anger even now coiled deep inside him.

And, in the background of all this turmoil, according to Queenie, was Stefan and Maddy, stepping in and out of the chaos.

The one nonnegotiable determinant in all of this was that Queenie would not in any way let go of Reese, and Reese wouldn't let go of her.

He kept studying his son, seeing Queenie in his eyes; yet Kirk's nose was on that little face, as was the same hair, the same shape of his face but Queenie's mouth.

As a reality check, tonight had been a big one. All those years Queenie had suffered were the years he'd lost himself. The years Reese had suffered, … all so unnecessary.

With his sister's confession, the police had allowed Reese to stay with Queenie. Good thing as Kirk knew he'd have World War III on his hand if anyone tried to separate them.

"Can we go home soon?"

He glanced down at Queenie, her arms strained as she carried Reese. He must be a dead weight in her arms. His son had crashed, the night's events too much for the little guy, his head on her shoulder. "Yes, the rest can be dealt with tomorrow."

"Or the next day," she whispered. "It will be days, maybe weeks, before I come back here."

He reached over and gently disentangled Reese. Queenie stopped him, still not able to let her son go. Kirk waited, his gaze compassionate, understanding, but unrelenting. Finally she eased Reese into his father's arms, but what really broke his heart was when she whispered, "Thank you."

CHAPTER 20

Tuesday, Morning …

QUEENIE WOKE UP the next morning, bolting out of bed to stand in the middle of a strange room. She spun around as she rubbed the sleep out of her eyes.

Reese.

They'd found her son. She raced to the second bedroom, finally remembering where she was. Last night Kirk had taken the two of them to his place. She'd struggled with Reese being in a separate bedroom, but Kirk had been adamant.

"The door is open. He's a strong young man, and, if he cries out, we'll hear him."

Finally she'd relented. Now she stood in the doorway of her son's room, tears in her eyes. It was really true. She had him back. She'd been so numb last night, then so very angry. With no way to release it, she had tossed and turned all night.

Until she had heard Stefan's whispered words. *Focus on the good. Let the rest alone.*

Words of wisdom. From that moment on, she'd focused on being grateful for the miracle of her son glued to her arms. And her anger drifted away. Leaving sadness behind. They'd missed so many years.

But you weren't alone all that time, were you? Stefan said quietly. *Remember about telling all your secrets?*

Sure, but I still don't know what you're talking about, she'd said in confusion.

Someone was with you and has been since you went looking for your son.

The pinkish-lavender energy? That was Reese, wasn't it?

No, Stefan said, a gentle humor in his voice. *It wasn't. But it's important that you find out who it was.*

He'd left at that point. She stared down at her sleeping son, remembering all the times she had thought of him as the lavender energy.

And she could see the energy around her sleeping son right now, but it wasn't lavender.

Neither could she feel the lavender energy around her now. "Hey, Reese, you there?" she called out quietly.

Nothing.

Frowning, feeling like she'd lost something special and not understanding why, she slowly made her way back to Kirk's bed, where she'd slept last night. She slipped under the covers.

Kirk's arm wrapped around her and pulled her close. "Feel better now that you checked he's still here?"

"I had to," she said apologetically.

He chuckled. "I know. I've checked too."

She shifted up on her elbow until she could look down at him. "Really?"

Opening his beautiful silver-blue eyes, he stared up at her and nodded. "Really."

Her heart gave a happy sigh. She beamed at him, loving his need to make sure his son was safe. Then she lowered her head to kiss him. "Good. I'm glad to hear that," she whispered before she brushed her lips against his.

Tucked up safe and warm in bed in the early morning

hours, their son sleeping a wall width away, being held by the only man she'd ever loved—well, if this wasn't what everyone would call perfect, she didn't know what was.

She slid a hand up his bare chest to gently brush his cheek. "Did you have plans today?"

His lips quirked. "Not today. Except maybe to stay in bed with the woman I love for as long as I can. What do you think? Have we got an hour before Reese wakes up?"

"Longer if we're lucky." She grinned. "And, as I recall, we never had a problem taking our time in bed. Of course it's been a while, so I might have forgotten."

"In that case, I suggest we refresh your memory," he whispered, reaching up to hold her gently, lowering her down until their lips met.

She let out the gentlest of sighs as pleasure rippled through her. It was sheer joy in knowing they'd come to this point, joy in knowing the pain of all the last few years was over. They were older, wiser, and so much better off today. And to think they had this moment, this point in time for just the two of them.

What a gift …

And she planned to enjoy it fully.

The gentle blending of mouths, accepting each other, was an aphrodisiac all in itself. Passion was slow to rise, but like any dry kindling, once the heat built, the fire wasn't far behind. Moving with slow assurance as someone who knew and was delighted with a gift inside a wrapped package, Kirk gently undressed her, showing pleasure with every change in her body since giving birth.

Her breasts were plumper, and they flushed pink as he cupped them gently, laved the nipples with his tongue. He buried his face between her breasts for a long moment, then murmured, "They are more beautiful than ever."

He took one nipple deep into his mouth and suckled. She cried out at the deep pulling sensation in her belly. Then he turned his attention to the other one. By the time he was done and moving to her ribs, she was mewling like a kitten.

"Dear Lord, I'd forgotten," she gasped as he nibbled on her hip bone, holding her firm as she twisted beneath his ministrations.

"I've never forgotten," he growled out passionately. "I was so damn confused, hating myself for my actions. But I couldn't stop myself from thinking about you, wondering how you were."

"And yet you didn't call me."

"I was going to," he admitted, gently stroking down her legs. "If you hadn't contacted me, I'd promised myself I'd come find you." He lowered his head and kissed her hip bone, letting his tongue trail up to her ribs. "I would have to."

She reached down and tugged his head toward her. He scooted up and kissed her passionately, letting her know how he felt about their years apart. The pain of their separation and the loss … God, the loss.

When he lifted his head, she was limp but needed so much more. She tugged him back down to kiss his again, her thighs widening to make a place for him. "You're home now," she whispered. "Just as Reese is."

He shifted his position so he was at the center of her body and held himself slightly aloft. "Not quite." And he slid inside.

Her body wept with joy as he filled her completely. She shuddered in his arms, already throbbing for more.

He leaned down, kissed the tip of her nose and whispered, "Now I'm home."

And he started to move.

Faster and faster, deeper and deeper, until she couldn't muffle her cries any longer, and he took her lips, his tongue driving deep in a matching rhythm. She let out a strangled cry, her body arching as the climax swept through her. He didn't pause but drove right through to let out a heavy groan on the other side. Shaking, his body still trembling in the aftermath, he rolled to the side and just held her close.

Tears slipped down her cheeks; she could hardly breathe, and talking was out of the question. She stared around the room, wondering at how her life had changed.

A light laughter—one she knew well—filled her heart and mind.

"Reese?" she whispered. But it couldn't be—could it?

"What did you say?"

"The spirit I connected with before—the one I thought was my son—is here," she whispered.

Kirk shifted so he could see the room. His gaze spun back her way. "That purple pinky thing?"

She stared at him. "You can see him?"

"Yes." Kirk nodded. "But it's faint. Like a mirage almost."

"Yes, it's always been that way. But I can hear laughter when he visits."

Kirk pulled the sheet up over them both. "So who is it?"

She didn't know but watched from the circle of Kirk's arms as the lavender energy floated closer until it was over her. It started to shrink into a smaller but more intense ball hovering in front of them. She gazed at it in fascination. "Who are you?"

No answer, just more laughter.

Then it lowered until it rested on her belly. And dropped lower yet again.

She gasped, her belly sucking in tight. But it sank lower and lower until it disappeared—inside her. She gazed at Kirk in shock.

"Did that just happen?" Kirk cried.

Just then Reese came running from the other bedroom. "Mommy, Mommy, she's here." His face was alight with excitement.

"Who's here, honey?" Queenie asked, opening her arms.

He tumbled up onto the bed and laughed. "Melly is here." He reached over and patted her tummy. "She's in here."

"And how do you know that?" Kirk asked, sounding dazed.

Queenie understood how he felt because she wasn't much ahead in this thought process.

"Melly told me," Reese said proudly. "And I believe her. She said you'd come for me. And you did. And she said she'll be with us soon too." His face screwed up as if trying to remember what he'd been told. "But she said we'd have a little wait first. But we should talk to her. So she doesn't get lonely."

And finally Queenie got it. A little slow but, given what she'd been through, maybe that was understandable. She smiled, a gentle loving smile, her hands covering her belly protectively. "So, my pinkish-lavender energy I was so sure was Reese wasn't my son," she whispered to Kirk. "It was our daughter, … waiting."

"Waiting? For what? And does this mean what I think it means?"

"It does indeed," she said with a beaming smile. "She's been waiting, just like you and Reese. She's been waiting to come home."

This concludes Book 13 of Psychic Visions: Itsy-Bitsy Spider.
Read the first Chapter of Unmasked: Psychic Visions, Book 14

PSYCHIC VISIONS: UNMASKED (BOOK #14)
CHAPTER 1

LACEY, INTENT ON capturing the photos she'd been asked to take, jolted when she heard Sebastian approach—that deep rumbling growl of his in the background.

He didn't fit her concept of an archeologist in any way. Yet, he seemed just as comfortable here among the rocks as he did as an angry overlord at the airport when he had first arrived. She could imagine him commanding a big company. It had something to do with his presence, that sense of power which emanated from him.

Heavy footsteps sounded the team's approach. Trying not to make it obvious, she quickly took photos as they studied their vandalized tools, very much needed to do this job properly.

His striking voice was hard as he demanded, "Are you sure you locked everything up, put everything away?"

Her cousin Chana said, "Yes. We have a routine. We do it every night."

He straightened and pivoted slightly.

Lacey pointed her camera and caught that jaw, the nose, the aquiline cheeks. *Click. Click. Click.* Then catching

Chana's gaze, quickly Lacey turned away. Chana stared and then frowned as she understood what Lacey had been doing.

Feeling the heat roll up her neck and cheeks, Lacey hid behind the camera. She changed the angle ever so slightly to get a panoramic view. She slowly, methodically took pictures of the entire circle around her. If nothing else, it would provide a hell of a memory afterward.

Finally the group walked toward him, standing still. Lacey stayed behind, taking pictures of the broken tools and footprints. It was so fascinating to see where people walked now versus where they had walked thousands of years ago. She couldn't help it. She bent close and took photographs of one shoe imprint and then another and then another.

"What are you, a detective?"

She gave a shriek and spun around to see Sebastian glaring at her. She took a deep breath, trying to stabilize her shaky hands. "I was thinking of the contrast," she said steadily but had enunciated very carefully, so there was no misunderstanding. "Of footsteps today versus the footsteps of a thousand years ago."

He stared at her suspiciously for a moment before he relaxed and gave her an approving nod. "That actually could make quite a story." He turned and strode away.

She let out her pent-up breath, only to suck it in again as Chana whispered angrily in her ear, "What are you doing?"

"Taking photos," Lacey said, hating her defensive tone. "What was I supposed to be doing?"

"You don't need to be taking pictures of the boss." Chana spun on her heels and followed Sebastian.

Lacey stayed where she was, needing a few minutes away from the group and Chana's prying eyes.

Lacey wandered the section, seeing stairs appearing out

of the dirt. No way to know how far down they went because the ground met the seventh step midway. They hadn't excavated any farther. She walked to the top of the stairs and snapped a photo as she took every step down, thinking about the people who had walked these stairs, carrying burdens, holding children by the hand—the old, the young, the weak, the pregnant. She moved carefully, and, where the stairs stopped, she bent to capture that partially buried step from many angles. The wonder of the past meeting the present flowed through her.

She gave a happy sigh and slowly straightened to realize she wasn't alone. She looked up to find Sebastian staring at her, an odd look on his face. She frowned and asked in a low voice, "Have I done something wrong?"

He shook his head and pointed to where she'd been crouched. "What is it you see?"

"I see where the past meets the future," she said quietly. "And I guess that probably sounds frivolous, but I look at it from behind the camera. I see the collision, not of the past with the volcano, but as the future reaches deep into the past."

That odd look crossed his face yet again. His gaze intensified as if probing into her psyche, holding her captive by his will alone. She stood uncertainly, her fingers fidgeting on the camera. And then, as if she had been finally released from his hold, he gave a quick nod and spun away again. Shaky, she sat down on one of the steps and took several deep breaths. What the hell just happened?

HE WOULD HAVE to find out more about his new photographer. Something about her was … familiar, … odd, …

insightful. She was a puzzle. He loved solving puzzles of the past. Puzzles of the present never interested him. They were too young, held no mystery, no depth. But something about her went beyond deep.

He really liked the answers she'd given to his questions. He could see an old soul reaching through the centuries. Did she realize she'd been drawn here and why?

He glanced back to see Lacey sitting, taking several deep breaths as if he'd unnerved her. Fine if he had. She'd unnerved him too. He walked toward Chana, seeing her stiffen, waiting for his condemnation. "If anything else happens, no matter how minor it may seem to you," he said in a stern voice, "I want to hear about it, and I want to hear immediately. Do you hear me? You don't call anybody else, including the rest of the team. You pick up your phone, and you dial me." He leaned forward just a bit, satisfied when she leaned back reflexively. "Do you understand?"

She took a deep breath and nodded. "I am sorry."

"I know you are," he said absently. His mind had already moved forward. "I'll be in Pompeii for the next week. We have lots of fundraising and a board meeting. I'll be on-site a lot. So, when you least expect me, I'll be here."

And with that warning and a hard look at the rest of the group, he turned and walked away, satisfied the team would follow his orders. Still, there was nothing like seeing things from his own eyes too. What he really wanted was to see what Lacey saw. He stopped at the edge of the dig, turned and called back, "Chana, come here please."

She raced over.

"What's the deal with Lacey again?" He watched the color blanch from her face. He shook his head. "It's fine that she's here. I just don't remember what the arrangement was."

"She's a middle-school history teacher, out for the summer holidays. I told her how we had lost our photographer, and she volunteered to come. She's really, really good. But she's not a pro, and we're not paying her," she said very clearly. "But we are covering her costs."

He shot a glance toward the woman who, even now, was absorbed in a pattern of rock on the ground just off to the side. The mystery of what it was, what it had been, remained buried beneath the ground. Her aura was cream-colored and glowing brightly, even from a distance … "Okay, that's fine."

"I'll keep an eye on her," Chana said quickly. "She's my cousin. She's really doing this as a favor for us."

He nodded absentmindedly. "I said it's all right. I do want to see the photos she takes."

"I didn't get her to sign an agreement," she said quickly. "If that's something you want, then we have to give her a contract."

His mind contemplated the issue. "I'll think about it. Depends on how willing she is to share her photos."

"She does this for joy," Chana said. "For the love of the world around her. She has a very unique insight into everything."

"And why is that?"

Chana lowered her voice. "I honestly think it's because she spent years caring for her dying mother—tried to make each moment count before she lost her. No treatment was working, so they knew the end was inevitable, and yet every day they tried to do something to make that day special. After her mother passed away six months ago, Lacy continued the practice. And coming here has been a dream of hers since forever. All I ever heard from her was how she wanted to come see Pompeii."

He'd just taken a step away when he heard that last bit. He spun around and looked at Chana hard. "What do you mean?"

He watched as his team leader shrugged her shoulders. "Honestly? She saw a documentary when she was young, like six or seven. Since then it's all she's talked about."

"And this is her first time here?"

Chana nodded. "I really want to make it a good visit for her. She deserves that. She's a good person, and she spent a lot of years of her life making her mother's life easier every day."

He kept his thoughts to himself, but he couldn't keep his gaze off Lacey. *What did she see behind that lens of hers? Did she see the people of the past? The death and disaster? The good? The evil? Did she see the masks?*

Voluntarily taking that walk of grief was hard. He'd only seen one person do it well—his own mother had nursed his sister to her early end. It took a lot of spirit, a lot of heart, but it could also break someone. And the breaks could be hidden inside where no one knew. That could make them weak, make them easily accessible, make them susceptible to all kinds of dangers.

He could admire what she'd done, but she needed watching.

A lot was going on here that nobody knew about, that nobody understood because they couldn't relate to the dark forces underneath. But anybody who had been *called* from halfway across the world, with a need instilled at such a young age—well, that meant that person needed to be here. He just didn't know why. But he'd find out. His visit just became open-ended. He didn't dare leave the site and Lacey alone …

Things happened here. People were doing things they weren't aware of. He'd seen the anomaly before—once, as a young man, just starting out at a Mayan ruin dig, where there'd been similar incidences to what he saw here. Only back then, they got much worse... ending with several deaths.

Deaths that had haunted him ever since.

This time he had to figure out how to stop it. When he'd heard about incidences on this site, his heart had damn near exploded in his chest. That was partly why he'd been so angry that they hadn't contacted him. They didn't understand the danger. And they definitely didn't understand how the darkness underneath was attracted to the light above.

The darkness especially loved the innocence, the energy, the purity of someone like Lacey. More than *liked*—it fed on it …

Book 14 is available now!
To find out more visit Dale Mayer's website.
https://geni.us/DMUnmaskeduniversal

Simon Says... Hide: Kate Morgan
(Book #1)

Welcome to a new thriller series from *USA Today* Best-Selling Author Dale Mayer. Set in Vancouver, BC, the team of Detective Kate Morgan and Simon St. Laurant, an unwilling psychic, marries all the elements of Dale's work that you've come to love, plus so much more.

Detective Kate Morgan, newly promoted to the Vancouver PD Homicide Department, stands for the victims in her world. She was once a victim herself, just as her mother had been a victim, and then her brother—an unsolved missing child's case—was yet another victim. She can't stand those who take advantage of others, and the worst ones are those who prey on the hopes of desperate people to line their own pockets.

So, when she finds a connection between more than a half-dozen cold cases to a current case, where a child's life hangs in the balance, Kate would make a deal with the devil himself to find the culprit and to save the child.

Simon St. Laurant's grandmother had the Sight and had warned him that, once he used it, he could never walk away. Until now, her caution had made it easy to avoid that first step. But, when nightmares of his own past are triggered, Simon can't stand back and watch child after child be abused. Not without offering his help to those chasing the monsters.

Even if it means dealing with the cranky and critical Detective Kate Morgan …

Find Simon Says… Hide here!
To find out more visit Dale Mayer's website.
https://geni.us/DMSSHideUniversal

Author's Note

Thank you for reading Itsy-Bitsy Spider: Psychic Visions, Book 13! If you enjoyed the book, please take a moment and leave a short review.

Dear reader,

I love to hear from readers, and you can contact me at my website: www.dalemayer.com or at my Facebook author page. To be informed of new releases and special offers, sign up for my newsletter or follow me on BookBub. And if you are interested in joining Dale Mayer's Fan Club, here is the Facebook sign up page.
http://geni.us/DaleMayerFBGroup

Cheers,
Dale Mayer

About the Author

Dale Mayer is a *USA Today* best-selling author, best known for her SEALs military romances, her Psychic Visions series, and her Lovely Lethal Garden cozy series. Her contemporary romances are raw and full of passion and emotion (Broken But … Mending, Hathaway House series). Her thrillers will keep you guessing (Kate Morgan, By Death series), and her romantic comedies will keep you giggling (*It's a Dog's Life*, a stand-alone novella; and the Broken Protocols series, starring Charming Marvin, the cat).

Dale honors the stories that come to her—and some of them are crazy, break all the rules and cross multiple genres!

To go with her fiction, she also writes nonfiction in many different fields, with books available on résumé writing, companion gardening, and the US mortgage system. All her books are available in print and ebook format.

Connect with Dale Mayer Online

Dale's Website – www.dalemayer.com
Twitter – @DaleMayer
Facebook Page – geni.us/DaleMayerFBFanPage
Facebook Group – geni.us/DaleMayerFBGroup
BookBub – geni.us/DaleMayerBookbub
Instagram – geni.us/DaleMayerInstagram
Goodreads – geni.us/DaleMayerGoodreads
Newsletter – geni.us/DaleNews

Also by Dale Mayer

Published Adult Books:

Psychic Vision Series

Tuesday's Child

Hide 'n Go Seek

Maddy's Floor

Garden of Sorrow

Knock Knock...

Rare Find

Eyes to the Soul

Now You See Her

Shattered

Into the Abyss

Seeds of Malice

Eye of the Falcon

Itsy-Bitsy Spider

Unmasked

Psychic Visions Books 1–3

Psychic Visions Books 4–6

Psychic Visions Books 7–9

By Death Series

Touched by Death

Haunted by Death

Chilled by Death

By Death Books 1–3

Charmin Marvin Romantic Comedy Series

Broken Protocols

Broken Protocols 2

Broken Protocols 3

Broken Protocols 3.5

Broken Protocols 1-3

Broken and... Mending

Skin

Scars

Scales (of Justice)

Broken but... Mending 1-3

Glory

Genesis

Tori

Celeste

Glory Trilogy

Biker Blues

Morgan: Biker Blues, Volume 1

Cash: Biker Blues, Volume 2

SEALs of Honor

Mason: SEALs of Honor, Book 1

Hawk: SEALs of Honor, Book 2

Dane: SEALs of Honor, Book 3

Swede: SEALs of Honor, Book 4

Shadow: SEALs of Honor, Book 5

Cooper: SEALs of Honor, Book 6

Markus: SEALs of Honor, Book 7

Evan: SEALs of Honor, Book 8

Mason's Wish: SEALs of Honor, Book 9

Chase: SEALs of Honor, Book 10

Brett: SEALs of Honor, Book 11

Devlin: SEALs of Honor, Book 12

Easton: SEALs of Honor, Book 13

Ryder: SEALs of Honor, Book 14

Macklin: SEALs of Honor, Book 15

Corey: SEALs of Honor, Book 16

Warrick: SEALs of Honor, Book 17

Tanner: SEALs of Honor, Book 18

SEALs of Honor, Books 1–3

SEALs of Honor, Books 4–6

SEALs of Honor, Books 7–10

SEALs of Honor, Books 11–13

Heroes for Hire

Levi's Legend: Heroes for Hire, Book 1

Stone's Surrender: Heroes for Hire, Book 2

Merk's Mistake: Heroes for Hire, Book 3

Rhodes's Reward: Heroes for Hire, Book 4

Flynn's Firecracker: Heroes for Hire, Book 5

Logan's Light: Heroes for Hire, Book 6

Harrison's Heart: Heroes for Hire, Book 7

Saul's Sweetheart: Heroes for Hire, Book 8

Dakota's Delight: Heroes for Hire, Book 9

Tyson's Treasure: Heroes for Hire, Book 10

Jace's Jewel: Heroes for Hire, Book 11

Rory's Rose: Heroes for Hire, Book 12

Brandon's Bliss: Heroes for Hire, Book 13

Liam's Lily: Heroes for Hire, Book 14

North's Nikki: Heroes for Hire, Book 15

Heroes for Hire, Books 1–3

Heroes for Hire, Books 4–6

Heroes for Hire, Books 7–9

SEALs of Steel

Badger: SEALs of Steel, Book 1

Erick: SEALs of Steel, Book 2

Cade: SEALs of Steel, Book 3

Talon: SEALs of Steel, Book 4

Laszlo: SEALs of Steel, Book 5

Geir: SEALs of Steel, Book 6

Jager: SEALs of Steel, Book 7

The Last Wish: SEALs of Steel, Book 8

Collections

Dare to Be You…

Dare to Love…

Dare to be Strong…

RomanceX3

Standalone Novellas

It's a Dog's Life

Riana's Revenge

Second Chances

Published Young Adult Books:

Family Blood Ties Series

Vampire in Denial

Vampire in Distress

Vampire in Design

Vampire in Deceit

Vampire in Defiance

Vampire in Conflict

Vampire in Chaos

Vampire in Crisis

Vampire in Control

Vampire in Charge

Family Blood Ties Set 1–3

Family Blood Ties Set 1–5

Family Blood Ties Set 4–6

Family Blood Ties Set 7–9

Sian's Solution, A Family Blood Ties Series Prequel
    Novelette

Design series

Dangerous Designs

Deadly Designs

Darkest Designs

Design Series Trilogy

Standalone
In Cassie's Corner

Gem Stone (a Gemma Stone Mystery)

Time Thieves

Published Non-Fiction Books:

Career Essentials
Career Essentials: The Résumé

Career Essentials: The Cover Letter

Career Essentials: The Interview

Career Essentials: 3 in 1